D0773033

PUSHBACK

John E. Stith

ReAnimus Press

Breathing Life into Great Books

ReAnimus Press
1100 Johnson Road #16-143
Golden, CO 80402
www.ReAnimus.com

Cover Art by Kavin King

ISBN-13: 978-0-9672984-5-0 (hardback)
ISBN-13: 978-0-9672984-6-7 (paperback)

First edition: November, 2018

10 9 8 7 6 5 4 3 2 1

Chapter 1

My day had been going just fine until I spotted what had been done to my car door.

From a distance it looked like a kid had drawn a familiar symbol in dust, but the Subaru was clean. As I got closer, my gut tightened even more with the realization that the damage was worse than I thought. I ran my fingertips over the surface. The two "dots" were in fact bullet holes.

A pair of bullet holes a couple of inches apart with a six-inch black marker circle around them. Below the bullet holes was an arc, also in black marker pen.

A smiley face.

Still in disbelief, I wanted to convince myself it was lifelike decal, not real. Again, my fingertip confirmed the rough depression and the hole.

The light-blue Subaru Outback was barely a year old. I'd bought it shortly after Allison's death, after I'd gotten out of the hospital. Unbidden, images of her in my old Acura shuttered through my brain. Allison happy in the passenger seat. Allison dead in the passenger seat.

I blinked away the past and looked around the parking lot, feeling angry and confused. Why would anyone do this? Downtown Colorado Springs felt benign. The July weather was great—partly cloudy but no threat of rain. The parking lot held barely more than a dozen cars today, a Saturday. No one was visible unless I moved a few feet away, at which point I'd be able to see Tejon Street afternoon pedestrian traffic and the cars traveling up and down Tejon. Exhaust from a vehicle swept by and then the breeze was crisp and clean again.

I scanned the second- and third-floor windows nearest me. Did someone just move back out of sight in that one?

I turned back to the vandalism. Why would someone shoot a bullet-hole smiley face into the middle of the driver's door of my Outback?

I'd just left the office, and was already running late to pick up Cathy. She'd convinced me to take her to my ten-year high-school reunion tonight.

And now I felt the all-too-familiar paralysis of indecision, a fight-or-flight crossroads I had blown through too frequently since I was a tween. My shrink says many people recover from PTSD, but she wasn't me. I felt an almost pathological need to avoid conflict, so flight was almost always way preferable to a fight. But as I looked around again, I saw no enemy. No one smirking and pointing. No smoking gun.

I took a deep breath and went back to the office to grab a spare *BTU Investments* magnetic business sign. Back at my Subaru, no further damage was immediately visible, so I slapped the magnetic sign over the bullet holes and marker pen and took a quick visual-inspection tour around the car. The gas-tank cover was still locked. Nothing propped next to a tire to puncture it when I pulled out of the space. I wondered if the engine compartment was hiding a bomb, and decided if people wanted me dead they wouldn't have alerted me this way.

A phone call to the cops was the right response. But then either I'd waste a few hours I could be spending with Cathy, and be no closer to finding the perpetrator, or just get frustrated by the voice-response system. My brain was already playing the tape. "Your crime is important to us. Please press four and then two for bullet holes in your driver's side car door. For passenger doors, press..."

I shook my head, baffled, and unlocked the car. The inside of the car door didn't show any exit holes. I wasn't a gun expert, so I assumed that indicated a small caliber weapon or a slow muzzle velocity or both. The engine caught, and I flipped the switch to lower the window. It started down smoothly.

After a few inches of travel, I stopped the window. It might work fine all the way, but I didn't want to risk the window getting stuck down before the ride into the mountains. Zip. The window went back up smoothly and closed all the way. Note to self: No drive-ins for the time being. Not that there still was one within fifty miles.

I forced the vandalism completely out of my mind. And then I proceeded to puzzle over it all the way to Cathy's office. I had no enemies. That I was aware of. I kept watch for anyone following me, partly thanks to old habit, and partly because of the bizarre damage.

My anger and sense of violation hadn't abated by the time I got to Cathy's office, so I tried even harder to force the feelings aside. I'd tell Cathy about it later. There were some important things about my life that I'd been afraid to share with her, and tonight was the night I planned to come clean about my PTSD symptoms and the reason for them. I could tell her about the bullet holes at the same time. What could go wrong?

The parking lot outside Cathy Whitley's veterinary office on Garden of the Gods Road wasn't very full, given a Saturday afternoon. I'd just shut the door and was ready to go inside and find her when she pushed open the glass door and headed happily toward me. She carried a small, red overnight bag.

My breath caught for an instant, and I realized how amazingly lucky I was to have a second chance I never expected. Allison's death a year ago had left me shattered, convinced my life was over. But now, against all odds, I had a new life.

Cathy's black hair swung gently side to side over her shoulders as she neared me. Those dazzling green eyes, and her broad smile, made my heart pick up a little speed. I'd been dating her for just under a couple of months. Those two months had been just long enough to get me hopelessly hooked.

"Hi! Miss me?" she asked. Impossibly, her smile seemed even more joyful. With the wrong lighting her nose looked slightly crooked. Her lower teeth were just a bit crooked. God, I loved her smile.

"You bet. Miss me?"

"Sure did." She dropped her bag on the pavement, wrapped her arms around me, and gave me a wonderful kiss. I reciprocated. The kiss was terrific, and it felt great that she wasn't afraid to show her affection within sight of her office. For several seconds in a row I forgot about the bullet holes and just breathed in her scent. Peaches maybe.

A few seconds later, we broke apart. I popped the trunk. Cathy tossed her bag inside, and I closed the lid.

I hesitated, wondering if the bullet holes in my car door indicated some level of threat for Cathy. What a bizarre thing to happen in downtown in the daytime.

At the time, I hoped they were merely random vandalism.

Cathy bent to re-tie a shoe. She'd shed her lab coat and now wore tight black pants and a white, short-sleeved blouse. My breath faltered.

She stayed very busy, primarily with work and off-hours animal rescue volunteering, and on top of that she'd just gotten back from a several-day seminar in Chicago, so we'd not had much alone time recently.

Cathy was like Allison in ways that probably spoke to my "type" — strong, intelligent, caring — but the two women were as different as an orchid and a rose.

Allison had been wealthy; her father could probably buy Nebraska. Or at least South Dakota. Her mother had died a couple of years back. Cathy's parents, both still alive, worked for USAA, the insurance company dedicated to serving the military; Allison had been a sixth-grade teacher. Cathy was a veterinarian, the first college graduate in her family. Allison was manicured. Cathy could put on her makeup in twenty seconds while she was pulling on her jeans. Allison had battled depression. Cathy was the most steadily upbeat person I'd ever known.

But both felt as rare as lightning striking a four-leaf clover nearby. For what had felt like the first time in my life, with Allison, I'd been truly happy. The aftermath of her death, the realization that someone so rare and precious was just gone — in an instant — was nearly unbearable. It was like the low points in my childhood all over again, only worse. My PTSD nightmares and hypervigilance had come back with a vengeance, but I think I was able to conceal them for the most part.

I still cried at very sad or very happy scenes in movies, but I thought Cathy just put that down to me being in touch with my feelings.

"You ready?" Cathy asked. "Road trip?"

I tried again to force aside my fears and questions about the bullet holes in my car door.

"You bet." I opened the passenger door for her. I was glad the bullet holes were on my door.

It wasn't going to be all that much of a road trip from a mileage point of view. I headed west, then south, and soon passed the Garden of the Gods park, a mostly wild area where enormous sandstone rock formations jutted from the earth like the scales on the backs of gigantic half-buried stegosaurs.

We left Colorado Springs behind us and followed Highway 24 westward, on our way up Ute Pass to the small town of Woodland Park.

My thoughts went back and forth between the bullet holes and Cathy. I wanted to talk to her about them, but I also wanted a longer conversation about some things I had neglected to tell her about myself. A car trip of less than a half hour wasn't the time.

Cathy turned toward me and put her hand on my thigh. "You're awfully quiet today. Everything OK?"

"Couldn't be better." Well, my passenger door could be pristine. "I got done what I needed to at the office. The decks are cleared for a couple of days. How about you?"

"I'm good. Melanie will cover for me Monday, and LuAnn next door will feed Freddy."

A guy on a motorcycle—I assumed it was a guy—roared loudly past us doing more than a hundred miles an hour. Our car breathed in a faint scent of hot motor oil.

Cathy shook her head slightly and said, "Well, at least he's wearing a helmet."

"Good. That will make it easier to figure out which piece is the head."

She gave me a wry grin.

The Subaru tire jolted over a pothole, and my knee twinged from the car accident last year.

I was struck by a feeling of déjà vu. In my case, although the details of the incident on Monarch Pass had gone through the dirty lens of concussion and were now upside down, murky, and fuzzy, I saw with crystal clarity most of that last trip with Allison, the trip that ended with her death.

I'd become a hermit after Allison's death, wallowing in loss and self-pity and physical pain, not looking for any new relationship. The nightmares started up again, with new ones about the Allison's death. At times the depression was almost unbearable, but the medication helped. I was constantly on edge and at the same time fatigued. Only a last-minute decision to go to a friend's birthday party had shifted the alignment of the universe. Cathy was there, along with a mutual friend I hadn't seen in easily five years. Cathy had lost Howard, her husband of several years, to a nerve disease that took him from sixty to zero in under eight months. The mutual friend, Debbie, pulled us both together and conspiratorially announced, "You both had people close to you die recently. You should talk."

So we talked. As we did, I watched the fire in Cathy's eyes. Pain flickered over the coals there, but a steady heat overshadowed it. OK, maybe not literally in her eyes, but in her gaze, her posture, her words, all consistent with the strength to find the next step on the rope bridge, scrambling over that board that had splintered and fallen into the chasm. And she looked appealing. Green eyes filled with gold flecks. Black, shoulder-length hair. A mouth with small creases that only enhanced her smile. A mouth I couldn't imagine sneering. She felt gentle. Strong but gentle. Her cheerful optimism was infectious. If she could get through this, maybe I could, too. I felt myself nearing the point of asking her out to coffee.

I was almost ready to risk rejection when Cathy related the advice she'd received from a friend, a fairly recent widow of maybe fifty. That friend had explained that for a while Cathy would be the new girl, the recently bereaved, and people would go out of their way to be kind, to make invitations, to include her. But before long, someone else would lose a partner. And then another survivor would take center stage. And another. And before much longer, her loss would be old news. From dust to dust. So the answer, according to this friend, was to, "Always be a 'yes.' And then you must reach out to others, and to that next person who suffers a loss." Accept every invitation. Stay connected to the world. Stay alive.

Crap. I realized that if I asked her out to coffee right then, I'd be putting her on the spot and she'd feel virtually compelled to say "yes," and I'd feel like a royal schmuck. Or, if she did say "no" I would really know it was a "no." Not just a simple no, but a "hell no, not even now" no. I was too fragile to risk the possibility, or too considerate to put her in that position.

Instead, I threw the decision into the lap of the gods, and took out one of my financial counseling business cards. I offered it, saying, "If you'd like to have coffee sometime, and talk, I would like that. Just call me if you want to."

She accepted my card with an enigmatic smile. It took her almost a week, but she called. She still has that card in her purse.

My nightmares started slowing down again. I'd had only a few this week.

A pickup raced up from behind us, sounding its horn as it overtook us. I realized I'd lost speed, and pushed down on the accelerator.

"You still with me?" Cathy was turned partway in her seat, amusement showing on her lips and in her eyes. I hadn't seen anything but cheerfulness directed at me, but I'd been in her clinic one day when a guy had brought in a dehydrated Cocker Spaniel he'd left alone too long without water. Man, I never wanted to see that look from Cathy.

"Sorry, lost in thought, I guess. Feeling lucky. Feeling appreciative."

"I'm feeling the same thing."

I smiled more broadly.

We curved around an old rock wall and then past a rock bluff as the divided highway took us farther up the pass. I swallowed and my ears popped again. My right knee hurt. The accident that killed Allison had, among other things, turned that knee into an altimeter and a barometer for weather forecasting. I was a human meteorological station.

My knee felt as strong as ever thanks to physical therapy, but it told me a big storm was on the way. The pain would be worse on the return trip, though.

At the time, I was thinking only about knee pain.

The sun went behind one of the hills ahead and Cathy folded up her sun visor. We passed the exit to North Pole, a Santa Claus winter-themed amusement park for young children, appropriately nestled in Christmas trees. My mind turned that quick glimpse into a disturbing and bizarre image of Santa and a few menacing elves facing off against Snow White and her posse of seven dwarfs, each brandishing a mean-looking pickaxe. That image I didn't share with Cathy.

Cathy leaned forward to put her sunglasses away in the glove box, and her blouse parted, revealing a black bra and cleavage.

Suddenly I was thinking not of bullet holes, but of what might be in store later tonight, after the reunion dinner. Cathy, as far as my experience went, always wore black lingerie, and now my thoughts were on removing some of it. Well, let's be honest—all of it.

We were near the exit for the tiny town of Crystola. Allison's father's estate was up in the hills to our left, though you couldn't get to it from here.

My old high school was even farther up the pass, but I'd gotten an email saying they'd picked a Mexican restaurant in Woodland Park to host the reunion dinner.

A car in the downhill lanes passed, giving me a quick glimpse of door-mounted advertising. My thoughts went back to the bullet holes and then on to the discussion I wanted to have with Cathy about my past. I needed to approach the conversation very carefully.

Cathy was very even tempered, good natured, but she had a couple of hot buttons, and pity the guy who pressed them. One was dishonesty. The man in her life before Howard had been a con artist named Terry. Terry not only broke Cathy's heart, but he made off with something north of twenty thousand dollars invested in some scheme he was able to make sound very foolproof. It turned out, too, that the woman he occasionally visited overnight was not in fact his sister. Cathy had no more tolerance for frauds. I'd try to smuggle a machine gun past the TSA before I'd knowingly disappoint her.

On the radio, "I Hope You Dance," came on softly, so I boosted the volume. The song spoke to both of us pretty strongly, with lines about one door closing. I felt like the luckiest guy on the planet, still being alive and having another opportunity for real happiness. I missed Allison, but nothing would bring her back. I periodically said my thanks to Allison, but Cathy was here with me. Cathy was my present and future. I hoped. With her, the nightmares had subsided, other symptoms had retreated, and I felt loved. I still didn't feel I deserved that love, but in time, maybe I would.

The land had flattened out a little now, and we passed a Walmart on the left, and the buildings grew in density. As with most places, Woodland Park had seen a series of chain stores replacing home-grown businesses over time. I recalled the fight they'd had over letting a major big box store into a relatively small community still home to a decreasing number of mom and pop outfits. Some of those folks were likely still moms and pops, but I wasn't so sure they were business owners any longer. Maybe in another thirty years we'd be down to a dozen different companies altogether. The dirty dozen.

We hit the thirty-five mile-an-hour zone. By now half the cars had their headlights on. Only very low hills lay ahead. The town sprawled around us, and the sky opened up more fully.

Woodland Park, at 8500 feet, is a bit less than half a mile higher than the Springs, but now that I had popped my ears again and equalized for the pressure change, everything felt the same. The main way to tell how high you are is to exert yourself. Although, now that I reflected on marijuana legalization, other people might have different yardsticks.

Our destination appeared on the right, a two-story Mexican restaurant. It was a tall building for the surroundings. I took a right into the parking lot but not before noticing a sign for Taco Bell, right across the next street. The pairing made it seem the larger restaurant was sending out runners.

We had to go well back to find a parking space. Next to an empty spot was a pickup with a bumper sticker reading, "I like big books and I cannot lie."

With the engine off, we relaxed in the silence. If I were in Cathy's place, I don't know that I'd enjoy an evening with strangers. I said, "We don't have to do this, you know. We could find another restaurant and just have a quiet dinner on our own before we check in at the B&B." I had dragged my feet, not wanting to go to this reunion, but

Cathy had virtually insisted. I was even more of a wreck in high school, and going back was reawakening some of the same feelings.

"Nonsense. I like meeting your friends."

I leaned in, and Cathy turned her lips to mine. Starting or ending a journey now had this fun little ritual as a perk.

My right knee complained just a little as I got out of the car, but it had healed well. I moved my right shoulder in a small circle to free some of the stiffness.

Cathy and I walked, hand in hand, to the front door of the restaurant.

We all go through life taking mental snapshots of way stations along the path. As Cathy and I walked through the door and into the restaurant, I vividly remember feeling great and thinking everything looked very normal, small-town, innocent, benign.

Chapter 2

The feeling of normalcy continued for a minute or two after we entered the restaurant and went through the inner door. I felt happy. Now that Cathy had convinced me to go, I had shifted gears and was anticipating having some old friends meet someone special in my life, someone amazing.

The aroma of Mexican food welcomed us. Onions, chili peppers, frying corn tortillas. Colorful curtains, with lots of yellow and blue. The wait staff bustled, and nearly every table was occupied. One booth held a pair of parents with a boy and a girl, both under ten. The children were busy drawing on large pieces of paper, looking content. For an instant I felt a twinge of sadness that children were not to be part of the possible future for Cathy and me. I sometimes felt the tug, but I also knew I wouldn't be an adequate parent. At one point I had promised myself no kids. People with better role models to emulate are the ones who should have kids.

To the right, at the bottom of the stairs, Cathy and I spotted a reunion welcome poster, and moved to it. A big arrow pointed upward to the second floor. An old picture of the graduating class had been enlarged under the banner, "Mountain Lake High School Class."

I started up the stairs, then hesitated. The class picture showed sixteen people. Two rows, young men in the back, young women in the front. Eight and eight. My class had had twenty. But the picture had my year on it.

I looked more closely and got my first twinge of unreality. They had gotten the picture wrong. It had to be a different class. But I didn't recognize the faces in the photo as being classmates ahead of me or behind me by a year or two. So they really had it wrong. How hard could it be to get the right class photo?

At least the school in the background was right. It was a long building in the "WPA Rustic" style, boxy, made from local stone. It could have been a National Parks building. The sixteen kids were posed right next to the school sign, just as my class picture had been taken.

"Someone must be embarrassed," I said. "This isn't our class." I took another look. One of the women in the front row was a stunner. Blonde, perfect-teeth smile, like a smiling model if you can imagine such a thing. I would remember her. I was wary of too-beautiful women, but I did have a minor in art appreciation.

The woman had bangs and straight hair that fell to about the middle of her neck. I had never seen her before. But I wished she'd been in our class.

Puzzled, I reached for Cathy's hand and tugged her toward the stairs. "Come on. We'll figure it out."

My knee twinged and my ankle snapped as we climbed, but I was used to that. The stairwell walls sported more school photos intermixed with the restaurant's own photos. Another of the school building, from a different angle. A group of teachers. There was Ms. Grayson, my cranky geography, political science, and history teacher. Runners on a track, too far away to recognize faces. Possibly a debate, shot from the back of the room. Five students singing. My free-floating unease grew.

We reached the second floor. Within just a couple feet of the top of the stairs, a table partly blocked the path. I felt uncomfortable, off-balance in the narrow space between table and stairs. Two nametags lay on the tablecloth. Hanging on the front of the table was a duplicate of the screwed-up poster on the first floor. Same banner text, same eight and eight students. Behind the table were two people about my age, late twenties. One was a muscular guy with medium-length hair shot through with brown and blond. Squared-off jaw. The guy's nametag said, "John Dyson."

The other person at the table was the stunning blonde woman in the picture.

She wore a name tag saying "Liz Bennet." Reading the tag was a reading-comprehension *and* focus challenge because she had on a *very* low-cut top. Her blonde hair was now curly, more like a grown-up Shirley Temple than her hair in the group photo. Her top was vivid red. Her bra was white.

I hesitated.

"This floor is reserved for a school reunion tonight," the blonde said politely. "Sorry for the inconvenience."

"No, I—er, we're here for the reunion."

"Oh, I'm sorry. I don't recognize all the spouses. But I don't know if we have enough dinners." She fingered the two remaining name-tags. "These are for Max and Joanne. I'm afraid I don't have you on the list."

I scratched my forehead, the feeling of confusion turning darker in my brain. Was this something like Candid Camera or Borat? "Hey, something's wrong here. I'm Dave Barlow. I'm a graduate of Mountain Lake High School. Maybe there's—"

I glanced at Cathy, who looked as baffled as I felt.

The blonde hesitated, shuffled a short stack of pages in from of her. "Say your name again?"

"Dave. Dave Barlow. Maybe if you got one of the people from the class."

"I *am* one of the people from the class," she said, puzzled.

"But I don't remember you."

"I'm sorry. I just don't get this," the blonde said. "We had sixteen members of the graduating class, and you're not one of them." She bent sideways to grab something from her purse, giving me quite a view, then straightened. In her hand was a copy of the school year-book. I had my own copy at home. At least this would clear things up.

She flipped open the book, revealing some familiar pictures, but as she reached the individual photos, my stomach lurched.

Even before she turned the book so I could see better, I knew this was wrong. I took a closer look as Cathy moved a small step away from me.

Eight and eight. The sixteen people from the group photo. There were Liz and John from right in front of me. They looked fairly similar to their pictures, but many people can transition from eighteen to twenty-eight without massive changes, apart from hair. I was not there. No one I knew was there. I searched the faces of people sitting at the booths and tables beyond. No face looked familiar. A central bar area had more people on stools. None of them looked familiar.

I steadied myself by leaning on the table.

"Something's wrong," I said. "There can't be two Mountain Lake High Schools?"

"Look," John said. "It might have seemed funny to try to get a free meal, but it's not happening. Maybe if you crash a larger party."

"But I'm not crashing. I belong here. What's going on?"

John rose from the table, looking for a moment less like a classmate and more like a bouncer.

A dozen ideas flashed through my head. I could maneuver past John and grill the people at the tables. I could call the manager and tell him the party here was a hoax. I could call the police, tell them — tell them what? Tell them I was going crazy? Was I?

The flurry of ideas died down. Even if I didn't have a super aversion to fighting, this was not the kind of problem a fight would solve. It would just make things worse. I turned, stunned and confused, to Cathy. "Come on. Let's get out of here."

"Just a minute, OK?" Cathy's confusion mirrored mine.

Fight-or-flight mode had kicked in with a vengeance. Flight was way out in front. I wanted to get out of here. As fast as I could. I tried my damnedest to avoid conflict, and if I stayed here, the situation had conflict written all over it. This just had to be a setup. I was not going crazy.

I scanned the crowd again, feeling my pulse race, sensing the perspiration on my forehead. "I really want to go, Cathy."

And then I looked at her face. Her expression had changed, hardened.

A chill raced down my back. I was that guy. I was the guy who left his dog without food or water. I was the guy who scammed her and broke her heart. I was a liar, a poser. She backed away from me, the look in her eyes something I never want to see again. Abruptly I was acutely aware of the damage that had been done by the boyfriend who turned out to be a con man. He probably made her feel she was partly to blame, that she was somehow a magnet for criminals and sociopaths.

Cathy wasn't going to cry. I could see the anguish on her face, but she was rigidly under control. "Is this your high school or not, Dave? Is this why you didn't want to come to the reunion?" She picked up the yearbook and looked closely at the sixteen faces and then at the cover.

"I dragged my feet a bit, but, no. This is crazy." Bad word choice.

"Yes. It is. Something's wrong."

"I agree. But you know me."

"I thought I did. But this doesn't make any sense."

I summoned calm and got nothing but more anxiety. "I don't know what the purpose is, why this is happening, but this is some kind of setup. I'm being totally honest here."

"Just a sec."

It was bad enough that this reunion was all wrong. But to have it affect my relationship with Cathy would be ten times worse. A hundred. The increasing stress level made me feel out of breath, struggling to get from the depths to the water's surface.

"Come on, please. Let's get out of here. I can make some phone calls and get to the bottom—"

"Wait. Just wait. I have to think."

I said nothing. There didn't seem any more I could say. I knew the damage con-man Terry had done to her. Maybe in her own way Cathy was almost as damaged as I was.

She couldn't meet my gaze. "Look, Dave, I'm sorry. I'm just not going with you right now. I need to process this, and right now I—I don't feel safe." She moved another step back, hitting the wall.

"But—how will you get back to the Springs?" My world was falling apart and here I was the pragmatist. Great response.

"I'll take a cab. I'll walk."

"Look, I can just drive you—"

"I said no!"

I stepped back. I hated that word. I tried so hard to avoid it. Normally I'd rather not even ask the question if "no" was a possibility. I would take the long way, walk instead of ride, if "no" was a possibility.

I had just turned invisible. The blonde said, looking at Cathy, "Several people here live in the Springs. I'm sure we can find you a ride or chip in for a ride." She cleared her throat. "You don't think your friend is dangerous, do you?"

I swung toward her and searched her eyes. I had trouble reading her, but I imagined I saw some compassion there. Or maybe just curiosity. Or perhaps that was what I wanted to see.

"No, I'm not dangerous." That was mostly true.

I looked back at Cathy. Her jaw clenched. Brow furrowed. Her anger was palpable. If anyone was dangerous, it was her. My pulse pounded so loudly other people must be hearing it. My tell-tale heart.

Her reaction seemed over the top to me, but I wasn't the one who'd been conned and lied to and cheated on. And I knew I had my own hot buttons. She was likely reacting as much to the past as to the here and now. Maybe I was the stand-in right now for all that was deceitful and manipulative about some men. And I certainly hadn't been entirely candid with her about my PTSD symptoms and the reason for them.

I stood there, feeling hollow. Two choices lit up — two paths. One, fight for Cathy, make a scene, push back. Two, retreat, avoid bringing more conflict into my life. I'd already had enough conflict to last a lifetime and I wanted no more. If Cathy was able to believe these strangers over me, what other hurdles lay down that road? Cathy's reaction robbed me of any remaining will to fight right now. I just felt numb.

"Something is very wrong here," I said carefully. "But it's not me."

Cathy said nothing. She would no longer meet my gaze.

I nodded. "I'll get your bag."

I'd taken a couple of steps down the stairs when she spoke. "Dave, I'm sorry. Maybe this is more about Terry than about you, but I'm scared. I just can't come with you."

I processed that for a few seconds and then nodded. "You want to just borrow my car? I can get back on my own. "

She shook her head.

Cathy's red overnight bag was in the trunk, next to my own bag. I retrieved hers and went back into the restaurant. Liz was waiting at the bottom of the stairs.

"I can give the bag to your girlfriend," she said. "Good luck."

I didn't get it. She seemed genuine, not ironic. I nodded and handed over Cathy's bag.

I turned toward the doors. I put my hand on the inner door and took a glance up the stairwell. I could see only to the landing. No sign of Cathy.

I pushed through the pair of doors to the cool evening air, leaving behind the second woman I had ever loved.

Chapter 3

Dave Barlow is nine years old. It's a Saturday morning in Dayton, Ohio and past time to get up. A March wind blows outside, and sun shines though shifting maple tree branches and into the south window. Dave lies in his bed, wondering.

He thinks about Clint Eastwood.

Last week, his mom and dad were away for an overnight. Before they left, Dave sat on the stairs and listened to them talking in the kitchen. Something about rescuing the marriage. Like it was a drowning dog. The night they were gone, Dave stayed over at the McCarthy's place down the street. Frankie is the same age, and his sister is twelve. Frankie's sister, Barb, is pretty, so Dave has multiple reasons for enjoying time spent there.

They have a TV in a room on the second floor. While Frankie's parents were downstairs, the three of them watched Dirty Harry*. In movies, some problems actually got solved. They didn't always go on and on and on.*

Dave lies in bed, wondering. Does he feel lucky today? And what is a punk?

The truth is he is likely to be lucky in the mornings. It's the nights when his dad comes home drunk or gets drunk at home. A couple of times his mom has thrown out the liquor, to stop his dad from getting drunk at home. That didn't turn out well.

Dave knows about the gun. The pistol.

On the top shelf in his parent's bedroom, in an wooden old cigar box, is a handgun.

The cigar box is all scuffed and beat up. The cover says "Fonseca." Inside it, nested on an old scarf, is a small pistol. It smells vaguely of old machine oil, like his dad's toolbox. The pistol has "RUGER" in capital letters on it.

Dave doesn't know how many bullets it holds. But he wonders. What would it feel like to put the barrel next to his head? To pull the trigger?

Would he be lucky? Would the gun fire and end all his problems? Would he feel anything? Or would the bullet just glance off, hurting like mad, making a giant mess, and making his life even worse?

Or what if he pointed the gun at his father? He could tell him he couldn't treat Mom and him like that anymore. But an adult isn't going to think a kid is really going to pull the trigger. His dad would just take the gun away and things would be even worse.

Or Dave could pull the trigger. Their lives would be better. Except for the whole going to jail and ruining his life part. And down deep he thinks his mother does love his dad. He could take care of one problem and have his mother hate him forever.

Maybe they will win the lottery. Maybe his dad will have a heart attack. Not one that kills him, of course, but one that convinces him to change his ways.

Now Dave can hear his parents downstairs. Their voices are soft, too faint to make out what they are saying. But his dad is not shouting. Maybe today will be OK. Maybe Dave won't make a mistake that makes his dad angry. Maybe his mom will do the same. It could happen. Dave has seen days like that. Days that look like the All-American family.

Dave gets out of bed. He pulls the covers up on the bed and shrugs on some jeans. He wears the t-shirt from yesterday.

Dave goes downstairs, wondering if today he will be lucky.

Chapter 4

As I stepped out of the restaurant I felt like I was back in the upside-down Acura, confused, concussed, hurting. Night was nestling in on the mountain town. In my imagination I was an ocean diver swimming in the presence of a cluster of octopi squirting black ink that slowly transformed from tendrils into clouds and gradually obscured the environment. Since I was ten, I've been visited by occasional and unpredictable dark images, sometimes silly, sometimes grotesque, in response to seemingly random stimuli.

Those dark images were part of what I'd intended to talk to Cathy about this weekend.

I sat in the Subaru for about forty-five minutes, hoping against hope that Cathy would knock on the window, saying how sorry she was that she had jumped to the conclusion that I was somehow lying about a thing as basic as where I went to high school. Later, I found it difficult to recall one coherent thought from that time.

The Bed and Breakfast was about fifteen minutes away. I had guaranteed payment, so there would be no refund, but I didn't care about that. I considered going back home. There, given that Cathy had been such a frequent presence, the house would feel empty, just like after Allison died. And then Allison's death and Cathy's distrust would be additive, making things even worse than right after Allison died. From past experience, I knew more than one nightmare would be in store tonight, so I was in no rush to try to sleep.

At least an empty B&B room would be closer to a normal experience. Cathy could find me there if she had a change of heart. I hated myself for holding out that hope. I was mostly an optimistic person, but holding out hope for something that was not to be was just sad. I drove.

The B&B had a Woodland Park address, but it was a bit outside of what I had considered "town." I got back on Highway 24 and went west. Soon I turned onto a two-lane asphalt road, then onto a smaller dirt road leading past an array of pedestal mailboxes, between ridges, and up the hillside. I passed a giant boulder larger than a house as the rough road twisted upward. The smell of dust mingled with the pine scent.

Even the B&B name mocked me. Pikes Peak Paradise Bed & Breakfast. The building sported giant white gothic pillars that would have looked right at home in front of a Southern mansion.

I checked in like an automaton, barely recalling whether the clerk had been male or female.

The room was everything I'd hoped it would be. Before. Fireplace. A king-sized bed. Three large windows onto a balcony. Outside, a pine forest fell away sharply, dimly lit by the stars. Pike Peak rose toward the sky in the distance. The difference between looking at this alone instead of with my arms wrapped around Cathy was unbelievable.

I flopped onto the bed feeling eighty years old. A faint scent of laundry soap lingered in the air. My right shoulder and right knee still hurt from the accident more than a year ago. I'd probably go to my grave complaining about the aches.

Pain seems cumulative. As I lay there on the bed, utterly alone again, the last car trip that had gone terribly wrong swam up from the depths, and the night Allison died came back to me. It was almost as though I were in the car with her.

~~~

The driver behind us maintained his distance even after I slowed. We kept climbing through the night toward Monarch Pass.

Traffic was negligible on this section of Route 50, but the headlights trailed us a hundred yards back. Perhaps the driver thought my

Acura was an unmarked State Patrol car. Or he just obeyed the speed limit. Some drivers are like that.

On the other hand, maybe he was deliberately following us. But for what reason? I cut off that thought. What felt like paranoia was, according to my shrink, mere hypervigilance.

The dark highway ahead snaked through the gaps between peaks. Spruce, fir, and lodgepole pines crept up the mountainside to our left, down the slope to our right. The drive back from Crested Butte had us close enough to the center of Colorado that someone using a state map for target practice would find us right in the bull's-eye.

I willed myself to ignore the car behind. After a relaxing breath, I risked a long glance at Allison in the passenger seat. Her features were easily visible in the pale light from the dashboard, and her short blonde hair backlit by our tail. She made me think of the old Clairol ads on the backs of my mother's magazines.

Allison noticed my glance and her smile intensified. Her hand resting on my thigh tightened as she looked back at me. *My fiancée,* I thought for the hundredth time in the past five days. I felt so loved, so happy, that my PTSD symptoms were barely an issue. I think I was good for her, too. As we'd been getting to know each other, she'd had frequent somber moments, bordering on depression like mine, but hers were rare now.

The only bump in the night was the unknown thing that was bothering Allison, and so far I'd been unable to coax her into revealing it. Naturally I was determined to make it about me. Maybe I'd said something wrong, a criticism or misstatement that would explain this slightly subdued mood.

As the miles raced under us, though, I was still happy, unaware of how short our engagement would be. Ignorance and bliss, holding hands.

Pine trees on our left whipped past our high-beams into darkness, set scenery constantly being swept into oblivion.

Allison turned to me. "You ready for me to drive?"

"Not yet. I still feel wired." I swallowed again to let my ears equalize the pressure as we continued up the slope.

"I think you've felt wired for five days now."

"More than that." I grinned. It's true that my tension had been higher than average for the past couple of weeks, but my normal state was to be more wired than she realized. Her presence in my life was helping me push out of that condition toward a more relaxed level.

"You shouldn't have been nervous. You foreshadowed the big question enough to know what the answer would be."

Five days earlier, I had asked Allison to marry me. I'd made dinner reservations at a popular restaurant. I had some of our favorite oldies playing in the car on the way. Not "Love Hurts" or "Rainy Night in Georgia," but "When I Fall in Love" and "Happy Together."

My plan had not anticipated a forest fire that started that same day. The smoke was so bad that in my totally sealed house the smoke alarm went off. Newscasts stressed the fear that the fire would travel up the mountain pass toward Green Mountain Falls and Woodland Park, near where Allison's father, Ben, lived. Ben Stuart could have paid enough people to spit on the fire to put it out in an hour. With bonuses for "above and beyond the call of nature" he could have halved the crowd size.

After a couple of days of heavy smoke and work stoppages, Allison and I had decided to hit the hills. Most of my investment clients were preoccupied with the fire, and Allison was on summer break, between continuing education classes. It seemed a good time to be elsewhere.

"Is anything bothering you?" I asked for the second time tonight. I felt I had a fairly good handle on Allison by now, knowing what it meant when she was very talkative, knowing what it meant when she was more quiet than usual.

She hesitated, a guarantee that the answer was "yes."

"Your dad?" Her father had been recently diagnosed with lung cancer. The doctors were still saying it was treatable.

"Nothing I'm ready to talk about, Dave," she said. "But it's not about you or about us. 'Us' is the best thing that ever happened to me." Allison smiled again, her good smile. She got high marks at conversation and body language. Only her handwriting fell below par. Reading notes from her reminded me of playing hangman. Some of the letters were unmistakable, but the ones in between had to be deduced from context. Maybe without telling me, she was thinking of abandoning teaching and had applied to medical school.

We'd spent last night and a lot of the day at Crested Butte. We passed through Gunnison less than an hour ago.

In a minute she said, "I have a new dream for you." Allison had a long-time interest in the subconscious at work.

"Shoot." I didn't point out that this was an easy way to divert the conversation from whatever issue was troubling her. Unless the dream was related.

"OK. In the dream I find a cat in a closet. I don't recognize the cat or the closet. The cat is one of those puff-balls — all white and fluffy and pretty."

"I think that means you want to have sex with me again."

"Shut up." She gave me a wide smile. "That's true, but that's probably not what the dream is saying." She squeezed my thigh again and moved her hand slightly north. I maintained admirable control of the vehicle.

We reached the summit of Monarch Pass, which was nothing special visually, but was the Continental Divide at 11,300 feet. We started down and the second lane went away. The driver behind me had lost his chance for an easy pass.

Perversely the guy closed the gap by half. I sped up a little to maintain distance, and he didn't press it. My pulse rate had crept up, but I took a few deep breaths to relax.

"Ok, the cat. The cat is beautiful and in the dream I have good feelings about it, but then I see it's been playing with a bloodied little mouse. The poor thing is so tiny and sweet and completely helpless given the cat's power over it."

"So I'm the mouse?"

Another smile. "So I put the mouse in a cardboard box, and I see someone else in the room. I hand the mouse box over. That person, I can't tell the age, the gender. It's almost like looking at one of the grays, you know, the aliens in the movies. You can't tell whether that's a cool guy or a sexy lady or what. No clue about age."

Allison went on. "The gray, or the person, whatever, takes the mouse in the box. I turn back to the cat in the closet, but it's no longer there. In its place is a dog, one of those small ones, a schnauzer I think. And then I woke up."

Being serious for a moment, I asked, "Does it mean anything to you? You feel any resonances?"

The road was turning to the left as Allison opened her mouth to speak. She was interrupted by a muffled *bang*! A blowout. The car shook and pulled to the right, hard. The hood tilted down on the right.

No way to change trajectory.

We crashed through the guardrail, careened off a boulder, and bounced over.

The airbags exploded. The car filled with mist. Allison and I let out discordant, scared yelps. In my head, reverberating echoes of gunfire blasted at me from all directions, but no one was shooting at us.

My stomach lurched. For a long moment the car sailed in freefall, and I coughed on a lungful of toxic fumes and particles. The car tilted. Tilted more. The view ahead was hidden. The one thought my brain flung to the top of the list was, "Now the airbag is spent, what's the next impact going to be like?"

I reached for Allison. I couldn't tell if we were headed for a tree or a flat spot, but when we hit, we crashed into something that hit back. Hard.

Chapter 5

The universe was black. A constant noise assailed my ears. Gravity was all screwed up. My chest ached.

I could not form a coherent thought. For a time, all I could manage was a crude version of "What's going on?" The world went black again.

For an instant I was back in a closet in Dayton, Ohio. A moment later I was in the kitchen in Dayton, blood pooling on the floor. Finally I remembered going over the side of the road. In Colorado.

My eyes opened, I think. I couldn't see anything. Right, it was dark. At least I hoped that was the only explanation.

Allison! I tried to call her name, but no sound came out. My throat burned. My chest throbbed. I moved my right arm toward her, and a sudden sharp pain lanced through my shoulder, as if someone had exploded a firecracker in the joint. The world went black again.

My eyes flickered opened again sometime later. Noise was there again, and I couldn't tell whether it was rushing water, or blood pounding through my veins, or ringing in my ears. Nothing made sense. My face and torso felt cold, my hands colder.

My head felt congested, under pressure. Something moved up my cheek. Slowly I realized I was hanging upside down. Blood was leaking from somewhere and travelling up my head and dripping onto the roof of the car. For a second, the surface looked like old diamond-patterned linoleum covering with blood. My breath was ragged, accompanied by a sharp pain on my right side that came and went, in time with my breathing. The air smelled faintly of fireworks and something I couldn't identify. An image of my mother in distress took center stage in my brain, but seconds later the curtains closed and the present grew visible again.

I sensed that Allison was motionless beside me, but I couldn't see her, let alone reach her. I could not hear her breathing. Oh, God, Allison. A picture of my mother, her arm raised level, flared in my mind.

A bright spark. Then gone. Seconds later it came again. From outside the car. Someone with a flashlight. Thank God.

I tried to call out and the world went black again, for seconds or minutes. Light flared again, nearing, jittering across the nearby brush, coming closer.

The light stopped on the passenger side. I tried to turn my head. This time I moved slowly enough that the piercing pain didn't put me out again, but I could turn my head only an inch.

A deep *thud* sounded. Another. And another. Then the passenger window cracked and bits of glass sprinkled down. Something metallic cleared more of the shards out of the way. Louder tinkling now as pieces of glass rained down on other pieces of glass.

I think an arm reached into the car, two arms. Someone leaning into the car. I had a split-second impression of facial hair. Someone was touching Allison. Her neck, her ear. Suddenly Allison turned her head to face me. The stranger's arms disappeared. Allison's eyes were closed now.

I tried to cry out to her, but my throat was too tight. I don't even know if I made a sound. Tears wet my eyes and escaped onto my eyebrows. The world went black again.

Noise woke me. I was still in the car. Lights, two this time, swinging over the ground ahead of me, coming closer.

Another shadowy figure reached into Allison's window. Seconds later, a man's voice said, "She's dead."

Back there in the darkness of distant memory I heard an echo of someone saying that before.

Pain shut out the world again.

The next sound was a man shouting, "We've got to get him out!" Light was lasering in from behind me, flickering light. The roof of the car and the cracked windshield seemed to be dusted with talcum powder.

Another voice, maybe a man, maybe a woman, "Be careful!"

Sometime later, a shape appeared at my window. I had the impression of hiking boots on the ground outside. The window was already gone, and my side of the car had shed a scattered pile of fractured safety glass. "We've got to get you out right away, Buddy. There's a fire behind your car." The man, I think it was a man, reached toward me with a knife.

I flinched, sending pain through the top of my head as if a knitting needle were driven into my skull. My right knee felt like it had been bent backward. The hand with the knife began sawing my seatbelt. When the threads parted and I fell, the pain blasted my skull. The world went black and lonely for a long time.

~~~

Involuntarily reliving that awful night just compounded my sense of loss. I lay on the bed in the Pikes Peak Paradise Bed & Breakfast and wiped my eyes. I took a couple of ragged breaths.

My departure from the reunion once again took center stage in my mind.

I already knew I wasn't going to confront Cathy with any proof, but I needed at least a little corroboration for my own peace of mind. To prove I wasn't going crazy. I sat on the edge of the bed and called Marty, the only friend from high school I kept in touch with. The real high school.

"Marty here." His voice in my ear was the most welcome thing in the past hour. I recognized his voice. Thank God.

"It's Dave. Dave Barlow."

I had a couple of terrible seconds as I imagined him saying, "Dave who?" but he came back with, "Hi, guy. We missed you. How are you doing? And what time is it?"

Relief flooded me. "I'm really sorry about the time. I'll explain later. I—must have gotten my wires crossed. I thought the reunion was this weekend." It would have been nice to see him. He knew about my history and cut me more slack than some.

"Oh, man. It was last weekend. I should have looked up your number and called." I could see an image of Marty leaning back with a beer in his hand. His medium-length black hair would be in the deliberately unkempt style. He would be stroking an imaginary beard as he thought about things. We'd learned not to talk politics in today's polarized climate, but that was OK. We probably agreed on most things anyway. It was the screamers on both ends of the spectrum who made it tough for all of us closer to the middle.

"No, it's all right. I'm just sorry I missed you."

"Next time you're in town?"

"You got it." I had another thought. "By the way, how did you get your notice? Email, letter, voicemail?"

"A letter. Are you on the mailing list?"

"I'll make sure. Thanks, Marty." My notice had come in email. I'd never seen a letter.

He hung up. So I was alone and screwed, not alone and crazy. I guessed that was better.

In the bathroom, I took an Ambien in hopes of sleep.

I thought one more time about the idea of calling Cathy. But the likelihood of just hearing the line ring and ring, or having the call shunted to voicemail, was too much. I wanted no more "no's" and no more conflict in my life. I'd rather walk into a biker bar and bet no one could kick me in the nuts hard enough to make me whimper.

Chapter 6

Today is not one of Dave's lucky days.

Most of the kids he knows look forward to Saturdays. Not Dave.

On Saturdays, Dave's father doesn't work. Fatigue and stomach troubles from his deployment overseas — he got out of the Army when Dave was six — mean that he misses a fair number of work days at the post office, but Fridays and Saturdays are currently his regular days off.

On those days, his father starts drinking earlier. He complains about the Army telling him his symptoms are all in his head. He complains about the meals Dave's mother fixes. He complains that Dave hasn't done his chores. If Dave is actually caught up on his chores, his father complains about jobs Dave didn't know were on the list. Dave's mother has tried to explain about PTSD, but at the moment it all sounds made up.

Most of the time, Dave tries to hide from his father. Out of sight, out of his mind.

Dave is bagging cut grass heaped after mowing the back yard when his father calls to him. "Dave, get in here." His father is at the back door of the garage.

In just those few words, Dave can hear the anger, the slightly slurred words. If only there were a way to have the confrontation out here, where other people could see. Maybe someone could step in and stop this.

Dave hesitates. He catches sight of his mother at the kitchen sink. Her eyes look hollow. She ducks her head, pretending she's unaware of what's going to happen. Seconds later she's gone from the window.

Dave promises himself that if he ever marries he's not going to find a weak woman. Not one who would let herself be victimized. Not one who would fail to prevent harm to her children.

"Dave!" *His father's voice is louder, angrier.*

Dave leaves the mower where it is. Drops the bag of clippings. He moves toward the garage at a precisely calculated pace. One as slow as he can possibly make it without further angering his father.

He glances at the neighbor's windows. No faces.

"Yes, sir," *Dave says as he reaches the door to the garage. He hopes being polite will at least keep things from being worse than they already are.*

"My hammer isn't in the toolbox." *From a yard away, Dave can smell the piney odor of gin.*

So that's what it's going to be this time. His father barely touches his toolbox or the tools on the pegboard at the back of the garage. But when he does, every tool had better be exactly where it should be. It doesn't matter if his father has loaned a tool to a neighbor and forgotten about it. Or if Dave is using it because the day before his father asked him to do a chore that required that tool and he is not finished yet. Rules are rules, young man.

Dave goes to the movies once in a while, or watches them on TV. For an instant he fantasizes about quoting a movie line and saying to his father, "Fuck you, asshole." *Or even,* "Frankly my dear, I don't give a damn." *Maybe,* "You talkin' to me?"

Like that would happen. "I'm sorry. I was replacing a board in the fence."

"It looks to me like you were mowing the yard."

"Well, yeah, right now. But earlier—"

"Don't talk back to me!"

I wasn't, *Dave thinks. He knows better than to say it.*

"You need to shape up. Be responsible."

"I try—"

"Shut up." *His father's voice is softer now. Some people might think that's a good thing, but Dave knows better.*

His father unfastens his belt buckle and pulls his belt out through the loops. Slowly. Deliberately. "Lean against the wall."

Dave's voice quivers. "Please, I'll remember next time."

"You're damn right you will. Do it!"

Dave leans against the garage wall as his father closes the door to the back yard. As the light is cut off, Dave can smell the fresh grass clippings he brought in fifteen minutes earlier.

"Please!"

"Shut up!"

The first lash against his butt makes it feel like his jeans aren't even there. Tears flow even before the second.

By the fifth blow, Dave has little space in his mind for coherent thought, but the hurricane of emotions whirls one vow to the fore. This stops with me. I will never have kids.

Chapter 7

A sound woke me.

I lay on top of the covers on the bed in the Pikes Peak Paradise B&B, feeling as far from paradise as was humanly possible. I opened my eyes. My watch said the time was 3:20AM.

Cathy had not showed up at my door. She'd not texted or called or emailed. I chided myself for hoping for such a thing even as I continued to hope.

I jolted even wider awake as a noise from outside intruded into the room. A sound like someone bumping into a table. I looked out the window onto the dark landscape but saw nothing.

On the bedside table, my phone was blinking. An incoming text message. Maybe it was Cathy!

I grabbed the phone, feeling my pulse racing.

But no, it was not from Cathy. I couldn't tell who it was from—the space where it should have showed a name or number was a string of zeroes. I stared at the message and felt chilly.

"How does it feel to be forgotten so quickly? Have a nice day. ☺"

What the hell?

Without pausing for thought, I shot back, "Who is this?"

No response. Eventually the phone's backlight went off, leaving me once again in the dark.

I puzzled over the message. The sender must have been the person who set up the fake reunion party. So I went to my ten-year reunion and people had already forgotten about me, as though I never existed. That was the message?

Of course no one had forgotten me. The party was rigged to put me in that frame of mind. But what was the message really saying? That I had forgotten someone too fast?

Allison was the obvious choice, but I hadn't forgotten about her. I thought of her every day. She had even joined my nightmares.

Maybe a forgotten investment client? Had I mistreated anyone, lost a lot of money for a client? Not everyone gained and not everyone listened to the advice they solicited. But I couldn't think of anyone who'd lost enough to seek retribution.

But clearly someone was angry with me. Angry enough to stage an elaborate fake reunion just to make a point, just to hurt me.

I realized I'd temporarily forgotten about the bullet holes in my car door and the happy face. And the text ended with a happy face.

So the vandalism had been a warning.

And the timing of the text. Maybe the sender figured I would have drifted off to sleep my now and the text would wake me, send my pulse racing, making it impossible to get back to sleep. Mission accomplished.

So if whoever it was, was angry about me moving on after Allison, that meant it had to be someone close to Allison. Or could it be someone close to Cathy, someone seeing me as a jerk for starting to see Cathy when Allison had been gone for only ten months?

I started putting together a mental list. If it were someone close to Allison, that meant it could be her father, Ben. Or her sister, Maddy. Or maybe a close friend. Certainly her father and her sister had the resources.

Who close to Cathy could have done this? Her parents, maybe. She had no siblings. I couldn't think of a friend who might feel strongly about her, but I didn't know everything about who she'd dated or who all her friends were.

As I thought about it, I realized the use of a restaurant bar was not actually a costly choice for setting this up. Two hired shills, for sure, "Liz" and "John." But the others in the "reunion party" could have been anyone. At least anyone in the approximate age range. Someone else could have been having a party and this con job just piggybacked on it.

Scanning, modifying the pictures, and printing a new yearbook. That was not like paying for a European vacation. Someone could have done it for less than a week's pay.

Still, it had to be someone really angry.

This had to be someone lashing out at me. But was it really about Allison and moving on? Maybe that was a red herring to shift the blame. In my office, Stan gave me a smile from time to time, but it always felt fake, forced. He had to be feeling the pressure from a new guy meeting his commission targets when Stan was having trouble. And I knew he'd been angered when one of his clients asked me for a second opinion.

The client, a restaurant owner in her fifties, asked me about "churning" and whether that might be happening to her account with Stan. After I took a quick look at her account, I told her I didn't have enough information to say anything conclusively, although my gut tightened as I reviewed the file. My lukewarm defense of Stan must not have been enough, because shortly after that she moved her account to another firm.

Stan could easily afford to set up something like this. I had no idea whom to really suspect, but I decided that when I made it back to the office, this disaster was not going to show on my face.

I rose from the bed suddenly and fumbled toward the door, a rash plan of action flickering through my brain. I jammed my knee against a table leg. A bolt of lightning surged into the joint and blew away all conscious thought.

When I could finally put weight on my leg again, I moved more cautiously to the door. I left my overnight bag where it was. I'd be back.

The B&B was quiet as I made my way down the stairs, out past the registration area, and through the small lot to the Subaru. The mountain air was cold. July was one of the few months the nighttime temperature stayed above freezing. At the moment it was probably low fifties with enough of a breeze to make it feel more like low forties. As I drove, the roads were deserted, like unused test tracks. Aside from light traffic on Highway 24, I noticed only a couple of sets of headlights as I drove back to the Mexican restaurant.

The place was closed. No surprise. Inside, a couple of safety lights shed enough of a dim yellow glow that the cops might be able to see burglars if they stood up directly under the lights. The parking lot was nearly deserted. The only vehicle there was an old blue or black Nissan that maybe would no longer start. I went to the door and peered inside toward the stairwell, trying to spot the reunion poster. It was gone.

Occasional cars cruised along the main drag a half-block away, but no headlights were directed my way.

I walked north, toward the rear of the restaurant, hearing little but my footsteps and the wind in nearby trees. I should have put on a jacket. A cardboard McDonald's fries holder skittered on the pavement.

The area around the dumpsters was more dimly lit than the rest of the parking lot. Two dumpsters with flat tops sat in the far northwest corner.

I sighed, thinking this was stupid, and nearly turned around. I imagined a solid yard-high mass of leftover food that even a Japanese game show contestant would balk at touching.

The top of the nearer dumpster was about five and a half feet tall, so I could just peer over the edge. The smell was actually not that bad. Probably the top layers of stuff were from tonight. Both dumpsters had lids that covered half of the top surface. Probably they should be totally covered at night, as a preventive against bears, but maybe the last person out was tired. Or thought someone else was making another trip.

The other dumpster looked more promising. On top, within arm's reach, were some cardboard boxes. I snagged a couple of them, nested them for strength, and gingerly stepped onto my makeshift stool.

They crunched under my weight. That was not going to work.

I circled the dumpsters. Behind one lay a couple of cheap, wooden produce crates. I put one in place of my crunched cardboard stool. As I stepped onto it, it flexed. But it held.

I could see better, but I had to use my phone's light to actually make out stuff in the morass below. Discarded food, empty cans and jars, more cardboard. But in the corner beyond my reach was paper refuse. Napkins and some paper cups mostly, but what looked like a small stack of flat pieces of paper.

I was trying to figure out how to get to that paper, and wondering vaguely how I would fend off a foraging bear, when I realized a vehicle was approaching. I ducked, trying get out of sight quickly while not moving fast enough to trigger the eye's automatic attraction to motion. The outline of the police lights atop the vehicle came into view.

Perfect. I wondered what the penalty for dumpster diving was here.

The cop car was driving north on the street just to the west of the restaurant, but it was at least eight or ten feet higher, on the other side of a retaining wall. Maybe they hadn't spotted me.

Even if there was no penalty for skulking, I didn't want the humiliation of a ride in the back of a police car and the hour of explanation.

The road was paved. Grit crunched under the tires as the car slowed near me. I kept my head down, having no idea if I could merely bluff my way through this, walking casually through the lot and explaining I was out for a nighttime constitutional.

The car stopped. The sounds of a distant radio dispatcher made my pulse rate flare.

The car started up again, and my ears said it was taking a right turn, taking it just north of me, again just beyond a retaining wall. I crouch-walked around the dumpster, heading for the corner, where I would be concealed from the parking lot.

For a brief second I felt more secure and then I remembered the produce crate. Crap. I scuttled to the corner and pulled it back toward me.

A mere second later, a brilliant white light shot from the stopped police car maybe fifty feet to the east of me. Light hit the area a couple of feet from me and I jerked sideways. Thankfully the dumpster sat directly on the ground, so they had no chance of being able to see my feet.

The light stayed there for long seconds. Maybe garbage was more valuable here than in my neighborhood.

Then the police car moved off and I began to breathe once more. The car rolled ten feet farther east and stopped again.

When the space next to the dumpster was suitably dark again, I peered around. The bright light was illuminating my license plate.

After ten or fifteen seconds that felt like minutes, the light moved, falling to rest on the license plate of the Nissan that also occupied the lot.

And then the police car was moving again, heading east. It sounded like it was moving farther away, and then I could hear it no longer. The only car noise was the light main-drag traffic just south of the restaurant.

I waited. In my imagination, the police car had stopped in sight of the parking lot entrance, and now a couple of armed cops were quietly making their way toward me, one on each side of me.

Crap. Wasn't there enough real crime in Woodland Park?

Minutes passed and with no sound other than wind in the trees and occasional traffic on the main drag. I was freezing. Much longer out here and I might welcome a nice ride in a warm police car.

I waited another five minutes as I considered walking right back to my car and getting the hell out of there.

Instead, I took cautious stock of the area and got back up on my crate.

I couldn't tell enough about the stack of papers that lay beyond my reach. But I could see some flattened cardboard boxes a little closer.

I snagged the boxes and pulled them toward me. They could form a crude bridge, using the same principle as snowshoes. Spread the weight over a large enough area and stay afloat.

Seconds later I was in the dumpster, already convinced this was a terrible idea. Some of the restaurant odors were here—cheese, chili peppers, onions—but they were overlaid with spoiled milk, rotting lettuce. My brain, being unhelpful as it was sometimes, conjured up a movie image from years ago, a character snooping or hiding in an industrial trash compactor, suddenly threatened by the machinery being put in motion. That image made me wonder if the trucks that emptied these dumpsters came during the day or during the night. And were they loud enough that I'd hear one coming over the beating of my heart? A person in a dumpster like this could be thrown into the back of a trash truck where the hydraulic press would make him indistinguishable from the rest of the garbage. People who claim it's a gift to be imaginative are not seeing the whole picture.

I crept forward, feeling the cardboard shifting unevenly under me, afraid I'd plunge off into the mushy and slimy leftovers. And then I did slip. *Yuck!* The feeling was worse than the fear. It was like rolling in mashed potatoes. That had been thrown up. And then gone rancid. I somehow managed to get back on my surfboard and calm the rocking. I leaned forward.

My fingers reached the stack of papers.

Was that the sound of the police car returning? I guess it was just my heart jack-hammering in my chest.

I grabbed the stack. As I backed up, I realized the cardboard had settled a few inches into the sea of refuse below. I leaned back over the side of the dumpster and swung my feet toward the waiting produce crate. I winced at a jolt of pain and my knee hit the dumpster. Where was the crate? There! I made contact.

Back on the pavement, I scanned my surroundings, half-convinced the cops would be right behind me, ready to tap on my shoulder.

The parking lot was deserted. I reached my car and stashed the pile of papers in the back seat.

I started the Subaru, and moved slowly out of the lot. I didn't spot a police car. Or a bear.

I ran the heat on high for miles until I pulled over on the shoulder. At least here, if a cop came along, I could just explain that I was drowsy and decided to stop for a minute.

The papers on top of the stack were kids' coloring and puzzle pages. I flashed on a T-shirt saying, "I went to Woodland Park, and all I got was a stack of greasy menus."

But deep down was pay-dirt. Folded into rough quarters was the reunion poster. With it were the photos from the stairwell.

Now that I had them, I wasn't sure what to do with them, or even if I wanted to do anything with them. But if I'd waited, I wouldn't have had the decision to make.

I drove slowly back to the B&B as my heart rate gradually approached normal.

My car smelled like rancid milk. Or was that me?

Chapter 8

The absolute worst day of Dave's childhood starts out as one of the best.

It's a Saturday in December in Dayton. Dave goes to a Toy Story *movie with Mike and Mike's mom at the Cinemark. What amazing animation. And the popcorn! Nothing better than movie popcorn.*

On the drive home, a light snow starts to fall, and thoughts of Christmas start to flicker at the edges of Dave's brain. Maybe this Christmas will be better. Like Christmases in the movies. Or like the day he went to work with his father. His father was happy, showing off the sorting equipment, and he seemed genuinely proud to introduce Dave to his fellow workers.

But when Dave waves goodbye to Mike and his mom, then opens the front door to his house, he can hear them arguing. More precisely, he can hear his father yelling and his mother placating. His heart sinks. Coming from the wonderful escape of a movie with a friend and arriving here is like falling through fractured ice and plunging into freezing lake water.

They're in the kitchen. His father is even louder than normal. He wanted steak tonight. Not salmon. He never gets angry because of who won the election or whether we should have troops in the latest country. It's always something like what's for dinner, or what mom is wearing, or where are the car keys.

Dave is about to creep up the stairs when his father paces to the side of the kitchen where Dave is visible.

"And you," he father yells. "You were supposed to be back an hour ago. Get in here."

Dave dutifully walks to the kitchen, starting to feel numb.

"Well?" his father asks. The smell of gin is on his breath. His shirt tail is partly out of his pants.

"We came straight back from the movie. We—"

"The hell you did! It's almost six. You—"

"He's right on time," says his mother quietly. She's wearing a lime-green blouse and dark pants. Her hair is a bit mussed.

His father turns toward her with exaggerated slowness. "You interrupted me." He moves toward her.

"I was just explaining—"

Without warning, Dave's father slaps her. An instant of shocked silence follows, then Dave's father shoves her against the stove. Her arm flies and smashes a pot sideways. Steaming water cascades over the stove top and onto the floor. Dave's mother cries out when the boiling water coats her arm.

"Shut up!" Dave's father yells. He slaps her again.

She falls to the floor. His father doesn't reach to help her. Dave does not either. Dave knows that when his mother rises, his father will hit her again. Experience is a brutal teacher.

Dave takes all this in, feeling completely helpless. He knows that nothing he can do will help. And at that moment something snaps. A neuron that has never fired before fires now. Dave can *help. If nothing else, he can divert attention from his mother. The movie lines flood through his brain and in an instant he makes an awful decision, one that will haunt him for a long time.*

Dave pushes at his father, who loses his balance because of the unexpected direction the threat comes from.

And Dave says something he will never forget. Ever. He says the Terminator *line. "Fuck you, asshole."*

The dynamic shifts as quickly as a static shock.

"What did you say to me?" His father asks, struggling to his feet. Disbelief makes his eyes go wide.

"I said stop hitting her."

Dave's father's complexion is ruddy much of the time from drinking. Now it goes even redder. He steps closer, bends forward, and punches Dave in the stomach.

Dave's breath is gone. He can't pull in another one. It's like his lungs are paralyzed. The pain is horrendous.

But at least his father is no longer focused on his mother.

Dave's father punches him in the face. Lightning shoots through Dave's nose and blood is flowing down his face, into his mouth. So much blood.

Dave steadies himself on the kitchen counter and he reaches for his nose, to stanch the flow, but his father shoves him sideways. Mixed in with the confusion Dave hears his mother scurrying away. Good. At least some good will happen because of this.

Dave's father hits him again, and Dave falls. The lights dim.

Dave realizes he has missed some of the action. He's on his back, breathing again, thank God, but his father kneels above him and slaps him hard. Fireworks go off right in front of Dave's face.

His father backhands him. More fireworks.

Then Dave hears a sound he has never heard before. A snick *or a* click. *Metal on metal. And then he hears something else he's never heard before.*

His mother's voice is ragged, but more forceful than she's ever been until now. She says, "Get away from him."

Dave's father seems to understand what's happening more quickly than Dave does. He rises, giving Dave the chance to wipe blood from his eyes.

His mother stands in the kitchen, a couple of yards away, and she's holding something.

The pistol.

She has the gun from the upstairs closet. The one in the shoebox. And it's aimed at Dave's father.

"Put that thing down," Dave's father says.

"Not happening. You are never going to hurt him again. You got that?"

You go, Mom, *Dave thinks.* Scare him good, and maybe he'll change.

"Look at you. You have the safety on," Dave's father says, moving toward her, but his voice doesn't contain his normal confidence.

"Stop!"

Dave's father keeps moving. He says, "You don't even know how much trouble you're—"

Blam! *In the small kitchen, the sound of the gun seems even louder than in the Cinemark with the volume way up.*

Dave's father's forward motion has stopped. He lurches. One hand rising toward his chest. Tears are streaming down Dave's mother's face. Blam!

Dave's father drops to one knee. Dave is now merely an observer, no longer a participant, frozen in place by pain and shock.

His mother moves cautiously closer, still crying. Dave's father slowly collapses on the floor, and then he's motionless. Blood pools. She comes closer. Aims the gun at his head. Blam! *Dave flinches. She does not.*

Methodically now, Dave's mother puts two more bullets into the body. The body seems to flinch each time, but Dave knows that's just the force of the bullets.

More blood pools on the old diamond-patterned linoleum floor, spreading under the kitchen cabinets. So much blood.

A scent Dave recognizes is in the air. Fireworks have been his only exposure to it until now. But he understands that it's the scent of gunpowder.

He looks at his mother in amazement. He had wanted her to stick up for him, but not at this price.

Then it gets worse.

His mother looks down at Dave. She's no longer crying, but her expression one of infinite sadness. She mouths something to Dave, as though she's lost the ability to make sound.

Her lips form the words, "I'm sorry."

Then just as Dave's fogged brain is putting it all together and he starts to rise and scream, "No!" she does it.

Dave's mother lifts her arm, bends her elbow, aims the pistol into her open mouth, and pulls the trigger.

Blam!

As his mother falls, it's like the world is in slow motion. Dave's brain is buffeted by another whirlwind of terrible thoughts, and among them is, No, Mom! This is all my fault! I should have kept my mouth shut!

Chapter 9

As soon as I got back to my room at the B&B, I flipped on the gas fireplace and turned on every light. Gas generally doesn't provide the same degree of heat of a wood fireplace, but it helped. I wanted to sit in front of a small sun so hot it melted the paint on the walls. Instead I took a super-hot shower.

By the time I stepped out of the water and dried myself, it was 4:45AM. I'm ashamed to admit it, but I checked for messages. None.

At least I felt warm now. And I didn't smell like rancid milk. Be thankful for what you have, right?

I moved closer to my pants, trying to ignore the stink from them. Unsure how best to clean them, I ultimately just went back into the shower and washed them under the hot water. Once they were mostly wrung out, I hung them over a chair and put the chair near the fireplace.

Unbidden, a scenario popped up in which my pants caught fire and I had to evacuate the B&B in my underwear. I moved the chair back from the flames.

At a small square table, I rifled through my treasure haul. A bunch of used kids' menus, a discarded adult menu, and the prizes, one of the reunion posters and two of the pictures that had been posted in the stairwell.

The two pictures seemed to be simple blowups of actual yearbook pictures, the ones I recalled from the stairwell. Runners on a track, too far away to be identified. Two people behind a long table at the head of a filled room, again too far to recognize people.

The poster showed the head shots of sixteen students, eight males, eight females. There were "Liz" and "John" mixed in with the others. I tried to recall if the other faces on the poster matched what I could remember about the group seated at tables and booths in the restaurant.

It was hopeless. Most of my attention had been focused on "John" and "Liz." Well, let's be honest. Mostly on Liz and her low-cut top. I'd glanced at the people on the tables, few of whom were facing directly toward me, just long enough to get a sense that the crowd could have been between twenty and thirty people, about right for a sixteen-person reunion plus some spouses or friends and minus a few people not in the mood for a reunion.

The student-body head shots were all black and white and a little fuzzy. So whoever decided to turn my life inside out was not only angry, but also cheap.

A closer look at Liz and John showed the two faces I remembered. The backgrounds were the same shade of gray. I looked more closely at the other photos, seeing something I hadn't noticed before.

I wondered where these photos had been taken. In several of them I could see very faint outlines around the person's hair or shoulders. Editing artifacts. Subtle, but indicative of the original photos having other backgrounds. The pictures had been edited to make them seem to all be in the same batch. The same class.

But again, the editing was cheap. Then again, it was intended to pass scrutiny for just a short time. I wondered if someone was banking on Cathy's fairly quick reaction, knowing she wouldn't immediately jump to my defense and start looking for holes in the reunion story rather than assuming I was the liar.

Unless Cathy was in on it, too.

I dismissed that. For one thing, I could not believe she was that good a liar or actor. For another... Well, it was just that one thing mainly.

And I couldn't see how she could gain from participating in this fraud. Who did gain? All I could see for sure was who lost: me.

After another ten minutes I gave up. I was exhausted and jumpy. If I stayed at the B&B and was lucky enough to get to sleep, that would cost me for another day since I would miss checkout time. Instead, I decided to head back home.

But first I went back to the shower. I could smell rancid milk again.

I knew the stress was getting to me. It was only after I got out and finished drying off that I had the thought, *Probably it's the pants.*

Chapter 10

As I drove down Highway 24, getting closer to Colorado Springs, the valley containing Manitou Springs dropped away from the road on the right. Some of the hillside to the left showed burned trees from last year's fire. I hated to think all that remained of my relationship with Cathy was a pile of cinder and ashes.

The 31st Street exit took me over tiny Fountain Creek, across the Old Colorado City narrow business strip, and into one of the residential areas making up Colorado Springs' West Side.

A few minutes later, I reached the top of the mesa and turned right onto Mesa Road, a two-lane leading past Holmes Middle School and through my neighborhood.

Cathy should have been in the passenger seat.

My house was built in the 60s, one of the smallest ones on the right, with a view across a valley to the foothills and Pikes Peak. It was a low house with stucco facing and tight construction.

A brownish-gray rabbit first froze, and then quickly hopped away as I pulled into my short gravel driveway. I backtracked and grabbed some junk mail from the box before returning and closing the garage door.

No dog or cat greeted me inside. I've always liked animals, but being gone so much just wasn't fair to a pet.

I looked at my phone to make sure I hadn't missed a call during the drive down. No calls. Strong signal. Cathy was not going to call.

Unfocused anger welled up again. I found the prescription bottle tucked away in the back of the bedroom closet and took an anti-anxiety pill.

Having opened some windows, I sat down on the living room sofa. The top of Pikes Peak was partly lost in some clouds at the moment. The ground behind the house fell away into a small park, opening the view of a distant ridge of houses, and the expanse beyond. I loved this view. I loved this house.

And I loved Cathy. I'd been nearly to the point of telling her that. I had reached, "I love your smile," and, "I love your sense of humor," phrases I thought would convey how happy I was with her but not trigger any, "Oh, my god, this is too soon," responses.

I was still blown away by finding two people to love. In the beginning, Allison absolutely amazed me, first by creating such a strong desire in me, and then by loving me, despite my visible flaws. Given all the people I can take or leave, I figured that was it after Allison.

And then the revelation came with meeting Cathy. I had a sense of how rare such women are. Sure, the world is full of wonderful women, but when you subtract the ones either happy alone or happy together, and factor in how fussy I am, and how much of a wreck I am, the qualifying population is pretty rarefied. Cathy had showed me there could be life after the death of a loved one.

But now Cathy was over. And why? God, I wanted her. But I knew from past experience that I could lose more than I gained by fighting against what was meant to happen.

A soft refrigerator whine joined the sound of the gentle cross breeze. I sat there, wondering why things work out the way they do. Hunkering down and letting the storm pass was historically safer than engaging in a fight.

Apparently someone had been willing to periodically check my mailbox and steal the reunion letter. That seemed to show determination. But my mailbox was next to the road, not mounted to the outside of the house, so someone could stop there pretty quickly with low risk. I stayed so busy with work that I really didn't know my neighbors other than to occasionally wave as I was driving in or out. Or someone could have bribed a letter carrier. That one seemed pretty remote to me.

I had surprised myself by digging through the dumpster for that poster, but for now I wasn't willing to go much farther. Tomorrow I'd call the restaurant and see who made the booking, but my gut said that would be a dead end. If I were patient this would go away on its own. And with something like this going on in my life, I knew from hard experience that Cathy would be safer if I just left her alone. Fighting back could be a shortcut to unintended consequences.

I kept thinking about the bullet holes in my car door.

Chapter 11

Dave is eleven and living in the Colorado Rockies not too far from Hart-sel. Nearby are locations with homespun names like "Schoolmarm Draw" and "Sawdust Gulch." He lives with his Uncle Mark, his mother's brother, a wiry man with sun-bleached hair.

Uncle Mark has his own son, but Randy left for college a year ago.

Dave listens to a conversation between Uncle Mark and Mark's wife, Brenda, who's basically nice. An air vent carries their soft words to Dave's bedroom after lights out.

"...worried about him," Uncle Mark says.

"Give the boy time," Aunt Brenda says. She's a sturdy, jovial woman, hard-working just like Uncle Mark. Dave sometimes sees his mother's eyes in her eyes even though Uncle Mark is the one who's related to his mother.

"It's been almost two years. He's got to move past this."

"Some people heal more slowly than others. Lord, that boy went through tough times. It wasn't just the – time when it ended." Dave of course knows she means when her mother shot his father. "And he blames himself for not being able to stop it."

"He was ten, Brenda." Uncle Mark's voice rises. "And I've told him about her asking me if Dave could come here for a while if something happened. I think she'd already made up her mind about what she was going to do."

"I know that, Honey. But in Dave's mind, there's always the chance that he could have found the key, some way to reach his father, some way to defuse the anger. His problem isn't totally predictable, and people do get past it. Not a hundred percent, but lots."

"Yesterday I saw that Webster kid pushing Dave around again. Dave's got twenty pounds on him. One good punch, and that kid would stop."

"Fighting's not the answer to everything. You know that."

"I do know that. But sometimes a man has to fight for what's right. If we don't fight alongside the folks in Fairplay for our water rights, there'll be that many more streets being watered in Denver and the Springs, and the fields out here will all be brown. Our wells will run dry."

"Aren't you exaggerating—"

"Brenda—"

"OK, OK. I do know what you're saying. But he's only twelve."

"You're never too young to stand up for what's right. Dave can't spend his whole life hiding from trouble. Sometimes it comes looking for you."

Chapter 12

I was not ready to go back to work Monday morning, but I pulled out of the garage and headed for the office anyway. I drove on autopilot, leaving my subconscious to handle the traffic lights and turns. A couple of drivers along the way paid even less attention.

Feeling at least ten years older than my real age today, I was still exhausted. I'd slept badly of course, despite the prescription.

I don't think Allison or Cathy suspected how often I had nightmares. A few years earlier, I'd done some reading about lucid dreaming, the kind of dreaming where you come to understand within the dream that you are in fact dreaming, and at that point you can actually exert some control over the dream.

One flying dream over the desert was simply stunning. And let's be honest, there were a couple of amazing sex dreams. If I could dream what I wanted all the time, you could just hook me up to a feeding tube and—

A car honked, and I stepped on the gas, moving through the green light on Uintah and continuing around the gentle curve past an estate that looked abandoned, the kind of worn-down relic of the past that kid detectives loved to explore.

I never really got the control over dreaming that I had imagined I'd get. I suppose I lost patience after a while. But I did get one benefit that was worth it all. If I had a standard variety dad dream, er, bad dream, it would continue like normal. But if I had a genuine nightmare, like I realized I was back in the kitchen in Dayton, looking through a red film at my mother's tears, something triggered in my brain and suddenly I was aware I was dreaming. I had entered the lucid dreaming stage.

Once I was there, in that state, I just said to myself, "I am not doing this tonight." And I woke up.

It was pretty much foolproof. I only rarely had extended nightmares anymore. Just lots of beginning clips. Short enough that when I woke, I would no longer scream or struggle. My adrenaline levels would still soar. My heart would still race. But the dreams were no longer as bad as the full-blown, extended nightmares had been. If someone lay next to me in bed, she usually didn't even realize I was awake.

Unless I reached over to caress her, to touch her skin beneath my fingers, to feel alive. To force the past back into the past.

~~~

I pulled into the downtown parking lot still on autopilot. A half-block up Tejon Street was our door, leading to a wide staircase going up. The smell of coffee was strong in the air. Like other businesses not dependent on walk-ins, we had offices on the second floor, above the main restaurants, bars, and shops doing business on the ground floor. My knee was OK with the stairs today, thanks to months of physical therapy.

The lettering on our door window said "BTU Investments" which made some people think we handled investing in heating oil or furnaces. Beth Tilden Underwood was a financial genius, but her name-selection committee could have produced more bang for the Beth.

Her normal response was that using "Elizabeth" and "ETU" was no better. If people were more concerned about image than results, let them find other financial advice.

I waved to Beth as I moved to my desk. She was on the phone, which was true much of the day. Beth was single again. Crowding fifty and still loving her job. If your numbers stayed down for too long, the talk with Beth was no fun, but ordinarily she was the most upbeat and cheerful person I knew. If she'd been on the *Titanic* as it listed to port side and the steerage decks were flooding, she'd probably savor the dazzling beauty of the Milky Way that dark night.

No one else was in yet. People mostly set their own hours. Beth cared more about performance than appearance or desk time. All of us made a fair number of home or office calls to clients.

Fortunately the market wasn't bouncing around as much as last year and was generally trending upward. Indicators were mostly positive. Unemployment and housing numbers were near expectations. The Fed had made no big recent policy changes. All of those factors taken together meant we were in a period of less-frequent hand-holding, and could spend more time on new-client acquisition.

I sat down at my desk, already wanting a nap. My line showed no messages, but I knew that because my cell hadn't received any notices.

My first order of business was a call to Violet to find out if I could see her. Her secretary said she could fit me in at the end of the day. I put 5PM on my calendar, but I wouldn't forget after a weekend like this one.

A check of my email revealed nothing I hadn't previewed on the weekend. One said Ricardo was sick today. Another email told me that a follow-up call to a client would be prudent. I picked up the phone and called Frankie Estefan. Or as he normally introduced himself, "Frankie Estefan, no relation." He was a software engineer with Lockheed Martin, one of the giant tech employers in town. Luckily for phone-tag-prevention, he was at his desk.

I answered a couple of easy questions for him and got ready to hang up. "Have a nice day, Frankie."

With his voice slower than his normal cadence, he said, "I'm sorry, Dave. I can't do that."

"Stop it."

He laughed and hung up. If that line had been used in *Ishtar* instead of *2001*, no one would remember it.

Gloria, our company secretary, arrived loaded with a box of donuts. She was newly married and her calorie burn rate was high so she was trim, and for the moment so was I, but my attraction for donuts made me cautious.

"Morning, Gloria," I called. And smiled. Once in a while I would get her a Morning Glory arrangement from the florist down the street, and every time her reaction was like it happened only once a decade.

Her husband was a lucky guy. Too bad morning glories weren't as easy as roses to get and keep looking good.

"Come and get them," Gloria called back. She was a good-hearted person, but she had somehow gone through school without mastering the ability to differentiate statements and questions with inflection. She tended to end statements and questions alike with a rising inflection, which transformed statements like, "I like cats," into questions. "I like cats?" The result was that people who didn't know her either thought she was a little dim or very indecisive.

Stan Marston wasn't in yet. Once he was, the competition was on, whether for donuts or dollars.

I tried to lose myself in my work. On good days, that's not too hard. Today it was like pushing a log uphill with a number two pencil. For a little while, though, I must have succeeded.

"Bad weekend, huh?"

I looked up. Denise stood in front of my desk. She must have had ESP. She was pleasant, hard-working, early thirties, away on vacation packages as often as she and her husband could get away. Most of the time at the office she wore half glasses—reading glasses that let her look at you over the top rim. As I thought about it, I realized she was a glass-half-full person and the glasses suited her perfectly.

"How do you do that? I mean it was OK."

She looked straight at me for maybe five seconds. "We need to have lunch today."

"You're on."

She looked at me for another five seconds and then retreated to her own desk. Ricardo was my mentor at the firm, but Denise was the rock, my best work friend. Where Stan would guard his knowledge, Denise would share as if she got frequent-flyer miles every time she imparted some hard-won tidbit. She was a good-deed-floats-all-boats person, while Stan was always the guy to suspect if your boat sprang a leak.

I still felt like a dishrag that had been put away dirty and wet and left to get moldy, but Denise made me feel a bit better.

That faint glow lasted until the morning mail delivery. It held the regular collection of inquiry letters and trade confirmations, but today an extra envelope was in the stack. No return address. Addressed to

Mr. Dave Barlow, Esq. Since I was not a lawyer, the title implied pretension. Or irony.

The note inside was short. "Hope you had a nice weekend."

I flipped the note over. No other writing. No brand markings. I held it up to the light. No watermark. The envelope was similarly generic and plain. The postmark was blurry, but it indicated Colorado Springs on Saturday.

I needed a donut. Maybe that would help ease the emptiness I now felt in my stomach.

It did help. For maybe twenty seconds. And then I felt worse.

The idea of checking for fingerprints occurred to me, but I rejected it. Whatever was happening spoke of planning. It seemed pretty unlikely that whoever it was would be easily tripped up by CSI 101.

But some Journalism 101 questions sprang to mind. "Who" and "why" in particular. Knowing either would likely reveal the other. But "what" was also interesting. What was the goal? To punish me for moving on after Allison's death? Or maybe it was something simpler, more universal. Maybe someone just wanted me to fail. Distract me enough from work, and I'd start losing clients. My numbers would slip. If the culprit was in the office, that could only be Stan.

Beth wasn't close to retiring, as far as I knew, but Stan would be the person most interested in buying her out when it came time. Until maybe a year or two earlier, he likely felt it was not necessarily a sure thing, but a very good bet. But my numbers and clients were growing faster than his. Stan was unfailingly polite to me, but there was always a sense of self-control at work, a brittleness that suggested underlying hostility or at least over-competitiveness.

If it was his plan to distract me from work, it was succeeding.

I tossed the note and the envelope in the trash. After a moment, I retrieved them and stuffed them into a desk drawer.

When Denise came back over to my desk for lunch, I was really ready. We started walking the couple of blocks to La Baguette.

The Colorado Springs downtown was healthier than in past years. Despite perpetually tight budgets, the main drag, Tejon Street, had improvements like attractive, flower-filled planters, enhanced intersections, and new buildings just to the south.

The scent of fresh bread and coffee met us inside. Without much delay, our croissant sandwiches and drinks were delivered to our table.

Denise ate a couple of bites before the interrogation began. "So, tell me about it. Last I heard, you two were going to your high-school reunion. What went wrong?"

"How do you know anything went wrong?"

"Come on, spill." She'd tucked her reading glasses in her purse. Unobstructed by the half glasses, her big brown eyes were piercing, as if she already knew everything.

"We'll, it pretty much couldn't have gone worse."

She just looked at me.

"This is going to sound weird." I took another bite, then launched into the story. "I mean off-the-scale weird. When we got there, the whole thing was a put-on. I didn't know anyone there."

Denise blinked. "I don't get it."

"Neither do I. The whole thing was a sham. It was not my classmates. It was some group of people apparently hired to pretend to be the people at the reunion."

"Why on earth—"

"That's the biggest question. I found out the real reunion happened a week earlier. My invitation went missing. I got an email inviting me to the phony one."

Denise had stopped eating. Fortunately the restaurant was busy enough that my voice carried only to her, and everyone else was still eating.

"What an exceptionally nasty thing to do! Who might be that angry with you?"

"I don't know. My only clue is a text I got afterward, asking me how it felt to be so quickly forgotten."

"Forgotten. Could that mean dating Cathy after you lost Allison?"

"See? You went right there, too. Maybe it *was* too soon."

Denise wasn't much of a toucher normally, but she reached over and placed a hand over mine. "It was not too soon. You needed to rejoin the human race. I watched you after Allison died, remember? You must have lost twenty pounds you could ill afford. You moved around like a ghost. You really had us worried."

"Yeah, well. Thanks."

Denise became aware of her hand and withdrew it. "Thank God you found Cathy. I think she rescued you."

"Well, that's another thing."

"What?"

"She didn't come home with me."

"That makes no sense. She knows you."

"This all made her question that. Before Howard, she had another guy in her life. Someone who turned out to be a con man who lied to her regularly. Long story. But it sensitized her. She's not going to get lied to again if it—"

"If it what?"

"If it kills her, but that's not what I meant."

"But surely once she's had time to reflect, she will realize what kind of guy you are and give you a call. Say she was sorry to jump to conclusions."

"No call."

"The phone works both ways. And it could be that by now she's so ashamed she can't bring herself to call."

"I'm—" I took a drink to give myself more time with the answer. "I'm not going to contact her."

"But that's—that's crazy. She's the best thing that's happened to you. Why not?"

I could tell Denise part of it. I couldn't bring myself to tell her my talent for getting others around me hurt. Or the bullet holes. I couldn't contact Cathy until and unless I resolved this and knew there would be no danger to her. There was no way on Earth that I'd draw someone else into a potentially dangerous situation. Not again.

"I need to take a step back. It could be that Cathy understood I was telling the truth, but thought that could be explained by someone retaliating against me for something terrible I'd done. Conversely, if she thought I was lying, then in her eyes I'm a bad guy for that, too. Maybe she was just totally confused. But if she's able to go with either of those scenarios, she doesn't know me the way I thought she did. Or feel about me the way I thought she did. I think she's a remarkable woman, one I'd love to spend my life with, but maybe it was too soon after Allison. Maybe I should have waited until I was more healthy."

Denise gave me her long look again, then took a bite of sandwich.

"I think you're wrong. I think you should call her right now and show her proof. You have stuff from high school, right, like a year-book or diploma at least? You have friends who went there."

"There's more to it than that. But it gets into an area I'm just not comfortable talking about. I know that sounds like I'm rationalizing. Maybe I can bring myself to contact her. But not yet." Fights with my father, rather than inoculating me against future conflict, had some-how damaged my immune system. A little conflict went a long, long way with me now, and I'd make great sacrifices to avoid any more.

"The longer you wait, the more firmly she may get set on this new path."

"I know that."

Denise leaned back in her chair and returned to the big picture. "Someone's really angry with you."

"I know that, too." I gave her my theories about Allison's father, or sister, or someone close to her. Or a client.

"I hear you on the phone with clients. I know how you treat them."

"Well, thanks."

"And you don't have any ex-clients, do you?"

"I can't think of one."

"You're doing a great job, Dave."

Her approval felt terrific. I recalled a quote I'd seen on a t-shirt: "Feeling gratitude and not expressing it is like wrapping a present and not giving it."

I leaned forward and said, "Thank you, Denise. I really value our friendship, and I can't thank you enough for being one of the truly great influences in my life."

For a moment, I thought I'd gone too far. She ducked her head and blushed. But then she smiled and looked me in the eye levelly. "You're a good man, Dave. Figure this out and get her back."

Chapter 13

By the time Denise and I got back to the office, Stan Marston was at his desk, talking on the phone.

Stan was a half-dozen years older than I was, and the only one in the office competitive enough to fist-pump when he beat you to a parking spot.

He was nice enough to people most of the time, but once in a while he'd wish someone a fond farewell on the phone and hang up, and then pick up the receiver again and slam it back down. If I were a betting man, I'd put a token on "heart attack at forty-five." Well, actually I was a betting man. I just bet in an arena where the odds were a lot higher and better managed than in Vegas. The Dow and NASDAQ take their hits from time to time, but if you're patient, spread your risk, and go with the relatively safe bets, you don't come out behind very often.

Stan waved at me as I crossed to my desk. I waved back. I didn't dislike him. I felt sorry for him. And he told good jokes.

I made a few calls and filled out a few forms and thought about Cathy only a hundred times by the time the phone rang. Blocked caller ID. At home, I would have let the call go to voicemail. In the office you answer.

"Hi, Dave. It's Daniel Else."

Who else? I wondered how many variations people had teased him with. My more serious thought was that he was calling the wrong guy. Daniel was one of Stan's clients.

69

"Hi, how are you." I would typically say his name, but not this time. I involuntarily looked at Stan, who had looked my way when the phone rang. Stan was still on his phone.

"I'm OK, but look. I, er, had a question for you."

"OK," I said slowly enough that he picked up on it.

"I know. I should be asking Stan Marston. But he's the subject of my question."

"It's a bit unusual, but shoot."

"I wouldn't ask but I've done some checking around and you really have a reputation as a straight shooter."

"Go ahead."

"I assume you know what churning is."

My stomach tightened fractionally. Of course I knew what churning is. It's when a client gives you a discretionary authority to make trades on his account, and you make trades not so much to increase the client's long-term bottom line, but to maximize your commissions. It can be subtle or significant. Regardless of the magnitude it's unethical and illegal.

"I do know."

"OK. My question." He hesitated. "Do you think it's possible that Stan is churning my account?"

Stan's gaze swept my way again as I tried to keep my expression somewhere between neutral and positive.

I framed my answer, worrying that my voice would carry to Stan's desk. "My first thought is that it's extremely unlikely. But I don't really have enough data to know that for certain."

Stan finished his phone call. He rose and stretched.

Daniel was silent. I pictured him in the jewelry shop he owned and ran. After a long pause, he said, "Is it possible for you to get more data? So you'd know for sure one way or the other?"

I hesitated. I didn't want to be having this conversation right now. I didn't want to be having this conversation at all. Stan moved closer to the window to look out on the street. Closer to me.

"I'm not sure."

"I realize you're probably friends. But I'd really like to know. And I'd rather not take my business elsewhere just in case. My gut could be wrong."

"OK. I'll see what I can do."

"Thanks, Dave. I really appreciate it." Click. He hung up.

Feeling a little James Bondian, I kept the phone to my ear, trying to figure out how to make Stan less suspicious, if he even was. "OK, you're welcome, Lillian. If I see the dog again, I'll call you right away.... Right. No problem.... Bye."

I hung up. Stan's gaze was on me. I felt I had to say something more. "Some dog is digging up a neighbor's garden. I didn't think people let their dogs run anymore."

Stan nodded cheerfully. I was half-expecting him to recommend paint-balling the dog or something worse. "Have your neighbor spray some vinegar on the plant leaves. The dog will stay away."

"Thanks, Stan." Ordinarily he was as helpful as obedience school for cats, but this actually sounded helpful. I almost wished I knew someone with a dog problem.

He smiled and walked back to his desk. Break over.

The phone rang a few more times as the afternoon went on. Each time, I had a flare of hope that it would be Cathy. But I also experienced a pained, "maybe it's for the best," feeling driven by not wanting to get her hurt by whatever was going on in my life. The last call came just as I was ready to head out the door.

"Dave Barlow?" the caller said. "My name is Ross Morse. You were recommended by a fellow I met at an event I attended last month. It might have been the symphony—not sure."

Ross has a very faint accent. One maybe in the very broad British/Scottish/Australian family. To a person in that group, I was probably labeling differences as diverse as US Southern and US New Englanders, but I didn't have much of an ear for accents. Unless he asked me to put another shrimp on the barbie or asked me to be a good chap, I probably wasn't going to narrow it down.

"How can I help you?"

"I'd like to start an investment account."

"I'd be happy to do that. Would you be able to come into the office—we're downtown on Tejon—or I could come to you."

"I was thinking I could just send you a check and you could send me whatever paperwork you need signed."

"Well, at a minimum, I need to get a sense of your goals and your current position. For instance, a person in his mid-twenties can afford to take a bit more of a risk—and potentially gain more—than someone who's only ten years from retirement. Being near retirement typically means minimizing risk so there's less chance you need funds during a downturn."

"May we do that by phone?"

"Er, OK." I always felt better meeting clients face to face, but I didn't want to lose a potential client by being too inflexible.

"Do you have a questionnaire you could email me?"

"I can do that."

I got his email and we agreed to talk again the next day. No alarm bells went off. I'd dealt with a number of clients too busy to want to come into the office, and the call seemed totally routine.

Chapter 14

After leaving the office I got into my hot Subaru, maxed out the AC, and drove about fifteen blocks north. We were in the middle of a pothole epidemic thanks to city government funding problems, but I hit only one pothole. The running gag was that right now, the only people not weaving on the roads were the drunks.

Around the corner from my destination was a convenient parking spot. I was lucky to be able to park this close to the Colorado College campus. I put my sunglasses in the glove box and set out on foot. The magnetic sign still masked the bullet holes. I refreshed my mental note to get the damage repaired.

The street was nice and wide, as were most of the older streets. The afternoon temperature had peaked at ninety-six. By now at almost 5PM it had dropped to ninety-three. Fortunately the humidity was characteristically low.

A short walk took me to a Victorian house built maybe in the 1920s. The neatly printed sign in the window said "Dr. V. T. Fencke, PhD, PsyD." I thought of her as Violet, but I didn't call her that.

The house was comfortable. Violet's assistant had stepped out, so I took a seat and waited. I started my breathing exercise to relax from the car ride. Traffic had been no busier than most days, but I'd still felt myself tensing up behind the wheel. Sometimes the smallest pressure set off overreactions.

A few minutes later a woman a few years older than me came out of Violet's office with a girl maybe six years old. The girl had curly blonde hair and dead eyes. Part of me started to ache for her as I wondered what she'd gone through and whether she would come out the other side. I wondered if I was out the other side or if I was just fooling myself.

I pushed away the feeling of paranoia. Violet had explained what I felt was not paranoia, one form of mental illness, but was actually hypervigilance, a PTSD injury symptom. A thorn by any other name still pierced the skin.

Violet's door stayed closed for a few minutes as, I assumed, she was recording her session notes. I glanced at the cover of an issue of *Psychology Today*. The cover article was "The Power of Touch." I didn't pick it up. I already knew that touch was energizing, soothing, and awe-inspiring, when the right person was touching.

"Dave." Violet stood in her doorway. She was a diminutive woman, probably in her sixties, with white hair. Cherub cheeks. One of Santa's elves if they grew to full height. She winked at me. How many people can say their psychiatrists wink at them?

I followed her into her office and shut the door without being asked. The smell of tea in the cup on her desk wafted my way. With the shortage of psychiatrists, most only did medication management, but Violet still did therapy also. She liked being part of the whole picture. Her bill, therefore, was higher than a psychologist would charge, but I felt comfortable with her and this way was one-stop shopping.

She settled into a desk chair that seemed two sizes too large for her body. Silently she looked at me for several seconds. Maybe she and Denise practiced together. "Tell me what's going on."

"Well, for starters, I think I need to go back to a weekly schedule." I'd started out monthly with her. After Allison died, I'd dropped to weekly. Since meeting Cathy, I'd gone back to monthly.

Violet waited for me to say more. Her expression remained neutral.

"And I'll probably need to refill my Paxil sooner than later."

Violet's silence helped me realize I was stalling.

"OK. Let me dive right in. I've apparently made a significant enemy. I got an invitation to my high-school reunion for last Saturday night. Cathy and I went up to Woodland Park, expecting a nice getaway and meeting some old friends. I dragged my feet a little bit because I could imagine that with our positions reversed I would not be all that excited to go to her high-school reunion. But she pressed to go, and I was up for it.

"Anyway, we got there, and it was a fake. They had a couple dozen 'classmates' there and a sign and pictures and stuff. But they weren't from my class. They were strangers, apparently paid for a performance for my benefit.

"Either it was too crazy for Cathy, or this hit one of her hot buttons. She dated a liar and a con man a while back and has zero patience for that anymore. It was easier to think there was one liar there, me, than somehow being in the presence of a couple dozen liars.

"Then in the middle of the night, I got a text. 'How does it feel to be so quickly forgotten?' I'm assuming that means someone is angry that I started dating Cathy after Allison had been dead for not quite a year."

Someone who didn't know me as well might have started out with, "How sure are you this was a setup?" or, "That would be a lot of effort and expense just to make a point."

Violet said instead, "Given this experience, how are your PTSD symptoms? Are they still mostly under control?"

"Yeah, mostly. Nightmares are ramped up, but most of them are kind of waiting in the wings. They start, but I can usually wake myself up before the really bad stuff starts. Lots of difficulty sleeping. More flashbacks, but under control. I feel jumpy most of the time, like the other shoe is about to fall, or a bunch of shoes are about to fall out of the closet. More dark images that come out of nowhere. I feel jumpier again. Oh, I said that. See?"

"The nightmares that do start. Are they from when your mother killed your father?" No weasel-wording or politically correct language from Violet.

"Not the majority. Mostly the car accident with Allison. I'm upside down in the car and I see people approaching. Or I see the car exploding. Stuff like that. One with Cathy hanging upside down in the car with me instead of Allison."

"These are all since, what, Saturday night?" She glanced subtly at the calendar. Two nights.

"Right. One starts, I wake up. Eventually I get back to sleep. Rinse and repeat."

"What do you see happening next?"

"For one thing, in the next few days I'll look around for another PTSD support group." That way I could talk this through with more time than the weekly appointment with Violet. "Keep up the exercise. Continue physical therapy on the knee."

"What else?"

"You mean like in the movies? Track down this guy—or whoever it is—and deal with him? Take him out in the woods and feed him to the bears?"

"Some people in this position might. 'Closure' and all that stuff. What about Cathy? Her presence in your life really seemed to be healthy for you."

"You know what happened when I fought back with my father. That's not going to happen to Cathy." I flashed on the blood flowing from my mother's body, spilling into the pool my father had bled. "My car's been shot up. I don't know where this is going."

"What happened to your mother was not your fault."

"I get that intellectually. Emotionally, not so much."

"So no contact with Cathy until this is resolved?"

"I don't know how it's going to get resolved. The more I think about it, the more my symptoms surface. I'm hoping this will just blow over. Whoever it is will feel he's gotten his pound of flesh. Time will pass. Maybe nothing more will happen."

Violet was silent for too long.

I said, "You don't think it will pass on its own?" My chest tightened. I'd been trying to convince myself this would stop by itself, but down in my mental subbasement, the supervisor was unconvinced.

"It might. But Cathy was a healing force in your life. Surely there's a way to demonstrate to her that you are totally honest, and that this is not a reflection on you. This is an anger response on someone's part perhaps, but you are not responsible. This is not your doing."

"I want her back. God, do I want her back. But the damage has been done. If she's willing to believe the worst about me, she doesn't have much faith in me. And I will not put her at risk."

Violet's lips compressed just a bit. If she were a poker player, it would be a fatal tell. It was small, but I knew what it meant: "I disagree. But I won't press it right now. I'll circle back to it later when you're totally unsuspecting."

In the near silence, an old grandfather clock ticked and cool air forced its way through a vent behind me. From somewhere outside came the sounds of a garbage truck laboring.

Well," she said finally. "Let's do some more exposure work. This new image, seeing Cathy in the damaged car with you instead of Allison. Tell me about that."

This was the most repetitive part of therapy. In theory, and I had to admit that in practice, going over and over the incidents, the images, slowly robbed them of power over me. It was a bit like listening to a favorite song so many times that it no longer felt special, that it became just another song. But this path with Violet led to increased functioning, not to less music enjoyment.

"Again, these are pretty brief images because I can shut off the dream. But I'm there in the dark car interior. I see past the passenger seat to a guy with a mustache or a beard outside the car window. He's bent down so I can see some of his face. I turn my head and look at the person in the passenger seat. Sometimes it's Allison, sometimes it's Cathy."

"And the man?"

"Just some guy. One of the rescuers I assume."

"So the emotion comes from the women."

I nodded. "Must be. When it's Allison, she just hangs there limply, like she's sleeping, except her hair is hanging straight up, since we're both upside down. I feel cold and afraid, and I wake up. When it's Cathy, her hair is hanging "up" also, but she's awake. She's looking at a map on her phone, or turning to me to talk. I feel—I don't know— ashamed maybe. Maybe afraid. It's so quick I'm not sure."

"Ashamed why?"

"I felt like a fool at the reunion. Embarrassed that she would think me a liar. I have my faults, but that's not me. Let her be angry at me for not being forthcoming about the number of nightmares I have, or the degree of insecurity I feel. Having her angry at me for something I didn't do is just wrong."

"You've never lied to her?"

I hesitated. That made me hesitate even more as I thought about my hesitation. "Maybe a little stuff in the 'does this dress make me look fat' category. I guess the biggest thing is I've not told her about my childhood. Or at least *that* part of it. And I've not told her about the nightmares, the dark images, the hypervigilance, the depression, the flashbacks. Mostly those things are in check and I'm the only one aware of them. Over time they were getting better before Allison's death. And before the reunion. I guess I thought I could be—whole—before I had to tell her this stuff. You know, in the 'some bad stuff happened in my life, but it's all over now' way."

"And you're OK with concealing that?"

"You know it takes me a while to open up. It takes me longer to work up to some things. I don't like it, no. But I'm not there yet. I love her, but there are things I've been afraid to share this early. But I was going to tell her on this trip."

"Just this?"

I thought. "I don't really know how she feels about having children. We're not at that point yet. I have mixed feelings on that. I made a vow to myself a long time ago to never have children. But sometimes I'll see a toddler or a youngster and I think it actually would be nice to have kids. And then again sometimes I think about my role models and I shudder. I wouldn't want to bring anyone into the world unless I'm a hundred and ten percent ready and committed. Parents should have to pass tests. Very difficult tests."

Violet looped us back around to the beginning. "And the image of Cathy beside you in the car occurred for the first time this past weekend?"

~~~

When Violet's session-timer bell chimed, I was in fact feeling better.

"You can get past all of this, Dave. I've seen the evidence. I know you."

"I understand. I still feel optimistic. The feeling can get buried way down deep sometimes, but I know it's there. I'll check with your secretary about Mondays for a while?"

"Tuesdays will probably work better if you can do that. I think we should do some EMDR work next time." EMDR was still a bit strange to me. Eye Movement Desensitization and Reprocessing had me recall events like the death of my father and the car accident, but included things like Violet moving her arm back and forth in front of my face. It was a bit difficult to accept the notion that it would help, but I trusted Violet and the process did seem to do me some good. I was starting to think about how to approach Cathy.

"Sure. Thanks."

I let myself out. No other patients were waiting. She'd slotted me in on top of her regular schedule.

Outside the day was still warm, the sun still nowhere near going down behind Pikes Peak. I loved having the peak right there and so high. It made city navigation dead easy. The mountains were always to the west.

Closer to the corner, I caught sight of several people down the street to the left, in the direction of my car.

At the corner I could see it was more like a crowd, between a dozen and two dozen people, weighted toward CC student age. Some on the sidewalk, some in the middle of the street. Several people had their phones positioned as though they were taking pictures.

They all seemed to be gathered about the spot where I'd parked my car. If Scarlett Johansson had been dressed in a bikini and was waiting on the hood of the car for me, maybe this reaction would make sense. But I couldn't think of any positive explanation.

Darker and darker possibilities zipped through my brain as I started running.

Chapter 15

I got close enough to see though the crowd and they were in fact looking at my car. My nice fairly new Subaru.

A cold feeling crept along my skin, and I felt angry and paradoxically tired.

The good news was that lying on the top of the car was a single red rose. The bad news overwhelmed the good news.

I edged my way through the crowd until I was a yard away. The two windows on the street side of the car were both broken out. The two tires I could see had both blown out. But the worst news was inside the car and was the reason for the blown tires.

The Subaru had been filled with wet concrete.

The gray fluid rose to the level of the bottom of the windows. The car had been slightly overfilled so some of the concrete had flowed down the driver's door and the driver's side rear door. The flow obscured the .22 caliber vandalism. A trail of concrete led down the street, tapering off in the distance, pointing the way in case I wanted to follow. I realized the sound I'd attributed to a garbage truck a while back had probably been a cement mixer instead. No trash pickup, just a large dump.

So much for this whole thing blowing over after the reunion incident. On the plus side, I no longer cared about the bullet holes in the door. In fact, the sun could go nova and it would be fine with me as long as I could just wrap my hands around the neck of whoever did this and squeeze. My anger flowed unchecked through my veins until I found myself wondering if this was how my father had reacted to lesser stimuli. I took another couple of breaths and convinced myself I wasn't him.

I turned away from the car. "Did anyone see this happen?"

At first no one said anything. Probably because they imagined having to talk to the police for an hour.

"Anyone?" I said. "Someone's been harassing me, and I just want a clue to what the guy looked like." Anger must have crept into my voice, because a couple of people stepped back.

But a young woman maybe twenty stepped forward. My guess was CC student. Ultra-short, threadbare jeans shorts and a tight black T-shirt. Sandals. "There were two guys. But I couldn't describe them. They both had those, you know, hard hats on all the time. Kinda average guys. White, but that's all I know."

"Thanks. That's a start." It was hardly worth anything, actually. Colorado Springs was probably seventy-five percent white, so white males between twenty and sixty might have only narrowed the suspects to twenty-five percent of the population. On *CSI* they'd add footprint residue picked up with infrared, a cigarette butt, and a brand of hat. With that they'd narrow it down to ten red-headed guys who all went to the same strip club on Tuesday nights, but that was *CSI* and I was here in the all-too-real world.

"Anyone else?" I called. "Anyone have any pictures of the guys or the truck, or any videos?" I shouted out my phone number. "Please help a guy out. Text me what you have, please. Or at least send me the YouTube link."

A young guy also maybe twenty, likely another student, came forward. He sported a backpack. He also wore sandals. "I took this. And I can post it and send you a link." He spoke with a New England accent and I pictured a young John F. Kennedy.

"Thanks." I watched the screen. He'd evidently been about halfway down the block, so far enough away that details of faces or license plates would be fuzzy, but the help from the woman and from this guy made me feel a little less alone. A gray cement truck was stopped next to my car and concrete was pouring through the chute and directly through the driver's window. Seconds later, there was a shout. Could have been "Done," or "Full," or "Stop." The rate of flow started diminishing. The guy raced for the cab passenger door, and the vehicle was laboring into motion even before the door slammed shut. Sloppy wet concrete continued to spill out of the chute as the truck lurched away.

"I really appreciate it," I told the guy.

I called out to the group and repeated my email address. "Please, if there's anything you saw or anything you recall that would be helpful, let me know. I would really appreciate it."

My words were punctuated by a *whoop whoop*. The sound a police car makes when it pops the siren but doesn't give it full rein. I recognized the sound, but at the same time I realized that the weirdness of all this was buffering me from reality, as if all this were happening to someone else and I was just an observer.

The crowd parted as people headed for either sidewalk. A police car crept forward and stopped next to my Subaru, the bar lights still flashing. The car was mostly white with a huge blue racing stripe along the side. I wasn't sure if the racing stripe was sending the exact message law enforcement was going for. The trunk bore a four-digit number in very large numerals that were easier read by people on the space station than by people on the street.

The lone occupant, dressed in a blue uniform with a utility belt Batman would have envied, exited the car and looked at me. I felt like I was in one of those movies where they ask for volunteers for a suicide mission and all the smart people take several steps backward. I was alone. The nearest other person was now the cop.

The cop, a tall black guy probably in his forties, said, "We got a call about some vandalism. I'm thinking this is the place." He had a very faint Southern accent, broad shoulders, and a neatly trimmed mustache. His dark eyes gave me the feeling he'd seen everything. Except maybe this.

"This would be the place," I said.

He surveyed the concrete-filled car. "This is my first one of these all day."

"You won't believe this, but it's my first ever."

"You see it happen?"

"No, but some of them did."

He and I looked around. The crowd was no more than a third of the size it had been.

He surveyed the crowd and called out. "Thank you for sticking around long enough to be good citizens. I just want to get your contact information and ask you if you saw anything that might be helpful. I will be quick. I promise."

The cop turned back to me. "I'll get your information when I'm done with them. My guess is you're not going anywhere right away."

I nodded.

"You have roadside assistance?"

"Yes."

"Good. When you call, put it on speakerphone. I've got to hear this."

~~~

I had to call AAA once and my insurance company twice. AAA said in this kind of incident, I should contact my insurance company. It was a bit hard to imagine their checklist included "car filled with concrete" but maybe it fell under "Act of God or dickweeds." The first insurance associate decided she was being punked. She remained polite but firm, like a parent who's slightly amused by your new hair color, but insisting you try again. Right now.

While I waited for the tow truck and for the cop to finish quizzing the bystanders, I took a few pictures of my own in case my insurance company balked. I didn't have the rider for concrete dumping, but from my conversation, I assumed the damage would be covered. I wondered if that would make it onto a future list of exclusions.

Finally I called a car rental company to ask about a rental. They had no Subaru Outbacks but they did have a Ford Focus and I made a reservation.

The tow truck arrived while I was finishing with the cop. Fortunately the tow truck had a flatbed and winch. I stood well back as the guy hooked up cables, imagining the damage if one snapped.

Before the driver started the winch, he got on his cell phone. I caught something about, "We're gonna need a bigger boat." He listened for a moment and then walked over to my car. The cop had no time to object before the guy stood carefully out of the path and opened the driver's door. Gooey concrete started flowing onto the asphalt. Even if the cop wanted the door closed again, it wasn't going to happen.

Apparently satisfied that he had lightened the load sufficiently to get the car onto the flatbed, the tow truck driver reached for the winch controls once more then hesitated. He must have had a firm mental checklist of questions because he asked me, "Do you need to get anything out of the car before I put it up on the flatbed?"

I shifted my gaze to the concrete coating the interior of the car. "Never mind."

We left behind an enormous, hardening blob of concrete. I suspected the "cleanup on aisle five" bill would be mine.

~~~

The tow company's yard was near the rental outfit, so I hitched a ride on the truck.

I was hot and tired and mentally exhausted by the time I'd walked from the towing yard to the rental company and started driving a black car that had been sitting in the sun all day. The Ford Focus sat in my garage now. It handled well enough, but I was angry about what had been done to my Subaru. And my sunglasses had been in the glove box.

As soon as I got home I worked like an efficiency expert on his day off. I ordered pizza and a liter of Pepsi. Then while it was being processed and raced to my door, I took a cool shower. My fresh clothes still felt cool when the doorbell rang.

The driver was one of the two regulars I saw most often. I gave him a decent tip, and went about consuming comfort food. On the back deck I moved a chair into a small patch of shade behind a piñon pine. I knew that suddenly coming out into the strong sunshine would have triggered one of Cathy's cat-like small sneezes. I would have given anything to hear that sneeze right now.

The horizon here is dominated by Pikes Peak. In the Springs, when real estate people talk about location, location, and location, they typically mean view of Pikes Peak, view of Pikes Peak, and view of Pikes Peak. Since it was July, the sun was descending toward Ute Pass, well north of the peak. In the winter, it would fall to earth much farther south, nearer Cheyenne Mountain, home of the underground NORAD complex.

The air was still warm, and the sun was still an hour above the mountains, but the air was moving in a slow but steady breeze, and in the shade I felt almost human again. Just very tired. Conflict siphoned off an enormous percentage of my energy. Today I hadn't been in a fist fight, or had to run for my life, or even confront an actual angry person face to face, but I felt like I had been in a war zone for a month. I knew from therapy that it was mostly mental; I essentially had a compulsion-level need to avoid violence and conflict. I willed myself to relax, but it didn't work. I still felt angry enough that I kept seeing images of my dad being angry. Trying to shift the focus from inside myself to the rational external world was only partly successful.

The land behind the house fell off to the southwest, into a small valley park that had been left wild. A faint scent of grass moved with the breeze. The land was sprinkled with piñon pine, thorny honey locust, Russian olive, Chinese elm, yucca, prickly pear, and varieties of grass.

I propped my legs up on a wooden crate and leaned back. My right knee twinged a bit. I'd skipped my regular morning run today, and I'd planned to visit the fitness center for some physical therapy on the knee after seeing Violet, but that plan had evaporated. I would see if Bruce had time in the next day or two.

I pulled out my phone and checked email. Nothing from Cathy. But there was a new text that I'd missed, again with the number somehow obscured. *"Good luck on your next detailing at Water Works. Have a nice day."*

Water Works was a car wash. Obviously the text came from my tormentor. I felt another surge of anger, anger somehow intensified by the absence of a target.

On the plus side, two of the bystanders had sent me pictures. I found what seemed like the best one of the cement truck. To the right on the rear of the vehicle was a rectangle—the license plate.

Colorado's typical pattern was three numbers followed by three letters.

I zoomed in on the plate on the cement truck. The picture was grainy and heard to read. The lettering read, "FOK YOU," making it invalid *and* a bad impression of Arnold Schwarzenegger.

So that was a dead end.

A link in one email took me to a video. It showed one person in a hard hat standing by my car. He then raced to the cement truck cab and got in just in time as the vehicle roared off.

In *CSI*, they would blow up such an image and see an iron cross earring on the perp, or some similar detail that just wasn't there. In this photo an earring would probably have been at most one pixel. Heck, the guy's ear was probably only four pixels. Other than getting the information that the figure was likely male and about a head and a hat taller than a Subaru Outback with flat tires, I wasn't seeing much.

I wondered how they had known where I was. One byproduct of being hypervigilant is that I paid too much attention to cars that might be following me, to the point that I'd periodically change routes if I thought there was a chance of someone tailing me. I hadn't noticed a thing.

Chapter 16

Multiple nightmares got past my defenses during the night, and by the time I should be getting up, I felt even more tired than when I'd gone to bed.

I rose on Tuesday knowing I wasn't going in to work. Not being right there when a potential client made an inquiry always carried a possible cost, but after the Subaru incident I realized I had to call on the proverbial 800-pound gorilla. Allison's father, Ben.

Two major events in three days gave me an awful feeling about what life might be like if I couldn't defuse this. I was a little closer to understanding Butch and Sundance's decision to flee to Bolivia. And my question was a bit like theirs: "Who is doing this?"

Maybe after visiting Allison's father, I'd get a taste of that closure stuff people keep talking about. I decided not to call ahead. Given his health, he was almost certainly there, and I didn't want to give him any extra time to prepare.

I looked out on the view to the west as I ate a light breakfast of toast and orange juice. The sky was blue and cloudless. It could be one of those days when it stayed like that all day long, or it could be one of those days when in another hour or two clouds would start peeking over Pikes Peak and the afternoon would deliver a thunderstorm. That part of the future I was fine with leaving as a mystery.

A text to my boss let her know I was taking a personal day. She knew it would hurt me more than it hurt her, so even without offering her an explanation I didn't expect any objection.

The Ford Focus, safe in my garage, had suffered no damage during the night. I started retracing my path from the weekend, winding through the west side of the Springs, toward Highway 24.

This time, the majority of the traffic was heading into Colorado Springs, so the traffic was lighter.

I passed the exit for Crystola Canyon Road, which dead-ended not all that far from Allison's father's estate, and I kept going on 24. The farther I went, the more hypervigilant I got. I kept checking the rear-view mirror to see if anyone seemed to be following me. If the same car showed up on my radar for more than a couple of minutes I would speed up or slow down or take an exit and get back on the highway.

I curved through Woodland Park about a half-hour later, glancing at the Mexican restaurant as I passed. No ring of police cars surrounded the dumpsters, so I imagined my midnight heist had gone unnoticed, or at the very least the furor had blown over. Dumpster diving was probably near the bottom of their crime-lord index.

If you didn't pay attention to the road through Woodland Park, it seemed like you were just continuing through town, but the road fed into town from the south-southeast, and left heading southwest. The highway up had taken me from a starting point east of the estate, then north of it, and a few miles later I was to the west of it, where the access road met the highway.

A left on Edlowe Road took me past a sign saying "Firestation 3" and led me closer. One prairie dog chased another across the road in my path. The road wound through rolling hills and mountain meadows. Pikes Peak was visible to the south from time to time. Another left, this time onto 281, a dirt road, was the only way in. On the left was a big group of pedestal mailboxes. I bet if Ben Stuart actually drove this road it would have been paved by now.

Ben had made his fortune the old-fashioned way, according to Allison. Ruthless ambition, intense competiveness, with a dash of family money and a pinch of luck. He bought a retail electronics store as the computer revolution was in its very early days. He leveraged those profits and bought another store, and another. He must have been channeling Archimedes who said something like, "Give me a stick long enough and a pivot and I shall move the Earth." Ben Stuart seemed to always find a way to be in the right spot, and he had never been afraid to use a big stick.

He even knew something many successful people didn't. He knew when to quit. In the late nineties, when the dot-com era made it seem the sky was the limit, some inner sense must have told him the sky was falling, because he negotiated a deal to sell the entire chain to an even bigger fish. Less than a year later, the clouds were forming and the bubble was bursting, and Ben Stuart was buying private islands and an estate in the Rockies.

I was amazed that Allison had come out as unaffected and as special as she had. I attributed that miracle to her mother, who'd died a couple of years before I met Allison at a charity run in the Springs. In the space of less than three years, Ben Stuart had lost the two most important women in his life, the first to cancer, the second in a car accident with me. More than once I wished I could have traded places with Allison.

I kept going on the dirt road until a right turn put me on a narrow paved road that wound through the pines. After a short time, the high wall surrounding the Stuart property appeared on the right. Rock pillars joined by thick wood beams. Ahead would be the gates. The land fell gently away from the road on the left side. On the right, the terrain rose gradually for ten or twenty yards and then reached its highest point. Pines dotted the area irregularly.

I passed a long section of fence, took a right into a driveway, and stopped at the eight-foot-tall gates. They weren't as thick as the blast doors at NORAD, but I bet a Humvee would bounce back on impact. Twin video cameras looked down on me from the tops of the hinges on either side. Another camera looked into my driver's window as I reached for the intercom button, round and red. I pressed it. With the window down, the air felt ten degrees cooler than in the Springs. The pine smell would have been relaxing at another time.

The delay was long enough to make me think I should have called ahead. Finally a *click* sounded and a voice said, "Yes?" Maybe if I'd called ahead the voice would have said, "Hello, Mr. Barlow. Come right in." Or "Hi! Go screw yourself."

"I'm Dave Barlow. I'm here to see Mr. Stuart."

"Do you have an appointment?"

I dislike people who already know the answers to the questions they ask. Except teachers.

"No, I don't. I was engaged to Allison and I need to speak to Mr. Stuart. It's important."

"Please wait." Implied but unspoken was, *We'll be the judge of that.*

This wait was longer. Maybe ten minutes. But finally the answer was, "Please come in and stop at the main house."

The silent gates swung open ponderously. I pulled ahead, leery of the gates reversing course too fast. I thought about my trusty Subaru. At least this was a rental.

The biggest difference on this side of the gates was the road. As the Ford moved ahead it began to shudder slightly as the tires traversed the cobblestone. I had been here only five or six times, but I knew that underneath the cobblestone driveway were heating coils strong enough to keep the road clear of snow in winter. It always struck me as overkill, because in a bad storm, as soon as you exited the gates, the public road beyond would be impassible. But the public roads were a non-issue since Ben didn't use them. And overkill seemed to be his middle name. With initials BS, I'm sure he had or wanted a middle name.

The road rose gently over the next twenty yards and then started down the other side. From that point much of the estate was visible.

The cobblestone road curved down the gentle slope until it swept under a huge peaked portico covered with gray slate singles. The scale of the portico and the mansion it was attached to was in the range of a resort hotel rather than a single-family dwelling, but then again with 30,000 square feet, ten bedrooms, and a dozen bathrooms, it was more like a resort.

Beyond the rooftop of the main building, also covered with slate shingles, lay Pikes Peak, looking even closer than in the Springs. Pine-covered rolling hills filled in the middle distance. I knew the far side of the roof was covered with solar panels.

A low rock wall circled the house a couple of yards out from the base. Huge windows rose from near floor level to almost the top of the high-ceilinged first floor. The walls were mostly covered with slate, except for horizontal wood accents. Two matching decks flanked the main entrance at the second floor level, but they were unoccupied.

Allison had been embarrassed about the opulence of the house. An article in *Forbes* had put the original price tag at north of $50 million.

Flanking the main house were the two guest houses, matching style, both of them larger and far more luxurious than my own single-family dwelling. Last I was aware, Allison's sister, Maddy, had lived in the one on the right until she got married. Up on a large, naturally level area, was the helipad. I flashed on *Back to the Future* and Doc Brown saying, "Roads? Where we're going, we don't need roads."

Circling the whole area at a great distance was the high wall I'd come through on the way in. Ben was extravagant and wasteful, but not to the point of putting in a lawn in Colorado. The area that hadn't been left wild was a mix of xeriscaping and stone paths threading though the pines that had been allowed to remain in place.

I parked the car, grateful for being able to avoid the shame of a clunker that dripped oil. I imagined a white-gloved staff assistant whipping out a car bib and whooshing it into place before a drop could fall.

As I walked from the visitor lot into the main entrance, I felt this was a bad idea. If Ben were responsible for my troubles, all this would do is give him satisfaction. I walked ahead anyway.

The delay at the intercom was offset by the immediate response when I rang the bell. As the door opened, bells were still reverberating.

"Come in, Mr. Barlow. I'm Christine." The greeter was a woman in her thirties, half staff and half model. Her eyes were the bluest I'd ever seen. Ben Stuart was the kind of guy who might have coined the abominable term, "spokesmodel." I recalled some of the ads where the "spokesmodel" extolling the virtues of the product was holding it right next to her cleavage, leaving some ambiguity about what was being offered for sale. At the very least it had to split the consumer's attention.

She led the way. We walked along real marble flooring through echoing chambers faced with lots of mahogany, past some very large family paintings. Allison, Maddy, and Ben's deceased wife, Samantha. We climbed a sweeping staircase, and went down a wide hall toward the south wing. On this trip I was more aware of the tour guide than the tour.

Christine stopped before a pair of heavy wooden doors that could have admitted a yacht. She gestured that I could go inside. The gesture was just like a spokesmodel's.

In the giant bedroom/observation deck, the windows were tall and wide and the view was spectacular. Somehow the addition of windows made the view seem even more magnificent than what I had seen when I entered the property. I caught a hint of cigarette smoke, but I suspected Ben Stuart hadn't smoked since the lung cancer diagnosis.

Ben sat partially upright in an oversized recliner. His hair was thin, wispy, short. His eyes looked like a snowman's eyes. He wore an oxygen tube that had not been needed the last time I saw him.

Next to him stood another woman. She was silent, looking more like a model-bodyguard. Stunning, twenties, and muscular. Maybe ex-military.

I came closer, but not close enough to set off the bodyguard. "Thanks for seeing me, Ben."

It took him a few seconds to respond. It was if his brain were as oversized as the house, and it took some time for the sound from the front door chime to carry all the way back to the pool. "What can I do for you, Dave?"

Ben's words were conciliatory and he was reclining, but the forcefulness of his personality came through in his eyes as they bored straight through me. He looked more like I had just interrupted him during a boardroom speech than just curtailed his nap.

Several thoughts coalesced as I registered his indifference and the strength he still radiated even as he lay there in the bed. I realized that Ben was my only true suspect and that somewhere in my reptilian brain I had already decided this all had to be his doing. But besides that I realized I didn't really know what to say.

Quit picking on me?

Maybe, *Fuck you, asshole?*

I went with, "I'm sorry your health isn't what you want it to be." And I got stuck there. Finally I said, "Some things are happening in my life. Some nasty things."

Something flickered over the model-bodyguard's face. Concern? Concealed scorn? Ben's face was chiseled in stone, totally unreadable.

"Whoever is arranging these things seems to be angry that I started dating someone after Allison. Someone who thinks I should have waited longer. Maybe I should have. For a long time I didn't think I would get past Allison's death. But the world keeps turning and all that. And I wound up being lucky enough to meet another amazing woman."

He breathed deeply. "That's what you wanted to say?"

"No, not really. I wanted to tell you that I miss Allison. She made me happier than I had any right to be. But she's gone and there's no way to bring her back. And although she died in the crash, I was not negligent. The car was in great shape. The road was clear. I was sober and doing the speed limit and totally in control of the car. I'm sorry. But I did not kill her."

Ben thought about that. The message was floating along lengthy corridors and through spacious rooms.

"I don't know what you're talking about." It wasn't clear if he was playing with me or being serious.

"I'm saying I think you blame me either for Allison's death or for moving on too soon, or both. I think that you're responsible for the harassment I've been experiencing." I took a deep breath. "I want the harassment to stop."

He glanced at the magnificent view before his gaze traveled slowly, deliberately, back to me. "I'd help you if I could. But this is all news to me."

Ben started to cough.

The model-bodyguard moved closer, intervening between me and Ben. I could sense that she had just shifted to orange alert. She shook her head. The message was plain. The interview was over.

It was my turn for the message to echo through eternity as I tried to parse the response and react. Part of me was convinced this was all his doing, but I had zero proof. Maybe I'd figured he would gloat when confronted with me. Or maybe, given his deteriorating state, he'd let slip some vital clue that would help me find proof.

But there was nothing. I was angry at him, angry at myself, clueless about how to proceed. But I had no leverage, nothing to force him to tell me what he was doing and why it made sense to him.

In the end all I could come up with was, "I'm sorry to have bothered you. I wish you the best with your health. I'll see myself out."

As I turned and walked from the room, I could sense the model-bodyguard going back to "at ease" or DEFCON 5 or whatever model-bodyguards used.

I think Christine walked with me as I retraced my steps along the wide hallway, down the stairs, and exited the distant main door. I couldn't be sure.

Chapter 17

As I walked back to my car, I was in a stupor. By the time I heard someone calling me, my unconscious mind told me it was the third or fourth call. I looked around.

Near the western guest house, a woman was waving at me. Maddy Stuart. Allison's sister.

I changed course and waved back, trying my best to pull back from the funk.

The path to the guest house was a series of octangular granite stepping stones, each about a yard across. I lost sight of Maddy as the path led me through some pine trees and then she came back into view.

Maddy was the prettier sister, trim as a gymnast, golden hair. She had kind of a girl-next-door look if you grew up in a neighborhood populated by the offspring of supermodels. She seemed nice enough but where Allison had been a bit apologetic about the degree of affluence in her family, Maddy was very able to cope. Where Allison had valued education to the point of becoming a teacher, Maddy's main academic focus was to employ a new word each day.

For all her looks and wealth, she'd always seemed a little insecure to me. I wondered if she could be the one behind my recent misfortunes, but I just couldn't picture her that way.

"Hey, you," she said once we were a couple of yards apart.

"Hi, Maddy. It's good to see you."

"You, too!" She gave me a warm hug and stepped back. "I didn't expect to see you here."

"Just paying my respects. I didn't expect to see you here either."

"Yeah, Kevin and I have a place in Kissing Camels, but we're going to be up here a lot of the summer. Kevin likes to get to the Springs at least a couple of days a week." She'd married Kevin Mayer last September. I'd gone to the wedding, but I'd still been on a lot of pain killers at that time, so not everything in my memory was vivid.

"Look, I'm sorry about your dad's condition. I didn't know—"

"Yeah, he was doing really pretty well until around the start of the summer, but the disease seems to be moving faster than the doctors thought it would. There's still an awful lot we don't know about how to cure people."

I nodded. I wondered if Ben could be responsible for my troubles, if his downturn and my starting to date Cathy had been a double whammy. But if so, how had he even found out I was dating?

"Daddy isn't one to give up, though. We're expecting another team of specialists to arrive in a week or ten days. Maybe they can halt or reverse the progression."

Ben had lung cancer, not one of the typically slow-moving cancers, like prostate cancer, but indications originally were that it was treatable. Beyond that I didn't feel comfortable trying to quiz Maddy enough to nail it down more precisely.

Early on I'd thought about visiting Maddy to see if she could be the one behind what was happening to me, but her warmth still undercut that theory.

"You're looking good," I said. "Marriage must agree with you."

There was the barest hesitation. "Where are my manners? I should let Kevin see you. And vice versa. Can you come in?"

I really didn't feel like it, but there was no point in being rude. "Sure. What's Kevin doing lately?"

To some people that would spur a discussion of business accomplishments. "He's been working on his golf game. He's hitting in the 70s."

I idly wondered why handicapping hadn't made the leap to tennis, or football. Clearly there were some football teams that could only win that way.

We went into the guest house. It had the same design motifs as parts of the big house, but was built on a human scale. Must be nice for Kevin, I thought, not having to worry about the day-to-day humdrum of a job. I couldn't recall his history clearly, but the "Mayer" name had been prominent in real estate. Very prominent.

After the foyer, the layout of the house differed some from the big house. We passed a vast kitchen with two peninsulas, a huge Thermador oven, a pair of SubZero refrigerators, a pair of microwaves, and a pair of waist-high wine coolers, one for red, one for white, I assumed.

We found Kevin in the media room, watching a golf tournament on a screen bigger than I realized they made.

We came up behind him, not wanting to disturb the putt.

"Look who's here," Maddy said as the ball rolled past the cup closely enough to change direction.

Kevin got to his feet and turned. Maybe he rose too fast, because the blood seemed to drain from his face. Or it could have been the lighting. But he seemed off balance for just a second.

"Hi, Kevin," I said. More than once, I'd almost called him Ken because his looks were a perfect match for a male companion for a Barbie doll. He was about my height, blond, model good looking. He would look just great with a sweater tied over his shoulders.

"Dave," he said on top of Maddy's reminder prompt, "Dave Barlow."

"To what to—do we owe the pleasure?"

"He came up to visit daddy."

"Just in the neighborhood," I added lamely.

"What can I get you? Bourbon, ice water, orange juice?"

"Some water would be great."

Kevin paused the game. Wouldn't want to miss any of it. We moved to a south-facing dining nook slash rec room. It was a pass-through away from the kitchen and lined with tall, wide windows. Again the view was magnificent.

Maddy brought a tray with three glasses, and Kevin brought an ice bucket. I settled onto a bar stool. Kevin used tongs to add ice to my drink. One cube missed the rim of the glass and instead of making the basket, the cube rolled off the rim and onto the floor. Kevin leaned over to grab it.

As he was discarding the dirty cube, I said, "You look good. Different, but I'm not sure why." I looked at him intently, trying to figure out what was different.

Maddy said, "Right, he shaved off his mustache."

Kevin turned. "Yeah. I got rid of it after we got married. Maddy said it tickled." He gave me a lopsided grin.

I nodded. Something bothered me, but it was one of those things that effort to recall just forces farther away.

"That's a specious argument, Kevin," Maddy said. "You said you decided that it looked like a blond centipede."

I puzzled over the word choice for a second and then it hit me. Word of the day. Well done, Maddy.

At the same time, Kevin's lip twisted just a fraction. I couldn't tell whether he didn't like the centipede story or the word-of-the-day habit.

"Maddy tells me you spend part of the time in the Springs."

"Yes," he said. "For me anyway, if you're not gaining in golf, you're falling behind. I get down there a couple of days a week."

I could have suggested that he look me up if he needed any investment advice, but I don't do that to friends, and it would have seemed a bit awkward advising someone already that well off. It would be like Kevin telling Tiger Woods his follow-through was sloppy.

"You're looking good," Kevin said. "I guess you've been able to rebuild your life after — after the accident."

"More or less." I looked at the mountain view and then back at him. "But some people and some things you never forget."

Kevin nodded.

Maddy was quieter now that we were a threesome. I felt as tense as a violin bow string, but I tried to let the mountain scenery and the cool, clean water do their magic. No luck. I drained the glass.

"I should be getting back," I said. "It was good to see you two."

They were polite but not insistent. Maddy showed me back to the front door and gave me another hug. She waited a moment on the steps as I walked the path back to my car.

Man, that hug had felt great. The film about Coloradoan *Temple Grandin* shed light on an autistic woman who felt uncomfortable with human contact. Not me. Today, I could have used a ten-minute hug if that wouldn't have been creepy and wildly inappropriate.

Maddy's hair smelled nice, too. Roses maybe.

Most of my recent thoughts about women centered on Cathy, but being here had me thinking more about Allison.

Chapter 18

During the drive back to the Springs, I let my mind wander where it would, focusing my automatic attention functions on turn signals and avoiding crashes.

Maddy seemed a little more tense than I remembered her, but I hadn't seen her all that many times. And she had certainly seemed warm. For now I had to cross her off my mental checklist of possible terrorists. In pencil.

And I couldn't see how Kevin Mayer could be behind this. He'd never even been that close to Allison. No reason he should be angry that I had started dating Cathy.

I missed Cathy's presence in my life. The only awful days since I met her were the ones after the reunion, but I knew that if I'd had such a bad day that I needed a ten-minute hug, she would have held on tight.

Only one other person came to mind when I thought about people who cared about Allison enough to punish me for moving on after her death. Sally Anderson had been a classmate of Allison's at Colorado College and Allison's best friend. They had graduated the same year, and Sally opened an antique store in Old Colorado City. She was right on my way back into the Springs.

Old Colorado City started out as Colorado City. Now it was basically a suburb of Colorado Springs, one with a very distinctive character.

I got off Highway 24 and jogged over to Colorado Avenue. Within a few blocks, many of the buildings were old one- and two-story red-brick structures, a mix of tourist shops, restaurants, bars, antique stores, jewelry shops, tee-shirt vendors, and an assortment of small businesses serving the residents. I passed Meadow Muffins Bar and Grill and the Rocky Mountain Chocolate Factory, wondering how many people still knew a meadow muffin was a cow pie.

I found an empty parking spot next to Bancroft Park, a one-small-block-square park next to a branch library, and fed the parking meter. The sky was still clear and blue, and the day was warming up. Mid-eighties so far.

At Sally's antique store, Old Colorado Pretty, a couple of customers occupied Sally's attention, so I turned and browsed a neat aisle between some old school desks with folding lids and real wood bureaus. Allison and Sally shared a love for old stuff that I didn't appreciate to the same degree. The house Allison had lived in was a small two-story Victorian about five blocks away.

The furniture gave off the odor of polish and stain and, though it all looked clean and fresh, dust.

"If I can help you find anything, just let me know," Sally called to me after the pair of customers left. I turned.

Sally smiled broadly. "Dave! What a surprise." She was about the same age as Allison and I were, but she had pure white hair. I'd never asked her, but I assumed it was the result of heredity, not choice. Seeing her surrounded by antiques, I wondered if she had been driven to antiques by having a look that felt old, or if she cultivated the look because she liked the antique era. She wore silver filigree earrings and a pioneer dress—lacy white collar, pale-pink print top and puffy sleeves, full white skirt.

"Hi, Sally. How have you been?"

Her hug felt good, unreserved. She seemed genuinely glad to see me, so I didn't grill her about making trouble in my life. If she were that good an actress, questioning her would be worthless anyway.

In answer to my question, she held up one hand, palm toward her, letting me see the new engagement ring. She smiled even wider.

"Who's the lucky guy? I assume it's a guy?" I felt good for her.

"It is a guy as it turns out. You don't know him. Alan Friedberg. He's a real estate agent. I met him just before Christmas, and we really hit it off."

"I'm happy for you."

"How about you?"

I hesitated. "Well, I started dating someone, but—I'm not sure if it's going to work out."

"You'll find the right someone. I know that's what Allison would have wanted for you."

"Thanks. I saw Ben today. And Maddy."

"They were down here, or you went up there?"

"Up there. Ben didn't seem to be doing very well."

"I heard that, too. I'm surprised. I thought that was a treatable cancer, the kind that lets you die of something else. Maybe Allison's death hit him so hard he just gave up."

I could sense no underlying blame for me in her manner. Just sadness at the outcome, sadness mirroring mine.

"What brings you here? Looking for some old jewelry? Maybe a nicely preserved suit?"

"Nope. I was passing through and realized it had been too long." It had been. "It's really good to see you, Sally. I think being engaged really suits you."

Understatement. It seemed to have transformed her. Sometimes I'd seen a quick somber expression darken her face in the middle of a crowd. Maybe that's why she and Allison had been so close. But no hint of that showed now. Just unadulterated happiness.

I left the shop and headed back to my rental car. It was a sign of the time that I breathed a sigh of relief when I could tell the windows were undamaged and there was no sign of concrete.

~~~

Since I had skipped physical therapy because of the concrete incident, I swung by my house to get my workout clothes and then drove up Centennial and then across on Vindicator to a strip mall anchored by a Safeway. Behind the grocery lay another branch library and Anytime Fitness.

Windows ran most of the length of the fitness center, a fact I appreciated more than I had before, because I could keep tabs on my rental car.

A half-dozen people were using the treadmills, ellipticals, and various weight machines. Bruce was chatting with a client, and he waved. When he got free he came over. Bruce was a buff, black twenty-something with one earring and he was one of the best sources I'd found for keeping fit, or in my case getting back in shape. He could talk nutrition, exercise, yoga, or attitude. After my insurance rehab benefit ran out, I'd asked around and found Bruce ready to take me the rest of the distance. My right knee gave me some trouble, and my right shoulder had its complaints, too. Both had been twisted past the maximum recommended values in the accident.

The right shoulder had just been repaired with arthroscopic surgery. I was regularly doing some light jogging around my neighborhood, and Bruce helped me keep increasing the strength in both knee and shoulder without overdoing it.

We said hi and caught each other up to date, but I left out the concrete incident and the reunion. Either incident would generate enough reaction that I'd spend more time reliving the recent past than I wanted to.

Today he had me mainly on the seated leg curl—the bender—and the leg extension—the kicker. One main goal was to strengthen the quadriceps on the front of the thigh without doing anything to reinjure the knee. I went through three sets of fifteen reps and then he had me move on to working on my shoulders, again trying to strengthen without overdoing.

As was often the case, Bruce had a new gadget to show me, and we talked while he observed and I pushed and pulled.

"So take a look at this," he said. He had his phone out and he held it so I could see. It showed his dog, a black lab name Barney, sleeping on the couch.

"I've seen pictures of your dog."

"Yeah, but watch." Still keeping the screen so I could see it, he reached over and pressed a button on the screen. He raised his voice and went into stern command mode. "Get off the couch!"

If I'd been on a couch, I would have gotten up immediately. On screen, his dog suddenly perked up and looked around. I was watching a live video.

"I mean it. Right now."

Obviously still unsure of where his owner was, the lab grudgingly got up, shook himself, and stepped down.

"Just call me Big Daddy," Bruce said with a grin.

"Well you are black. 'Big Brother' would work, too."

"I know. I considered that one."

"So we're seeing live video from your house?"

"Exactly. I've got a laptop with its webcam on the dining room table. I see the video here, and if I want to talk, it comes out the laptop speakers."

"What does Julia think of this?"

"It creeps her out. She's in the house, she closes the laptop. She's got kind of a thing about privacy."

I nodded. I knew his wife. People might not try to hack his system to watch his dog, but his wife was another matter.

"So you can't use this to keep her off the couch?"

"If I don't mind sleeping with Barney in the doghouse for a month and eating from the same dish."

Chapter 19

At the office, I returned a couple of phone calls I'd let go to voice-mail. In email, the new client, Ross Morse, had already responded to my questionnaire and was ready to transfer $400,000 into his new account with us. The questionnaire didn't address how people came into money, so there was no way to tell if he'd gotten an inheritance or he was a scrupulous saver or he flipped houses. He seemed to be on a good track for a thirty-five-year old. He'd even completed the wire transfer request, so I clicked *approved*.

I pushed the rest of the buttons required to move things to the next step. I was glad to see that he was investing for the long haul. I'd love to give planning advice to former day traders, but not too many of them still had money to invest after the recent turnarounds. Gaining while nearly the whole market is rising is one thing. Bucking a losing trend by playing with short-term trades is more like pulling that long handle and waiting as several rolling icons come to a full stop. The short-term market can drive people crazy when the tiniest indicator change gets magnified by thousands of automated trades. Some days it would be more stable if housecats were chasing reflections and accidentally pouncing on the buy and sell keys.

Everyone else had been gone an hour by the time I got caught up with the day's work. From my computer I could enter transactions for only my accounts, and only the accounts I had discretionary authority for, or a verified transaction request from the customer, but I could view transactions for the whole company. I called up the client list and found Daniel Else. Stan Marston was the investment analyst responsible for his account, and Stan had discretionary authority. I looked at Daniel's age, his stated goals, and the amount he had invested. One of my clients, Annie Holmes, had a roughly equivalent profile. Similar age, similar risk choices, and she had about eighty-five percent of Daniel's balance.

I pulled a transaction and commission report on both accounts. In the previous year, Daniel's account showed one and a half times the number of transactions, and almost double the amount of commissions compared to Annie. For the year before that, the reports were much closer to one another. Same for the year before that. Over all three years, Daniel's rate of return was very similar to Annie's, if you ignored the commission cost. But the commission cost was a few percentage points higher for Daniel, so his net was lower.

So, what had changed? Had Stan entered a micro-managing stage of his career? Had personal finance pressure made him less concerned about keeping client transactions to a minimum rate? I put a copy of trade dates and details on a working file and started slogging through them in detail, looking for reasons the trades might have happened on those dates. Maybe a new CEO had been hired and the CEO compensation ratio had doubled. Maybe the price-earnings ratio had been rising over time. Maybe a new product had tanked, or an old product had come out of its patent-protection period.

In the end I concluded most of the trades could be justified, but they weren't in my opinion all completely necessary. Daniel could have paid five or ten thousand dollars more in commissions than he needed to, or I could have been wrong in second-guessing Stan's moves.

I leaned back, rubbed my eyes, moved my shoulders forward and back to relieve the stiffening. A car on the street below moved past, generating the annoying *boom-boom-boom* from speakers better suited to an auditorium. Music from a nearby bar floated up. The sky outside was starting to darken.

Daniel answered my call after two rings.

"Daniel, I've gone over transactions for the past few years, and your commission costs are slightly higher than what I would have expected, but they don't seem to be in a fraudulent range."

He was quiet for a moment. "You used some qualifiers there, so I'm not 100% sure what your recommendation is. Do you think I should stay with Stan?"

He was really putting me on the spot. I thought about it. "This is a little like a report card in school. I can't do a pass-fail. But I'd give Stan an A minus or a B plus for last year and a half. For the two prior years, I'd give him an A."

Again he was quiet as he digested this. "That's fair," Daniel said finally. "I know this wasn't easy, but I appreciate your being straight with me and for getting back to me quickly."

"No problem at all."

"One more question. If I did want to make a change in investment counselors, would you be receptive?"

This one needed no delay. "No. I'm sorry. I can't take clients of my co-workers. And even if I were tempted to break my rule, if I provided information that made you move from Stan to me, you couldn't be sure I was being objective. And I don't want to cause trouble for Stan or create tension between Stan and me."

"I knew I asked the right guy. Thanks, Dave. If I run into anyone looking for an investment house, I will absolutely steer him your way."

~~~

Wednesday morning, I felt better. I could use a flipping-digits safety sign like factories do. Thirty-six hours without a dirty trick.

Wanting the energy boost from a morning run, I put on my good running shoes, sweat pants, and a tee-shirt. I stuck my phone in a pocket and went out the front door.

I surprised a pair of mule deer, a doe and a fawn. Mom bounded away in the energetic four-footed bounce, her white, black-tipped tail flopping as she ran. Junior followed her at a more relaxed pace. I waited until I was sure my presence wouldn't scare them into traffic.

Jogging along Mesa Road concerned me because some of the morning drivers paid scant attention to the thirty-five mile-per-hour limit, despite having just driven by a school, but a roadside trail offered a reasonable setback for most of my path. It was early enough today that traffic so far was very light.

I crossed the street and started running southeast, parallel to the road. As I ran, I tried to keep in mind all of Bruce's advice on how to run without stressing my knees. Lean forward, land on the midfoot. Keep my knees bent most of the time.

The morning air was crisp and clean, one of the many reasons I loved Colorado. On the other side of a cross street, the trail became a sidewalk. I passed the church, reached the traffic light at 19th, and turned back. It wasn't much of a run, but I felt pressed for time at the office, given how much time I'd lost yesterday.

I was back on the path, running northwest, when I sensed the first indication of trouble. No cars were visible ahead, but the engine noise from one coming up behind me grew louder, throatier. Without thinking, I adjusted my path a foot to the right, crowding the outer edge of the asphalt trail. The only thing between me and a barbed-wire fence was a narrow strip of grass populated with plenty of yucca with their arrays of porcupine-like sharp spines.

A fraction of a second later came the crunch of gravel as the car moved out of the lane and its tires bit into the debris left by past rains.

I started to turn to see how close the car was. A split-second glimpse registered a series of micro impressions—dark pickup—close—too close—side mirror. I started to dart farther to the right.

Wham!

The side mirror slammed into my left shoulder, knocking me forward, spinning me to the right.

~~~

Once when I was younger, I loved playing with a toy fire truck, partly because I could run the siren and flash the lights.

For just a moment I was back there, pushing that truck along the linoleum in the kitchen. And then, abruptly, I was hearing the siren wail up close. But not from a fire truck.

I was flat on my back in what had to be an ambulance. From the road noise and the vibrations, it was moving faster than thirty-five miles an hour, and at first I was tempted to complain.

"Hello! Everything is under control. You got hit by a vehicle, but you're in an ambulance on the way to Penrose. What's your name?" The speaker was a thin guy in his twenties or thirties.

"Dave Barlow."

"Good. What year is this?"

I told him.

"Good. Who's president?"

I blinked and said, "These are things *you* really should know."

He laughed politely. "I need to know your memory is working OK."

I told him my guess as to who was president, and he bought it.

"Do you feel any pain?"

"My foot," I said slowly. "I think my left foot doesn't hurt. That's about all."

I was exaggerating, but not by a lot. I had a splitting headache. The left side of my back felt—I don't know, just felt *bad*. The backs of both of my legs felt like someone had practiced Sewing Machine 101 on them. My right cheek smarted. A bee had stung me on the inside of my right elbow.

"I can crank this up some, but I want you lucid." He pointed to an IV that explained the bee sting.

"I think it's under control," I said. Actually, whatever they were giving me was not only starting to take away the pain, but it relaxed me to the point that my fear and anger seemed to just hide in the corner for a while. I could get used to this.

The ambulance slowed for an intersection and took a left turn. I felt happy with the system of sirens and flashing lights and getting priority through traffic just for me. It was good to be the patient.

I decided it was nap time.

Chapter 20

The lights were brighter when I woke again. And they were moving. Oh, I was moving. I was on a stretcher, moving along a hallway. Someone behind me was pushing me along, like I was on an expensive go-cart.

They wheeled me into a room the size of a bedroom. One with lots of ceiling lights and built-in cabinets. And a sink. The fog lifted a little and I realized I was in an emergency room. I could smell cleaning solvents and maybe rubbing alcohol.

A gowned man positioned my bed and locked the wheels. He looked down on me and held my wrist as he got my pulse. "Who's the president?"

"Seriously, don't any of you guys know?"

He grinned. "How's your pain level? You know the ten code?"

"Probably a six. Seven when I laugh." They must have given me something to make me loopy.

He finished hooking me up to some cables. "The doctor will see you in under ten minutes. We'll be monitoring, but press this if you need anything."

"Can I just ask?"

He'd been on his way back out of the room. "I'm not going to be here. That's why—"

"No, I mean I really need my phone. It's in my pocket. I've got to tell my boss I won't be in to work."

He hesitated. Probably against the rules. But he fished out my phone and handed it to me. "Be quick."

I had a little difficulty focusing, but I placed a call to Beth at BTU Investments. I got her voicemail and left a message. "I'm going to be late today. I had a small 'accident' while I was jogging, but I'm OK, and I'll be back as soon as I can."

I terminated the call and was trying to remember how to silence the phone when it rang. Beth must have called back immediately without listening to my voicemail.

But the caller ID said WHITLEY C.

Cathy.

I desperately wanted to talk to her. I also very much wanted to keep her out of whatever was going on. Maybe it was the drugs they'd given me for pain. Maybe it was a concussion.

I answered. "Dave Barlow."

A short silence. Then, "Hi. It's me."

"Hi." I felt ready to climb out of bed and go see her for coffee.

"I've been trying to find a way to say how sorry I am. For not—for not believing in you."

"It's OK." Wow, I was eloquent today.

"No, it's not. I've been feeling awful, the more I thought about it all. I was trying to find a way to apologize. And a friend called me at the clinic and told me about the *Gazette* article about your car. That was your car, right?"

The concrete incident seemed like ancient history now. That couldn't have been only two days ago. "Yup, that was mine."

"What's going on, Dave?"

"I wish I knew."

"Look. Could we get together for lunch?"

I spotted a giant clock on the wall. It was still early in the day. "I—" I hesitated, waffling between, "I want that more than I want any-thing," and, "Please stay away for now. Because of the crazy things going on, I'm dangerous to be around."

In that brief hesitation, an announcement started over the PA. Some PA systems are garbled, like the staff is having a big joke on the customers. This one was perfectly clear. "Code Blue. Room twelve. Code Blue. Room twelve."

"Where are you, Dave?"

"I—you know, I'm not absolutely certain."

"Where are you?" Her voice rose. She was a pro at emergencies. Even in my short time dating Cathy, I'd seen more than one person rush into her office with a dying or injured animal and she was the epitome of grace under fire. "Goddamnit, where are you?" Her voice was shaky.

"Penrose, I think."

Perfect timing. A doctor walked into my cubicle. She gave me a frown when she saw the phone. She was maybe forty, so she'd probably had lots of experience with people trying to waste her time.

I said, "Look, I've got to call you later. My first appointment is here."

I shut off the phone, earning a *that's better* expression.

"I'm Dr. Bentson," she said. "I hear you took a spill."

"No, I think they gave me a shot. IV. Whatever."

She parsed that. "Not a pill. A spill."

"Yes. Yes, I did."

She frowned again. I wasn't making a good first impression.

She checked my vitals again. You just can't be too sure about those vitals.

I realized I was still feeling loopy, but I couldn't do anything about it.

She pulled up the sheet and looked at my legs. Then my chest. She touched my chest a few times with an ice cube, I think. "Can you roll over?"

For some reason, the idea of a doctor trying to teach me how to roll over seemed funny. I laughed. That was a mistake I wouldn't repeat soon. It seemed like another good time for a nap. No one else seemed to have gotten the nap memo. It was if people were deliberately trying to keep me awake.

I woke more when they were taking an X-Ray or an MRI scanning cats or one of those *look inside* things. Once I was back out in the hallway, I could better understand why dogs love car rides. The journey was doing me good. With each light I passed beneath, the fog in my brain seemed to clear a bit more. I thought about yelling, "Faster! Faster!"

The nurse wheeled me back into the room I'd been in before. At least it looked very similar. One difference was that the visitor's chair was occupied. On it were a purse and a white lab coat.

Another difference. Cathy stood there looking tearful.

Man, the lengths I had to go to, to get her attention.

"Hi," I said. I tried to wave, but my arm was held down.

"Hi," she said. "How are you?"

"I'm actually a bit sleepy."

The nurse finished locking the bed in place and told me the doctor would be back soon.

"Are you all right?" Cathy took my hand. She looked around, apparently saw no one or no one whose disapproval she cared about, and she leaned over and kissed me. Hard at first, then tender.

"Better now," I said. I actually sighed.

"What happened?"

"As best as I can piece it together, I'm in the emergency room."

She compressed her lips. Beautiful lips. Black, shoulder-length hair that looked a little helter-skelter today. Wonderful green eyes flecked with gold. She waited. I realized she knew that much.

"I went out for a jog." Somehow I had the presence of mind to give her the sugar-coated version that even I was having trouble accepting. "Apparently someone strayed from the road. I got pushed hard and fell. I'm fine."

She swallowed.

"I'm fine, really."

Dr. Bentson came back in with a clipboard. It looked like the kind of clipboard that would list suggested tire pressure, oil filter status, and a recommendation for a new air cleaner.

She didn't ask me if I wanted synthetic oil. "Is it all right to talk about your status with your friend present?"

"She's welcome to stay."

Cathy stayed. I probably couldn't have gotten her out of the room with tear gas.

"All in all I would say you are pretty lucky."

I knew that. When I woke up, I knew it was going to be my lucky day. Then I glanced quickly at Cathy. "I know what you mean."

"You've got deep bruising on your back on the left side. It's going to be ugly for a while. You're lucky the car's mirror was rounded and didn't hit you squarely, would be my guess. What may hurt more is that part of your back and part of the backs of your legs were punctured by yucca spines. You're loaded up with a tetanus shot and I've got a prescription for antibiotics. Take them all per the directions even if you feel fine. You've got some abraded skin on your cheek and elsewhere. You'll have cream for that."

Cathy brushed a hand against her lips.

I hoped *elsewhere* wasn't a euphemism for somewhere I really didn't want damaged. Particularly with long, sharp spines.

"My biggest concern actually is the mild concussion. Your brain got rattled around a bit, so take it easy. No roller coasters, that kind of thing."

"Is it safe to ride with her?" I pointed my chin at Cathy.

Cathy rolled her eyes. "I think that means he's recovering."

Doctor Bentson frowned again.

"I'm sorry, doctor. I will take it easy, and I really appreciate your care. Are there some painkillers on the list?"

"Yes. As soon as you can, switch to regular ibuprofen, but stay ahead of the pain. No alcohol. Have someone check on you to make sure you're doing all right. I'll give you a checklist of things to avoid or to be careful with."

She looked at her clipboard, her own checklist, I guessed.

"Who's the president?" she asked.

"Couldn't you ask me for the cube root of 125? Or the capital of Kazakhstan?"

"Be well, Mr. Barlow." She gave a raised-eyebrows glance to Cathy that probably said, *You're going to have your hands full.*

Chapter 21

This was not how I imagined getting back with Cathy would look.

She was fairly quiet on the drive home, probably wanting to make extra certain there were no accidents. I felt like a sick cat on the way back from the vet. At least it hadn't been that special one-time visit to the vet.

At the back of my mind was, *I should be at work,* but that was surprisingly easy to deal with. I looked over at Cathy and felt all was right with the world. She just had that power. She must have felt me looking at her, and she glanced back at me for a safe amount of time. I loved that smile.

She pulled into the driveway and braked to an extremely gentle stop. Something must have been in the air today because she sneezed. Most people have the reflex to draw in a breath when they feel a sneeze coming on. Cathy deliberately breathed *out,* to minimize the sneeze. The result was like a small cat sneezing. I smiled as I did every time.

Inside, she helped me get situated in a recliner where I could see the view to the west. Kitchen noises came and went and she handed me a nice cold glass of orange juice. She made sure a blanket was giving me just enough warmth.

"I'll be back in a half-hour. I'll get your prescriptions. All they ask for is your date of birth, and I know that. Can I get you anything before I take off?"

"No, I'm good. Cathy, I can't thank you enough—"

"Don't be silly. You get some rest." She gave me a kiss and headed for the door. She was going to make a wonderful mother, but I was still afraid I didn't have it in me to be a good father. Sometimes I was certain I carried the Barlow family curse and it would be best if it died with me.

As I was thinking those cheery thoughts, I must have nodded off, because the next thing I knew, Cathy was back, rustling paper and plastic in the kitchen. Moments later she came out with a couple of pieces of toast. "You should have something more in your stomach for some of these pills."

"Thanks." I gave her a grateful smile.

She looked wonderful. She'd parked her white lab coat somewhere. She wore a crisp white blouse and snug black slacks that looked extremely nice on her. I took my interest as a good sign that the yucca spines had not speared my *elsewhere*.

She sat down beside me. "I just want to say how sorry—"

"Stop right there. I would have done the same thing in your shoes. You're back. That's all I care about."

She digested that. Her green eyes were glistening. She leaned over and kissed me gently for quite a few seconds. Her black hair fell in my face. What a nice kiss. Finally she leaned back. "OK. What's happened since Saturday night?"

"Well, one of the first things I did was to call Marty, one of my high-school classmates. One of the real ones."

I took a bite of toast, and savored the taste.

"The actual reunion was the week before. It would seem that someone intercepted my invitation and sent me an email with a different date."

"So all those people. They were all fakes?"

"They had to be."

"But who would—" she foundered for words. "Who would go to this length to do something like that?"

"That's the big question. In the middle of the night after the reunion I got a text. It said, "How does it feel to be forgotten so quickly?"

"I don't get it."

"I think it means someone close to Allison is angry that I started dating you so soon after Allison died."

"But it was almost a year."

"I know. But in the grand scheme of things, I felt guilty a few times that I was enjoying life with you when Allison was dead."

"Right," Cathy said. "Survivor's guilt. I felt it, too. But going on with life is no betrayal of Allison. Or Howard."

"I know that. Anyway, I decided to just hunker down and see if the storm would pass. And then Monday I came back to my car and found it filled with concrete. A few hours later, another text, gloating or goading."

"Any text about today?"

"Not so far. But the day is young."

"The article said you were near CC when your car was filled with concrete. What brought you there?"

I hesitated. "I had an appointment with a counselor. A psychiatrist. But I don't think I'm ready to talk about that."

Cathy opened her mouth, shut it. Then, "First of all, lots of people see counselors. But OK, forget that for now. Any theories about who's doing this?"

"Maybe a disgruntled client. Or a friend of Allison's. I thought Allison's father was the most likely candidate. I drove up there yesterday. He has an estate a little past Woodland Park. He seems pretty ill, some kind of cancer, and I couldn't really get a reading out of him. He denied it, but I just don't know."

"Can you go to the police?"

I was just about to explain my thoughts about contacting them with a complete lack of evidence when the doorbell rang.

Cathy started for the door.

"Wait," I called. "Let me. Just in case." I didn't want her going to the door in case this was another incident with my mystery man. I struggled out of my chair, feeling pain in my back and legs more intensely than before.

"You can be pretty stubborn, you know," Cathy said. She softened it with a smile. We both could, but I didn't see an upside in pointing that out.

It wasn't a mystery man. It was a cop. Not the same one as from the concrete incident. This one was a serious woman in her thirties, her hair swept back in a bun. I almost asked Cathy, *How did you do that?*

The cop gave me the once over and apparently concluded that she was at the right house.

"Mr. Barlow? We've not been able to locate the vehicle that hit you. But can I ask you a few questions?"

"Sure. Come on in."

I introduced Cathy and the three of us took seats in the kitchen. Cathy was a natural entertainer and asked the cop if she'd like some juice. Not this time.

"Another driver came on the scene just in time to see the incident. She decided correctly to come to your aid rather than chasing the vehicle. Can you tell me anything about the vehicle?" I supposed she didn't tell me her version because she didn't want to precondition me.

"Not much. I had just a split-second warning that it was drifting off the road. I turned and got a quick impression of a dark-colored pickup."

"The witness thought it was a black Ford pickup, probably an F150, but she couldn't tell any more than that. But just so you know. She said the driver didn't 'drift' out of his lane. The witness reported that the driver deliberately swerved to try to hit you. If you hadn't dodged, the truck would have hit you squarely."

Cathy gripped my arm.

I nodded, trying to absorb a confirmation of what I already suspected. Did the mystery man want me dead or just really messed up?

Or maybe a different possibility. If Stan were churning accounts, and found out I was looking at his records, how far would he be willing to go?

"I suppose F150s are pretty common," I said at last.

"Extremely common."

There wasn't much else to say about what I was starting to think of as the F150 incident. It bothered me a lot that I had enough incidents that I had to name them. If they found the F150 driver, great, but if I told the cops my thoughts about Ben and Stan at this point, it wouldn't really give them anything tangible to act on.

As I said goodbye to the cop, she said, "Be careful, Mr. Barlow."

You don't have to tell me twice. Well, maybe today, but not normally. Unless it's to eat my spinach.

I sat down in the recliner again, and then immediately got back up. Standing was less painful than putting pressure on my back and legs.

Cathy watched me as I paced slowly. "What are you going to do next?"

"I'm thinking about lying down, but not on my back."

"And after that?"

"Have you ever been to Bolivia?"

She raised her eyebrows.

"I don't know. I'd forgotten about it with everything going on, but I'm supposed to be at an all-day seminar in Denver tomorrow. Keeping up with investment law."

"And about what's going on? About what's happening to you?"

"I don't know. I just want to keep a low profile. Maybe by now whoever's responsible is feeling he's gotten his pound of flesh. He's destroyed my car and put me in the hospital." I was still a bit out of it because of the drugs, but I refrained from saying, *What else could go wrong?*

Cathy didn't look happy with that answer, but she didn't offer any great ideas on how to solve this either. She picked up the doctor's instruction list. "I think you need to take a shower or a bath. Bath would probably be better for soaking the yucca punctures, but that might hurt too much. What do you think?"

"Shower."

On the occasions that Cathy and I stayed the night, either here or at her place, we usually showered together. It was a wonderfully intimate and life-affirming way to start a day. Today I expected I'd shower alone, but Cathy followed me into the bathroom. I don't think I'll ever get tired of seeing her take off that black lingerie.

I stopped short in the bathroom, and my skin felt cold. On the bathroom mirror, written in large lipstick letters was, "Get Well Soon!"

"Damn these people!" Cathy said. I'd heard her swear only twice now, and both times were on my behalf.

She took a tissue and began quickly wiping away the letters. The lipstick smeared, but she used a stack of tissues and kept wiping until you could no longer tell anything had been written there.

"Now," she said. "Where were we?"

"I think you should go," I said when she turned back to me.

"What are you talking about?"

"Someone tried to kill me. And that someone has been in this house. You're not safe here."

Cathy took this in. "Are we going to a motel then? I'm not leaving you right now. No one's going to attack us in the house in broad daylight."

She didn't know that, but I didn't have the energy either for driving someplace or for arguing with Cathy. Once she made up her mind about something, it would take a dozen circus strong men to change her course.

"At least get a chair and stick it under the doorknob."

She smiled. "Be right back."

She was. We took turns taking a piece of clothing off the other person. For a moment, the depression, the hypervigilance, the lack of self-worth, were all banished. But then fear resurfaced. Maybe someone had done more damage inside the house. How did someone get in? I took a deep breath and willed myself to ignore those thoughts. I would worry about them before it got dark.

When I turned my back to her to toss my running clothes in the hamper, she gasped. I looked in the mirror. A huge portion of my upper back was an angry red welt. Here and there were small red circles and dots, thanks to the yucca. The backs of my calves were bandaged. I felt a bit like Frankenstein's monster without the bolts. So far.

Cathy gingerly removed the bandages and exposed maybe a dozen of the red punctures. She brushed her fingers lightly over spots between the punctures, and then kissed me lightly several times on my back. She turned me around and lifted her mouth toward mine and kissed the abrasion on my cheek. Say what you will, I felt very much better.

The hot spray from the showerhead stung. Not as bad as the initial pain, but right up there.

Cathy soaped my back and the backs of my legs. And let's be honest, she was quite a bit more thorough than that. The degree of pain I felt pretty much insured nothing more was going to happen, but I was mightily relieved when I confirmed that my injuries didn't extend to *elsewhere*. Cathy looked happy, too.

Once she had gotten the yucca punctures clean again, we just hung on to each other for minutes and let the hot spray flow over our bodies.

In the bedroom, I lay chest-down at her command, while she applied new antibiotic cream to the punctures, and started to put fresh dressing back on. I bet I was one of her most cooperative patients. I was so cooperative that during the process, I fell asleep.

When I woke, the slant of sunlight through the window suggested mid-afternoon. I glanced to the other side of the bed and found Cathy's gaze on mine. She snuggled closer and I put an arm around her. I barely cried out at all.

"Thank you," I breathed. "Thank you, thank you, thank you." And then my brain got into second gear. "Shouldn't you be at the clinic?"

She smiled. "Tomorrow is another day."

Chapter 22

Traffic was heavy as I drove south toward Colorado Springs early Thursday evening.

I was beat. Sitting in an extended meeting all day wore me out more than if I was pushing myself all day long. My only exercise had been constantly shifting positions to try to find the least uncomfortable posture for my back and my legs. I thanked the gods that I hadn't been speared in the butt. Or elsewhere.

I-25 always seemed to be under construction or slowed by an accident between the Springs and Denver.

Despite my exhaustion, I was ready for a late dinner with Cathy. I would get a nap for maybe ninety minutes and then meet her. With that to look forward to, the bruises and punctures from yesterday seemed less important, though the bruise on my back had evolved into a huge eggplant-blue mass.

I exited on Uintah and took a right on Mesa. I wondered, as I'd wondered aloud with Cathy yesterday, if the amount of pain inflicted so far was enough to satisfy the mystery man. Or woman.

I slowed for a trio of mule deer crossing the road and flashed my lights so the motorist ahead would know something was up. The deer made it safely across and I accelerated.

It was only in the last hundred yards that I first started getting nervous and then angry.

Traffic was moving very slowly along Mesa Road, but between vehicles I could see that my mailbox was missing. I had enough to worry about without that.

And then I got closer and realized it was not just the mailbox.

I pulled to a stop behind a gawker, stunned. And angrier than I can remember being.

My house was gone.

I was so angry that it was all I could do to signal my turn and wait for an opening in the slow-moving oncoming line of traffic instead of just crashing through like a bumper car rampage. I drove onto where my driveway had been. Technically the driveway might have been still there, but it was no longer well-defined by gravel. I got out of the rental car and walked forward, in shock.

One of the problems with hypervigilance is that it picks and chooses the moments. I could be completely wound up about whether the guy behind me in the checkout line was the same guy I saw on a wanted poster in the post office, even if he looked like Mr. Rogers. But I'd had not a glimmer of worry that someone might raze my house. If I had, I could have alerted the neighbors or at the very least installed one of those fake barking dogs. But this—this took me completely by surprise.

The lot had been leveled, crudely. From the edges of the properties on either side of my house, most evidence of a house was missing. It didn't take a Sherlock Holmes or a Miss Marple to see the clues, though. Heavy equipment tracks bit into newly turned dirt where the bushes in front of my house had been ripped from the ground. Maybe my basement was still there, but if so it was filled in with debris from the main floor of the house, and dirt pushed against it.

I felt sick.

It was a bit like my house had been scraped, to make room for a new, more expensive house. It happens all the time in some neighborhoods, and of the houses on my block mine might have been the cheapest, and hence the best candidate.

But as I walked deeper into the lot I saw the space hadn't been scraped in the traditional sense. The wreckage of the above-ground portion of my house had apparently been carried forward by a bull-dozer blade and pushed down the ravine. The slope looked like the aftermath of an explosion, with scattered pieces of concrete, stucco-covered wall segments, a mangled table lamp, a crushed sink.

In the rubble would be the telescope Allison had given me. Photos of my mother. A rock paperweight my grandfather had given me before he died. Client files, artwork, books. I kicked through some of the surface trash and found only two-by-fours, concrete, sheetrock, dirt, and mangled electrical wiring. Whatever was left of my possessions was deeply buried.

I had to turn away I was so angry. And then it got worse.

My phone chimed with an incoming text. The screen seemed to be tinged in red, and I could barely read the letters on the screen. The message said, *"If you see your girlfriend again she gets everything you get. Have a nice day."*

Chapter 23

I was sitting on a piece of periscope-like concrete that rose to a height of about a foot when the first police car arrived. I now had space for a fleet of them if they all wanted to investigate.

My body was a giant collection of throbbing aches. My pain pills and my anti-depressant pills were somewhere below me in the wreckage. My right shoulder ached from the car accident, my left from the hit and run. My back actually only hurt when I moved, but I thought I could feel every yucca spine puncture individually. No doubt the mental stress was compounding the physical symptoms.

The police car pulled to a halt in the dirt and a cop got out. The same guy I'd met during the concrete incident.

I waited, numb, while he surveyed my property and looked at the rubble flowing down into the ravine. Finally he came over and stood by me.

"Man, you must have really pissed someone off, big time."

"You want to listen in while I call my home insurance company?"

"No. Sorry about that. The car was one thing. This—wow."

The presence of a police car apparently motivated my neighbor to the northwest to approach. Maybe she felt with a police presence I wouldn't beat her up for not stopping this. She was a woman in her sixties I guessed. She wore one of those hats that gardeners and Vegas dealers wore, like a ball cap but with only the green visor and strap. I knew her to wave "hi" but I didn't know her name. I could see where maybe that had been a mistake.

"Hello," she said to the cop. She nodded to me. "I can't help but notice—"

Please don't say, *Your house is gone.*

"—that the scrapers did a poor job. They pushed stuff down into the park instead of scooping it all up."

"They weren't scrapers," I said.

She looked around the lot, bewildered. "What were they doing then? I thought you had decided to upgrade."

I looked at her house. It was probably worth twice as much as mine had been worth, but really? Mine was *that* bad?

"They were vandals, not scrapers."

"Oh, my. This is something new." She looked back at her house as though she should be back there right then, just in case.

The cop took over. "It's not a new fad, ma'am. Someone has been targeting this fellow here. You have nothing to worry about."

She took a couple of steps toward the ravine and pointed at the avalanche of rubble. The flotsam of my house. My belongings. "Really? Look at that."

I rose, feeling anger rise inside, and started walking back there. "I'll get right on it." I bent over and retrieved the only household possession I could see, a shoe.

I tapped the shoe against the heel of my hand a few times, shaking the dirt out of it, and trying to calm down. The neighbor was just being a little slow on the uptake, seeing things from her self-interested perspective. That would change as she got the new information processed.

The cop said to her, "I'm sure the insurance company will take care of the cleanup, ma'am. But in the meantime, there are questions we need to find the answers to."

I wondered crazily if I had the bulldozer-damage rider on my policy. The home insurance call was going to be even tougher than the concrete incident call.

The cop asked her, "When did you notice something was happening here?"

"A couple of hours ago. A man came to my door. He showed me some papers on a clipboard. He said he had all the permits in place and he was going to scrape the house."

That part was smart, I supposed. As long as the neighbors thought it was legit, they wouldn't call the police.

Another police car arrived on my dirt. "Just a moment, ma'am," the first cop said, and he walked over to meet a pair of cops in the other car. The pair, both beefy guys in their forties probably, consulted with him briefly and then split up. One started taking photos of my dirt, and the other walked toward my neighbor on the other side.

"OK," the cop said when he returned, "What can you tell me about the man?"

"Tall. Kind of thin. Big full gray beard and dark glasses. Ball cap. He wore it right, not that backward way the retards do."

Maybe it was best after all to not know my neighbors better. I wondered if ZZ Top had done this.

"Anything else?"

"Dirty coveralls. Big thick work boots."

Great. She had a reasonably complete description, but I bet by now that guy was only tall and thin. The beard, sunglasses, hat, and outfit were probably in some dumpster already.

The neighbor woman turned to me. "So this really was vandalism?"

"Yes, ma'am," I said.

"I'm sorry for your loss. You would be welcome to have dinner with Fred and me tonight." She glanced back at her house, and I saw that a beagle had found something to stand on so he could look out the window. *Hello, Fred.*

"I may take you up on that. Thank you for the offer." My intense anger had abated. Now I felt lost, alone, and partly numb.

Another car pulled up. Cathy's. I started for her, but she was way faster than I was. She pulled to a panic stop, flipped the car door open, and raced over to me. "My God, Dave. Are you OK?"

"Physically. But you've got to get out of here right now."

"What?"

I could tell the cop had pricked up his ears.

"I got a text a few minutes ago, from whoever is doing this. He says if I see you again, you will get the same treatment I'm getting."

It took her maybe two seconds. "Well screw that. I'm with you."

"No, you're not. I am not dragging you into this."

"I know. I'm volunteering."

"It's not happening. I can't explain it all right now, but there is no way in the world I'm going to let you get hurt by this. No matter what."

There must have been something in my voice or my expression that added to my words and convinced her of the impossibility of negotiation. Her eyes filled with tears.

"I am so sorry, Cathy, but you've got to get out of here and stay away from me. I will contact you if I feel I can do it safely."

"But, Dave—"

"I won't take that chance. Unless you're safe, I'm headed for Bolivia."

She nodded. "Find this guy. Deal with him."

This conversation was right in front of a cop, but I doubt that concerned her any more than it did me. There was always Bolivia. She rocked forward on tiptoes and gave me a kiss on the lips. And she left.

She got behind the wheel and wiped the tears away. Moments later her car was running and moving back toward the road. She paused there and gave me a quick wave. Then she was gone.

"The dinner offer is still good," my neighbor said.

"I'd like to see the text," the cop said.

I pulled out my phone and showed him.

"Can I take this for a day? Have a guy downtown take a look?"

"It's about all I have left," I said. "How about if I bring it down to police headquarters tomorrow?"

He nodded.

I looked back at the road. Slow-moving traffic spooled by, but Cathy's car was gone. I wondered if one of the other cars held my tormentor.

My neighbor said, "Do you like bean and weenie casserole? Frank begs for it."

Chapter 24

After the cops departed, I sat on my concrete rock and called my insurance company to share the bad news. I couldn't really say the whole misery-loves-company thing was borne out. The rep sounded incredulous at first, and I felt even worse for having someone think I might be making all this up. Thankfully my house insurance wasn't with the same company that handled my car insurance.

As it was, I had to ask to talk to the representative's supervisor, and then the supervisor's supervisor. It was a lot of fun.

My body had stiffened as I sat on the concrete. I felt like an old man when I rose and walked to my car. The stream of gawker-mobiles had dwindled, and traffic was more like normal.

It was only after I had driven five or six blocks that I remembered that I'd lost out on a bean and weenie dinner.

A low-cost motel on Colorado Avenue quoted me a tolerable number for a weekly rate. I could have gotten an even lower rate if I went for a year, but that was too depressing to even contemplate.

No mint on my pillow. But the place was clean and the walls didn't seem to transmit every little noise from outside.

I lay on the bed, chest down. I'd really been looking forward to a nice meal with Cathy and the pleasure of her company. Now my appetites had disappeared.

My phone had a good signal here. I entered half of a text message to Cathy before I halted, thinking about the warning.

Whoever sent the recent text not only knew about Cathy, but he knew I had reconnected with her, or at least knew that I'd spent time with her yesterday. Therefore, I'd been watched, or listened to, or somehow monitored. Maybe someone had even put a bug in my house. If so, disposing of the bug was one problem already solved.

And my tormentor knew I'd be out of the house long enough today that he'd have a window of uninterrupted time for a spin around the lot with a bulldozer.

When it came to Cathy, I had to assume my actions would be known. And I didn't know the extent of that monitoring, or the parameters of the warning. Did "see Cathy" mean just meet her physically? Or did that include a video call? Or a text?

One thing I knew. No matter what, I would not allow my actions to cause harm to her.

I put the phone down.

Instead of calling her, I just thought about her. A month earlier, we had climbed Pikes Peak together. A good part of one day took us from Manitou Springs, near the bottom of the Cog Railway, to Barr Camp, roughly the midpoint of the trip. We'd spent the night in our sleeping bags in a lean-to and the next day went up the rest of the way. Cathy was thrilled as we passed the tree line and simply ecstatic when we reached the summit. Her tennis strength had served her well. We'd made reservations on the Cog Railway and took the train down, mostly as an act of kindness to me because the downward journey would have been risky for my knee.

~~~

In the morning I left another message for Beth, explaining that I wouldn't be in today. My perfect-attendance record really had been thoroughly shattered.

Instead of going to work, I got in my rented Ford Focus and found a McDonald's drive-through on South 8th and bought an Egg McMuffin and a McCoffee and some McSausages.

No home, using a rental car, buying fast food. It would not have been a huge step to being homeless. As for depression, fatigue, hopelessness, they were right there with me. I wondered if Violet did house calls.

I continued on, aiming for just south of downtown. Police head-quarters was a modern brick building that had more in common with a bunker than with a convention center, though I supposed that made sense. The building was set back from Nevada Avenue, with a nice water-sucking lawn out front. It looked to be four stories. The upper floors had the very wide but short windows reminiscent of missile-launching bunkers. The ground floor had a long series of square win-dows spaced closely together. Three flagpoles gave them room to fly the US Flag, the Colorado state flag, and what seemed at first glance to be a CSPD Flag. I wondered idly what other city departments had their own flags. I concluded there were many things I didn't know.

The visitors' lot at the north end of the building offered quite a few empty parking spaces. A few minutes later I was sitting in a confer-ence room—maybe they called it an interrogation room—with Detec-tive Winchester. At least his name wasn't Beretta or Magnum or Colt.

Detective Winchester looked to be in his fifties. Roughly the same body type as the two cops in the second car last night—beefy but not fat. Civilian clothes, more than nice enough for mowing the lawn, not quite nice enough for formal church. Bushy eyebrows. His nose was reddened as though by sunburn or bar-burn. He had both a file folder and a tablet computer with "Colorado Springs Police" and a picture of a police car emblazoned on the cover. I suppose we were still in the transition era from paper to electrons. Or he personally liked having a backup. To start out, he reviewed a summary on the tablet screen.

"So, Mr. Barlow. It looks like someone is targeting you. Or you've really had a run of bad luck." Cop humor, I supposed.

I waited.

"In just five days, I see your car had a run-in with a concrete mixer, you were hit by a passing truck, and your house was vaporized." He tapped the screen and more information came up.

"There was one more incident," I said.

He looked up and raised his eyebrows.

"I went to a high-school reunion in Woodland Park last weekend. It was all faked, apparently to drive the point home that I was forget-ting about my dead fiancée too quickly."

He frowned. "There was a homicide, too?"

"No. This was an accident more than a year ago."

He frowned again, so I gave him the back story. In the middle of talking about the accident, I had the strangest thought.

So much was happening to me, all caused by some external force. What if somehow Allison's death was all part of a larger picture? Nah. I dismissed that idea as too preposterous even as I wondered where the thought had come from. All these recent things sprang, in someone's mind, from my starting to date Cathy too soon after Allison's death.

"Well, that's interesting." Detective Winchester leaned back in his chair and thought about all this for a minute. "I can't investigate the reunion. For one thing Woodland Park is not in my jurisdiction, and another it's not clear any law was actually broken—"

"But—"

"But, it's useful information that may help shed light on the rest of this. And I have a friend in WPPD. I'll talk to her and see if anything has gone on up there that might have a bearing. A car abandoned near the restaurant. Any nearby break-ins or reports."

I wondered if there might be any security cameras aimed at the parking lot or dumpsters there.

"Look, if you see a complaint about dumpster diving Saturday night, that was me."

His expression was deadpan.

I explained about the reunion posters, and the potential evidence they might have contained, like fingerprints.

"So, did you bring the posters in with you?"

"No. They're now part of the buried rubble that was my house."

"You think this was a very elaborate way of destroying evidence?"

"No. For one thing, whoever did this wouldn't even have known I had them. At least I don't think so. For another, I think the home destruction incident was more about continuing the string of torment."

He nodded, considering this. "You have any suspects? People with good reason to do this kind of thing?"

"No one has a good reason to do this kind of thing," I said. "My main candidate is Allison's father, Ben Stuart. He lives near Woodland Park." I thought about Stan, too, but those thoughts didn't rise to the level of talking to a cop about them. Yet.

"Not *that* Ben Stuart." Detective Winchester probably wasn't talking about a guy who had bullied him in junior high.

"Right. The *Forbes* list Ben Stuart."

The detective got up and paced a couple of short rounds.

"Ben Stuart is not the kind of guy you just bring in for questioning and let sweat in an interrogation room for a couple of hours."

"Does that mean you can't investigate?"

"No, of course not. It just means that we need to exercise a bit of caution. No going off half-cocked."

Well, I was fully cocked at this point, but I didn't share that. I said, "I feel certain Ben Stuart isn't running around the Springs doing these things. He's old. And ill, maybe dying. I assume he's hired someone, or more than one person, to do his dirty work. If it's even him. I talked to him this week, and I didn't get any sort of confirmation that he's behind this. It could even be someone with a completely different purpose. Like a competitor at work. A rival in love. Who knows?"

"You have any names to go with those other theories?"

"No. I really don't have any theories." I thought about Stan at work, and my checking into the charges of churning. But the reunion pre-dated that.

He made a couple of notes in his folder. "OK. We'll be following up to see if we can find anyone who 'borrowed' a cement mixer or bulldozer. If a black pickup is stopped for any reason, we'll see if the driver can be connected to you. We can take a look at security footage at sites where the machinery could have been taken, whether lawfully or not."

"Thank you for taking this seriously."

"Why wouldn't we?"

"I don't know. It's all so bizarre to me."

"Bizarre or not, we've got clear evidence that something's going on. I don't want to get your hopes up too high, though. This is not necessarily an easy one to resolve."

"I understand. I appreciate your looking into it." I hesitated. "Just curious. How many cases do you handle per year?"

"The whole department? Around 40,000."

"Ouch."

He nodded. He took another glance at his tablet. "It says here you're supposed to see a tech about the texts you received. I'll send one in."

We shook hands and I was left alone in the room. If I were maybe one percent jumpier than I already was, I would have tested the lock.

Moments later the door opened again and a woman about my age came in. She was dressed in civilian clothes, too. Maybe Friday was casual day. She wore skin-tight black jeans and a tee-shirt that just reached the jeans. One nostril pierced. I couldn't see her tongue or other possible piercing sites, but I had the typical where-there's-smoke-there's-fire reaction. When you see one tattoo or one piercing, your mind wanders. I wouldn't say she had raccoon eyes, but I did wonder if she washed all her food under running water.

"Hi. I'm Caitlin. I hear you've got some texts on your phone that I should look at." She gave me the forehead scrunch and the raised eyebrows I often see during press interviews when someone is in the process of soliciting a question or just got asked the question best left unasked. I also see it on people reacting to an awful punch line of a terrible joke.

I handed her my phone, one of my last worldly possessions.

She sat down and started going through screens. Moments later she looked up. "Wow, you seem to have stepped in it."

"Yes. Yes, I have."

After a few minutes of looking intently at the screen and making some notes she looked up. "I can't tell the number these were sent from."

"Right." I knew that much.

"But I've noted the exact times they were sent. I can match these messages against whatever phones and computers we currently have warrants for. And I can keep them on file in case any new phones or computers are confiscated or examined in the course of other investigations."

"OK, thanks."

She tapped the screen a few more times and handed the phone back. "There. I put my number in. You should call me if you get this crazy person off your back."

I smiled politely as I left, wondering who was crazier.

Chapter 25

My sleep the night before had been even more troubled than normal. Too many nightmares despite my ability to stop them before they ran on longer. The short-term fix was a power nap in my car. I parked the car in the shade of a tree near America the Beautiful Park, in sight of the stargate, a huge round water sculpture intended to rotate slowly on giant bearings. The "stargate" was my name for what the city called the Julie Penrose Fountain. A movie and a television series had aired a few years ago, set in Colorado Springs and mostly filmed elsewhere. The show featured the stargate, an enormous round gateway to other worlds.

Dirt in the water apparently proved more of an obstacle than expected, so the stargate either never turned, or only on special occasions. Since it was before noon and a nice breeze was passing through the car windows on the way from Denver to parts south, the temperature was perfect for a nap.

I woke, feeling unrefreshed. My shoulders, legs, and most of my back ached. I couldn't shake the feeling that I was but one step away from living out of my car. And it wasn't even my car.

Time to take stock. At least the police believed me. So they had a chance of discovering who was doing this. A near-compulsion-level feeling pushed me to leave it in their hands, to not get into the fight. I knew where entering the fray led. And I'd already had my lifetime supply of conflict.

But I was beyond angry. It was hard to say whether the destruction of my house was the tipping point, or the sheer amount of hate and spite required to deliberately cut me off from Cathy. Regardless, I had been pushed off the edge. Humpty Dumpty was either going to be an omelet ingredient or land on two feet.

I would not risk harm to Cathy, but whoever was doing this had finally tipped the scales. I worked so hard to avoid conflict in my life, but even I, as it turned out, had a limit. I finally realized I'd rather be dead than live with the status quo.

Whoever had kicked over this rock was going to find a nasty surprise. I was done with sitting back and hunkering down.

I knew, too, that although the cops would add these incidents to the queue of bad things to investigate, I was not the only victim who needed help from the police. No one had more time to spend trying to get to the bottom of this than I did. Aside from sleeping, and needing to hang onto my job. I made a mental note to talk to Beth on Monday about reduced hours for the short term.

I needed a right-hand assistant, a team of investigators, a fully-stocked office, and a mission control communications center where every clue was monitored and cross checked against every suspect and every incident. I settled for driving over to an office supply store on 8th Street and buying a laptop and a phone charger for both home and car. My phone was nearly dead. Thankfully my credit card was in my wallet and not filed away in my pile of dirt.

As I walked out of the office supply store I grabbed one each of several real estate and rental booklets and a free copy of the latest *Colorado Springs Independent*, the *Indy*.

The shady spot at the park had worked well for my nap, so I drove back there. With my phone charging back up, I used my nail clippers to defeat the plastic packaging on my purchases, and about twenty minutes later succeeded in sharing my phone's data connection with the laptop. I was ready to browse the web with a bigger screen.

Detective Winchester was leading the effort to check on cement trucks, black pickups, and bulldozers. That left the reunion for me.

"Liz" and "John" were convincing enough to make Cathy think I was a liar. I would have recognized Scarlett Johansson and Brad Pitt. Probably. And the cheapness of the posters suggested no one had hired Oscar-winning actors and flown them in for the charade.

So, what did that leave? Either very talented liars, or maybe local actors.

On the campus of University of Colorado at Colorado Springs was Theatreworks, probably the big dog in local theater. Unless the big dog was the Fine Arts Center. Or the Pikes Peak Center. But as I thought about it, the idea of hiring an actor accustomed to playing Hamlet or Lady Macbeth for a fake high school reunion gig sounded unlikely.

I decided to start with venues that were better known for less classical tales. On my list went places like the Iron Springs Château Melodrama Dinner Theater, the Millibo Art Theatre, the Dinner Detective Murder Mystery Dinner Show, Black Box Theatre. I wondered vaguely why some venues went for the British spelling.

I was also surprised at the extent of live theater events. Churches, restaurants, schools, community theater. I saw a notice for a high school play coming up, and I was thankful I could narrow the field a little before I started driving.

Presumably I was following the footsteps of the person who had set up the reunion incident. Unless he, or she, just happened to know a group of actors, he probably looked for venues the way I was looking. And if he was trying to cover his tracks, he wouldn't use anyone who knew him. So a theater company without an Internet presence might be fair to ignore. Unless he saw a sign when he was driving by.

I could second guess this forever. Instead I shut the laptop and switched on the ignition.

After a moment, I turned the ignition off again. A couple walking by gave me an odd look. I pulled the laptop back out.

I called up an image search and entered "Colorado Springs theater." That didn't help much. It showed me pictures of the Peak Theater downtown and some other area movie theaters and sets, show posters and a few actors' photos. I tried "Colorado Springs actors."

More interesting. Lots of head shots. Elvira showed up since Cassandra Peterson graduated from high school in the Springs, but I was pretty sure I hadn't seen Elvira at the reunion. I clicked on a few pictures at random and realized that modeling agencies and talent agencies were another avenue to explore.

The ache in my back and shoulders made me shift position again.

I kept looking. A photo of Kevin Spacey in Mexico showed up, making me wonder about the validity of the search. I clicked through and found the picture accompanied a wire story that had been shown on the website of one of the local TV affiliates.

More scanning. Dance studios. Lon Chaney, who was born in the Springs. I supposed Nikola Tesla would be next because he'd done a lot of experimenting during his time in the Springs. Now there's one guy you probably didn't want as a next-door neighbor. A photo of a murdered prison director. More search imperfection—a lion enjoying a birthday party.

Five screens later, I stopped.

The shot was a profile, making it more difficult to be sure. But I thought it was "John."

I clicked through. For some reason it took me to a page on the *Indy*, but the page didn't have the photo. I felt warmer.

I downloaded the original photo to my laptop, and went back to the main image search page. There, I clicked on the camera icon and it let me upload the photo and search for similar images.

There. The picture was used on a page for a *Gazette* article about an event at Stargazers, a large movie theater that had been converted into a venue for plays and other special events. The picture said he was George Thomas. Even better, the same page had another head shot. Bingo.

It was the same guy; I was sure of it.

I searched for his name and found it was way too common, so I added "Colorado Springs." He was apparently a client of Peak Talent Agency. Another article said he was in an upcoming play at Stargazers. But not for another week.

I saved the better head shot on my laptop, and I put a copy on my phone.

This time when I started the car, I had no second thoughts. I drove over to Stargazers. It was east of downtown, just off Pikes Peak Avenue. I'd love having a nickel for everything around here named for Pikes Peak.

When I neared the building, I recalled a friend telling me it was the "breast theater in the Springs." The tan roof—some would have called it a dome—was huge and round, with an oversized nipple on top. In early afternoon, the parking lot was nearly deserted, but not totally empty. An old red Chevy sported the bumper sticker, *Auto Correct Has Become My Worst Enema.*

The door was locked. I shaded my eyes and peered inside. A couple of people were behind the concession counter, evidently preparing for an event tonight. Another time, I would have come back later. Anything to avoid a potential confrontation and an angry response. Instead, I knocked on the glass, hard.

At first they ignored me. But after I kept at it, a young guy, maybe a high school kid, approached.

"We're closed," he shouted through the glass.

"I just have one question," I shouted back.

As he came closer to the door, I pulled out my phone and displayed the picture of George.

"Is this guy going to be here tonight?"

The guy turned around and walked away. I sighed, ready to start pounding again. But he wasn't ignoring me. He was consulting. The other person behind the counter was a high school girl. The guy consulted with her, and she headed toward me.

"I really need to talk to him," I shouted. "Is he going to be here tonight?"

She got close enough to peer at the image. Her complexion was flawless, as though she'd just been airbrushed. "Not until next weekend," she said. She had long brown hair and bangs. Apparently theaters attracted beautiful people. "But he's got a gig at the MAT."

"What's the MAT?"

"It used to be the Manitou Art Theatre, but they moved it to the Springs. It's the Millibo Art Theatre now. So still the MAT. Down on South Tejon."

"Thank you so much. I'm sorry to bang on the glass and cause you trouble." That was so unlike me. I tried to wipe off a smudge.

"No problem." She gave me a beautiful smile.

I took Pikes Peak back to Nevada Avenue and headed south through downtown and then to Tejon Street.

The Millibo Art Theatre was in a repurposed church. The building was red brick with pairs of very tall and very narrow windows. The roof was white, a huge one so dominant it was a cousin of an A-frame, but there was space under the eaves for one story.

I knocked on the door, but here I could summon no response. I looked around.

This must have been the neighborhood for repurposing. Across the street was the old Ivywild elementary school that had been closed about a decade earlier due to declining enrollment. It had been bought and transformed into a newly opened commercial and community center.

Parking was tighter at Ivywild, but that was fine. I parked between two other cars in a spot that would not be ideal for a concrete delivery.

Inside the old school, a fair amount of the space had been taken over as a brewery. The old gym was now a place to show movies or host events and meetings. I found the Bristol Pub and ordered a Coke/Pepsi, annoyed at the marketing strategy that resulted in typically having only one choice. Obviously the customer is not always right.

I was sitting there, tying to get more comfortable, resigning myself to having to wait a few hours, when I glanced up and took in a breath.

I saw a woman I recognized. From the reunion.

Chapter 26

Two women had just walked in to the Bristol Pub and had taken seats near the door. One was maybe forty with long black hair and lots of jangly bracelets. She was a total stranger.

The other woman was closer to thirty. She wore skinny jeans and a tight tee-shirt with spangles. She had curly blonde hair.

"Liz" from the reunion.

A waiter was taking their orders. He gave me the impression that he knew them, but some waiters treat everyone that way. I ducked my head, not wanting her to spot me while she still had an opportunity to flee.

I tried to move slowly and calmly, to avoid any accidental attention. I shifted sideways from her, trying to keep my head tilted a bit away from her line of sight.

I was lucky. A couple of men were picking that time to leave. I tagged along, close enough to use them for concealment, but far enough away to avoid being creepy or to make them think I wanted to talk to them or I was pushing them to move faster. As we neared the table, we edged past "Liz" and her friend, and seconds later I was in the hallway, around the corner.

My breath came way too heavy, and erratic. Part of my typical reaction to stress. I took several deliberate and slow breaths to try to get under control. "Liz" was the only face I'd actually run up against in this mess of vandalism and attack. I wanted to punch her, and I wondered if I were actually capable of such a thing. I also wondered if I was helping to write my own Dave and Goliath or if this had the potential to turn out more like *Bambi Meets Godzilla*.

I stood there, wondering if I should call the police and then mentally reviewing how poorly that could go.

As I collected my wits, I had at least one good thought. I took out my phone and went into the camera ap. At the very least I would have that level of evidence. I leaned around the corner, and saw part of her profile. She was looking more away than toward me. I put the camera into video recording, so as long as I came away with one good frame, I had that much. I took a deep breath and moved closer. Before she noticed me, I put the phone down at my side. Maybe having the audio would be helpful.

I didn't know whether she would try to run, and, if so, how I'd deal with that. Or if she would try to bluff it through. *Who are you, stranger? I've never seen you before.* Or call for a bouncer friend to say I was hassling her. What she actually did, surprised me.

I moved closer. She didn't see me yet.

I covered the last yard or so and raised my voice, not to a shout, but just loud enough to be sure of being heard over the noise. "Hi. Could I talk to you for just a minute?"

She looked up, apparently puzzled by the interruption. Her friend stopped talking and looked up at me. For an instant, "Liz" had a blank expression.

And then she smiled. She said, "Hi. I didn't expect to see you again. How did it go?"

I was dumbfounded. *How did it go?* "I, ah, really need to talk to you about it. Just for a couple of minutes."

"Sure!" She didn't object in the slightest. She said to her friend, "I'll be back in five, OK? Watch my purse."

"Liz" and I stepped out into the hallway where the noise level was lower.

I was about to launch into questions, but she beat me. "So, did you get the gig? And how did your girlfriend take it when you told her?"

I blinked. That was definitely not going the way I'd imagined.

"Let me back up for just a sec, OK? Can you tell me what you were told about the reunion party?"

"Sure. You're an applicant for a pilot for a new reality TV show, right? The producers wanted to see your reactions under stress. You looked pretty stressed, but you must have known something like that could happen, right?"

I didn't know where to start. But at least I now understood that this woman wasn't in on the deliberate torment. Lucky I hadn't punched her in the face. Hypothetically.

"Look," I said. "I am not angry at you. I'm not interested in pressing charges or doing anything at all that hurts you."

Now she started looking confused.

I went on. "You were lied to. The reunion thing was part of a plan to deliberately hurt me. I just want to find out who's behind it all."

"No. No, I was told—" She had very pretty eyes. I could see in them the confusion, the attempt to suddenly view the reunion party in an all new light.

"Just a sec," I said. I stopped the recording on my phone and called up the web browser. I went to the first of several bookmarks on the local news sites. I showed her the headline. "On Monday, someone filled my car with concrete."

I touched the screen again. "On Wednesday I got hit by a pickup truck mirror." Another bookmark. "On Thursday my house was destroyed."

Her face had gone white. "Oh, my God. That was you? All those things were done to you?"

"I'm not angry with you," I reiterated emphatically. "You were lied to and used. I just want to find out who's doing this. And make it stop." Finished with the web, I put the recorder back on, just for the voice part as a backup to my memory. Sometimes when I felt a lot of stress, it could make my memory less than 100 percent.

I could see why she had gotten some acting gigs. Real or faked, her anguish showed all over her expressive face.

"I am so, so sorry," she said. "I never—"

"I know that. I just want to learn anything I can that might help me follow the trail back. Tell me about it. Did you get paid in cash? Was it done all over the phone?"

"No, not cash. That would have made me suspicious that this was a prank rather than a real gig. I got the job though my agency. The client asked for about thirty people who could pass for late twenties, right? George and I had the most acting experience—a lot of the rest were models—I'm Holly Baxter. The guy who was at the table with me is George Thomas."

"Nice to meet you, Holly. Dave Barlow."

"God, I feel so awful."

"Don't. You thought you were doing me a favor."

"Hang on a sec. Let me get you a card."

She didn't wait for a response. I couldn't have held her there against her will anyway. But seconds later she was back and she handed me a thick, glossy, double-sided business card bearing her photo and a second card that was nice but not lavish.

She pointed to text on the fancy card. "There's my agency contact. Marion is great. My home address and phone. This other one is my real estate agent card. I love acting but it doesn't always pay the bills."

"Great. What can you tell me about the client? And the payment?"

"George and I got fifteen hundred each, less commission. I think the rest of the crew, the diners, got a free meal and three hundred. I didn't actually meet the client. Marion did. I'm certain he gave her a check. A few days before the gig, Marion called and said the check cleared. It could have been a figure of speech, but I think she meant a literal check."

"The client was male?"

"I think so. I think Marion said that."

I wanted a copy of that check. Or the invoice. And a description of the client. I thought about driving downtown to the agency right then, wondering if I'd be able to convince Marion to share. And then I had another idea.

"Is there any chance that you would be willing to visit Marion this afternoon? Get a copy of the invoice if you can? Find out anything you can about the client?"

Holly hesitated. She looked at her watch.

"I would pay you for your time," I said. "I wouldn't expect you to run around town for free."

"Don't be silly. I want to do this. I need to do this. I think I have enough time. I'm in a show at the MAT across the way that starts at six."

She looked at her watch again and said, "I have just enough time to do this and get back for the show. The show finishes around eight-thirty. Meet me in the Blue Star for drinks."

I nodded.

She pointed, even though we couldn't see it from here. The restaurant was a block and a half away, just across the street on the far side of the MAT. "What about your girlfriend?"

"She won't be available."

I could have sworn I saw a slight uptick on the edges of her mouth before she touched my arm briefly and ran back to her table. Seconds later she flew by with her purse. She almost rammed a middle-aged couple on their way in, but successfully dodged them. I hoped she wouldn't have an accident on the way to or from the agency. At least her reaction time was good.

~~~

The Blue Star was a very nice, upscale place. Tall ceiling and exposed ducting gave it a faintly industrial feel. Wood flooring and a giant circular mirror like a porthole almost gave the impression of being aboard a ship. The kitchen bordered the dining area, and in one corner was a giant glass-paneled wine-storage area.

I was starving, so I found a table instead of sitting at the bar. The metal-bound menu was classy, and the selection looked fabulous. Scents drifting past from other people's dinners made me hungry.

I had plenty of time to peruse the menu as I waited for Holly, and the waiter was attentive enough that I felt guilty arriving early.

I waited at a table along the wall. Several new arrivals started filtering into the restaurant, probably signifying the end of the show at the MAT.

I looked at my watch. Holly should be here.

And then she was. She stepped into the part of the restaurant I was in, looking breathless. I waved and she joined me.

At first I thought she was high, and then I realized she was high, but with adrenaline. She greeted me and sat, alternating between fanning herself with a program from the MAT performance and looking at the menu to decide. She wore a low-cut frilly black top, and a short skirt. Play to your strengths I assume. She looked very nice.

"Woo!" she said as she fanned herself. "I love acting. I love being out there playing someone else. And I love the applause."

I was far more curious about how things went with Marion than the show, but I forced myself to be polite. I settled on a steak and she went with salmon. Holly was fairly curt and dismissive with the waiter. Cathy would have treated the waiter as though a favor was being done for her.

With our orders in the queue, Holly was able to gradually unwind.

"I'm actually famished," she said. "I was going to have a snack with my friend when you interrupted us."

"Sorry about—"

"Don't worry about it. OK. Here's the scoop. Marion met with the guy one time. She pretty much insists on meeting people face to face at least the once. She's probably read too many stories about people being kidnapped and sold into slavery or something."

"I'm not sure how often—"

"Oh, it doesn't matter. Anyway, the guy, the client, was in his forties she thought. He had glasses and a beard and a really full head of hair."

I translated in my head as she spoke. *Disguise.*

"He was almost a foot taller than Marion. She's a bit short, but that still puts the guy probably at six feet and some change."

"And he was thin," I said.

Holly looked puzzled. "No. A bit overweight. Not obese. But nowhere near thin. Marion pays attention to people. That's her business. But he did have very thin hands. She thought that was unusual for someone who was overweight."

But thin hands were not unusual for someone in a fat-suit disguise.

"And, ta-da!" Holly pulled out a letter-sized page of paper. Printed on it was a copy of the check. Front and back. She pushed it over to me, very happy with herself. "Marion's bank lets you go online and see the checks deposited in your account."

"Wow, Holly. I couldn't ask for anything better."

"I know, right?"

I looked closely at the printout, and felt less confident about how helpful this would be. The back just showed Marion something's signature. The front showed everything I could have hoped for: the bank and account routing numbers, the check number, both in the upper right and accompanying the routing stuff at the bottom. The amount was $14,400. And that probably didn't include the restaurant's charge for the dinners.

In the lower right was the signature. The name was stylized to the point of illegibility.

In the upper left was the name of a firm, and a PO box address. The worst part was the name of the firm.

Demolition Department.

The name was disheartening. It said the person behind this was so confident in shell companies and holding entities that he was essentially taunting me with the business name. It was probably incorporated in Bermuda and firewalled behind a string of empty business fronts. Someone expected me to see this. And wanted to twist the knife in the process.

"Is that helpful?" Holly asked in the silence.

I hated to dash her spirits, too. "I'm sure it will be. I'll do a search for this address, and I'll search for this business name."

"Right, there can't be too many companies called 'Demolition Department.'"

"I really don't think so." So far I wasn't sure there actually were any at all. I didn't know what proof a bank asks for when it issues checks on a Doing-Business-As name.

My mind was racing nowhere.

"Anyway, I hope this helps," she said. She took a sip of her drink. "This is a great place. Probably my favorite place is the Briarhurst in Manitou Springs, but this is terrific, too."

A woman passed by our table. She wore an oversized purse over her shoulder, and as she moved, the purse hit Holly's water glass and it spilled toward me.

Cold water spilled into my lap and I jerked to my feet. A fair amount of the water sloughed off before it had a chance to absorb, but

I was still very wet. I looked like I'd just been in a very scary scene in a horror film.

"Oh, my God, I'm so sorry," she said. Her voice was breathy. "I am so clumsy." She grabbed a napkin and started dabbing at my pants.

"Hey!" Holly said, even before I did. I would have objected soon. I'm sure of it.

"I got it," I said, taking the napkin from her. I started drying myself, and then decided this would better be continued in the men's room. "I'll be right back."

"I am *so* sorry," she said again. I glanced up at her face. Very cute. Blue eyes. Dimples. Light freckles. Straight blonde hair. The quick scan from toes to head registered a second later as curvy but trim.

"No harm done. It's just water." I looked at Holly. "I'll be right back."

She nodded. The clumsy woman was still apologizing to Holly as I moved away.

The men's room had a good supply of paper towels. I glanced around as my pants dried out. Solid red walls. Decorated by someone who really liked photographs of Marilyn Monroe.

By the time I got back, Holly had a new glass of water and the area around the table looked better. I got a commiserating smile from a guy at a nearby table.

"Are you OK?" Holly asked.

"You know, of all the stuff that's happened this week, this really was not as bad as it could be. I almost got fondled by a pretty stranger and I'm having a nice dinner with another pretty woman."

Holly had to be used to compliments, between being a very pretty woman and an actress, but she ducked her head as though embarrassed by praise.

I took a long drink of water and we continued our meal. When I'd said, "nice dinner," I had really underestimated. The meal was terrific, the medium-rare steak cooked to perfection. I was a bit puzzled that I didn't see the woman who'd knocked over Holly's water glass because the room wasn't all that large, but maybe she'd been on her way back to her table just before leaving.

"So, what is your next step?" Holly asked after a few more bites of food.

I thought about it and had another drink of water. "Try to track down the company. I need to find out who's doing this. And then maybe I can figure out why. And stop it."

"So this is all for no reason?"

"There's always a reason for people to do mean stuff. Whether that reason will make sense to me is another issue. It would seem that—"

I paused. "Is it pretty warm in here, or is it just—"

Holly looked back at me, puzzled. "Are you all right?"

I thought about it. I thought some more. "No. I'm not. I'm feeling nauseous. And very hot."

Holly put her utensils down, probably having the same thought I was having. *Food poisoning?*

The feelings ramped up higher. I was sweating. This was coming on very quickly.

I had a new thought, inspired by this week's chain of events. Especially the hit and run. It wasn't enough to strip me of my possessions and force me away from Cathy.

Maybe someone wanted me dead.

Seconds later, I was on the floor, vomiting. The pressure made me light-headed, on the verge of passing out.

"Holly," I cried. "Call 911. Make them pump my stomach. I think someone poisoned—"

I threw up again.

Chapter 27

My nightmares didn't cooperate with my orders to halt. They kept going. I dreamed about throwing up. A lot. I was in a scene in *Alien* with someone forcing a foreign object down my throat. I was in sick bay aboard the *Enterprise* being monitored. I woke several times, but other than being aware of good lighting, I didn't know where I was.

When the dreams finally faded, I opened my eyes. The overhead fluorescent lights looked familiar.

My throat felt raw. My body felt like I'd just been put through the wash cycle *and* the dry cycle at an industrial Laundromat.

"Are you really awake this time?" A feminine voice sounded from nearby. Cathy?

A face swam into view. It wasn't Cathy. "Holly?"

"Right! How are you feeling?"

"I—"

"Yes, how are you feeling?" another person asked.

Dr. Bentson. I recognized her from a few nights ago. Time to re-check those vitals.

I said, "I'm back in the emergency room."

Dr. Bentson checked her clipboard again. That was probably a non-standard response. "Any pain, nausea? Any complaints?"

Man, did I have complaints. "All the old stuff. Plus my throat hurts. Has anyone been standing on my chest?"

"The sore throat would be the gastric lavage—stomach pump. Your friend was pretty insistent, but we would have done that any-way, given your symptoms. We followed that with charcoal infusion to soak up toxins left behind." Dr. Bentson turned to Holly, maybe taking in the low-cut frilly black top. "You're new, right?"

Holly blinked.

"Never mind. You're a lucky man." This must have been one of her standard lines. "We went ahead and cleaned out your stomach as soon as it was safe to do so. When we know in advance what the toxin is, there are some available antidotes. Not knowing makes it more difficult. The full toxicology report will take a few days to a week or more, but your EKG showed peaked P waves, which led us to find your potassium level was *way* up. Your symptoms and your subsequent recovery after the procedure both suggest poisoning as the explanation for your symptoms. Your symptoms were severe enough that lack of rapid attention could have resulted in your death."

"Thanks, doctor." I turned my head. "And thank you, Holly." In the first few bad moments, I had wondered if Holly had poisoned me. Given what happened, my suspicions now rested on the woman who bumped over Holly's water. The confusion could have allowed her to drop something in my drink.

Holly looked pleased. She still seemed to be trying to compensate for participating in the reunion, albeit unknowingly.

I turned back to Dr. Bentson.

She said, "Is it your chest that hurts, or your abs?"

"My abs, now that I'm thinking more clearly."

"The pain is likely just from the muscle contractions when you were throwing up. The actual gastric lavage isn't hard on the chest."

"What are your recommendations?"

"Well, a good deal of caution would be in order." That must have been doctor humor, based on seeing her twice in one week. "Lots of fluids and rest are the main things. You want to continue to flush out any remaining residue of the poison. Who's your family doctor?"

"Doctor Hammerstrom."

"I'll have the toxicology report forwarded. His office will be in touch in case there are any changes to my recommendation or any additional follow-up is needed."

"Thanks very much. Am I free to leave now?"

"You're welcome. Yes. A nurse will be in with your paperwork." She turned to go, then stopped. She actually smiled. "I mean this in the nicest possible way. Don't come back."

~~~

Before I was allowed to leave the ER, I'd had to talk with a cop. Apparently poisoning diagnoses required police notification. I told him what I could, but it wasn't all that much.

It was still dark, early Saturday morning, as Holly drove her red Mustang south on Nevada Avenue, taking me back to where my car was parked at Ivywild school. I felt so crappy I didn't even care if my Ford rental had been fed to a car crusher or set on fire.

Some people spend parts of Saturday morning mowing their lawn. Or reading the *Gazette* while basking in the fresh air and slanted sunlight. Or packing a picnic for an outing in the park.

Well, that wasn't going to happen.

"Thank you for all your help tonight, Holly. Sorry to ruin your evening."

"That's all right." She gave me a tired smile as she waited for a red light. "I hate the feeling of being used. I like being able to even the scales a little."

"You've gone way above and beyond. I'll try to find a way to say thanks."

"Well, keep my card so when you start looking for a new house you'll have a real estate agent to help."

"Will do." I checked my pockets belatedly and realized I still had my wallet in my back pocket and in my shirt pocket were Holly's business cards and the folded copy of the reunion invoice. But my shirt smelled like vomit. Some of the shirt buttons were missing and it had a couple of long cuts in it.

We continued south in companionable silence. The car passed through downtown. Most of the taller buildings were on our right. Only a half dozen or so rose higher than six or eight stories.

Holly pulled up behind my rental Ford. No obvious damage had been done to it.

"Are you sure you're going to be OK to drive?" she asked. She almost seemed sad the adventure was over, but it wasn't over for me.

"I'll be fine. It's still early so traffic is light. I'll be careful." I sat there, not quite ready to exert myself by getting out. "Thanks, Holly. I really appreciate everything. Your running over to the agency to get that invoice. Staying with me in the emergency room. If you ever need a recommendation, let me know. Or investment advice."

"Let me know how it all turns out, will you? And call me if you need a place to stay. I've got several listings and access to lots more."

I might send her a postcard from Bolivia. "I will." I hesitated. "I'd give you a hug, but I think I threw up on my shirt."

She gave me a wry grin. And she hugged me.

She waited while I got into my car and started the engine. I gave her a thumb's up, and she gave me a wave. I rested in the driver's seat until her tail lights disappeared around a corner.

I pulled out of the lot and proceeded with what felt like the caution of a drunk trying not to run into anything or get pulled over. I caught myself just before I took a turn that would take me toward home. Instead I turned toward the motel.

On the way, I had to wait a few minutes for McDonald's to open before I grabbed an early breakfast. And a giant Coke. Doctor's orders.

No tornado or flood or bulldozer had done any apparent damage to the motel room. I finished my breakfast, thought to put out the do-not-disturb sign, and crawled into bed. Alone.

I slept so long that it was dark again when I woke.

Hunger, or poison aftereffects, gnawed at my stomach. I got up long enough to go to the bathroom and fill up again with water, and I went back to bed. When I woke, it was light again. Sunday morning.

I don't think I'd ever felt so alone, even after my parents passed. The curtain let enough light in around the edges to indicate it was clearly morning. Some other day, I might have chosen to be alone, knowing that at any time I could have changed my mind and called a friend. Today, I knew that contacting Cathy would only bring harm to her. I could have called another friend, but I just felt drained.

Still, as someone famous had said, when the going gets tough, the tough go shopping. Maybe it was Ben Franklin.

After another awful, but convenient, breakfast I promised myself I'd eat a healthy lunch or dinner. Maybe both. But first I found a K-Mart and started looking for shirts and pants. I was ready to drop, but it wasn't from shopping.

With three pairs of pants and five shirts in the shopping cart, I realized I wasn't finished. I added a dozen sets of briefs and tee-shirts, five two-packs of socks, and a light jacket.

The checkout counter had no customers waiting. An impossibly cheery woman of about forty greeted me and congratulated me on my taste. I was ready for her to glance at my current attire and say, *Not a moment too soon*, but she didn't. On one bicep, she had a large rose tattoo that was obviously out of warranty. I wondered about the tattoo business model that involved pain and money to buy and then required even more pain and even more money to return.

Only after I was out of the store did I start to worry that this harassment could extend to making problems with my credit cards. *Mental note: make a significant cash withdrawal soon, and hide the bills.*

I drove around to the back of the store and parked near a dumpster. The clerk might not have said it, but it really wasn't a moment too soon. I threw my old shirt over the side, following it with the packaging and pins from a new shirt. It still had creases, but it was way better than what I had been wearing.

Inside my car, I swapped out old trousers for new. I pulled ahead and tossed my old pants through the open window and over the lip of the dumpster, in a reverse drive-through action.

In a nearby patch of shade, I took a few deep breaths that felt a bit cleaner than before. The change of clothes helped. I should have been in advertising. *Now, with twenty percent less vomit!*

I checked my phone for messages, finally aware that I had not seen a taunting text following the poisoning incident. Nothing. Maybe this was like Vegas. The occasional small win made you think you still had a chance against the house. In this case, I was more and more convinced the house had to be Ben Stuart. I knew where I was going to be tomorrow.

But today I had some preparations to make. I dialed Bruce's number. He wouldn't be at the fitness center today, but that wasn't what I needed.

"Hey," he said.

"Hey, yourself. I've been thinking about your dog cam. I really want to get one. Did you buy it locally?"

"Nope. Got it on online."

"Damn. Do you think anyone local sells them?"

"Maybe Costco. But tell you what. Julia's been giving me enough grief about it, how about if I just sell you mine for what I paid?"

"You'd do that?"

"Actually, you'd be doing me a favor." Bruce must have had one of those phones with a speaker so loud people nearby can hear. In the background Julia said to him, "Give him that damn thing. I don't want it in my house."

Bruce said, "She's weakening my bargaining position."

"Not a problem. I would be happy to pay. How do we do this?"

"Done deal. Come to the house. You can get it right now." In the background, Julia said, "You should take it to him. Right now."

I grinned, knowing the grin would carry over the phone line along with my words. "I'll be there as fast as I can get there. Give me directions?"

Bruce lived in a neighborhood called Holland Park, on the west side, a few miles north of the parking lot I was in. I got onto I-25 and got off where Fillmore climbed to the west, one of the steepest major roads in the Springs. I made my way through an idle construction zone, keeping watch for anyone following me.

To the north, Centennial Boulevard swung downward in a gentle curve through the Holland Park neighborhood. I passed Hans Brinker and Amstel without seeing any windmills or dikes. Next was Amsterdam Drive and I took a right. One of the houses near the intersection had tulips growing in the front yard. I found the address Bruce had given me. A bi-level or what they called a raised ranch, with a large blue spruce out front. Wooden stairs led up to a front deck.

Bruce opened the door before I rang the bell. Right there in the doorway with him was Barney, his black lab.

Julia was there, too. I'd met her a few times at the fitness center. Her normally black hair was tinted very gently reddish. She had red nails today. She looked happy. Maybe happy that the dog cam was on the way out. She said, "Dave, you're not married, right?"

"No, I'm not."

"That's good. Because if you were, your wife probably wouldn't even let you bring this into your house."

"Well, I don't have a house so that's—" I caught myself too late. I blame it on the fatigue.

"What are you talking about?" Bruce asked. "You've got that nice house on Mesa."

I hesitated, not really wanting to get into it.

Bruce must have sensed my reluctance. "Come on. Have a seat. I'll show you the stuff."

I sat on a leather couch that backed up to a trio of tall windows on the front of the house. Opposite was a three-quarter wall that hid the kitchen without rising to the vaulted ceiling. On the wall was a large-screen TV. Barney looked at me enviously, I imagined. I got to sit on the couch. *Suck it, Barney.*

"What do you mean you don't have a house?" Julia asked.

I sighed. "Did Bruce tell you about my car?"

"No. What about your car?" She turned to Bruce, who was just coming back with a glass of water for me. "What do I have to do to get you to tell me what goes on?"

Bruce handed me the water. "Sorry. It's been a busy week. Someone dumped a load of concrete in his car."

"What?"

"Someone—"

"I heard that. What's going on?"

I took a sip of water. "Someone has decided to make my life difficult for a while. It'll pass. But after the car, someone demolished my house." I decided the hit and run and the poisoning were just too much to add to the mix right then. TMI.

"Damn!" This was from Bruce and Julia simultaneously. In the same way owners sometimes resemble their pets, people in sync sometimes have the same responses. At least they were not finishing each other's sentences. They both demanded more details.

After I gave them a quick info dump, Bruce left the room. He came back a moment later. He took away my glass of water and handed me a Coors. "If I had something stronger on hand, you'd have it."

Julia said, "So your wanting the dog-cam has something to do with all this?"

"Right. I don't know if it's my vandal-cam or a burglar-cam or a spy-cam or what yet. But I want to see if anyone tries to tamper with my motel room. And my car." I looked at Bruce. "Can one of these monitor my car?"

"It's not as easy with the car. Let me think while I'm getting the stuff."

He came back shortly carrying a box of stuff. A bit sheepishly he pulled two digital clocks from the pile.

"You had *two* of them?" Julia asked.

"I didn't think it would bother you that much."

"You didn't think—"

"Let's talk about this later, OK?" He fixed a hard stare on her.

"OK. But we are not done with this."

"I got it." Bruce pulled more stuff out of the box and put it on the coffee table in front of the couch. It was like looking at a shelf of merchandise in a surveillance specialty store.

He put one of the clocks in my hand. It looked like a regular digital clock you might put on a bedside table or a kitchen counter. "This does everything. Built in camera of course. The picture isn't terrific resolution, but it's good enough. Connects to wi-fi. Motion-sensing recording. It can record to a flash card and can send files to an ftp site. Put the app on your phone, and you can be notified any time the dog is on the couch."

We must have gotten into territory Julia didn't find all that entertaining. "I'll see you later, Dave." To Bruce: "We are not done with this."

"I *got* it."

I turned the camera/clock over in my hands. No heavier than a clock without the camera. Dangerous in the hands of a teenage boy.

"You have Wi-Fi at the motel?"

"Sure."

Bruce waited a second until Julia moved down the adjoining hallway. "These cameras are great. You can get them to look like room deodorizers or computer speakers, or tower fans, smoke detectors, wall sockets, lamps, whatever. There could be a dozen of them in this room right now and you wouldn't know."

I looked around, inventorying a wall clock, an old-time radio, lots of books, several lamps, a couple of potted plants, knick-knacks on the fireplace mantle. "*Are* there a dozen?"

Bruce gave me a hint of a grin and then his best straight face. "Of course not, man."

I could better understand why he was willing to part with these two. I just didn't want to be around if Julia found another nanny-cam in the house. I wondered how long the very notion of privacy would take to crawl away under a porch and die.

Bruce gave me a thorough run-down on the cameras and helped me download the app. When he was done, he took a quick glance down the hallway and moved over to the mantle. Sure the coast was clear, he grabbed an insulated thermos mug and brought it over. He gave me a quick look, then stuffed it in the box and piled some cables over it.

He lowered his voice. "If you were to get something for the car" — he winked at me—"a thermos mug would be a good choice. Battery operated, rechargeable, would not look out of place in a car. The model I'm thinking of doesn't have any wireless communication, but the battery can last several days. It records on a flash card and only records when there's motion. You would not get an alert if someone moved in its field of view, but you could find out later. Assuming the car is still there."

"I can't thank you enough for all this, Bruce," I said at the door, ready to leave. "This stuff might literally save my life."

"Don't mention it. And I mean literally don't mention it." He winked again.

I lowered my voice. "Aren't your worried about what happens if, you know?" If Julia found out there were more nanny-cams, life could get pretty uncomfortable.

He leaned in conspiratorially and grinned. "It's a risk. But with Julia, make-up sex is absolutely sensational."

Chapter 28

I put the nanny-cam clock on the night stand in my motel room. The existing clock, I unplugged and put in a drawer, just to reduce suspicion in case anyone thought about two clocks. I hoped the maid didn't think I thought she was stealing. I put the second nanny-cam clock on the bathroom counter.

With the nanny-cam app set up on my phone, I walked into the fields of view of the cameras, satisfied that in both cases my phone chimed and showed me a still frame of me walking.

The nanny-cam mug went into the back seat of the Ford Focus, in the corner diagonally opposite the driver's seat, where it might naturally have come to rest if I'd tossed it in back. If I were carjacked by someone who wanted me to drive, I'd probably want it in the other corner. You have to go with the odds.

The whole discussion with Bruce had me sensitized to surveillance. I thought back to my question about how someone knew I was at the Blue Star. I started to explore. The glove box had much less in it than my own car had. No sunglasses, old maps, tissue, pens. In the gaps between the seats, this car was also cleaner than mine was. No lost coins, no fuzzy French fries. A thorough search of the car's interior revealed nothing.

I went through the trunk. It, too, was cleaner than my car was. It didn't smell like old machine oil. That left the engine compartment and the exterior. The engine was cleaner than the one in my car. This whole process was making me feel like a bit of a slob.

The engine compartment held several things I could not identify, but they all seemed to fit where they were. The finish matched what it was next to, or the wires had the same colors as nearby equipment. Every year cars became a little more high-tech, a little more foreign, and held fewer things you could service on your own. I wondered when car mechanics had to start worrying about some of the same stuff computer engineers worried about.

In the right rear wheel well I found a foreign object.

It was magnetized, like someone's hidden key carrier. At first I thought it was welded in place, but then I realized it was just a very strong magnet, much stronger than anything I'd seen before.

The box itself, smaller than a deck of cards, just bore the legend, "Positioner 6500." I thought for a moment and then put it back where I found it.

In the comfort of my motel room, I searched for the unit on the web. It was a GPS tracking unit.

As I looked at the specs, I wondered if it had been put there by the car rental company, to make sure I didn't speed or leave the state. Or had it been put there by my nemesis? I bet if the rental company had done it, it would have been wired in so it didn't depend on a battery that had to be charged from time to time.

The box periodically grabbed multiple GPS signals to determine where it was. Either on demand, or every minute, it transmitted its current location over a cell phone network. Someone at a computer or a phone anywhere seeing one-minute updates could tell where I was within a mile or two if I was going really fast, or within a few feet if the car was stopped. Apparently the civilian use of GPS had started out with a more relaxed goal, but inventiveness and the profit motive had spurred developers to look at more satellites simultaneously and to use error correction signals built into the GPS broadcasts. Now, these things could probably alert me if I were going the wrong way in a specific lane.

I decided to leave it in place, rather than alert someone that I had found it. Now that I knew about it, if I needed to be in stealth mode, I had the option of removing it.

The GPS discovery in the car made me think about monitoring in the motel room. I went through the room contents piece by piece. If the cable box or the smoke alarm had something built into it, I couldn't tell. Everything else seemed to be stock equipment, incapable of monitoring me. Then I noticed a vent high up on the wall that separated the main room from the bathroom.

I got a screw driver from the guy in the office by saying I had a loose shelf and I'd be happy to fix it. I labored for almost ten minutes on stubborn screws, thinking that if I'd put my nanny-cams in when I first arrived, I could have saved myself a lot of effort.

The vent held nothing but some grit the flowing air wasn't capable of dislodging unless Tim Allen of *Tool Time* fame souped it up. I wondered if he'd had a hand in the new breed of public restroom hand dryers that felt like they had to be securely bolted to the wall or they'd fly around the room.

With the vent back in place and the screw driver back in the motel office, I felt exhausted again. I lay down.

At some point I woke up briefly and opened the window to let in some night air. The breeze must have been traveling west tonight because the faint train whistle sounds carried all the way from a couple miles to the east.

I'd listened to those train whistles in the middle of the night with Allison more than a year ago now. More recently, I'd listened to them with my arms around Cathy. From a few blocks away, the sounds would likely have been bothersome, maybe even sleep-depriving. Or perhaps lonely.

With a companion in my arms, the sounds felt comforting and nostalgic, summoning the memory of train whistles from when I was five or six. Today, lots of coal trains travelled through the Springs on a north-south route.

Cathy was more observant than I was, at least about some things. The whistles had always sounded random to me, the squawking of a *get off my tracks* hand at the controls. But Cathy had noticed the vague similarity to Morse code, and looked it up. It turned out that aside from some truly random short bursts that actually were *get off my tracks*, the others were deliberate patterns of long and short blasts. The messages ranged from *visibility obscured* to *fire on the train* to *train has come apart*. Fortunately I'd never heard the worst ones. The one I heard ninety plus percent of the time was the *Long Long Short Long* sequence that indicated the train was approaching a road crossing. That's what sounded now.

My grandfather had been a ham radio operator, and he'd told me that he could recognize a number of other operators by their signature, something about how they spaced the dots and dashes and how long they were. The same was true here. I didn't know any of the engineers' names, or anything about them aside from their occupation, but I knew at least several different engineers drove through the Springs. The spacing between the dots and dashes would be longer or shorter. The longs would be very long and drawn out, or they'd be not much longer than the short. The short itself would come right after the second long, or the gaps would be longer, maybe to emphasize that was the short one.

The signals were more audible at night, maybe because the city noise abated, or perhaps because I was less preoccupied with life's zigs and zags.

Tonight I was acutely aware of the emptiness surrounding me on the bed. I wondered what Cathy might be doing, and I felt completely, utterly alone.

I wondered what the weather was like in Bolivia.

~~~

Monday morning I swung by Wells Fargo on my way to work. The staff was participating in another weird customer-service experiment where everyone in the bank professed to be interested in what I had for breakfast and what was on my agenda for today. The good news was that my bank account was still functioning, so I took out a couple thousand dollars. About a third of it went into my wallet. A third was tucked into the back seat of the Ford. The remaining money went into a locked drawer at my office.

Beth and Stan were the only ones in the office. I'd greeted both. My inbox held more messages than I liked, and I started triage. Two clients had finally responded to a prior request that they come in and do an annual update on their goals and positions. The new client, Ross Morse, who had just put $400,000 into his account, had experienced a reversal and he asked me to send a check for fifty thousand to his company. A long-time client had talked to his cousin and the cousin felt his portfolio "didn't make sense."

I handled the stuff that just couldn't wait, then went to see Beth.

Her fingers danced over the keyboard as she nodded to indicate she saw me and she'd get to me in a second.

When she finished, she gave me a big smile and waved at the visitor's chair. I sat.

"I'm having some troubles on the home front," I said. "My plan is to be out of the office a fair amount this week, but I wanted you to know this is not an indication that I have any problems with you or the job. I love working here."

Beth turned and gave me her full attention. "Are you all right? What happened last week?" I knew about happy drunks. Beth was an ever-cheerful workaholic.

I gave her the short version: reunion, car, house.

"My God, Dave. Have you gone to the police?"

"I've seen more of the police in the last week than most people see in their lives. The good news is that they seem to be taking this seriously. Maybe they'll get this solved without my help, but there are some things I've got to do. And no cop is going to be as motivated as I am to get this resolved."

Beth nodded. "Ricardo's on vacation for another ten days, but Stan and Denise would be happy to take up some of the load."

It was true that they would. And Denise wouldn't even give me any grief about it. But losing face time with clients, and not being there when new clients expressed interest was like having a slow leak in a tire. In all four tires. One more reason I needed to get this resolved.

I was on my way out, almost at the door, when I heard my phone ringing. I was tempted to just let it go, but I got there in time.

"I'm glad I reached you." The woman's voice held a touch of a Southern accent. "I'm a friend of your late fiancée, Allison Stuart. I teach in the same school. My name is Sharon Kelso. Maybe she's mentioned me?"

I remembered the name. "What can I do for you, Sharon?"

"Ever since a conversation with Allison, I've been meaning to move some funds into a better investment. When my mom died about eighteen months ago, I came into a large sum of money, and it's just sitting in a savings account. I know from Allison that that's basically throwing money away."

"I think you can do better, true."

"Look, I waited too long. I'm leaving on a trip early in the morning. Is there any chance that I could meet with you long enough to sign forms, do whatever's needed?"

I thought about the day. I already had plenty I wanted to do, but none of it paid the bills. "Could you meet me in my office around four? I'm downtown."

"Sure that would—oh, I'm sorry. I just remembered a commitment I can't get out of. Allison said you sometimes meet people in their homes. Is there any chance you could do that this time?"

I sighed, softly enough that she wouldn't hear me. "All right. What's your address?"

She gave me an address in Black Forest, which used to be a remote community, but was now touched by the northeastern sprawl of the Springs.

No sooner had I put the receiver down than it rang again. The new call was from Tina Vasquez, a pharmacist in her fifties. After the pleasantries, which sounded strained to me, she said, "I'd like to transfer my funds to a new account at Edward Jones. I have the account number. Is there any problem with that?"

"No, certainly no problem. I'd be happy to do that right away. For your safety, I do need it in writing. The form is on our website. You could bring it in or mail it, whichever you like."

"Thanks." Her voice shuddered a bit, as though in relief.

I hesitated. Normally, requests to move to a new investment counselor or financial entity were automatically approved. If people were treated with courtesy, sometimes they came back, but if they were hassled on the way out, the odds went way down.

"Tina," I said tentatively. "I will absolutely do this, and you don't owe me any explanation, but so much has gone on in my life during this past week, I have to at least ask. Is there anything wrong? Have you gotten a negative message from me, or anything?"

At first I thought she wouldn't say anything more, but I was wrong. "This is going to sound silly, like I'm overreacting."

"Trust me. I've gone to enough counseling that I know your feelings are never wrong. That's what you feel."

"Well, I was in Starbucks on Friday. This is—" She stopped herself. "Anyway, two people came up behind me in line and they were talking. With each other."

"And?"

"And one of them mentioned your name and BTU Investments. He said the SEC had just put you on a warning list for questionable practices. That he was pulling his money out before he got burned, too."

My heart was racing by now. I sat down, trying to figure this out. I said, "That's not silly at all, Tina. It's very serious. And I really appreciate your telling me. Can I just ask you a couple of questions?"

"Uh, yes."

"Was either of these people a tall, thin guy or a very pretty blonde with blue eyes and freckles?"

"Well... one of the men was pretty tall. I didn't pay attention to his weight."

"Can you tell me anything else you noticed about these people?"

"Not really. They were both men, both in business suits. The tall man, I don't know, maybe forties. Glasses. Oh, and a toupee I think."

"Why do you say that?"

"A feeling more than anything. It looked like his real hair, brown, but it felt like a toupee. I can't say why. The other guy was shorter. Also with glasses. That's all I can remember."

"That's a wonderful help," I said, exaggerating. "Listen. As soon as I see that form, I will transfer all your funds wherever you say. Your balance is going to be very close to—" I scanned her account and gave her the present value. "But I'd like to recommend you do a couple of things as well. One, call the SEC yourself. Ask if they actually have any complaints on file about me. Look up the number yourself so you make sure you're talking to the real people. Also, call the Better Business Bureau. Ask them the same question. I don't actually know if the SEC will tell you about complaints that are in the works, but I know the BBB will."

"So this—are your suggesting this conversation was faked?"

"Do one more thing for me. Search for my name on the *Gazette* site during this past week. Someone filled my car with concrete and my home was demolished. Someone is very angry with me, but I really don't believe it's a disgruntled client. I think the conversation you heard is part of this."

"My gosh. I'm so sorry."

"It's OK. Just go ahead and get me the form and I'll take care of it for you right away."

"I don't know now if I will."

"If I get the form, I'll do what you ask. If you learn enough to make you hold off, that's fine. I hope to have this situation resolved in the next few days." I had no real timetable except that if it wasn't resolved in the next few days I'd shoot myself.

Chapter 29

I drove northwest into the Rockies, following Highway 24 up Ute Pass. The day was overcast, probably the first mostly cloudy day in a month.

I'd given Beth a heads-up about the attempt to convince Tina something was wrong at the firm. There wasn't much she could do about it at this point, but she needed to know.

Taking several deep breaths helped calm me down. I occupied myself during the trip by trying to maintain regular, relaxed, deep breathing. I had no idea if what I had in mind would work.

The road twisted and turned for much of the way to Woodland Park. I kept watch to see if anyone seemed to be tailing me, but I couldn't spot anyone consistently in my rear view.

Woodland Park was getting a breather from the heat also. The clouds were scattered, lower in the sky than down on the plains.

After I took the exit onto Edlowe Road, I kept going for a few minutes until the road took a gradual ninety-degree curve around a small hill. There I pulled over, out of sight of anyone who might have been following from a distance.

I waited ten minutes. The only vehicle that passed me was an old red pickup with two cowboys in it. They must have been hauling firewood. I let them get well ahead, and then followed.

Belatedly it occurred to me that if someone were following me, it could easily be the person who placed the GPS tracker in my wheel well, and he or they could probably have seen my dot on the map stop. They would just have to wait for it to start up again. Assuming they were even on the road behind me. They could have anticipated where I might be going and have led me here. Or they could be sitting in a downtown bar laughing over drinks and waiting for another of my clients to wander within earshot. I supposed with Tina, they had followed her around until they found her in a suitable public spot. Again, the nature of this operation suggested significant resources behind it.

Pikes Peak lay ahead of me now, mostly obscured by clouds.

Today the wall around the Stuart estate seemed even longer. And higher. The wait after pressing the red intercom button seemed longer, too.

I was admitted, though. I parked in the same spot as last time, and again I was met by Christine, the spokes-greeter. Ben Stuart must have been a cleavage connoisseur. She was a bit somber, I thought, as we made the trek to Ben.

"Is everything OK?" I asked.

We walked a few more paces, passing what could have been a sitting room, and then the library. She said, "It's rough, seeing him this way."

I supposed even Darth Vader had acquired some good buddies.

"What's the prognosis?"

"I don't know, actually. But each week he seems a little bit worse. Today he's actually slightly better than a couple of days ago. He goes up and down."

I imagined the Dow Jones during a sell-off. "I'm sorry." I meant I was expressing sympathy for Christine, not that under the circumstances I would be sorry to see him die.

Her cool blue eyes lasered in on me. "Are you?"

I stopped. She stopped with me. Behind her were some giant paintings of family members. I looked at a four-foot-high oil painting of Allison. She was looking directly at me. "I loved her. He blames me for her death."

Christine turned to gaze upward also. "You were at the wheel, right?"

"That's true. Maybe that's all that matters."

We resumed the trek.

A different model-bodyguard was on duty with Ben today. This one was Asian. The common threads remained fitness and cleavage. She was silent.

Ben did seem slightly more alert today. He still rested in his oversized recliner. This time I took the liberty of sitting down next to Ben where he could easily see my face. His sunken eyes tracked me. He smelled of hand lotion.

"I thought I should bring you up to date," I said. "I know you've done a lot of damage this week, but I wanted you to know that you're risking a lot. I'm sure you enjoyed destroying my car, demolishing my house, trying to turn a client on me."

Ben was silent, inscrutable.

"But the hit and run and the poisoning went too far."

I readied my first exaggeration. I had not gone to Detective Winchester yet about the poisoning. So many attacks, so little time. I'd talked to a cop, but I hadn't brought in the Ben Stuart angle.

"Now the police know you're trying to kill me, so if I wind up dead, you're going to have to have some serious explaining to do. And I know about the tall man, and the blonde woman. This morning the tall man tried to con a client of mine, and she got a photo of your guy." Another lie. I'd really had a pretty good relationship with the truth until this point in my life.

Ben was still silent.

"So it's only a matter of time before this guy is found. We have cell phone video of the cement truck guy to corroborate. I have a lawyer starting to chase down the chain of companies that start with the Demolition Department." Another lie. "That will eventually trace back to you. The urgency of that search might not be as high right now as the hunt for the Unabomber, but just think of the headlines if I'm killed. 'Billionaire hires hit man.' People will come out of the woodwork volunteering to help with the paper trail. You made some powerful enemies on the way up. I bet some of them still have the resources to spare. Some of them would love to see you behind bars, even if it's only for a month or two.

"So do your worst, Ben. I don't have any animosity toward you, honestly. You probably even think you're doing something noble because Allison died on my watch. But you're not going to be able to do this without any repercussions. Even if the information comes out too late to directly affect you, Maddy could be hurt by this. So just stop. You stop now, and I will stop. Allison is dead and nothing will bring her back. And I'll have lost the house and the car. But I can rebuild my life."

Still no response.

I rose. "Think about it."

I started for the door. I was almost there when he said, so softly I was unsure I heard him, "Wait."

He summoned his bodyguard. She leaned over while he whispered in her ear. He finished and she approached me.

"Would you be so kind as to let me turn off your cell phone for one minute? I will not damage it."

He'd taken my house and my car. Even if took my phone and never gave it back, so what?

I handed it to her. She switched it off and set it on a nearby table. She moved to a cabinet and withdrew something that vaguely resembled a curling rod for hair but it had lights and emitted a constant tone. She methodically swept my body with the wand until she flipped it off and nodded to Ben. Obviously Ben didn't want any possible recording of this conversation.

Ben tilted his chin up toward me in a *come here* gesture.

I came closer and so did the bodyguard.

When I was about a yard away, Ben opened his mouth. "I am *not* trying to kill you. I am not doing anything that could possibly have that direct result."

We stared at each other long enough for me to win one of life's smallest and most meaningless victories. He blinked first.

"But the other things are your doing?"

Ben had said his piece. He closed his eyes, dismissing me.

I said, "Maybe somebody got the wrong memo. Or maybe someone thinks there'll be a bonus if I'm dead. This needs to stop."

Ben didn't open his eyes again. I glanced at the bodyguard before retrieving my phone. A nod said it was permitted.

As I walked toward the door, I was struck by the difference in how I felt now versus the last time I was here. At that time, I'd had the reunion fiasco and the car incident. And I had felt whipped. Now he had thrown in the house and two passes at me that could have killed me. But I felt energized. The bastard was not going to do this with impunity.

I would get past this if it killed me. OK, there had to be a better way to put that. But an inner heat that was new to me was burning. And it felt good.

Christine showed me out. Of course I didn't need a guide. This journey would be burned into my brain forever.

Outside, I took some deep breaths in the cool mountain air. I glanced over at the guest house occupied by Maddy and Kevin Mayer. No sign of them at the moment.

On the drive back to the Springs, I thought about what little Ben had said. He wasn't doing anything that would have that *direct result*. That was a bit like lawyer-speak, carefully parsed. I might die of a broken heart, or I might decide to kill myself because I couldn't take it anymore. Or I might get hit a non-fatal blow by a truck mirror and hit my head on a rock. Hey, accidents happen. But harming me was the goal. Not killing me.

I wondered about whatever had been slipped into my drink at the restaurant. I don't think I drank the whole glass, and I still wound up feeling like murder was the goal. How carefully could you measure stuff like that? *This* much will make a healthy, 170-pound guy feel awful, but *that* much would kill him. Could even an MD be that sure of the difference? Or maybe someone in the chain didn't particularly care.

Despite Ben's denial of what felt like attempts on my life, he had tacitly admitted he was behind this. I knew about the tall guy, and I felt certain the freckled blonde was in on it. I wondered how many more were on Ben's team. If only this kind of team wore jerseys.

~~~

"What kind of gun do you want?"

The gun store on South Nevada Avenue wasn't very busy when I got there around noon. Just wait for another national election. The guy behind the counter looked like he would need a gun only for con-

frontations that involved terms like "battalion" and "SWAT." I wondered if his nickname was "Bear."

"I hear Glock is good," I said.

"What model?"

"Ah..."

"Glock is like Ford. You want a Mustang or an SUV?"

"Maybe a Ford Focus. Something that will keep someone from
shooting back. Doesn't have to be fancy. Needs to be reliable."

"Size matter?"

He was looking at me as though he were talking about something
else.

"Smaller, I guess, unless that makes it less reliable."

"Glock 19. Compact. Nine millimeter. Good seller. Good gun."

I waited. If I'd been shopping for a new TV, I'd probably get a
three-minute lecture that included twenty terms that were meaningless to me.

"Can I look at one?" I asked finally.

He unlocked a cabinet and handed me a pistol vaguely smelling of
oil. The finish felt very slightly slippery, the way soap and shampoo
bottles feel in the supermarket. The sides of the grip were speckled.
The top edges of the barrel and the front edge of the trigger guard
were squared off.

"Where do I put the darts?"

Bear gave me a slight frown. Maybe he knew Dr. Bentson.

"Sorry. Can you tell me just a little more about it?"

"Ten rounds. Takes a magazine. You can buy extra magazines.
Could use fifteen, but, you know, government pussies."

I wondered if I had any hope of surviving a firefight that went on
for that many rounds. "So how much for the gun, two magazines,
and, uh, twenty bullets?"

"Box is fifty rounds."

This was like buying hot dogs and hot dog buns. I wondered if I
should buy more magazines. "OK. How much."

"No holster?"

"Nope." I flashed on an image of a cigar box.

He gave me a price. Higher than I'd expected, lower than a Ford
Focus.

"I'll take it."

"You can't."

"Excuse me?"

"Background check. Supposed to be instant. It's running about a day."

Twenty minutes later, the background check paperwork was behind me. I turned toward the door. "So I can pick it up tomorrow?"

"Probably."

"Will you call me?"

He took my number. They always say they'll call.

Chapter 30

As I stepped outside the gun shop, my phone made a chirp I didn't recognize. It took me a moment to realize it was the nanny-cam app, alerting me to activity in my motel room. My heart started thudding.

Seconds later I got a glimpse of the person who was invading my territory. She was probably completely unaware of being photographed and having her picture sent over the wires.

A maid.

Unless the team took the precaution of finding a twenty-something, tired-looking young woman dressed in a maid's outfit and who was taking the time to change the sheets on my bed, my guess was that she was not the criminal mastermind behind my harassment. The worst she could probably do was short my sheets. And maybe eat the mint that could have been on my pillow.

Police headquarters had been my next planned stop, but since I was already south of downtown, I decided to make another stop first.

The Blue Star restaurant parking area was empty. It wasn't yet officially open for business. I parked in front, got out of my car, and walked around the three sides of the building. The restaurant butted up to Bristol Brewing just to the south of it. Most passers-by probably never saw them, but two large murals adorned two walls of the building, one to the north, the other on the side farthest from the street. The north view showed a restaurant scene mostly in red. The rear showed a humongous wine bottle and some grapes the size of basketballs.

I hadn't noticed the hardware before, but now that I was sensitized by my exposure to the nanny-cams, I spotted three small surveillance cameras.

As I rounded the corner to the back, a guy a little older than me was hunting for his key to unlock the back door.

"Hey," I called.

He jerked his head around, startled.

I stopped. "Sorry. Just wanted to ask you a question."

He looked more at ease now that I had stopped approaching. He had the build of a football player, so he really didn't have a lot to fear from me.

"There was some trouble here Friday night. What are the chances I could look at some of the footage from your security cameras?"

"Nil to none. The owner feels it's private. We've had people claiming a legitimate need when what they really wanted was to see the license plate on a car driven by a woman they tried to pick up."

"I understand. Can you at least tell me how long you save the recordings?"

He looked me over. Did I look like a stalker?

"At least a week."

"Thanks."

My next stop was police headquarters. As I waited for Detective Winchester, I pictured him snacking on a donut. Blame *The Simpsons*. I wondered how old the *dollars-to-donuts* idiom was. And how long before the meaning was completely reversed when the cost of a donut greatly exceeded a dollar?

"I don't have any new information for you yet," he said as soon as he stepped into the conference room. Again he had both his tablet computer and his paper folder. I suppose in another era he would have worn a belt and suspenders. Or maybe cops shared a motto with the Boy Scouts. They both wore uniforms.

"Actually, I had some new information for you. And a request."

He sat. "What's the request?"

"Can I tell you that after I've given you what I have? It will make more sense."

He seemed reluctant, but he said, "Shoot." Cop jargon maybe.

"I talked to Ben Stuart this morning. And he essentially admitted he was behind what's happening to me." Except for the statement that he wasn't trying to kill me. But did I believe anyone who'd destroyed my house and car?

"But you didn't get a notarized affidavit or a certified audio recording of this, I suppose." I supposed all cops were sticklers for that elusive thing called proof.

"No. That was more for my benefit than yours. But something else happened." I decided to omit mention of the con job on my client, but I needed to give him the details on the poisoning.

He made some notes while I went through the poisoning incident and emergency room visit number two. He didn't seem all that surprised by the idea that someone almost killed me. Again.

When I was done, he looked through his notes. "When your doctor gets the toxicology report, have him send a copy to me."

"Will do."

"So, what's the request?"

"The Blue Star Restaurant has video surveillance from Friday night. But they'll only save it for a few more days. Can you make them give you a copy? I want to see what car that blonde was driving, or if she was with anyone."

Detective Winchester considered that. "That's not unreasonable." Someone else might have said *that's reasonable*. Maybe cops come at things from a different perspective. Maybe to them people were possibly guilty until certifiably innocent.

~~~

The day had gone too fast. I headed out of the parking lot for my four o'clock in Black Forest, wishing Sharon Kelso lived near downtown. At least this would be my last stop of the day. I looked forward to relaxing in the motel with some comfort pizza. Maybe that could take my mind off my troubles for ten minutes.

This was Cathy's afternoon for volunteer work at a local hospice. Mainly she read to terminal patients and kept them company. To me it would be amazingly demanding emotionally, to befriend person after person who would be dying soon, some of them children. But

Cathy found the strength. She was cheerful, upbeat, and a great listener.

I wished I was there with her.

As I traveled north on I-25, I thought seriously about calling Sharon and cancelling. But since I'd already said yes, cancelling would mean I could likely write off a potential new client, friend of Allison's or not. It would have been better to have just said no right then and tried to schedule something for when she got back. But if she was a teacher and she'd already done her mandatory summer continuing education, she might not be back for a couple of months.

The Rockrimmon exit, which led west toward Bruce's fitness center, fell behind me. In the distance to the right lay the hill that was home to UCCS on the slopes, and a cluster of transmission towers on top. Farther north was the chalky white face of Pulpit Rock, looking a bit like an ancient fortress. Or maybe a pulpit.

Traffic was heavy but typical. Some people doing the limit, a few slowpokes, many people pushing over the speed limit by five miles an hour. And then we had the ten percent crazies, weaving between lanes and going anywhere from five to twenty-five miles an hour faster in an effort to get home two minutes earlier. There really must have been something wonderful waiting for those folks at home.

I-25 curved to the right as the road went past the massive Air Force Academy solar panel array on the west side of the Interstate and then jogged back to the north. The sun was still well above the foothills to the west, but its exact position was frequently hidden by late-afternoon clouds.

I passed over an interchange where the Interstate crossed N. Gate Blvd. To the west, as the name implied, lay the north gate of the Air Force Academy.

As the road continued its gentle slope upward toward Monument Hill, I took the next exit, heading east on W. Baptist Road. Here the land was grassy, mostly level. In the distance were the dark ponderosa pines and the ridge defining Black Forest. The divided highway took me through a sparsely populated commercial strip and on into a thinly populated residential strip. Soon the road changed from Baptist Road to Baptist Assembly Road, what seemed like an unneeded distinction to me. As the trees became a bigger fraction of the scenery, the road narrowed to two lanes, occasionally cutting through small bluffs that rose on both sides.

Houses were now much less frequent, and set back into the trees, rather than having fences coming within twenty feet of the roadway. Side roads earned stop signs rather than lights. After a stop sign, the road became Hodgen Road.

I was realizing that "Go right on Baptist and left on Goshawk" was shorthand for a much bigger distance than it had sounded. I was already running late. The road started dipping down to grassland and the trees fell away. Dwellings now seemed more like ranches than single-family houses, but maybe they were just houses owned by people who liked a lot of space.

A dark line appeared on the horizon to the east. As the road rose again, eventually the line resolved into another treed ridge. At Vollmer Road, solidly back in the trees, I slowed for a flashing yellow light, then around a jog to the right, presumably for a property line, ancient by Colorado standards, a toddler by European standards.

Around this time I started feeling paranoid. After the hit and run and the poisoning, I was now in a world where things that used to seem impossible now seemed possible. I pulled over onto the shoulder.

I could turn around right then. I wondered if I was having a spidey-sense moment or if I was acting like a scared rabbit. Were these people going to make me fearful of every shadow, or was I going to live my life? I knew Sharon was a friend of Allison's. It wasn't like I truly knew her as a person, but I'd been introduced once at a party. I could play safe and blow off this appointment. Then, assuming for the moment that this really was legit, she would look elsewhere for an investment counselor. And she might tell all her friends about "unprofessional behavior."

I finished chiding myself for being so quick to start living in fear. Having a backup plan couldn't hurt, though. I dialed Bruce's line. I would tell him where I was and ask him to call the police if I didn't call him back in twenty minutes.

No bars. Crap.

I resolved to go a little farther and call when I had service.

Minutes later the green street sign for Goshawk appeared. A left took me onto a narrow dirt road leading through the trees, through a clearing, and deeper into the forest.

I stopped again. Still no bars. I resumed my journey.

Fences lined many of the properties. I got the feeling people this far out valued their privacy. I remembered visiting a client in the Springs who lived next door to a home that sported a warning sign with an image of a gun, along with words to the effect that nothing in the house was worth dying for. My reaction had been that probably no possession in the home was worth killing a human being for, but we all see the world differently.

I was definitely going to be late, but since I had no service, going back to call Bruce would make me even later. Goshawk. I knew that was some kind of bird of prey, but I couldn't picture anything but a generic image of a falcon. Now that I thought about it, I was probably ten or fifteen miles north of the town called Falcon. I wondered what it was with killer birds out here.

About a mile farther along the road, it turned to the right. Finally a dilapidated fence and a neatly lettered sign saying "Kelso" appeared. The sign felt comforting. I turned in. The driveway was deeply rutted and overgrown with grass, angling deeper into the woods. I didn't bottom out in the Ford despite it not being a truck or an SUV, but it felt close at times. I pulled up in front of a slightly run-down log farmhouse that didn't feel in keeping with the smooth, polished voice I'd heard on the phone.

I checked my phone for a signal. Still no bars.

I shut off the engine. My hand stayed on the key. I felt like going home, and then felt foolish. But I also started feeling even more paranoid. I surveyed my surroundings.

No other car was in the driveway. Rutted tracks led around the side of the house, so Sharon could have parked around back. I got out of the car and listened. Wind through the pines was the loudest sound. The air held no hint of booming woofers, growling mufflers, ringing phones. Instead of the sounds of civilization or the uncivilized sounds of civilization, the faint sounds of bird calls were all that reached me. I just about got back in the car and got out of here.

This visit was seeming like an even worse idea all the time, but I walked to the porch. Three wooden steps led up to a wooden porch about six feet by ten. It was bordered by a railing.

The wood's appearance suggested one of those scenarios where you plant a foot and it goes right through a plank, but the flooring felt solid enough.

The house didn't have a doorbell. Instead, a small pull cord was mounted next to the door frame, presumably to ring a bell inside. I stood in front of the door and reached for the pull. And I hesitated.

The pull cord looked new.

I was feeling like a finicky cat who had found medicine in the mix too many times. I'd seen too much stuff like this in the movies and my thudding heart pounded louder. Instead of pulling the cord, I knocked. Loudly.

The sound was jolting in the quiet. I found myself reviewing the pros and cons of staying. On the pro side, if Sharon were legit, I could make some money. On the con side, everything else. No sound of footsteps came from inside. No "Coming!" rang out.

I peered in the window. Rising hair on the back of your neck is actually a real thing.

The interior was hard to resolve, partly because it was dim, and partly because the window was dirty. I shifted position, thinking about how foolish I would look. Fear of looking foolish had probably motivated more bad decisions than I could count. And after those bad decisions, I always felt worse than foolish.

I moved my head again, trying to see inside. And then I felt chilled. I was sure I was looking at a line that stretched from near the door to a dark doorway eight or ten feet away. I couldn't be sure, but a faint gleam looked to me to be a barrel. A gun barrel. Pointing at the door.

My brain replayed a gun scene from the past. I saw muzzle flashes as my mother shot my father. I don't know if the muzzle flashes were there in reality or if my memory had been enhanced with scenes from action movies. I felt sick and afraid.

I took some deep breaths and looked around. I saw no one. I could see no one in the house either, but that made sense if the door was booby-trapped.

Chapter 31

Decision time.

I could get back in the car and race back to town. Safer. And I'd never know for sure if my fears were justified. I wanted to get back in the car. God, I wanted to do that. My face was hot and a wave of the shakes hit me for a couple of seconds. The fear was almost overpowering.

But I also wanted this business to stop. I'd gone so long keeping my head down and avoiding conflict, that confronting trouble head on was giving me a sense of accomplishment.

And maybe there was a clue here. Maybe not a cigarette butt with lipstick on the filter. For one thing, not as many people smoked now in Colorado. But something maybe. A piece of paper on a notepad where the top note had been torn off after writing something cryptic. Or a phone with a caller ID list. Something.

I looked around again. I still saw no one in the vicinity. That made sense. If you knew someone was about to shake a beehive, you might not stick around.

Near the porch were some old two-by-fours. I took a closer look, and an idea started forming. The phrase, *I'm getting an idea*, probably ranks well up the danger list, somewhere near, *Watch this!*

Still, I got down there and very carefully, wary of black widows, kicked one board away from the others. Several inches from one end was a knot. The knot had shifted halfway out of the board.

I brushed some cobwebs off the board and pushed on the knot, but it was too stubborn for my fingers. I tried to be quiet, for no valid reason, like stooping under helicopter blades that were spinning a yard over your full height. When I swung the knot at the corner of the wood porch, nothing happened. But on the third swing I got lucky and the knot popped loose.

I stood as far from the door as I could and still reach the pull cord. No one had answered the door yet.

The cord had about six inches of play. Carefully, very carefully, I pushed the knot on the cord through the knothole in the two-by-four. Somehow the word "knot" made it seem they were meant for each other. I moved back farther, until I hit the railing on the porch. That put me about a yard from the door frame.

I twisted the two-by-four like a screwdriver until the knot was caught below the board, between the board and the side of the house.

I have to admit that only then did it occur to me that I could have gone around back and tried another door.

But that was no guarantee of safety. And at this point, if I was wrong about all this, the only thing I was guilty of was knocking a knot out of a two-by-four. And then pulling the bell cord.

I tried to calm my breathing.

I pushed the far end of the board downward, trying to keep the knot trapped below the two-by-four.

Blam!

The blast noise sounded even louder than the gun my mother had used. I saw her standing over my father and some part of me expected another *blam* and another.

I realized my eyes were closed. I opened them. The wooden door had a roughly circular hole through it at waist level, the size of a softball. God. The blast had torn out the lock and forced the door open. The gap between the door frame and the edge of the door was a couple of inches.

There are times you really hate being right.

I was tempted to go into the house to see if I could find clues. Maybe the shotgun had prints or a serial number or something. But self-preservation finally outweighed that impulse and I started to move off the porch toward my car.

Blam! A shot sounded from somewhere on the far side of my car. A slug punched into the wall inches from my arm. *Damn it!*

I wasn't aware of a decision-making process. No decision tree, no pro/con list, no thoughtful reflection. One second I was on the porch getting shot at and in the next second I was inside the house, out of sight of the shooter.

Another *blam* sounded from outside, muffled this time. I wondered why he hadn't shot at me as soon as I had started sniffing at the bait instead of gobbling it up, but I assumed he'd been counting on the Welcome Wagon to blow me out of the saddle.

The house wasn't all that large. Single story, maybe with a basement, maybe not. The smell of gunpowder hung in the air. The room was split between a kitchen on the left and a tiny living room on the right. A hallway led deeper into the house. The darkened hallway was where the shotgun sat, duct-taped to an old recliner. A light but strong cord, like you'd use for Venetian blinds, stretched from the side of the door frame over to the chair. This time I did go through a short conscious decision process. Try to hide, or move right on through and out the back?

I moved for the chair and the shotgun, which blocked the hallway. Keeping the shotgun aimed anywhere but at me, I pushed it closer to the front door, where any follower would at least have a pause. I wondered if a shotgun held a second round, one I could use against my attacker. Probably the only way I would know for sure right now was if I did a test fire, using up the one thing that would protect me. That wasn't going to happen.

I was at the back door before my second-thoughts period began. What if there were someone else out there waiting? My body still in motion as the thoughts were occurring to me, I opened the door. But something I'd seen in the kitchen pulled me back, something I couldn't even identify consciously. I waffled there and moved a foot or two back toward the kitchen.

That indecision saved my life.

Crash! I probably jumped six inches in surprise and fear.

Another booby-trap. A horizontal beam now blocked the door, still vibrating. It was supported by a two-by-four that led upward to a point just above the door frame on the outside of the house. Opening the door had apparent triggered a gravity release and the beam came pivoting downward, swinging into the open doorway.

The worst part was that the beam was lined with nails set every inch or two, protruding wickedly for maybe six inches. Had I not stepped back, my chest cavity would have been stitched open.

I shuddered. I went back to the kitchen to recheck what my brain had tried to tell me. There it was. In the ceiling was a square access panel for the attic. It was positioned so no one could get there without moving furniture, but I had a thought. And at the back of my mind was the idea that if I got higher, maybe I could get a cell signal. At the very least, I would be doing the unexpected.

I wasn't even sure if I had enough time, but in my extremely hasty decision process this looked like my best chance.

I pushed a chair out of the way and moved the modest kitchen table three feet. While standing on top of it, I was just tall enough to reach the square access panel into the attic and push it aside. I hopped down to the floor.

I considered stopping right there. I could run out the back right now, and have them delayed by thinking I was up there in the attic. Unless someone could see me right now from outside. Probably not.

I pushed the table back in place. My heart pounding, I climbed onto the kitchen counter. From there I climbed on top of the refrigerator. I crouched there, about a yard away from the opening to the attic.

I wasn't sure now if I could make the jump to the opening. But staying where I was, I was just waiting to be killed.

I jumped. My fingers caught the far side of the attic opening. I pulled with all my strength, certain I would have time and energy for only one try. I made it. Kind of. I was part way into the attic, my head and shoulders in, supporting myself with my elbows.

Another energetic push got my belt buckle and everything north into the attic. I scrambled all the way in, twisted my body around, and pulled the attic access panel back into place.

I was in near dark under the pitched sides of the roof. But a small amount of light came in from two vents, one on each end of the attic. I moved quickly away from the access panel, thinking that would be the worst place to be. If only one person were here and trying to kill me, I could maybe surprise him if he stuck his head into the attic, but then his partner or the others on the team would know right where I was.

By the time I was at one end of the attic, in the darkness away from the light coming in the vent, I had maybe two seconds to wonder if my impulse had taken me to the worst possible place or a better place before muffled steps sounded from below. I was taking out my phone when I heard a single word.

"Shit."

In this case, I knew it wasn't *Shit, we're going to crash,* or *Shit, the bank is foreclosing,* but *Shit, Dave's not dead.*

My turn. *Shit, there's no cell signal.*

Finally, I realized one more risk I carried with me. I put my phone on silent and put it away as quietly as I could. God it was hot and musty up here.

I thought I heard murmured voices from below. Could be two people reassessing. Could be one person on a phone, if he had a carrier with service here. Or a landline. I hadn't had time to search for one. *Shit.*

Now that I was up here, all kinds of second thoughts were occurring to me. Maybe I'd left a mark on the kitchen table. Maybe I'd disturbed dust on top of the refrigerator. Maybe they could just torch the house.

Seconds later I knew their short-term plan.

Whoever was doing this was thorough, almost as if he was taking delight in being thorough. I could have been shot while standing on the porch. But the shotgun booby-trap had been added. The beam-of-spikes booby-trap had been a second layer of attack.

Now, maybe because they thought I'd left the house, but weren't totally certain, the shooting started.

It was a few isolated shots at first, near the access cover. But then the serious firepower started. It had to be two weapons on semi-automatic fire, shots blasting every half second, stitching deadly rounds through the attic flooring. *Blam-blam-blam-blam-blam.* I heard other shots that didn't seem to come into the attic. It sounded like the gunfire was also directed into closets and the crawlspace, any place where someone could be hiding.

I was sure it was at least two weapons. Two people down below walking from room to room, each putting ten or twenty rounds through the attic flooring. Maybe they figured that method would attract less attention than starting a fire in the forest.

I really didn't know, but I imagined some of the residents out here were strong outdoorsy types who liked chopping wood, camping, and target practice. I could visualize someone a mile away hearing all this and saying, *Hear that, Edna? Sounds like the Hendersons are doing a little target practice again.*

The shots were coming closer to me now. I had no alternative but to stay put. If I tried to scurry from here to a place they'd already peppered, I'd be signaling my presence.

Closer. They must have really liked shooting to expend so many rounds just in case. I was sitting cross legged, and I pulled my legs in tighter, aiming for a smaller profile.

Blam! A knife sliced through the outside of my left thigh. Somehow I managed to ignore the desire to cry out. I clenched my jaw and bit my teeth against the pain.

Another bullet blasted through the floor on the other side of me. And another. I was lucky I wasn't a bigger target than I was. Finally they stopped shooting. Silence fell

I couldn't tell how much I was bleeding. I rolled up my pant leg just past the place the bullet had gone through the edge of my flesh. I twisted the material bunched on the inside of my thigh, and the pressure around the perimeter of my thigh formed a crude tourniquet.

The pain throbbed with my pulse, but it wasn't in the spectrum that would make me throw up or pass out. I shifted position as quietly as I could, in hopes of finding a position that relieved a bit of the pain.

I wondered what my hunters' next move would be. They'd shot up the place pretty well, but they couldn't be sure that I was up here, or whether they had injured or killed me. If I had gone out the back door, I could be on the way to getting the police. They couldn't stay in the house indefinitely just on the chance that I was up here.

As I followed my chain of thoughts, I caught a glimpse of motion through the vent next to me.

Two figures, both wearing ball caps, exited the back of the house. In seconds they were past the limited area I could see. I would have given anything to know if that was the entire team or if people were still waiting below me.

If they saw no sign of me out there, they could be back at any time. I thought about prying one of the vent slats loose, but they could be watching.

Carefully I started for the vent on the opposite side of the house, trying to minimize the pain and the noise. I stayed on the rafters as best I could, not wanting to fall through a weak part of the ceiling. I passed a lot of bullet holes on the way, each a tiny glimpse of dim light.

As I neared the access panel I'd used to get into the attic, I passed still more bullet holes. Ammo must have been pretty cheap. It was near one of the bullet holes that my level of fear grew, and I had a better understanding of their decision to move on to the property behind the house.

Gas.

I could smell natural gas. Or more precisely I could smell the odorant the gas company added so people could readily detect leaks. Or detect deliberate attempts to release lots of gas.

I didn't know if their plan was to blow up the house, or just gas me. In either case, they could leave, knowing I couldn't hide up here forever. I moved on. My path took me nearer a vent between the attic and the room below. The gas smell was even stronger. I almost coughed, but was able to stifle the urge.

I reached the other attic vent.

Below the vent was the porch roof. That was all I could see. A platoon of thugs could be waiting in the driveway, but I had no way to tell.

I felt my leg. My pant leg was sticky with blood and probably a little sweat. In the dim light it was impossible to tell them apart. The gas smell grew stronger.

No human sounds came through the vent. But people could be waiting just outside. No way to tell.

I seemed to have made it across the attic floor unnoticed, so I took one more risk. I rolled down my pant leg, feeling the blood begin to flow again. After using a key to start two tears, one on each side of my cuff, I ripped upward as quietly as I could. Then I took the two ends and tied them together to form a tourniquet that shouldn't need my constant attention.

I lay on my back with my legs resting lightly on the vent. Kicking out the vent and scrambling down was the only plan I had. I wondered if I'd have enough time to get into my car and race off. Or if they'd sabotaged the car or blocked my access.

Too many questions. The only certainty was that as the house and attic continued to increase the gas-to-air ratio, there would come a point where I could no longer breathe. And at some point a spark or a flame could produce a giant explosion. I tried to remember if I'd noticed any candles on my way through the house. If they'd closed the back door and left a burning candle there, time was really running out.

Once I started kicking, there would be no extra time for decisions. I had to have my plan in place.

I would not go for the car. That could waste precious seconds to try to get it started and then navigate an exit. The car's running engine would be a magnet for attention and firepower. If I busted out the vent in one crash, the sound would be short-lived and they might be far enough away to just say, "Did you hear something?"

I took a deep breath and steadied my nerves. And then I jumped as a spider crawled across my cheek. Crap!

I swatted it away, trying to curse as quietly as I could.

OK, ready again. Feet apart. I didn't want to bust a hole and have my legs caught and be trapped. I wanted the grate out of there. I tested the grate by pressing lightly. The boards creaked softly.

Now or never. I wished I had some clue that I could leave behind in the event of my death. Almost as bad as the idea of dying was the notion that the killer would go unpunished rather than being weeded out of society.

Crash! I rammed both feet into the vent. It was a good blow. One side of the vent had come loose. I gave the other side a blast. It tottered, then fell, then skittered down the porch roof and fell to the ground with a crash.

It made a lot more noise than I had hoped, but I was moving even before the toppling was done. I grabbed the side of the opening and pulled myself forward.

In my first glance, I saw no people. Beyond the porch and to one side lay my Ford Focus. Farther out in the driveway sat a black Ford pickup. An F150. I wondered if it had a dented mirror or a replacement mirror. But I didn't dwell on it long. My body stayed in motion.

I scrambled through the vent and onto the angled porch. My plan had been to creep down the porch to a point nearer the lip, and then grab the edge as my hands went past. Already the weaknesses in my plan were showing up. As soon as I hit the porch roof I was in motion. Involuntarily. I was sliding uncontrollably because the pitch was greater or the surface was slicker than in my imagination.

I considered it a minor miracle that I was able to re-aim my body on the way down, and I was able to grab the gutter as I went past. In my imagination I could hang on for a second to completely brake my velocity. In real life, the gutter started coming loose as soon as some real weight hit it. I went down.

I hit the ground and rolled. My right knee hit a rock and stung with the impact, and my wounded left thigh burned with flaring pain. For a millisecond I wondered, if I lived through this, what list of bodily complaints I'd have by the time I was in a retirement home.

Even before I reached my feet, the sounds of running footsteps sounded. Coming toward me, of course.

The footsteps had sounded from the left, so I ran right. Gunfire boomed loudly from behind me. *Serpentine*, my mind commanded, dredging up some old movie scene, the closest experience I had to running for my life. Until now.

I had run maybe ten or twenty feet when the world ended.

Chapter 32

OK, the world didn't actually end. It just felt like it.

The house exploded. I had no idea whether a flickering candle had finally ignited the increasingly deadly mixture in the house, or if a stray bullet caused a spark, or what.

I felt like a wall had fallen on me. If I'd been right in the actual blast area, I would likely be dead or unconscious. Luckily I'd been far enough away from the house.

One instant I was run-limping and the next I was tumbling away from the house while toothpicks, splinters, and two-by-sixes blasted in every direction, including mine. Dark, choking, war-zone smoke roiled around me. Heat from the fire felt like an awful sunburn. Shingles peppered the surroundings, some still falling to earth. A connected pair of interior walls still stood upright somehow, but the rest of the structure looked like a helter-skelter bonfire. The odor of charred wood was thick in the air.

My head rang. My whole body vibrated. Groggy, I got to my feet and teetered upright, dazed, unsteady. In my whirling attempt to steady myself and continue running, I caught sight of my rental car. Man, those guys were going to be pissed. They weren't going to just pump up the tires and empty the litter carrier and send that one out again. It looked like a demolition derby car that had come in last. Or maybe one of those cars they jumped over in a tractor where the tractor doesn't quite go the distance.

I ran. It was a little like a pin-the-tail-on-the-donkey after-party run, a drunken, lurching, stumbling scurry that needed course correction every half second.

I caught a glimpse of the black pickup again. It seemed far enough out to be undamaged. I wondered if I'd gotten lucky and the blast had taken out my two hunters.

But then, aside from meeting Allison and meeting Cathy, when had I ever been that lucky? My average level of luck was confirmed a second later.

Blam! Another shot came my way. From somewhere behind me came a voice. I think it was male. My hearing was a little funky. The voice might have said, "Move the truck."

I ran. Serpentine, but now it was more by choice than from complete lack of equilibrium.

Another shot. Another miss. At least I thought it missed. I didn't register any more pain.

The one good thing was that the shooter wasn't right behind me. The explosion must have slowed him down, maybe even more than me.

I ignored the pain in my complaining right knee, and the newly complaining left thigh.

Ahead of me was not really a clearing, but a thinning in the trees. To the right, the trees grew thicker, mostly ponderosa pines. I went right. Anything that could stop a bullet or offer concealment was fine by me.

I heard only single shots behind me. Maybe the hunters had used up their automatic weapons ammo in the house.

The next shot also missed. The gunfire sound seemed farther away. Maybe the shooter was more shaken up than I was, and losing ground. I ran faster. Under my feet lay a bed of pine needles.

A huge cloud of black smoke wafted over me. I coughed and looked back. For the moment I could see nothing of my pursuer. I swung to the right again, and tried to run even faster. My lungs ached along with the rest of my body. I started to run out of the cloud of smoke and veered back into it, trying to stay right on the edge of it. The edge grew more diffuse as I went deeper into the pine trees.

The last shot was now more than fifteen seconds ago. Presumably if I couldn't see the shooter, he couldn't see me.

The wind shifted. Abruptly I was in the clear again. I stepped around a tree and looked back. A lot of the pines nearby had been "limbed up," the lower branches missing as a fire-mitigation effort. Grass fires could race pretty fast, and if they reached some low-hanging branches then they could start an explosion into the pine canopy.

My pursuer trotted into sight, not running full out. And he was aimed for a spot maybe fifteen or twenty degrees away from me.

The worst thing I could do was to show up as fast motion in his field of view. That old evolutionary imperative to provide heightened awareness of predators. I stayed where I was, debating. Even though he was not aiming directly for me, he was closing the distance.

I started backing away from his position, trying my best to keep this tree between him and me. As part of his head came into sight, I moved laterally, slowly, and kept walking steadily backward.

Something touched my back, and I jumped. I'd backed almost to another tree, and I forced myself to move slowly around it. I wore no fluorescent orange or really bright colors. As long as I moved slowly enough I had a chance of being almost invisible.

I repeated the process with another tree. Now I was moving almost at a right angle to his travel. I tried to make out his face, but he was just too far away for that and the ball cap didn't help. I could have been pursued by Tom Cruise and I wouldn't have been able to iden-tify him.

The only vague impression I had was of body type, and while he seemed of average or taller height, I would not have described him as a really tall slender man. Maybe the slender man was his accomplice.

Retreating behind another tree, I caught a glimpse of the shooter again. He had a hand up to his head. Maybe he was calling the other hunter. I pulled out my phone. Still no service.

If he was communicating, maybe that meant he'd had the foresight to bring walkie-talkies into the cellular dead zone. I grew more nerv-ous about the position of the other hunter.

Another thought. Was this guy a gifted tracker, or a city boy? I looked at my path from the last tree. I could see a couple of patches of flattened grass and disturbed pine needles. Walking backward made it more difficult to pick up my feet and place them carefully.

I guessed my pursuer was about a hundred yards away now. Much of the time he was invisible thanks to the mounting number of trees between us. My breathing slowed a bit, and my thudding heart decided to give me a break and slow down a little. I could maybe have just waited there until my hunter gave up. But that wasn't foolproof, and I didn't know where his accomplice was.

I kept moving. Moments later I had to second-guess my decision.

A frantic barking jolted me. They say you need to be the most afraid of dogs that don't bark, but this guy, a German shepherd, was giving away my position. My path must have taken me toward another property out here.

I wanted to run. But the dog might get even more excited by that. At least right now, he was maintaining his distance as he barked. I started walking at top speed. Moving along. Nothing to see here, dog.

As I skirted the property, the dog stayed where he was, but I caught a glimpse of my hunter headed my way. Safely away from the dog's territory, I ran.

The hunter was gaining on me. Apparently he'd recovered from the explosion. Dark smoke rose in the distance, and for the first time I heard a distant siren. That was good news on a couple of levels, one of which was that my ears still worked.

The guy was still gaining when he hit German shepherd territory. Maybe it was the fact that he was running right near the dog, or the running was compounded by the distant sirens, but an angry commotion started up, built from even more frantic barking and growling, with some swearing added in. Then three rapid shots. *Blam! Blam! Blam!* The barking stopped.

I felt sad for the dog. He'd just been in the right place at the wrong time. But I kept running. The altercation had delayed my pursuer enough that he had disappeared again. I shifted course once more.

The sun was just above the mountains to the west by now. Darkness would be my friend, I thought, unless these guys had night-vision equipment. They had shown a tendency to be thorough.

My run took me into a denser copse of trees. As soon as I was through the densest part, I could see a barbed wire fence ahead. Beyond it was some rocky ground, and beyond that lay another dense copse of trees. I raced up to the fence and deliberately snagged my shirt sleeve on it. A small piece tore off and I made sure it was fixed to one of the barbs. I stuck a foot through the fence and pushed a heel into the dirt as far away as I could reach.

That done, I extricated my leg and ran ten or fifteen yards at a ninety degree angle from my old path. My hunter emerged on the run, bare seconds after I hid behind another pine.

He must also have felt time pressure to make a decision. Sirens in the distance, the possibility of a forest fire to drag even more emergency vehicles into the area. I waited behind my tree, listening intently, not daring to try to peek in case he saw the movement, or he experienced the *I'm being watched* awareness.

He hesitated at the fence, as I read the sounds. Maybe one or two seconds later, I heard a jolt in the ground, and heard footsteps racing across rocks.

I dared a look. He was racing away from me now, following the trail. I gave him another ten seconds, by which time he reached the other trees. I began backing away again, slowly enough to avoid, I hoped, triggering any peripheral vision awareness.

Five minutes later I felt much safer. Unless he was a trained tracker. But a trained tracker wouldn't have fallen for my misdirection. Unless maybe he had only a second to decide. He knew that the farther out of sight I was, the greater the chance that I could get back into cell coverage or stop at someone's house.

I checked my phone. Still no signal. This was a fairly large area to not have coverage. They had shown a high degree of thoroughness. I wondered if that extended to using some kind of phone jammer.

I kept moving, keeping watch in the direction he had gone.

Minutes later I reached an obstacle.

A pond lay just to the right of my path. Skirting it and continuing almost straight would take me across a road where I'd be visible for a long way. Going right meant a long trek around the pond. I wouldn't be able to stick to the water's edge because there was no concealment. That pretty much dictated the route straight ahead, across the road.

Being on the other side of a road would be a good thing. I just didn't want to be spotted.

I approached the road cautiously. Soon I was near enough to see a long way left and a long way right. I could wait and flag down a vehicle, but there was no guarantee the vehicle would be friendly.

I gave the decision three more seconds of thought and then strolled across the empty dirt road. If someone way down the road caught sight of a runner, that would be bad news. But someone strolling across, that would be a resident. Someone other than a target.

I was halfway across the road when in the distance an engine roared. Tucked away behind distant trees, almost out of sight, a black pickup came into view, racing toward me.

Binoculars.

Of course. These people were thorough. They probably even had a checklist like my new best friend, ER Dr. Bentson.

Chapter 33

I ran. I was almost to another grove of trees when the black pickup skidded to a halt. Three blasts came my way. *Blam! Blam! Blam!*

I reached the trees as the pickup's horn began to honk. *long short long short long short.* That had to be a signal to the other hunter. Now I had two people on my tail again. *Who were those guys?*

I thought about trying to double back and read the license plate on the truck, but decided I'd prefer be uninformed and alive rather than risk being knowledgeable and dead. If all test pilots made the same choice, we'd probably still be flying biplanes and wearing goggles.

This time I discarded subtlety. I just ran as fast as I could. My only concession to the need for evasion was to alter course from time to time and to stick to the densest areas of pines. Maybe I could just out-run them. My right knee hurt like hell, and my left thigh ached all the way into the bone. But I was alive, and no matter how much pressure Ben Stuart might apply, I preferred it that way. But what I really would have preferred was to be home watching a movie or reading a good book.

I topped a rise and went down into a shallow gully that was a bit deeper than my height. Instant course correction. I turned left and ran at a right angle to my former course, grateful for the certainty that for at least twenty or thirty seconds I was out of sight, and out of the possible path of bullets.

I tripped. A tree root had been exposed as the ground near it had washed away. I went down painfully, and now my back, where the pickup mirror had struck me, started aching again. I picked myself up and kept scrambling along. Any minute without gunfire is a good minute.

A chain-link fence appeared on my right. I ran to it, scaled it, and ran on. Or, more accurately, I limped over to it, clumsily leaned over the top and leveraged my weight until I fell over the other side. I brushed some leaves back into a more random array and moved away from the fence.

I checked my work and decided that any evidence of my latest detour was pretty subtle. The sun had vanished behind the Rockies, so my hunters would be facing a bigger challenge as more time passed. The sounds from the distant sirens had faded now, and I could detect no evidence of a brand new forest fire. That was good. People not too far from here had gone through Colorado's worst property-loss fire not much more than a month ago.

My phone still reported no signal. If these guys were using a phone jammer, it must have been a powerful one. Of course, equally possible, my phone carrier was trying to get me to upgrade by switching off the older transmission standards.

A noise in the distance behind me made me freeze. Slowly I moved behind the nearest pine tree and listened. Nothing but the wind moving through the pines. Ordinarily I loved that sound, but right at the moment it could be masking the noise of approaching hunters. Of course it had also helped mask the sounds I made as I ran from them.

Maybe I should have just waited where I was. Unless they had dogs or some high-tech infrared detectors, they couldn't know exactly where I was. I'd traveled far enough that the area I could possibly be in had widened enough that I should be the needle in the haystack. As long as they didn't try to explode the haystack again or set fire to it, maybe I was safe. They couldn't look for me indefinitely. I assumed.

I started moving again, more cautiously now, going for stealth and leaving no trail rather than my former frantic race for survival. I kept moving away from my last sighting, making sure the circle of possibility was steadily growing, making the odds steadily worse for them.

I looked at my phone again. Still no signal. I switched it entirely off, on the slim chance that they had ties to law enforcement or other assistance that could take advantage of the fact that I was now voluntarily carrying a device that would let the government know roughly where I was at all times. At least the government would only use that power for situations where it was truly for my benefit or because they had clear and present and legal reasons. *Oh, good one, Dave.*

Through the trees to my right, a building, maybe a house, came into view. I veered left.

I'd walked another twenty feet when from behind me came the sounds of running. I whirled. A dog, a boxer, was heading straight for me, silent but for his feet pounding the pine needles.

I ran.

You'd think a man with long legs and weighing probably double what a dog does could outrun the dog, but no. All too often those things that sound like they make sense if you're drunk and making a bar bet really turn out to be nonsense. Or maybe the four legs to two ratio was a huge advantage.

He was gaining on me. Of course the dog could have been a female, but in this context, I think all dogs are male.

My heart was pounding again, my breath ragged. I covered maybe fifty feet as the sounds from the dog grew louder. My foot caught a wire on the ground, but it wasn't stretched tight. I carried it forward with one stride and left it behind. I could hear the dog panting now.

I gave it ten more feet and I whirled and stopped. I had the notion that I could maybe feint and grab its collar as it lunged at me. That was wrong.

The dog didn't lunge. In fact, it stopped altogether as though it were now considering how best to bring me down. It paced back and forth about ten feet away.

I finally put it all together. The dog had stopped just on the other side of the wire I had tripped on. Invisible fence.

He was trapped on the other side. I could see the collar as he paced back and forth. A client had showed me his system once. The wire forms a huge circle, or whatever shape. Inside the wire, doggie has his run of the property. The fence triggers a shock from the collar, which contains a battery needed to deliver the charge. Until it runs down.

Thank God for Duracell.

I began to calm down to the point of wondering if my flight had alerted my hunters. No moving shapes showed through the trees. My

brain grudgingly exited fight-or-flight mode and shifted into rea-
soned paranoia. This was an obstacle I could put in the path of my
hunters.

I started jogging, now paralleling the invisible fence wire, which
glinted in the dimming light from time to time. My path took me farther away from the last known position of my hunters.

The boxer paced me. Just a boy and his dog out for a run. Now that
he was kind of on my side, I looked at him more favorably.

I'd traveled around maybe forty-five degrees of the giant circle of
the fence when ahead of me a driveway led back toward the building
I'd seen earlier. I waved at the boxer. In my imagination he'd enjoyed
the run and wished it were longer. Seconds later I carefully scaled another chain link fence, wary of sending vibrations far enough for a
distant observer to detect.

I think I was heading north, given the brighter sky to my left.
Normally the Rockies are the unmistakable indicator of which way is
west, but the trees blocked the horizon in every direction.

The light was gradually fading, which was good news as far as my
pursuers went, but if I stumbled into someone's back yard, darkness
might make the homeowner more unwelcoming to uninvited guests.

Gradually, as the possibility of pursuit seemed a bit less likely, I
realized my wounded thigh was throbbing. I paused and loosened
my makeshift tourniquet. It hadn't been tight enough to stop all blood
flow, of course, but it was been putting a good deal of surface pressure right near the wound. I'd been incredibly lucky. The bullet had
grazed me rather than going through lots of flesh.

The pain got worse for several seconds as more blood seeped out,
but then the pain dropped closer to its steady state level. I gave it a
minute and then tied the pant strips back in place. I moved on.

Another fence came into view ahead of me. This one was taller,
probably six feet high, also chain link. It stretched a long way to both
sides of my route. On the other side was an array of stacks of lumber,
some covered with protective tarps, some in multi-level bays. The
lumber yard looked like a potential hiding place that would serve me
until it got darker.

I struggled over the fence and moved on.

Stacks of plywood in various thicknesses. Two-by-fours in several grades. Two-by-sixes, four-by-fours. The cut-wood smell reached my nose and felt inexplicably comforting. The path was laden with wood chips that would not show much of a trail.

I limped along a path between rows of stacks. Ahead the wood gave way to uncovered piles of rocks and gravel in various sizes. I hesitated, thinking that finding concealment among the lumber would be easier than sitting near a pile of rock. I retraced my path, looking for a nook I could rest in for an hour or two. I was exhausted.

I found a space between a stack of one-by-tens and a pile of sheetrock. It looked like no one would be able to see me there unless they got within ten or twenty feet. No binoculars would help.

But while concentrating on hiding, I'd let my guard down.

As I carefully lowered myself into sitting position, trying to avoid doing additional damage to my wounded thigh, I heard a terrifying sound.

A male voice, close enough for me to easily hear even if he hadn't raised his voice, said, "Hold it right there."

I froze.

"Stand up slowly. Turn around. Slowly. Keep your hands visible, away from your side."

I followed instructions very carefully.

I was facing a man of maybe forty. Blue jeans and a plaid shirt. Was this the other hunter? He didn't wear a ball cap. What he did have with him was a nasty looking shotgun. Two huge barrels, both pointing in my general direction.

At least he hadn't shot me yet. But, hey, I'd really managed to piss off someone.

He kept the shotgun ready in the crook of his arm as he reached into his pocket. Walkie-talkie?

He pulled out his phone and touched the screen. Seconds later he gave the phone a disgusted look. He was having connection problems, too. He aimed the flat side of the phone toward me. I flinched at the flash.

But he'd just been taking my picture.

He checked to make sure he had a good likeness I guess, and then said, "Get off my property or I'll call the cops. I see you back here again, and you won't like what happens."

"I already don't like—" I started.

He leveled the shotgun at the center of my chest.

"Look," I said. "I'm really sorry to be here. But could you do me a favor and just go ahead and call the cops?"

He looked at me more closely now, probably taking in my rolled up pant leg, my bloody calf.

"What's your story, son?"

"Two guys are hunting me, trying to kill me. It's possible you're in danger too, if your flash caught their attention."

He absorbed this. "This have anything to do with the explosion and fire at the old Johnson place?"

"If it's a log cabin and you're talking about earlier this afternoon, then yes, it has a lot to do with it."

"You pulling my leg, you'll wish you hadn't."

"I'm being straight with you. Would you also call an ambulance? I've lost some blood and my thigh is hurting." I shifted my leg carefully and glanced down at it.

"You can walk OK?"

"More or less. I got here from the Johnson place under my own power."

He looked carefully around the horizon, keeping the shotgun aimed at me the whole time. "We're going to take a walk. You first. I'll give you directions. Nice and steady. No sudden moves."

The guy was cautious. But that was OK. If my hunters found us, I'd want someone armed and competent nearby.

He followed me about ten feet behind. Five times he gave me single-word commands, left, right. We traveled one or two hundred yards like that. Ahead lay a house, a low, sprawling ranch house.

As we got near the front door, he took another sweep of the horizon. Satisfied, he said, "OK, Listen up. I want you down on the ground. Face down. Arms outstretched. Head away from the front door.

I complied.

He knocked on the door. Seconds later the door opened. He said, "I'm OK, hon. But I need you to call the sheriff's office. Tell them to send an ambulance, too."

"Sure, Henry."

He said, "Wait. This will sound alarming, but don't worry. I want you to say to them, 'I fear for my life. There are some people in the area with guns. It has something to do with the old Johnson place exploding.' Tell 'em that, and we don't sit at the bottom of the stack."

She drew in a quick breath, then said, "Got it." The door closed again.

"Thank you," I said.

"Just you be telling me the truth."

I lay there, uncomfortable but somewhat comforted. I worried about the hunters showing up before the sheriff did. I thought back to Ben Stuart's words. *I am* not *trying to kill you. I am not doing anything that could possibly have that direct result.* Would such a sweet old guy lie to me?

Chapter 34

I was starting to wonder if they gave out frequent passenger miles for ambulances. Maybe having the lights and siren running was considered an upgrade. At the moment, the siren was definitely off, and I suspected the flashing lights were off as well.

I'd answered questions for the sheriff's deputy who had arrived around the same time as the ambulance.

The fire was under control, thankfully. The explosion had created a burn area larger than a typical house fire, but the sound of the explosion had helped people to investigate right away and get it contained. I was told the house looked like the aftermath of a frat party in a war zone.

The deputy showed some incredulity as I talked about being in the attic as the floor was ventilated, but the fact that the house had exploded was fairly incontrovertible. The good news was that I wasn't under arrest. It had been full dark by the time I'd answered questions for the deputy and the EMT team. As they readied me for a ride, I thanked Henry and his wife.

Since my bullet wound was considered not life threatening, they were transporting me back to my familiar emergency room by driving at a good clip but not in emergency mode. That was fine by me. Lights-and-sirens mode can spawn additional emergencies.

~~~

An EMT wheeled me into the Penrose Hospital emergency room, the home away from home that for the first time I saw while I was on the way *in*. I felt like one of the cast in a *Jackass* movie.

Naturally, Dr. Bentson was the first MD to check on me.

I said, "Don't you ever go home?"

She looked at me with what I took to be disapproval. Two ER visits constitute bad luck. Maybe three made her see me as a repeat offender. But then she said, "Don't you have a life?"

"I'm trying to hang onto it."

She looked around with exaggerated thoroughness. "What, no girlfriend this time?"

"Only the first one was a girlfriend. The second was basically a passerby."

"I think you mean innocent bystander." Wow, Dr. Bentson had a side to her I hadn't seen before. Maybe she didn't really open up except to third-timers.

She looked at her clipboard. "So what is it this time?"

"A bullet wound."

"Of course it is." She read some more stuff off the clipboard. "A grazing hit on your left thigh. I have to give you high marks for variety."

"I do my best," I said.

She put the clipboard down and grabbed her stethoscope, and then paused and looked intently at me. "What's going on, Mr. Barlow?"

"Someone is trying to kill me. Trying pretty hard."

She nodded. Maybe that was easier to process if you're an ER doctor rather than if you were an architect. She checked my vitals and then looked under the snug wrap and the bandages the EMTs had put in place.

Finally she looked back at my face and said, "For a wound like this, we can use a local anesthetic, but maybe a quarter of the time we use a general. Do you have a preference?"

"Let's go with the general. Besides being squeamish, I'm exhausted."

"I should re-clean your yucca wounds, too, while I'm under the hood."

"I'd appreciate that.

She nodded again. "I have to tell you up front, though. We do not give quantity discounts."

~~~

I got out of the hospital in the early afternoon. I wanted to be out sooner. They wanted me to stay longer. On the plus side, the yucca-spine punctures now barely bothered me at all. Amazing how you calibrate to new levels of damage and pain.

A cab ride took me to a different car rental outfit. I was glad they apparently don't compare notes on customers. Of course I hadn't yet told the first company about the fate of the Ford Focus. I'd had just about all the abuse I could handle for the moment.

I slid behind the wheel of a blue Toyota Camry that still had new-car smell. At least that's what I hoped it was.

The last Camry I'd been in had been a compact. This one was bigger. It took the same kind of gas, though, and at this point I cared about little else. The luminous blue speedometer pointer was one of the easiest instruments to read.

After getting a change of clothes from my motel room, my next stop was in response to a phone message.

The same guy was behind the counter at the gun shop. He looked up idly when the bell activated by the front door went off and I walked in. Always vigilant.

"Thanks for calling about the gun."

"The gun?"

"The Glock 19. You called me."

"Oh, right." Of course Colorado had a bad rap from the whole legalizing recreational marijuana thing, but it really did seem like a number of our citizens stayed pretty high, whether on alcohol or drugs. I wondered what John Denver would have made of it. He'd testified before congress that "Rocky Mountain High" wasn't about drugs but about the sense of peace he found in the Rockies. Seriously, man.

After I paid him, he gave me the CliffsNotes Instant Gun Shooting and Gun Safety Course. I was buying a deadly weapon that fit in my hand, and getting less information than if I had just paid for a cell phone, and part of the info was useless. I didn't care whether the gun had a firing pin or a "striker" or that it was a gen 3. As least I was pretty clear on which end the bullets came out.

A heightened sense of power washed over me as I walked to my car and deposited my purchase. *Mess with me now, you son of a bitch.*

I looked at the pistol. *And where were you yesterday when I needed you?* Given the lack of an active safety switch like they show in the movies, probably the safest place for it for now was the trunk. As I put the gun and the ammo there, I thought about the nanny-mug-cam that got left behind in the Ford. I would apologize later to Bruce and reimburse him.

After closing the trunk, an afterthought made me open it again. I ejected the magazine from the grip of the pistol. I pulled cartridges out of the box and loaded them in the magazine. I put the magazine back in the pistol, the pistol back in the trunk, and re-locked the trunk. If I really needed the gun in a hurry, I might have time to get the trunk open, but I didn't want to have to mess with jittery hands while I tried to stuff in cartridges. The gun-store guy made it sound as easy as tossing pennies down a wishing well, but under pressure it would be more like cramming bowling balls down a gopher hole.

~~~

Another phone call, this one cryptic, sent me to the office, wondering what was going on. Beth said simply, "You'd better get in here."

As I walked into the office, I was already feeling guilty about the amount of time I'd been absent recently. That was very much unlike me. The looks I got on the way in intensified the guilt. All eyes were on me. Stan's expression, I thought, contained some degree of satisfaction.

Beth was in her office. She looked more stern than usual.

"What's up?" I asked. In addition to the guilt around being absent so much, I felt a tinge of resentment at not being told what was going on.

"Have a seat, Dave."

"OK." I sat.

Beth took a file folder from her desktop and opened it. She leafed through a couple of pages and slid one toward me. "We've been notified of some fairly serious allegations."

Oh, man. I really did not need this right now. "What kind of allegations?"

"Take a look at this page first."

I scanned it. "I don't get it. This new client, Ross Morse, put four hundred thousand into a new account recently. Then he asked for a withdrawal of fifty thousand. I sent the check out. End of story."

"Who was the payee on the check?"

"His LLC. I think it was Redwood Properties. Something like that."

"Maybe Redfearn Properties?"

"Yeah, that sounds right. So?"

Beth handed over another sheet of paper. It showed the structure of Redfearn Properties, LLC, and contained a couple of signatures.

In the list of managers was my name. And my signature.

Beth said, "That says you're one of the officers of Redfearn Properties. Meaning you issued a check for a significant amount of client funds and sent them to yourself."

"But this is insane. You know me, Beth."

"Is that your signature?"

"It looks like it. But it has to be a forgery." I recalled reports about an election in Texas years ago. I no longer recalled the candidates, just the fight. One side was so adept at smoke screens and manufactured issues that the opposition had to deal with a new diversion almost every day. They eventually ran out of energy and momentum by virtue of having to react to the endless string of diversions. An incumbent with a good record was out.

I could not help seeing the similarities.

"Look, Dave. I'm prepared to believe you. But I can't just ignore this. I'm bound by SEC rules and Colorado state law. I have to cooperate with an investigation of this. I have to cooperate with the police."

I leaned back, feeling completely overwhelmed. "I know, Beth. And you can't let my problems drag down a company you've built from the ground up. What's the next step?"

"I have to put you on administrative leave. I'm confident we can get this resolved in a week or two."

I didn't ask her whether I'd be on salary during that time. I knew how tight margins were. "Can I officially be on vacation, drawing vacation pay, until my paid time off is used up?"

"Sure."

I rose and turned to leave.

"Dave? I do know you. I know this isn't you. We'll get it figured out."

I nodded. We'd have to. I couldn't deal with an endless string of this. When the ship is taking on twice as much water as you're bailing out, the quotient has to change or the end result is inevitable.

I felt like slinking out, regardless of not having done anything wrong. I ignored my desk, ignored any messages, and headed for the door. Gloria and Denise stood in my way.

Gloria have me a silent hug and a peck on the cheek.

Denise took off her half-glasses and gave me a slow look with her brown eyes. "We know you've done nothing wrong, Dave."

My throat felt tight. I swallowed. "That means a lot, you two. Thank you."

From the corner of my eye I saw Stan, still at his desk. His body language said *ambivalent*. He glanced my way and then back to his screen. He rubbed one palm over his mouth. Took a deep breath. But he stayed where he was. I looked back at Gloria and Denise. I gave them a grin that didn't match my inner dread. "I think I'm going to miss you most of all."

Denise caught the allusion. "So we're both the scarecrow?"

"No. You've already got way more brains than me. I'm the one stuck in this mess. It was just a goofy thing to say. I will miss you two, and I will find my way out of this."

Denise gave me a hug and said, "See you around, Dorothy."

I left them in the office with tears in their eyes. I have to be honest. Bolivia was looking better and better all the time.

By the time I reached my latest rental car, I was thinking of a different part of "The Wizard of Oz." "Pay no attention to the man behind the curtain." *Well, Ben, you have my full attention now. I'm going to rip that curtain into shreds and expose you to the world.*

To that end, my next stop was police headquarters. On the way I passed Waterworks car wash. One silver lining in getting a new rental car every few days was that I had no need for cleaning my car. I hardly even needed to buy gas anymore. I could get used to this. But I doubted my insurance company could.

After I had a short wait in the police headquarters lobby, Detective Winchester met me.

"We've got a copy of the Blue Star video from the night you ate there. It's waiting for you. We wouldn't know what we're looking for since you don't have a photo of the woman."

"Any luck finding video showing someone 'borrowing' a cement truck?"

"Not so far."

He led me back to an office and let me take over the computer there. "They have three cameras. The recorder is motion activated, so there's no dead space to skip over."

He showed me three files and explained the controls that would let me pause, fast forward, rewind, and jump forward and back. The controls were actually pretty idiot-proof, not a lot different than watching a movie on cable, except this time, I knew who did it, but not whether she'd appear in this movie or not.

He was about to step out when I said, "Interesting story. I got shot last night."

He raised his chin. I guess enough goes on in the Springs that one shooting more or less can fly under the radar. Or he already knew about it and wanted to hear my take on things before he admitted it. I brought him up to date. He made some more notes in his paper folder and his tablet, and left me to it.

I settled in to go through the Blue Star surveillance recordings. Three files. All three started at 4PM. One for the street out front, one for the side of the building, one covering the rear parking. The recordings all ended at 4AM. I spot-checked. During daylight the video was pretty crisp. By full dark, the video was grainy and took on a black-and-white feel. Every frame was time-stamped. The program showed the actual elapsed time for each of the three files. None were near the actual twelve hours because of the motion-activation cir-

cuitry. The longest recording was the one showing the front of the restaurant and Tejon Street. It took up almost five hours.

Cars arrived, people exited their vehicles. People left the building
and approached their cars. Sometimes they stopped and talked for a
few minutes before getting in and driving off. Some just left immediately. Undoubtedly some parties met each other inside, but now and
then a couple would arrive, wait five or ten minutes outside, and then
be joined by another couple or a single.

I started on the Tejon Street video. I arbitrarily decided that coming
in the front door was the most obvious candidate, if I spotted her
coming in, then I'd be able to see if she parked around the corner on
Tejon Street. If she came around the corner, I could note the time and
be able to look at much less of the side or rear cameras.

The angle on the front camera wasn't great. The view was mostly
looking down on people. Being able to read a license plate was going
to take some real luck. Recognizing the freckled blonde was not going
to be a slam dunk. I worked with the assumption that she'd come in
on her own, but remained open to the idea that one or more accom-
plices had come in with her, or that she tagged along with some other
arriving guests, just to confuse surveillance. I also kept watch for a
very thin, tall man.

I sped up the video whenever I could, but running it more than
double or triple speed increased the risk of missing something. It was
tedious work, keeping me wide awake only because the stakes were
so high. This was my best, and last, shot at a clue. Maybe someone in
Black Forest had a surveillance camera that could see the road, but
canvassing all the residents would be a nightmare.

Then again, I wondered if one of my neighbors on Mesa Road had
a security camera that could have spotted the black pickup or the cement truck. If I told people that some maniac was going around town
and destroying the homes of random people, I might get some cooperation.

I kept at it. Detective Winchester stopped by and I just shook my
head. Nothing so far.

I changed tactics. I decided to zero in on the time of interest. True,
the blonde could have arrived very early, but maybe not. I had come
into the restaurant around eight PM. Holly probably got there around

8:45. By shortly after nine I was getting a free ambulance ride. Well, not free—I hadn't seen the insurance bill yet.

I saw myself arriving. I'd been earlier than I thought—7:50PM. My face wasn't recognizable, but my shirt was. The gait felt like mine. A group of four arrived six minutes later, probably for an eight o'clock reservation.

Two more groups arrived in the next ten minutes, and at the point the camera was mainly being triggered by traffic on the street. I kept watch for a black pickup.

At 8:33PM a group of five entered. At the back of the group was a trim, fair-haired woman, straight hair. She could be the one, but the group didn't fit. I put the viewer into reverse, going slowly.

The group of five collectively put one foot behind another as they backed away from the restaurant like they'd just heard of a bomb threat. Farther. Farther.

There.

Four people had car doors magically open for them as they pulled their hands away from the car. They all backed into their respective seats in the car. And the extra woman started backing across the street, ready for a bad accident.

I ran it forward. The blonde had fallen in line behind the foursome as they hit the sidewalk. But there was no indication of recognition. No one turned to greet her. The group just turned from four to five and proceeded toward the front door. I noted the time: 8:33PM. But I could not get a good view of her face. And, just as bad, I wouldn't be able to see what vehicle she drove.

I ran the video ahead.

At 8:44PM Holly ran across the street just ahead of some passing traffic. I recognized her outfit, her curly hair.

The straight-haired blonde came out at 9:02PM. Maybe she'd just had a drink rather than a meal so she'd seem natural. I was absolutely convinced it was her now, but I could not get a clear view of her face. She waited for passing traffic, and then walked across the street, out of sight of the camera.

At 9:08PM an ambulance appeared. It double parked behind some customer cars and left the lights flashing. The surveillance system apparently recorded no sound, but by this time I assumed the siren was off. If the earliest ambulance had been built with one switch that controlled both the lights and the sirens, I bet Rev 2.0 had separate switches. Two EMTs moved quickly, efficiently, but not at panic speed. People who knew their business.

At 9:14PM they were carrying me out. Holly was hovering, as close as she could stay. They loaded me in the back. It looked like Holly was arguing with the EMTs, gesticulating hands, rapid movement. They refused to let her into the back of the ambulance with me. One EMT drove and the other joined me in the back. Holly raced away, presumably to get her car.

Seconds later all that was visible was a slowly dispersing crowd of bystanders and a couple of restaurant staff, as well as a few cars starting to move again, now that the flashing lights were gone. I watched the cars carefully, looking for a black pickup.

No black pickup showed. No pickup at all. And I couldn't see into any of the passing vehicles.

I leaned back, discouraged. I knew barely more than before. This confirmed only what I pretty much already knew and it added no useful information.

I ran through it again, looking for anything I missed.

I arrived. Holly arrived. The straight-haired blonde arrived. The blonde left. I got a ride to Penrose emergency room.

Holly.

The straight-haired blonde crossing the street.

It clicked.

Across the street was the Millibo Art Theatre and its parking lot, a former church parking lot. What if the blonde parked there? Probably some people did since the lot was so large. And Holly might have an in with the MAT people. Maybe she could convince them to let me see their video surveillance. If they in fact had cameras. And if the data hadn't been erased already.

Chapter 35

I pulled out my phone and called Holly. The call went to voice-mail. At the beep, I said, "Holly, this is Dave Barlow. I know you've done a lot already, but I need one more favor. Can you call me?"

I was going back over the sections where I could see the straight-haired blonde when Detective Winchester checked in again.

"I found her," I said. "But I'm afraid it's not too helpful."

I showed him the sections.

"I see what you mean." He took a seat next to me. "I knew there would be nothing we could use in court, but this doesn't even give us enough to help find her."

I nodded. "I feel better with a little external corroboration, but I understand."

"The direction she's walking—" He made a thoughtful face, as though he was visualizing the scene. "She's walking across the street. Isn't there a church or something there?"

I explained about the MAT. That the building used to house a church.

He said, "Maybe they've got video coverage. I'll check into it."

"Please. In the meantime, I know someone who might be able to help me get access."

With a mechanical pencil he made a notation in his folder and then he touched the screen on his tablet several times adding a to-do item to what looked like an enormous list. He double-checked the blonde's arrival time and departure time with me.

He was saying, "Anything else I should—" when my phone rang.

The caller ID said it was Holly. I held up a finger. "Hey, Holly. Thanks for calling me back."

"Sure, what do you need?" She sounded happy. Most of my days lately had made me feel tired and down, as if I were assigned to painting over graffiti, only to see new stuff appear after I'd moved a few feet away. It was nice to have *something* go right.

"I'm trying to track down the woman who spiked my drink in the Blue Star. I'm at police headquarters now, looking at Blue Star surveillance video. I've spotted her, but the video doesn't have a good view of her face, and she didn't park in the Blue Star lot. She came from across the street."

"From the MAT?"

"Maybe. I was thinking that since you know those people you might be able to talk them into letting me look at their video of the parking lot. If they have any security cameras."

"I'm on it." The line went dead.

I didn't know if Holly was one of those people who don't say goodbye on the phone, or if we might have just been cut off coincidentally, or whether she'd call back. But Detective Winchester was waiting.

"I may have some help," I told him. "I'll keep you posted."

He made me promise to let him know what I found and then showed me out. As we walked, I wished Cathy had been the feminine voice on the line. Getting friendly cooperation from Holly was a good thing, but not nourishing the way hearing from Cathy would have been. Before Cathy came along I was putting one foot ahead of the other and getting through life. But getting by was so much less than feeling joy and excitement. And happiness.

I hadn't even reached my replacement rental car when my phone rang again.

"Holly?"

"Got it. I talked to the owner, and she's fine with letting you look at the video."

"That's great! When can I do it?"

"Right now. She's already getting ready for the evening show. I'll meet you there."

"I can't thank you enough, Holly."

"Hey, we've got to get this stuff to stop, am I right?"

I could not have asked for a better sidekick. I should have been calling her "Robin." But probably no one really wanted to be the side-kick. Robin possibly saw himself as the hero and viewed Batman as an older mentor. Or a creepy older guy with an interest in boys.

"You're right. I'll be there in ten minutes."

The sky was partly cloudy as I drove south on Tejon Street to meet Holly. I kept watch for a black pickup. The only one I saw was coming north as I was coming south.

As I pulled into the MAT parking lot, Holly was waiting outside. She wore skinny jeans that were closer to the paint family than the clothing family, and her top was similarly tight. Trying to read the lettering on her t-shirt was like looking at a funhouse mirror, but I was no longer one to give up easily. The letters said, "Don't try any-thing funny. This could be serious."

I'd been missing talking to Cathy, missing her laughter, her smile, her friendship. Now I also missed the physical side of things. Holly gave me a tight hug, and I missed the physical side of things even more.

"We were rehearsing when you called. Not a minute later, Steph walked in. How cool is that?"

"And Steph can let us see the video?"

"Right."

She led me inside. We went through the lobby and along a corridor that opened onto the stage and tiered movie-theater seating. We kept going into a back-stage room.

Mounted on the wall was a nice-sized monitor. In a rack to the side was some equipment that I took to be the recorder, and a keyboard and mouse. No desk or chairs, but we could get by.

Holly said, "I'll find Steph. She can set us up."

Moments later Holly returned with a woman in her forties wearing oversized round glasses. She gave us a quick tour. Fortunately their setup was very similar to what I'd already seen, so the learning curve was no more than a couple of minutes. They had five cameras. Two on the large parking lot north of the building, one on the narrow lot to the west, and one each on the other two sides.

"Thank you so much for letting me see the video," I said as she started to move away.

"Thank Holly. She made the difference between a favor and a court order. She's a big part of our success."

Holly beamed like a lonely girl just invited to the prom.

I started with the camera showing the eastern half of the large parking lot since that was the side closest to the Blue Star. The view showed a central row of grille-to-grille parking spaces. Closer in, another six slots. Far to the right were four parallel-parking spots. And beyond the central grid was a dirt strip that allowed another single row of cars to park more haphazardly.

I looked at my notes and skipped ahead to shortly before nine on the night in question. The lot was about ninety percent full. Their video also jumped over sections without motion.

"There she is!" Holly yelled right in my ear. "Oh, sorry." She gave me a wry grin. "This is great."

It was good but not great. The straight-haired blonde walked into frame from the left side, moving briskly. The time stamp was a couple of minutes earlier than I expected, but that just meant that at least one of the two independent surveillance systems had not had its clock set right on the money.

The shot was from lower than on the Blue Star video, but I could still barely make out her face. My imagination was filling in the missing details, so I was sure it was her, but the picture was nowhere near what law enforcement would need to take action.

We watched her travel across the parking lot to the right, walking east. Next to a parked car near the right-hand edge of the frame, she stopped.

"What's she waiting for?" Holly said with her indoor voice.

"She tailgated a foursome into the restaurant, I suspect because she didn't want to be easily identified as a single visitor. I think she waited until she saw a group she could slide in with."

"That bitch."

I smiled at Holly.

"Just sayin'."

According to the time stamp, she waited there almost five minutes, giving the impression of impatience. Then she moved away quickly.

I sped ahead as fast as I dared. At the time I expected, she came back into view, moving even faster than before, but not running. Not enough to attract attention. At the left edge of the screen, she vanished.

"Let's look at the next camera," I said, and selected that recording.

I found the time on the recording where she had initially come into frame. There she was. I put the player into reverse and normal speed. She briskly walked backward.

Beside me, I was aware of Holly holding her breath.

Near the left end of the center row of parking spots, the blonde backed into a car. On the passenger side.

"She was with someone," Holly exclaimed.

I nodded. "But I can't see into the car. There's just not enough light."

"Can you tell anything? You recognize the make and model of the car?"

"No. Other than saying it's a sedan and made in the last ten to twenty years, I think, I can't tell." I used my phone to take a picture of the screen image. "Maybe if I take a picture to a car salesman or a car buff, I can find out."

"Great idea."

I jumped ahead. At the expected time, the blonde came back into view, walked fast over to the sedan, and got in. I froze the video while the car door was open. "The dome light must be deliberately turned off. I don't see any extra light."

"Crap. So this hasn't helped?"

"No, it's been a big help," I said, pretty much discouraged. "I really appreciate your—" I hesitated.

"What?"

I reached for the controls again. "Look there." I pointed to another car.

"What?"

"Look at the headlight flare." As another car passing through the lot went by, the headlights momentarily lit the license plate and windshield. I couldn't read the plate, but it gave me an idea.

I let the video roll. Moments later, the sedan's headlights came on and it eased out of its space. I took some more stills as the car changed orientation. "Maybe these will help my car buff."

The car passed out of view without me being able to see the blonde or the driver.

I jumped back to the starting time, when the blonde got out of the sedan, and I played it in reverse. The car had pulled into the lot ten or fifteen minutes after I'd gone in. It waited there several minutes before the blonde got out. This time I let the video run.

Five recorded minutes passed. Another five. Another five.

There. A light flared on our mystery sedan. Probably headlights coming in from the road to the west of the lot. I backtracked a couple of seconds.

I found the single-frame key and started tapping it, moving forward a thirtieth of a second at a time. Holly and I both leaned forward toward the screen.

The light was brighter in the next frame, but for some reason that frame was fuzzier. I hit the frame-advance key again.

In that frame and in the next, light from the other car's headlights hit the car and driver of the sedan.

It was hard to tell, but the emblem on the front of the car reminded me of the styled "M" on Mazda cars.

I stared. Overall the frame was fairly clear and sharp, but we were looking at a pretty small portion of the picture. The driver's features were not even as sharp as you'd get by looking at one of the background bystanders in a typical courthouse-steps interview, but it was just sharp enough that I thought I recognized his blond good looks.

"I'll be damned," I said softly.

"What? You recognize him?"

"I think so. That has to be Kevin Mayer. He's Ben Stuart's son-in-law. He's married to Maddy Stuart, Ben's daughter."

Chapter 36

I stared at the still frame showing Kevin Mayer. This all made no sense to me. I got out my phone and took a picture of the image on the screen.

Holly stepped back from the monitor. "So, what does this mean? And can you show this to the cops?"

"I'll tell the cops about it, but I don't think there's anything they can do yet. I think this is Kevin, but the picture is so grainy that I can't be certain. I don't think it's the kind of thing that would hold up in court. And I can't figure it out."

"What do you know so far?"

The backstage room at the MAT felt warmer than it had been. "Do you have some time? It might help me to talk this through. We could go back to the Bristol Pub."

She glanced at her watch. "Sure. I'm good for an hour at least."

"Great. Just make sure no one spikes my drink." I grinned at her.

"You got it."

The sun had dipped below the mountains by the time we walked from the MAT across the street to Ivywild School. I realized how little I had eaten during the day.

"Can I get a sandwich in the Bristol Pub?" I asked.

"Not sure. But the Meat Locker has sandwiches."

A few minutes later we were in the Ivywild school in the Meat Locker restaurant, sitting at a table with drinks in front of us. We were in an alcove to the side, where the only traffic would be for adjacent tables. I'd ordered a sandwich. Holly had a latte and declined the offer of food.

"OK," I said. "I'll try to make this very brief. Just the key points."

"Got it." Holly was attentive, like a game-show contestant ready for the next challenge.

"I guess this all started a little over a year ago. I was engaged to Allison Stuart. She was one of two daughters of Ben Stuart."

"I've heard that name."

"He's a very wealthy guy. Made gazillions in business, then retired. Anyway, Allison and I get engaged. This was at the time of the Waldo Canyon fire."

She nodded. Everyone in town knew about the fire.

"We took a trip out of town and we were driving—*I was driving*—over Monarch Pass when a tire blew. We went over the side and Allison was killed." As I talked, a too-vivid image of Allison hanging by her seatbelt obscured my view for a second.

"Oh, my God."

I swallowed hard and waited a moment for my voice to get less shaky. "Since then, I've had only a little contact with her father, Ben. We both took it hard, of course. Lately his health has been failing." I took a sip. "And then a couple of months ago, by random chance I met Cathy."

"Is she another daughter?"

"No. Completely unrelated to the Stuart family. No connections at all. Anyway, Cathy and I started dating. Not long after that, things started to go off the rails."

"You started having fights with her?" It was good Holly was interested in this, but she seemed eager to run with the ball before knowing which direction I threw it.

"No. I mean the reunion. She was with me then. And then a couple of days later my car was filled with concrete."

The light in Holly's eyes dimmed a bit as I said "reunion" but she recovered.

"Other stuff, too. Like the poisoning at the restaurant. And yesterday someone shot at me, doing his best to kill me."

"Oh, my God." She demanded I tell her more about yesterday afternoon, so I did. Fortunately her interest stopped short of wanting to see the bullet hole.

I went on. "Twice recently I've seen Ben Stuart. He's as much as admitted he's behind this. I think he's angry because he feels my carelessness killed his daughter. And I think he's angry that I was able to find someone new in my life."

My sandwich arrived.

"That looks terrific," Holly said. "I could be your food taster." She was trim enough that it looked like tasting was as far as she got with meals.

I grinned and cut part of it off for her. "So here's what I don't understand so far. One, Ben told me basically he's messing with my life but not trying to kill me. But the evidence says someone *is* trying to kill me."

"He could be a liar."

"True. But I can't figure out why he'd lie about that. We were alone, in a place that wasn't bugged. He even swept for listening devices."

"OK."

"The next puzzle, maybe the biggest puzzle, is seeing Kevin on the video. By the way, can you ask your friend to not erase that video? Even better would be if you could get a copy of it."

"You got it." She got her phone from her bag and touched the screen. "Note to self. Get copy of the video from Steph." She put her phone back and looked back at me. "So why is it funny to see Kevin there?"

"Kevin is married to Ben's only other daughter, Maddy. He's the son of rich parents, and he's married to a rich woman. So he's rich. I can see Ben doing all this to get back at me, knowing that if he's caught, he's dying anyway. But Kevin is my age, give or take, so basically he's fairly young and rich and I can't see him risking all that just to humor his father-in-law. And he probably barely knew Allison, so he shouldn't be personally angry about the car accident."

"Maybe he's doing it for his wife, Maddy you said?"

"Well, Maddy's relatively young, too, and rich. I can't see her risking an easy life for this. I guess the straight-haired blonde could have been brought in, though, because I'd recognize Kevin and Maddy."

"Maybe it isn't Kevin in the video then. You said you can't be certain."

"I can't. But the coincidence involved in seeing someone who looks just like one of the core family members just seems too much. I think that's Kevin."

"So what's next?"

"For one thing, I need to find out more about Kevin." I looked at the time. "The time you mentioned is up. I should let you go."

Holly didn't seem ready for the adventure to be over. My nightmare, her adventure. "Are you going to see Cathy?"

"No. She's off limits for the time being." I explained about the threat in the text that came after my house was razed.

"Wow. This guy is awful." She picked up her purse and we headed outside. Just outside the door, she said, "Look," starting tentatively. "I've got a computer at my place if you need to use the web to find out more about this guy."

I looked hard at her. She looked directly back. I had the distinct feeling the offer was for more than just some web surfing.

Holly stood there in the gathering dark, her eyes luminous, her lips slightly parted. *Must. Use. Impulse. Control.*

"That's really generous, Holly. I absolutely appreciate it. But I don't want to put you in danger any more than I have already. If this guy gets angry when he sees me enjoying life, he could extend his threat to you."

It would all be so easy, and such a buffer from the storm. But I wanted to be back with Cathy, and Holly was just the person to jeopardize that.

I also saw little good in hurting Holly's feelings. "If things were different..." I kissed her cheek. "Thank you more than I can say."

Holly took it well. "OK then, take care of yourself. And tell me how it all comes out." She gave me a very tight hug. Her breasts compressing against my chest, her warm cheek against mine, lifted my, er, spirits.

She waved goodbye as she headed for the MAT. "Get that bastard, OK?"

I watched her go, simultaneously grateful for her help and wondering if there was a way she could actually be in on this. She was part of the reunion and she was an actress. Maybe she had brilliantly ad libbed when I confronted her and took an opportunity to "work" with me to see what was going on in my head.

No. I just couldn't buy it.

I stood there for five or ten minutes, thinking about Cathy and how much I wanted to call her, to see her, to talk to her. And let's be honest, to undress her and feel that strongest of human connections. I felt so alone. The time with Holly had helped me think things through, but I just wanted my life back. And Cathy.

I realized more than that, though. My PTSD symptoms had been less in evidence lately than at any point in a long time. I'd spent years keeping my head down, tying to avoid conflict at almost any cost. But apparently there had been a cost. Right now I still faced some huge obstacles, ones I might not even overcome, but I felt more alive than I had in a long time. On some level, fighting back seemed to be therapeutic.

I found my rental Camry where I had parked it. It seemed to be unmolested, and it started up just fine. I wondered for the first time if I should be looking under my car for explosives when I came back to it. I had made the transition from thinking that sitting down on a whoopee cushion was the worst I'd likely encounter, to thinking turning an ignition key could be my last worldly action.

It was full dark now, so all but a very oblivious couple of drivers had their headlights on. I started heading for my motel room, but in the last few seconds before a traffic light, I looked and saw an open lane and moved over. I headed for my old house. My lot, that is.

It looked much the same as the last time I'd been here. A bit like the leveled ruins of a half-dozen mom and pop stores being torn down to make room for a generic big box store selling products made by people on the other side of the globe. Who knows, maybe that's what the remaining mom and pop stores had to sell now, too.

I stood near the lip of the hill and communed with the birds that were starting to quiet down for the night. A couple of towhees were calling back and forth to each other. *Chirp, chirp, trill.* The call of a dove, or perhaps an owl, though less likely, sounded in the dark. My very question. Who?

Ben Stuart? Kevin Mayer? Kevin had to be part of this, but why?

I missed my house. I missed Cathy. I missed my life. But, by God, I was going to get them back.

I got into my car and drove down Mesa and then down 19th to Uintah where I pulled into the parking lot of my favorite mom and pop place, Cy's Drive-In Restaurant, that seemed to be a holdover from the fifties or sixties with pictures of Elvis and Bogart. The drive-in that time forgot. Not re-created after the fact like Gunther Toody's, which was also good, but a true original. Their burgers were wonderful, and made from local beef. I hoped they resisted the onslaught of chains headquartered a thousand or more miles away. I paid for a burger, a chocolate malt, and some deep-fried mushrooms, happy to do my part in keeping the dream alive.

In my motel room, which seemed to have been unmolested except by the maid, I ate my haul and fired up the laptop. I knew a fair amount about Ben Stuart, but what did I know about Kevin Mayer? Aside from the fact that he could sometimes be found in the company of a freckled blonde about his age and not his wife. And that one or both of them had access to a drink additive that could not possibly be on the bartenders' short list.

You have to love the Internet. People complain about free-for-all government wiretapping, as I do, and then freely post online who they're dating, what they had for breakfast, and the size of their latest stool. OK, most people don't do the last part. But it does make you wonder how so many people drop their phones in the toilet.

If Kevin Mayer was Mr. Average, I might have been limited to Facebook and other social media sites. But family money lifted him into a wealth of news stories.

Once upon a time, Kevin Mayer was born to Warren and Suzanne Mayer. Warren and Suzanne as a team founded Mayer Sprayer, a garden tool company centered on a high-pressure washer and other tools powered by pressure from a garden hose. "Safer than electricity and gas. Quieter than electricity and gas. Everyone has a garden hose. Not everyone has a long extension cord or a can of gas."

Some things I vaguely remembered. The Woodland-Park-based company had done very well, becoming one of the latest and greatest things.

Then I saw some things I'd either never known or I'd forgotten. The company had had a big battle with investors about how the profit share was to be calculated, the Mayers claiming some big expenses, like a corporate jet, that the investors thought should come out of the Mayers' profits.

At about the same time, Consumer Reports had done an in-depth article about the Garden Washer and their line of accessories. They concluded that the tools worked as advertised, but at a huge cost of wasted water. The Mayers countered that the water went into the garden anyway. But the damage was done.

When buyers and stock holders hear a horror story and then a re-traction, they tend to retain the horror story. Selective memory. A bit like a dog easily hearing "Dinner!" but being preoccupied when the owner says, "Off the couch!" Sales went over a waterfall. Loan payments on business extensions were overdue. Investors sued. Mayer Sprayer was hosed.

I couldn't find anything to show that the company or Kevin's parents had ever recovered. So Kevin had gone from little rich boy to little average boy. Not long after, around the time Allison and I went off Monarch Pass, Kevin and Maddy had gotten engaged. And then, a few months later, in September, they were married. Kevin had gone from riches to rags to riches.

Kevin had attended college at the University of Minnesota in Minneapolis and had come home three years ago with a Masters in Business Administration. He'd come back from college, probably all ready to pursue the American dream to start at the top, but the company had begun its eighteen-month death throes already. It must have been like watching a winning lottery ticket go through the laundry in a pants pocket.

But none of that explained why Kevin would participate in a scheme that could land him in jail and throw away his future with Maddy. Except that no one really goes into a scheme like that expecting to be caught.

On the city government site, where real estate was assessed and documented, I found Kevin and Maddy's address. They were in a typically upscale house on Camels View, a street inside Kissing Camels, a gated community that took its name from a rock formation in the nearby Garden of the Gods. The map indicated their house was along the golf course. Maybe there was something to be learned by going over there and saying, "Hi."

Not tonight, though. I was tired and hurting. I could ignore the pain some of the time, but now the recently patched bullet wound made me take another pain pill. And the pain pills made me drowsy.

I kept being pulled back to one question. *Why Kevin?* The reunion seemed to have been set up by the tall man, and I didn't see how that guy could be Kevin. Just not the same build.

I started compiling an incident list. Reunion, concrete, black pickup mirror, house, poisoning, Black Forest ambush. What patterns could I see? For one, the pickup mirror and the Black Forest ambush both featured the black pickup.

Then I recalled something that had puzzled me before.

Taunting texts. I thought back. The reunion, the concrete incident, and the house razing were all followed up by texts. But not the pickup mirror, the poisoning, and the ambush.

So the non-lethal incidents had all been followed by taunting texts. The deadly stuff no. Why would that be?

One explanation occurred to me, but it was just too far out. There could be two teams at work. But that would imply I'd so pissed off two separate people that both of them had it in for me. And I still couldn't see Kevin risking so much on me. Two teams, both run by Ben, compartmentalized so that exposing one team would keep the other safe? That made barely more sense.

Fatigued from the past couple of days, I gave up.

I lay in bed for a long time with the lights out. The latest pain pill was gradually kicking in. I missed being able to curl up next to Cathy. For a second I wondered what Holly was doing right then, and my thoughts went immediately back to Cathy. I believe I was still thinking about her when I finally fell asleep.

~~~

In the dream, Allison and I were in a car. Headlights behind us. Allison telling me about some dream she'd had.

Headlights gained on us, brighter and brighter as they came closer, growing in size until it felt like there were two suns in the rear-view mirror. The road ahead held our long shadow, and trees to both sides were lit as though a photographic flash had gone off and it lasted for several seconds.

Then all was dark and we were in one of those flying cars Popular Science *had featured before I was born. I pulled the stick back, pulling the wheel toward me, and nothing happened.*

Light flared again, like a nearby nova.

Darkness again. Silence.

Flashlights flared in the distance, visible through a spider-webbed window.

They came closer. Closer.

Someone knocked on the window. Thud. Thud. Thud. *I looked over to see who was knocking. And there, his face lit like a jack-o'-lantern's by a flashlight pointing up from under his chin, was someone I recognized.*

Kevin Mayer.

Chapter 37

I woke still feeling tired. I had the feeling that I'd been troubled by dreams, a raw free-floating unsettled sensation, but whatever I'd dreamed about was now murky.

Allison had been very interested in processing her dreams, in becoming a more fully integrated person by narrowing that gap between the conscious mind and the vast unconscious reserves. She'd made it a deliberate intent, a habit, to recall her dreams, and she was far more successful at that than I was.

I lay in bed, missing a few more recent weekend mornings that Cathy and I had lingered in bed. A few times I'd fixed her breakfast in bed. And once or twice, dessert.

It would have been so easy to call her. And so easy to get her to join me in the bull's-eye. I didn't touch my phone.

In the motel parking lot, I checked my new rental car for the presence of another GPS tracker. Nothing.

I'd eaten a number of crappy happy meals in the past few days. Combined with the recent wear and tear on my body from running full-tilt through the woods and getting shot, the net result was that I was feeling run-down. I didn't have to be in the office today—good news, bad news—so I treated myself to a sit-down breakfast at Village Inn. Still restaurant food, but a step up from drive through. The breakfast rush had subsided by time I walked into the one on Garden of the Gods Road. I sat where I could keep watch on my car.

With two pieces of French toast, some orange juice, and a couple of strips of bacon inside me, I felt ready for the morning.

A mile or two south of there, on Nevada Avenue, was a Kmart. I found a cheap, white, bucket-style golf hat or tennis hat that would serve as a partial disguise. I thought about buying some white tennis shoes and a sweater to tie around my neck and decided that was going too far. Instead I found a windbreaker with a pocket. A pair of sunglasses larger than my regular ones completed my ensemble.

The Kmart was just north of Fillmore Street, which led the direction I wanted to go. I headed west, over the Interstate, through the under-construction interchange, and up the steep hill to the top of the mesa.

A left on Mesa Road would have taken me to my house, my lot that is, but I took a right. Soon the amazing rock formations in Garden of the Gods were visible on the left. Some expensive new houses were going up also on the left, several startlingly close to the subdivision's perimeter wall for such lavish homes. I imagined some people on the right side of the road were sorry to have the view obstructed, but that's life near the Rockies when you don't control the viewshed.

A minute later I drove slowly around a traffic circle opposite the front gate to the Kissing Camels gated community. I wasn't going in that way. One or two guards occupied a small peaked-roof structure at the center of a large green median. Beyond them lay an iron gate on rails barring the way in unless they pressed a button.

The exit road was completely open. I could have driven right in if it were an emergency and I didn't mind people being on my tail immediately. I was hoping for something more subtle than that today.

I kept driving. The stone fence beyond the sidewalk was only two or three feet tall, no real barrier to someone just walking in, but beyond the wall was an open, grassy strip maybe fifty yards deep. Anyone hoping to cross it unnoticed would have an easier time buying a tube of travel-size toothpaste at Costco.

Houses beyond the grassy area were mostly low, one-story homes with earth-tone walls and roofs. As I continued, the stone fence gave way to a wrought-iron fence. The road curved gently to the right and trees started to fill the barrier strip. There was no parking here, though, so it still wasn't right for my approach.

Next up was another entry road, this one unmanned, but an iron gate stretched across the road just behind a key reader. I was keyless, so I kept going.

The road curved back to the right again, now passing even more expensive houses paradoxically built much closer to the road than the less expensive houses to the southeast. Mesa Road crested a gentle hill and a lookout point on the left went by. Directly ahead in the distance lay one of the biggest eyesores in the region, the scar.

The scar was a site of an enormous gravel-extraction area where a mountainside had been turned into a clear-cut graded slope gouged out of the Rockies. The beautiful view of the mountains was one of the area's very biggest attractions, but it was cheaper to dig for gravel right here in plain sight than to go miles into the foothills and quarry it where only a few people would notice. That profit-over-esthetics battle had been waged for decades.

The quarry company was making efforts to rehabilitate the land, planting grass and trees to slow rain run-off. Their efforts were complemented by tens of thousands of volunteer hours from citizens. The scar had once been unmistakable from as far away as the horizon, a huge white scab on the dark mountains, but now it was turning green and looking a bit more natural so you'd notice it only if you were within ten or twenty miles of it. It definitely looked better, but some said it would always look unnatural, forever a reminder that we favored low cost over the natural look of the mountains.

Property taxes in the Springs remained a bit under the national average. Part of the population claimed that was exorbitantly high, while others said that explained the habitually high number of potholes and the money-saving programs to turn out street lights and cut down watering of parks. As the arguing continued, another new huge scar was expanding north of the first one.

The road swept down from the mesa at a steeper angle, passing a luxury property overlooking Garden of the Gods. At the base of the hill, Mesa Road fed into 30th Street and I went right, heading north. In less than a mile, on the left was the entrance to the Navigators, a Christian ministry that had bought the Glen Eyrie property, including the Castle that General Palmer once called home.

On the right was what interested me, a rest-area parking lot big enough for more than a dozen cars. I pulled in, joining only two other vehicles, both empty.

I was a bit more paranoid and observant than I had been a couple of weeks ago. One of the vehicles was an old red Volkswagen mini-bus, and the other was an old yellow Chevy Malibu. To the east, straight ahead of my car, rocky open space swept up to the western edge of the flat-topped mesa.

I got out of the rental Camry. I considered leaving my new gun in the trunk, but in the end decided to play safe and take it with me. I donned the windbreaker and put the gun in the pocket. The possibility of getting arrested for carrying a concealed weapon without a permit crossed my mind and vanished into the darkness.

I locked up and followed a concrete path that led toward the gradual slope. For the next part of the trek, hiking boots would have been nice, but once I reached the top of the mesa and wanted to appear to be a resident just out for a walk, hiking boots would look wrong.

The morning was partly cloudy, in the low seventies, a perfect Colorado day. I turned onto a wide asphalt trail that led around the base of the mesa. At the intersection was a sign warning about the danger of flooding. Bizarrely, the base of the sign was wrapped with a crocheted something or other, vaguely like a sock open on both ends.

I took the asphalt path north for maybe ten yards and exited onto a narrow dirt path that led the direction I wanted to go—up toward the mesa top.

To the south, a man and a woman walked with their dog on a leash. No one seemed overly interested in just one more hiker, and from any distance at all, no one could see that I was wearing loafers. Enough people came the way I was traveling to maintain a trail through the rocky landscape. I kept following the trail upward, as the grass and yucca gave way to low-lying three-leaf sumac and scrub oak. The ground was sprinkled with milkweed, prickly pear cactus, yucca plants. The rocky trail was bordered by lots of young green tumbleweeds that looked nothing like the stiff and prickly rolling brown husks we would see in the fall and winter. The air was clean and dry, the slope mild by Colorado standards. The faint smell of the dust I kicked up almost made me sneeze.

The trail curved left, but a narrower dirt trail spun off to the right. The narrow trail petered out near the top of the mesa and the land turned steeper, rockier. I climbed another twenty yards past some Siberian elms. This was the only stretch where hiking boots would have gripped better. An anemic barbed-wire fence presented a minimal barrier. Previous hikers had also apparently ignored the "No dumping or trespassing" sign because the strands had been stretched and repositioned for easy passage. Near the top of the rise was a second barbed-wire fence, but it ended right there and a mere two paces took me around the left end of it.

A dirt road led away to the left, following the lip of the mesa. A paved turnaround connected to a paved road following the mesa edge to the right. According to the map, this was the end of Hill Circle. Directly across the road lay the Glen Eyrie reservoir. No checkpoint. No wall. Just another barbed-wire fence that was easy to cross, even with my tender knee and aching thigh.

The reservoir was roughly circular, a bit more than a couple of football fields across, surrounded by gentle rock-lined banks. During the Waldo Canyon fire I'd seen it several times on the news as helicopters hovered over it, rippling the surface with rotor-wash as they used huge hanging buckets to scoop up water that they then flew over the fire and dumped. Today the scene was peaceful, deserted.

To the north I got a clear view of a large telecom company campus, the Mountain Shadows residential area, and the nearby burn scar, populated with burned toothpick-shaped residue of pine trees. On the eastern horizon lay the Cragmor area neighborhood and the campus of the University of Colorado at Colorado Springs near the top of the ridge.

A look back toward the path I'd taken to the top said no one was following me.

I walked along the path that ringed the reservoir. Eventually the path headed southeast, almost directly toward my destination. To my right lay part of a golf course. Beyond that lay a pond about a third the size of the reservoir. The golf course almost completely circled the pond. Nearby a foursome in two carts drove past me on the course.

When the path around the reservoir curved again, I had a choice. I decided to get off the path and cut across the course. No one was approaching at the moment, so I figured I'd be safe.

On the other side lay the continuation of Hill Circle. I could have walked along the road all the way from where it reached the mesa top, but my way was shorter.

Very expensive homes on large lots bordered this part of Hill Circle. I walked east, just a neighborhood guy out for a walk. Now my loafers looked right at home.

Houses started appearing more closely together. Big, clipped, water-sucking lawns divided by large circular driveways. Beyond the next few houses I could see either another golf course or a continuation of the one I'd crossed earlier. I had little use for golf. Taking a long walk in a scenic location and talking with a friend was good, but conversations on golf courses tended to be quick spurts between shots where everyone was preoccupied with the score and moving quickly enough to avoid holding up the following party.

I took a right at the next corner, Camels View, having seen three golf carts and two regular cars in motion so far. Large houses lined both sides of the road now, with golf courses showing in the distance between the houses on both sides. No sidewalks for some reason, but all the individual mailboxes were housed in oversize pillars along the curb. More lush green lawns.

This was Kevin and Maddy's street, so my relaxed stroll now felt more tense. I tilted my tennis hat farther down in front and adjusted my sunglasses. My gait might trigger some sense of familiarity if they saw me, so I tried my best to change it by walking more slowly. I wished I had a dog as cover.

I was just thinking about whether to risk calling Kevin to see if he was at home, and trying to remember the block-my-number code, when ahead of me on the right a late-model blue Mazda pulled out of a driveway and headed toward me. I was too far away to see for sure, but something about the driver's vague outline made me think of Kevin. Or I remembered the car from the MAT security recording.

Quickly I put my phone in video recording mode. I turned toward the house in front of me and held the phone as though I was taking photos of the house, but I used the front-facing camera so I was actually recording myself. And whatever happened to show up over my shoulder.

The Mazda travelled past me. As I saw it on the screen, I subtly maximized the time it was on screen. Seconds later it stopped at the corner I'd turned in at, and took a right. It was gone.

In the renewed quiet, I played the video. Seconds later, came the closest approach. I could not believe my luck. Yesterday, Holly had been a big help. Today, I arrived at Kevin's Colorado Springs house just as he and Maddy were driving away. I hoped they were going somewhere that would take them a long time. Like the emergency room. Or for a root canal.

As I got closer, I confirmed that the house I'd determined was theirs was in fact where the car had come from. It was a huge, sprawling two-story house covered with beige stucco. Circular driveway. Most of their neighbors had about six carefully placed and manicured trees each. Kevin and Maddy probably had a dozen evergreens and a couple of trios of aspens. Gray, peaked roofs. Lots of skylights. Manicured lawn just like all the neighbors. Low bushes butted up against most of the walls I could see. Two large flowerbeds.

Aside from the possibility of being recognized by Kevin, this was the most difficult stage. I didn't want neighbors calling either the cops or Kissing Camels security. I also didn't want neighbors coming at me with golf clubs. There was probably an oversupply nearby. I had this sudden bizarre image of being pursued by a slow-moving crowd, not of brain-seeking zombies, but plaid-pants-wearing, middle-aged men with raised golf clubs. Foursomes of the dead.

I did not stop and look around furtively. My heightened senses told me that would be a guaranteed neighborhood watch red flag. I walked calmly up to the front door and pushed the doorbell button.

My mind raced as I listened for a bell or footsteps, trying to decide how to play it if someone else was home. That decision tree was pruned. No response.

My fail-safe plan was that if I couldn't get in easily from the front, I would quickly but casually move off and then circle back around from another direction, come at the back from the golf course and quickly jimmy a door or break a window. I tried the doorknob just in case but things were not to be that easy.

I turned and moved toward something that had caught my eye.

The garage had a keypad on the door frame.

Feeling a thousand eyes on me from every house in view, I moved calmly to the door, as though I had every right to be there. Thanking the Internet, I tried Kevin's birthday, with and without the year, using the year as two digits then four.

No luck.

From the corner of my eye I spotted a dog walker, an older man who was slowing down as he approached. I tried another combination as I began to perspire. No luck.

The man had stopped right in the middle of the sidewalk.

When I finally tried Maddy's birthday with a four-digit year, the door started rumbling upward. I turned and gave a friendly wave to the old guy. I wondered if he was a next-door neighbor, or neighborhood watch, or had just run out of juice right there. At least he didn't have a golf club.

Chapter 38

As the garage door crept upward, I wondered if I'd find a black pickup inside Kevin and Maddy's garage.

No pickup. Just a black BMW sedan. Maybe this was Maddy's car and they'd driven off in Kevin's car. I put my sunglasses in my shirt pocket and stuffed my golf hat into a back pocket. It was a tight fit, but I didn't care if it looked rumpled. They came that way.

At the entrance to the house, I pushed the garage door control button and the door started rumbling downward. I prayed I was alone in the house and that Kevin and Maddy weren't the kind of people who set booby traps for intruders. At least not in their own house.

I moved inside. A narrow laundry room led from the garage to the kitchen.

In the living room, thick carpet with swirls of earth tones stretched as far as I could see. I moved cautiously toward the front of the house so I could see the dog-walking gentleman.

He wasn't there. No, wait. There he was. He was continuing his path, nearly to the other side of the house now.

My breath came easier. My heart seemed to slow a bit.

I looked around. Huge vaulted-ceiling living room. No beeping from a security system. No flashing panel. Maybe since the house was in a gated community and a thief would presumably be limited to taking stuff he could carry away on foot, Kevin and Maddy didn't feel a need for an additional layer of security.

I had no idea if they were headed to the store for milk or if they were going back up to the guest house on Ben's property, not to return for days. I looked for clues.

Bad news. On the kitchen table lay a cell phone. That could be cause for coming right back, though they could be gone for hours. But odds were they weren't going to the mountains. At least the stove was off, no crock-pot steamed on the counter, and the microwave wasn't counting down.

I hurried my search, paying only superficial attention to the luxury surrounding me. This home would really be a castle in some countries. And in many neighborhoods in the US.

As I started on the kitchen drawers, it occurred to me that if Ben and Kevin managed to maneuver me into breaking and entering, or at least entering, having me thrown in jail for a crime I had really committed would be a terrific coup for them.

I thought about leaving right then. If I were gone before anyone arrived, people might be suspicious, but they wouldn't *know*.

I stayed.

The kitchen was fairly well equipped but sparsely populated with personal possessions. I didn't know if this was their second home and their first home was the guest house in Ben's enclave, or vice versa. For all I knew, this could be house number five.

I found some extra keys, a grocery list, personalized notepad, opened bills, pictures of family and, I assumed, friends. No straight-haired blonde. No tall, slim man. Maddy looked very nice in a bikini. She was a bit prettier than Allison, and her body looked trim and curvy at the same time.

Off the kitchen was a pantry I left for later. Off the living room was a large media room. Given the possibility that they'd be back at any time, I decided I'd better triage. Step one was to determine the scope of my search.

A large lower level was divided into three rooms—a utility room housing the boiler and water tank, a guest bedroom, and a living area with exercise equipment and another large-screen television. The guest bedroom, at the rear of the house, had two windows with window wells. They faced several trees, so I mentally tagged this as my emergency escape route.

Neither window had a screen. In the Springs we had Miller moth season for a week or two, but fairly few mosquitoes. I made sure one window opened silently, then closed and re-locked it.

The level above the main level held the master bedroom suite, a home office that looked more masculine than feminine, and another guest bedroom. The windows were high enough off the ground that I really didn't want to be caught up here. I decided to search this level first, starting with the master suite because it was farthest from the street and hence farthest from any early warning of surprise guests.

I wondered about the response from the local security people if they got a call. Would they send several cars and surround the place, or just send one car in case they were dealing with a mistaken or un-informed neighbor? Probably I'd be OK if they showed up. It was Kevin and Maddy's return that had me most worried.

A sudden noise made me jump. Just a ringing phone. After four rings it went silent.

The master bath looked out on a golf green. And of course Pikes Peak. The windows were set high enough on the walls that guys could walk around with a reasonable expectation of adequate privacy. Belatedly I thought that if I'd consulted with Bruce about another spy cam I might have been in a better position to get more clues. But I'd be leaving behind an obvious clue. Better to come back again if I had to.

The medicine cabinets revealed nothing suspicious. Neither did the drawers in the bathroom, or the toilet tank, or the shelves in the adjacent walk-in closet. Maddy had a large selection of negligees. Kevin had a huge collection of shirts, favoring stripes. Standing in the closet, I wondered how easily I would hear the garage door opening when they returned. Now that I thought about it, I didn't know if they actually used the garage all the time, or if they frequently parked their car in the circular drive.

I had to go with the assumption they mostly used the garage. It did rain from time to time after all, and occasionally in July it hailed. Plus, there could be some homeowners' covenant against vehicles parked outside.

The office seemed to be Kevin's office. His desk phone caller ID log didn't show me anything that immediately shouted *clue*, like calls from a cement mixer rental outfit or Home Razers 'R' Us. I pulled out my phone camera and took a picture of each unique entry. I would go data mining later, assuming I got out of here alive.

His computer was password protected. I used my set of birthday-date guesses and some of the most popular favorites like 123456, but nothing worked.

One desk drawer just held office stuff like a letter opener, stapler, post-its, extra change. Another held bulkier stuff like envelopes, a box of tissue. No pistols.

The file folder drawer held, wait for it, file folders. I thumbed through them as fast as I dared. No receipts for a black pickup or an automatic weapon. No membership renewals from Evil Henchmen, Inc. I photographed a property rental agreement and draft copy of a will. One page said pre-nup notes. I photographed that. I also photo-graphed copies of their marriage certificate, a contract for a new Mazda, and the annual vehicle registration receipts. Some people grasped at straws. I had a fistful of stuff I'd probably never make sense of.

I slid the drawer closed with the side of my elbow, conscious of the possibility of leaving a slew of fingerprint evidence.

A pair of large bookcases held more knick-knacks than books. I looked through both, looking for anything hidden. Most of the books looked like recent popular fiction, not the kind of older classics that might contain a hollowed-out compartment.

On the second bookcase were several boxes of ammunition. A box of .22 cartridges. Three boxes of 9mm Luger rounds. On the far side of that bookcase was a gun safe. It was black, kind of old-timey looking, like an old safe that had been stretched vertically until it was between four and five feet tall but still less than two feet wide or deep.

I tried out some dates on the combination lock, but my attempt was half-hearted. I didn't see myself taking away a weapon even if I got into the safe.

I jumped again as the phone started ringing once more. I looked at caller ID. It showed no name, likely a cell phone, a repeat from the list I had photographed.

In the guest bedroom, I glanced out the front window. No angry crowd with pitchforks. Or golf clubs. I couldn't see anyone on foot at the moment, but a Toyota minivan rolled by without slowing. The bedroom held nothing interesting, less in fact than a motel room because there was no Gideon Bible.

I hurried downstairs, listening intently for the vibrations or sound of a garage door opening. As long as I was close to the door from the laundry room to the garage I opened it so I would hear better.

The guest bedroom on this floor was as sanitized as the one upstairs, so that search went quickly. If I'd been in rip-up-mattresses mode it would have taken a lot longer, but I still had hopes of getting out of here without letting anyone know I was checking things out.

In the media room, the home entertainment center proved barren of clues. Nothing stuffed in the movie boxes I sampled, other than a range of films heavy on chick flicks, comedies, and action fests, light on documentaries and children's films.

Downstairs the search went quickly. That floor held very little in personalization other than a number of paintings and wall hangings, none of which concealed anything of interest behind them.

Frustration was mounting. Nothing I'd found so far really called out, "This is important."

I went back up to the main level. Nothing in the ice cube trays or the freezer that looked suspicious. Most of the containers in the pantry were unopened, commercial products.

I stood, turning slowly around as I wondered what I had missed, worried the garage door could start rumbling upward at any minute.

And then I realized what I hadn't searched.

The garage.

I reached the garage and made sure the door was still down and the Mazda slot still empty. If Kevin and Maddy were keeping secrets, maybe they'd want them protected from prying eyes by being in the gun safe or concealed somewhere I'd missed. But if Kevin were keeping secrets from Maddy, maybe the garage would be a good place. It was traditionally more of a guy place than a gal place, and if he needed to take something with him, like a Colt .45, when he left the house, the garage was one place he could grab it at the last minute without Maddy noticing.

At the back of the garage was a wide workbench that seemed more for storage than for woodworking. A couple sets of metal shelves flanked the workbench. Near the garage door, where I'd be instantly visible if the garage door opened, were a set of golf clubs and some tennis racquets. No lawn mower or snow blower. Presumably the homeowners association took care of lawn care and snow removal.

On the work bench was a large red toolbox. Nothing interesting in it.

I picked through the litter of tools on the workbench. A hammer, a few screwdrivers. Spray cans of paint, WD-40. Some glue. A few rolls of tape. No bent-up truck mirror. No bottles of rat poison.

Below the workbench were some old cans of paint, the kind the builder leaves behind so you have matching touch-up paint if you need it. I guess either they hadn't heard that some latex paint, once frozen, doesn't match the original color too well, or they heated the garage in winter.

In Maddy's black BMW I rifled through the obvious places, especially the glove box. Nothing.

I moved back near the door to the laundry room and scanned the rest of the garage again, feeling frustrated. This had been a big risk for next to nothing.

Because I was right here, I moved to the workbench, bent down, and lifted the cans of paint. Three of them were heavy and sloshed as I shook them.

The one at the back was lighter and didn't slosh at all. Its lid showed fingerprints in the dust.

I tried to pry open the lid without mussing up the undisturbed dust. The lid was stuck tight. The closest screwdriver in the mess on top was a large flat-edge, just right for opening the can. How convenient.

The lid came off easily with the right tool. It had been pressed in place barely more than hand tight.

Jackpot.

Inside, wrapped in a thin towel, was an old cell phone and an unmarked pill bottle.

The cell phone was a flip-top model, years old. It was off. I pressed the *Answer* button for several seconds and it came to life. It booted more quickly than new phones, but still took fifteen or twenty agonizing seconds. The screen indicated it was a pay-as-you-go carrier, the kind you can load up with minutes and not get a bill for a year unless you run out of minutes.

I looked at the caller ID log. Primarily one number, and it showed up multiple times. On the outgoing log, only that number showed up. I photographed both screens and the number of the phone itself. *So, Kevin, you're keeping secrets from Maddy.* Good to know who might be on your team and who might not.

There was no indication of waiting voicemail. I checked the text log. Interestinger and interestinger.

The log went back only to Sunday.

Other person: See you tonight?

Kevin: Can't. M is in town after all. Tomorrow?

Other person: OK. XXX

Kevin: XXX

I supposed the XXX's were kisses, not a reference to an adult movie.

The next traffic wasn't until Monday.

Other person: Made call. He'll be there at 5.

Kevin: Preps done. Meet you at 4.

Monday was the day of the Black Forest ambush.

The latest messages were from last night.

Kevin: M goes back tomorrow. I'll have a couple days in town. See you tomorrow at noon?

Other person. Nooners. My favorite. XXX

Kevin: Me too. We can figure out the next step. This will all be over soon. XXX

I quickly photographed the screens. This wasn't proof at the Detective Winchester level, but I felt certain Kevin had to be the guy in the MAT surveillance video. And the person at this other number was almost certainly the straight-haired blonde. The log didn't go back far enough to show one of the taunting texts. That might have been enough for Detective Winchester to act on, except that this was tainted evidence since Kevin hadn't exactly just handed me his phone and said, "You bet, Dave. I'm happy to waive my rights. And sure, take whatever you need. You're free to use it any way you see fit in a court of law." As I thought about it, though, I supposed the texts were sent via an Internet site that allowed the number to be blocked or spoofed.

I switched off the phone and tucked it back into the paint can.

The unlabeled bottle of pills was an oversized amber vial with a child-proof lid. The pills inside were about the size of baby aspirin but these were white octagons with some tiny numbers on them. The bottle must have contained more than a hundred of them, enough that Kevin wouldn't miss a few, or if he did he might assume he miscounted somewhere along the way. I wondered how many they'd needed to poison me.

I had just put two of them in my pants pocket when I became aware of a new sound. An idling engine.

The sound grew louder and I fumbled to get the lid back on the pill bottle. I tossed the bottle inside the can.

The sound was louder still. The car must have been right outside the garage.

I put the paint-can lid back in place. If I had to, I'd race right out into the neighborhood and start pounding on doors, demanding that someone call the police before Kevin shot me.

With the same screwdriver, I tapped the lid down. Still the door was not rising.

I bent down and put the paint can where I found it, trying to leave the semicircular handle in the same orientation I'd found it in.

The door started rumbling. Daylight showed beneath it.

I jerked my head up and bounced my skull on the bottom of the workbench. I raced for the door to the laundry room.

The door moved higher. I heard raised voices.

One said, "Thanks. Maybe dinner next weekend?"

I reached the laundry room door by the time the garage door had risen a couple of feet.

I was through the door faster than a car salesman can say, "Exclusive of dealer prep and documentation fees."

I closed the door, taking time only to make sure it was actually closed, and I raced into kitchen, through the living room and down the stairs.

I split a fingernail on the window in my haste to get it up. Thank God no one was nearby. I awkwardly scrambled through the window and then managed to push it shut behind me despite the outside lip being much thinner than the inside.

I stood, and edged sideways. For the moment, I was invisible to anyone inside the house. But it was only a matter of time before some golf foursome came by and wondered what was going on. I donned my sunglasses. I reached for my back pocket and didn't feel the golf hat.

Oh, there it was. It had just shifted. I put it on.

I strode casually but quickly to the nearest evergreen, wondering if I were visible from the master bedroom window and if Kevin or Maddy were in that room. Maybe they were in the kitchen, looking out.

No cries arose. I navigated around the tree, putting it between me and their house, but exposing me to the neighbor's house.

I kept moving away as if I were either out on a walk, or just inspecting the perimeter of my lot. Reflections on nearby windows kept me from seeing anyone who might be watching me.

I reached the golf course and kept walking north, casually but with deliberate speed, and seconds later I was out of view of Kevin and Maddy's house. No sirens. No loud shouts.

I kept walking north, along the boundary between the golf course and the other houses on Kevin's street. My path was probably unorthodox but, I guessed, not forbidden. As I noticed people looking out on the view, I waved jauntily. *Howdy, neighbor. Hi, there.*

I stopped shaking about halfway back to my car.

Chapter 39

No one had come following me as I walked back from Kevin and Maddy's. Clouds rolled over the mountains and thunder rumbled, announcing the possibility of lightning, as a monsoon-season storm approached. Many summer days along the Colorado front range started with a clear, crisp morning. Clouds came in over the mountains in mid-afternoon, and the high point was an afternoon downpour with wind and sometimes hail. Then, typically, it would clear up in an hour.

The pattern was holding so far today. The rain waited until I crossed the last stretch of golf course. As the first drops fell, I thought about the pills in my pocket. And my phone. Getting the pills or my phone drenched was the last thing I needed. I wrapped the pills in a Kleenex from my back pocket and put them inside my wallet.

The phone was tougher. A couple of years ago I'd accidentally dropped my phone in the toilet. Distaste had promptly given way to practicality and I fished it out immediately. But it died despite my speed. Maybe water got in the headphone jack. Anyway, the experience made me paranoid, er, more careful.

The battery in this phone was not removable, or I would have taken it out. I did the next best thing and powered off the phone.

I ran. Now that rain was falling, a runner would look even less out of place. Part of the remaining path was right along the rim of the mesa. Golf hats are fairly inadequate protection against a lightning strike.

Given the number of golfers and fishers struck by lightning in Colorado, you might even wonder if golf hats *attract* lightning.

Most people struck by lightning survive, technically. But half of them wind up with some long-term issue, like brain damage. So the odds were not up to what my investment clients like to see.

An angry, blinding flash hit the earth maybe a hundred yards from me. The deafening blast came almost simultaneously and then echoed off the foothills. I ducked reflexively, like that would help. It was in the same category as holding up a defensive hand while someone blasted at you with a Colt .45.

I ran faster. Like that would help, too. At least it would reduce the time I spent on the target range. As far as I could tell, I was the only one out in this. Maybe the golfers had received a warning.

My breath was a little ragged by the time I reached the lip of the mesa and headed down. On the plus side, my skull was still at normal temperature.

Another stunningly close bolt crashed to earth behind me like one of God's lawn darts. Just after the second barbed-wire fence, where the trail was the steepest, I lost my footing and bounced down a foot or two on my butt. Fortunately no yucca plants were positioned to slow my skid, and the gun stayed in my windbreaker pocket.

I was drenched by the time I got down the hill and into my car. Desperate to know if my phone had survived, but not wanting for my impatience to guarantee that it died, I left it off as I hurried back to my motel.

In the motel parking lot, I put the gun back in the trunk, grateful I'd had no need for it. Inside my room, I shed my soaking clothes and toweled myself off. My wallet and phone went onto the bathroom counter where I started playing the hair dryer over them. Setting on warm, not melt, Captain.

I changed into dry clothes, then opened my wallet and pulled out the tissue-wrapped pills. The tissue was slightly damp, but the pills had survived. I transferred them to a fresh, dry tissue, and placed them on top of the microwave where they might be safer.

That left the phone and its contents as the outstanding big question. I left the phone off and carefully unplugged the tiny flash card. I made sure it was dry, and plugged it into a slot on my laptop.

Success. I was able to copy the pictures from the card onto my laptop. I relaxed a bit.

A loud rap sounded over my head. Another. Another three. Suddenly the roof sounded like a dump truck was unloading a huge load of gravel.

Outside it had begun to hail in earnest. I peered out through a gap between the curtains. Pea-sized hail to start with. Then the size changed. Still some pea-sized, but now mixed in with hailstones with the diameter of a quarter.

They got even bigger. Not quite golf balls, but almost. And so many of them, it was like being the focal point of a thousand driving ranges. I could see the dents appearing on the hood and roof of the rental Camry.

I was such a disappointment to the car rental people.

My phone stayed off. I would leave it off as long as I could, in hopes of it surviving the downpour. But the laptop worked just fine on the motel's Wi-Fi.

I found a site that gave much of the same information that used to be found in the "Physicians' Desk Reference." It looked like the pills were in a class called "statins" for reducing cholesterol. They were a surprisingly big business.

I was mainly interested in whether an overdose of this particular stuff could explain my spiked drink. Some of the overdose symptoms sounded bad, but not immediate, like liver damage and kidney failure. I kept reading. The first list had been for gradual overdoses. I found the single massive dose section. Nausea, vomiting, blacking out. Actions recommended: stomach pumping.

I leaned back. It sounded like it could have killed me if rapid action hadn't been taken.

So this was new verification that Ben's statement had been a lie. Or maybe he was unaware of the possibility of mission creep. It could be that his team showed a zeal for their task that Ben had not anticipated when he'd maybe said something along the lines of, "Bring him down."

I moved on. The main phone number calling Kevin's hidden cell phone was the prime piece of data. I started searching for it. Nothing. It was a cell, or maybe a line provided by an ISP, the kind of number that didn't get fed into the phone directory. I could call it and try to bluff my way through, but I held onto that thought.

I searched on the only other number in the phone. This time I got a hit. It was a doctor's office in a medical complex just off Fillmore Street. Their site indicated it was an office that held several GPs as well as some nurse practitioners and ancillary staff.

Their site was the kind that tried to look friendly and approachable. Beside the credentials of each of the key staff, bios also indicated their favorite pastimes and a little bit about their families.

I drew in a quick breath.

On the page of nurse practitioners was a familiar face. Staring back at me from the screen was a cute blonde with straight hair, bangs, and freckles on her cheeks. She wore a broad smile showing perfect teeth. *Hello, Tiffany Boyle.*

Vivid blue eyes, slight dimple in each cheek.

It was of mild interest that she liked skiing and caring for the ill, but I started searching for more information than that.

Several minutes later I got some. She had graduated from the University of Minnesota, School of Nursing. Perhaps she'd met Kevin while he was in Minnesota and had moved here at the same time he'd moved back.

Hoping enough time had passed and my phone was dry, I turned it back on. My short run of good luck was holding. It fired up and looked OK.

I transferred a picture of Tiffany to the phone in case I needed to show it to anyone. I also found a picture of Kevin Mayer and put it on the phone. I was feeling a rush from the success. Almost as an afterthought I emailed it to Detective Winchester.

I had a name and a picture to go with the couple who tried to poison me, and very possibly the couple who had tried to shoot me and gas me in Black Forest.

The Internet turned up no indications of a criminal record for either Tiffany or Kevin.

Finally, I moved on to the rest of the documents I'd photographed in Kevin's home. I had just called up the pre-nup notes page when a loud knock sounded on the door.

When my heart started beating again, I cautiously approached the door, mindful of that awful movie image where a killer fires through the peephole a second after it darkens. I pulled the curtain aside.

This maid was taking years off my expected life.

I opened the door and told her I didn't need services today. She masked her disappointment well. I left the door open for a moment and stared at the dents in the roof and hood of the rented Camry. Lining the parking lot were snow-banks composed of melting hail. Like millions of tiny snowmen had been discarded on the same day. Shredded leaves ripped from nearby trees formed a confetti spectacle on the pavement. Crap.

Back to the laptop.

The prenuptial notes spoke to an imbalance of assets between Maddy and Kevin. He'd put in a short table indicating that in the case of her death or their divorce, he'd be entitled to an increasing percentage of assets as their marriage aged.

The rental agreement was for a vacation cabin somewhere near Woodland Park. I noted the address.

Nothing really jumped out at me as I went through the rest of the stuff I'd photographed. I went back to the best thing I had. I knew Tiffany Boyle's name and where she worked.

I knew where that medical office was, but I didn't drive by there yet. Instead I headed for a camera store downtown.

I walked out with a compact Nikon, equipped with the highest zoom I could get for my budget, and a bean bag that would serve as a dash or rooftop tripod.

I made a few calls but turned up no one local who could sell me a long-range microphone. Three people would have been happy to order one, and I placed an order for one that should be in town in a couple of days, but I wanted one for tomorrow. Tomorrow noon was the only time I knew where Kevin and Tiffany were going to be together. Maybe I'd be able to follow them to her home. The text messages suggested that Kevin was leery of having Tiffany in his Colorado Springs home even when Maddy was away.

I reached the medical center parking lot just before the end of the work day. Faces were still a bit small in the Nikon's display, but the long zoom made a world of difference over my phone's camera. I was parked in a spot where the shade covered my windshield and my car was at a slight rise from their office door.

Five patients, I assumed, exited the building during my first twenty minutes of watching. I left the camera recording video just in case I missed anything the first time around.

Two people came out in green tunics and trousers, one man, one woman. The woman was not Tiffany. Five more minutes passed.

There she was.

I let the camera record until she passed out of the viewfinder. Then I held the camera in front of my face, zoomed out a bit, and tracked her as she made her way through the parking lot.

She passed through five double rows of parking spaces and arrived at the outermost ring of spaces. Probably staff was discouraged from parking in the nearby spaces.

She slowed as she dug through her purse. Seconds later she had keys in her hand. She kept moving, and seconds later she stopped.

A black pickup. The F150.

I tried to keep the camera steady while the zoom and my heart rate both worked against me. She got in the car. Running lights flared, then the white reverse lights clicked on. Colorado requires license plates on the front and rear, so I should be able to get a shot of the plates no matter which way she went.

She faced the truck toward me. As she finished backing out and turning, I zoomed in and got a good view of her face. I tilted the camera down and got several frames of her license plate before the car's motion made tracking with full zoom impossible.

I zoomed out and recorded her as she left the lot. So I knew her name, where she worked, and what she parked there.

With the camera on the passenger seat, I followed.

I had to be careful, because presumably she knew what vehicle I was driving. I got through the access-road stop light barely in the same cycle as her, four cars back.

It was easy to avoid getting too close. The problem was keeping up. She drove aggressively, as did too many other drivers, so I had to punch it a few times just to stay within fifty yards.

I mainly did OK until she ran a red light. Too bad the voters nixed Photo red. Were 7-Eleven cameras next to be prohibited?

When the light turned green again, I followed Circle Drive south, hoping I would get lucky and spot her. No luck.

I was disappointed to lose her, but buoyed by what I *had* learned during the day.

Given my newfound free time, I opted for another sit-down restaurant meal rather than more fast food.

After dinner I went back to my home away from home, the Penrose Hospital Emergency Room. I asked if Dr. Bentson was on duty yet.

"She doesn't take appointments," the orderly at the desk informed me.

No, I thought this was Jiffy Lube. "I was in a couple of nights ago with a bullet wound and she asked me to stop by and just tell her how it was doing." I exaggerated. OK, I lied.

He glanced at a screen.

"All right. But she isn't here until 9:00 PM, and you'll have to take your chances on her schedule. If things let up, she may come out. If we have a steady stream of emergencies, you're out of luck."

I nodded. "Thanks."

I found a seat in the waiting area where I could sleep if I needed to. A man and woman in their thirties already appeared to be sleeping.

Once I had been in the chair for five minutes, the activities of the last few days began catching up with me. Or maybe it was the feeling of safety. Probably here in the emergency room waiting area no one was going to mess with me. The threat level going down a notch or two, albeit temporarily, coupled with being sedentary, my energy whooshed out of me and I fell asleep.

Someone poked my shoulder. I roused, groggily. The lighting was different now. It was completely dark outside. The clock said it was 2:35AM.

Doctor Bentson sat beside me, looking quizzically at me.

"Eh, what's up, doc?" I guess I was groggier than I thought. Maybe it was something in the air at the ER.

"You had a question for me?"

"Right. Thank you for making the time." I pulled a tissue-wrapped pill from my wallet. "Do you think some of these crumbled and dropped into my glass of water, could explain my poisoning visit here?"

She took the pill and turned it over in her palm, looking thoughtful. "Where did you get this?"

"It's probably best that I don't say, other than I may be getting closer to resolving my string of unfortunate incidents."

She held my gaze for a moment. "I would be surprised, but when the toxicology report comes back, I'll check." She confirmed that it was a statin and told me the proper name. "While it could produce many of your symptoms, it wouldn't be a first choice for a rapid poisoning. If you ingested a lot of this, it's predictable that you would start throwing up most of the dose. If this was used on you, throwing up might reduce the dose to a non-fatal level all on its own. My guess is that you were suffering from potassium poisoning, not a statin overdose."

She jogged my thoughts into a new path, and I asked her a couple of follow-up questions. She gave me her thoughts. I was trying to think of other questions for her when an orderly called out to her, "Doctor Bentson. Two GSWs on the way. Five minutes out."

She rose, and so did I.

"Thank you, Doctor."

She said, "Be careful out there. Try not to get shot anymore." And she was off.

Very good advice. I would follow it if I could, but I couldn't make any promises.

Chapter 40

I was in place in the medical center parking lot comfortably before my noon appointment with Kevin and Tiffany. The good news was that this appointment didn't require any medical paperwork to be filled out, no blood tests, no urine samples.

Tiffany's black pickup was parked two spaces away from where it was yesterday afternoon, and I was in a good spot to watch from a distance. An old elm tree, one of the survivors left standing, shaded my current rental. Fortunately, depending on one's perspective, the parking lot held several other hail-damaged cars so mine didn't stand out.

My camera had a fresh battery charge, as did my phone. My car had a nearly full gas tank. I was backed into the parking space so I could follow quickly. The only thing I was missing from my movie watching of stakeouts was a coffee can or a juice jug for, well, a bathroom away from home. These people were pressing me to many of my limits, but not all of them. So far.

A blue Mazda came up the aisle toward Tiffany's pickup. It pulled in right next to the pickup, about as far as possible as one could get from the doors leading to medical offices nearby.

Perfect, the Mazda was on this side of the pickup, and, like the pickup, the driver was on this side. I shifted the camera's line of slight slightly down from where it had been and there he was.

Kevin Mayer.

The image was nice and sharp. I left the camera in video recording mode. If I wanted still frames, I would be able to grab them from the video.

He was looking at his watch when the passenger door opened. *Hello, Tiffany.*

She leaned into Kevin and they kissed. A long, passionate kiss, not just a peck on the cheek. Excellent. I double-checked the blinking *record* light. All looked good.

I felt disgusted with myself at the thought, but I had now had enough video that if nothing else I could blackmail Kevin into stopping this wave of attacks. Unless Kevin and Maddy had an open marriage.

I was feeling pretty self-satisfied when a couple of things happened.

First, Kevin and Tiffany finally broke off their kiss. Kevin seemed to have a phone in his hands now, and he started looking around the parking lot. So did Tiffany.

Second, my phone chimed. I almost ignored it because the sound it played was the sound of what had basically proved to be my maid alarm from the nanny-cam in my motel room. I pulled out my phone and looked at my screen anyway.

Holy crap! It was the slim man. He was in my motel room.

I vacillated. I wanted to follow Kevin and Tiffany. I assumed they were probably not going to have sex right there in his car in the medical center parking lot, so they'd likely head for her home. Then I'd have more data and another place I could learn more. On the other hand, I had no information at all on the slim man. I had Kevin's name and address. I had Tiffany's name and phone.

I started my car and turned out, going away from Kevin and Tiffany. I made the large loop around the lot and came out on Fillmore Street.

There, I gunned it. I turned into the universally hated, dickish driver, completely self-centered and contemptuous of other people. I weaved through traffic, taking big risks just to get one car length ahead. I ran one light that had just turned red, getting honks from several cars. I was sensitive to the remote possibility that my departure had been noticed by Kevin or Tiffany and that they were tailing me, but my rear view showed no sign of a black pickup or a blue Mazda. Anyone following me would either be even more suicidal, or sporting red and blue flashing lights.

As another red traffic light appeared in my path, I took a right at the light, a left into a convenience store parking lot, and zoomed through the lot, narrowly missing a kid on a bike. One hundred percent asshole.

A driver waved at me. I think it was a wave, but I couldn't see all his fingers.

I took I-25 south, moving at least ten miles an hour faster than the craziest drivers already abusing the speed limit. More honks. This was very bad for my karma.

I tore up Highway 24 as fast as I dared. The traffic was lighter than on I-25 so I had more functional brain-power left over, and I puzzled over things. Was it just a coincidence that as I was monitoring Kevin and Tiffany that the slim man decided to do something in my motel room? Or were these people all somehow one step ahead of me? If Kevin knew I had seen the texts on his hidden phone, then he could expect me to show up at the medical center around noon today. And then the slim man would have known he had a window of opportunity. But if Kevin knew I'd be there, would be have engaged in some passionate kissing with a woman other than his wife? Maybe he just didn't care.

And what was the slim man doing at my motel? Maybe he was placing a bug. Maybe he was doing some more vandalism. This whole business of specialization seemed more and more bizarre as I learned more. It didn't make a lot of sense that Ben would have one team in charge of trying to kill me and having a separate guy merely trying to make my life hell.

Until now, until the recent acquisition of the video in my camera, I had no leverage to get Kevin to explain what was going on. Maybe the slim man could be persuaded to shed some light on all this. Or if I could do some spying on him, maybe I could learn what was motivating him, without him having to tell me anything. But that all depended on me being able to follow him. Or at the very least see what kind of vehicle he drove, and maybe get the license plate.

I flew through another stoplight one second after it turned red. It would take me years to get this karma back.

I was afraid I was too late. I was almost there, but the remaining light ahead of me turned red, and two cars in each lane slowed to a stop ahead of me. There was no way to pull off or take a spur-of-the-moment right. I banged my hand against the steering wheel and braked to a stop.

The phone screen showed a series of still frames. In one was the slim man, but it wasn't a great picture. He was backlit by the open door, so his features were shadowed. Maybe a better image would be in the actual video on the laptop. But as I sat there looking at the screen, I realized one reason the doorway was bright was that a large silver car was parked in front of the door.

I looked up at the intersection ahead and seconds later a silver Oldsmobile Cutlass pulled onto Highway 24 ahead of me. It came from the road that led to the motel. Maybe I hadn't pissed away every single ounce of karma yet.

If this wasn't the car, I'd get back to the image on the phone and try to enhance it later. At the moment, this seemed like my only hope.

When the light changed, I followed. The Olds traveled northwest, heading for Ute Pass, which led to Ben Stuart's estate. Three other vehicles traveled between our cars, and I let a fourth and a fifth pass. I couldn't afford to be spotted if this was my guy.

We all travelled through another light and then another. The silver car was easy to keep in sight, and he was driving like a law-abider. Ahead, he moved into the left turn lane in front of Red Rock Canyon, puzzling me. I slowed enough to make a Jeep swerve around me to the right and honk his horn.

Two hundred yards behind him, I took the same left when traffic permitted, and I saw where he was actually going. The road that led to Red Rock Canyon curved west and became High Street. I wondered how many marijuana jokes those folks had to endure lately.

The good news, if I recalled correctly, was that this was only one way into this neighborhood. Unless that was the bad news and I was entering a trap. I took the curve in the road. On the left was a split rail fence bordering the western edge of Red Rock Canyon open space.

On the right were parked a lot of recreational vehicles. In the distance, the Olds took a left at a T intersection.

Both sides of the road now held single-family houses, some small and modest, others larger and upscale, but short of McMansions. The mix continued all the way to the stop sign. I waited at the stop sign, indecisive. I'd lost sight of him when he took a left turn here.

But I couldn't have totally lost him since this area had only the one main route in and out. I took a right, went a half block, did a U-turn and stopped. I called up a map on my phone. The road in front of me led to another left turn which ended in a cul-de-sac. Probably no more than ten houses there. Ahead of me on the right, another road intersected. Again, probably no more than ten houses, these all more upscale with large lots. My money was on the large lots. Ben's estate was a couple stages higher than lavish. Kevin and Maddy lived very upscale. My first guess would be that this guy was upscale, too.

I drove straight ahead, aiming for the eventual left turn and cul-de-sac, taking a chance and heading into the lower-cost road. The traffic was now virtually non-existent because of the small number of houses and the lack of a thoroughfare. My car would stand out. But so would a lone person on foot. I took the left-hand choice mainly so I could rule it out.

The road curved left and ahead I could see the cul-de-sac. I scanned houses as I drove. No sign of the silver Olds. No garage doors closing. I swung around in the cul-de-sac loop. The evidence wasn't conclusive but my bet was still that the tall man was on the other road, Crystal Valley Road. A sign at the corner said, "Red Rock Canyon Estates." I stopped near the sign at the intersection and thought.

Seconds later I returned to the spot where I had first parked and looked over the map. The huge Red Rock Canyon open space where Allison and I had taken walks was to the southeast, and the whole neighborhood gave me the feeling that someone out for a walk would garner less attention than an unfamiliar car on a road serving fewer than ten houses.

I started to lament my lack of binoculars when I realized I didn't need them. I had my camera. Lots of binoculars were eight or ten power. My zoom was thirty power.

I grabbed the camera and my golf hat disguise. As I walked to the intersection, I pulled my shirt tails out of my pants to give myself an alternate look. I took a deep breath and turned the corner.

Very nice first impression. A low brick wall paralleled the road on the left. A two-tiered set of matching walls rose over head height on the right, doubling as a retaining wall. The road was paved, with concrete rain-run-off gutters on both sides. Between the gutters and the rock walls were neat strips of gravel. The walls themselves were irregular, earth-toned brick. A series of signs warned of no parking, fire lane. Given only one way in, the road needed to be resistant to rain and fire.

The low wall on the left ended. Thirty yards later, the walls on the right dropped down to nothing. Ahead I could see the roof of the nearest house.

The road curved to the left and more rooftops became visible in the distance. On the left was a pair of multi-mailbox structures favored by the shrinking post office. The number of locks seemed to be much greater than the number of houses I could see on the map, and I didn't know if that meant room for expansion or if some of the buildings were multi-family dwellings. No sign of nametags, and hence no reason to investigate further, so I didn't. Next to the boxes was a place to sit. It occurred to me that if I had difficulty locating the house belonging to the tall man, I could set my camera in the grass far up from the road, leave it recording for a day, and come back and see which box he opened. I could maybe get a better picture of him that way, too.

On the right side of the road, undeveloped land gradually sloped up to a ridge top maybe a hundred yards distant. Scrub oak and shrubs dotted the hillside, and wide swathes of grass filled in much of the rest. I felt too exposed on the road, and the vegetation on the slope offered easy concealment if a resident were to drive by. I moved up the hill.

I couldn't go all the way to the ridge top. As I got closer, a row of houses come into sight, so I satisfied myself with being about two-thirds of the way up the slope. At that level, I began walking parallel to the road below, keeping conscious of nearby concealment if I needed it. I was far enough away from the road and high enough that by simply staying motionless as a vehicle passed, I would be mostly unnoticeable.

By now I could see what seemed to be all the houses on the road. No sign of a silver Olds parked in front of any of them.

I found an ant-free zone and sat on a roughly flat rock positioned so I was invisible from the road's closest approach. I pulled up my camera and started my survey. The viewfinder showed a panoramic view of the massive sandstone rocks in Red Rock Canyon and parts of Colorado Springs beyond. The houses in the foreground were mostly very large and expensive places, perched on a strip that then dropped into Red Rock Canyon. The residents could just walk down a gentle slope and be all ready for a hike.

One at a time I trained my camera on the windows in each house. I saw no glimpse of the tall man, no sign in a window saying, "Look here!"

A noise on my left distracted me from my task. A Jeep was incoming. I trained my camera on it, but at full zoom I couldn't keep it in view. I zoomed out.

I zoomed in when it stopped at a distant house. A young couple dressed in jeans and plaid shirts got out and went into a house. They were strangers to me. Back to my scan.

Twenty minutes later I put my camera down. Nothing so far.

I breathed in, aware of the light scent of dirt and vegetation. The day was moderate, partly cloudy. White, puffy clouds, not thick, dark, lowering clouds. No imminent threat of a storm. I finally became more aware of the big picture.

I'd been using the long lens of the camera to scan windows in the houses below, so far totally without success. But right here in plain view was the park all the houses overlooked. The westernmost section of the park was a flat, grassy strip no more than a few hundred yards wide, less than that in many places. At the far edge of the flat strip, the land rose into the rocks. Along that edge ran the Contemplative Trail, one of the many trails in the park. It ran through immense boulders, many far bigger than a house. From there, I would have a view of the other sides of all the houses.

Maybe the tall man parked in the back of his house. Probably the windows in the houses were designed to take maximum advantage of that beautiful landscape. So perhaps I'd have better luck spotting the tall man.

I was just starting to get to my feet, to go back to my car and reposition my search, when a garage door on one of my target houses began to rise. And out came a silver Olds. On a street with this few cars, the odds were vanishingly small that two people had a Silver Olds.

I readied my camera again. As the driver finished backing out, he stopped, put the car in a forward gear, and started moving away from the house. In that second or two while he was stopped, I got some video.

My camera continued to record as the tall man and his silver Olds drove right to left on the road below, so I had a clear shot at his face.

He was a stranger to me. No glasses, no goatee. None of the disguise descriptions I could remember. But I was sure he was the guy. Closely cropped, light-brown hair. Hard features, angular. Maybe mid-forties, but I'd look again at the video and blow it up. I had more new information to share with Detective Winchester.

The problem was that none of my new information fell into the elusive category of proof. It was more in the category of, "In case of my death." That gave me some thoughts for later.

But for now, I knew where the guy lived, and I knew he wasn't home.

Once he was completely out of sight, I moved from the bushes that had offered me some concealment and hurried down the slope. I was less worried about being noticed now.

At my car, I opened the trunk. I tucked in my shirt tails and donned a light jacket even though the weather didn't demand it. I stretched, taking in my surroundings. No one seemed to be nearby, so I pulled the Glock out of the trunk and stuck it in the back of my pants. And then I perceived more value in having a holster.

When the gun salesman had given his pitch, the lack of an actual safety had seemed unimportant, even an advantage if one needed to fire right away. Now, with the gun stuck my pants, I was having second thoughts.

I walked briskly. As I passed the road I'd originally come in on, I could see all the way down it. A car was heading my way in the distance, but it wasn't silver. I kept moving, round the corner, onto the tall man's street.

I passed the brick walls and the community mailboxes and kept going. By the time I reached the tall man's house, the combination of the unneeded jacket and the tension made me feel quite warm.

His house was enormous, larger even than Kevin and Maddy's Colorado Springs home. My view from the hillside above blended with what I saw on the ground and gave me a fuller picture. The roof was a huge series of peaks, some seemingly at completely random angles. Huge windows faced in most directions. The building kind of cork-screwed around, with the small tail-end being the three-car garage.

The house rose three stories above ground. The roof was a mottled gray, and the siding a charcoal gray. He, too, had a huge lawn which would have been more appropriate in a Eastern state with a lot more rainfall. Recessed pop-up sprinkler heads dotted the lush, green grass. On the lip of the hill facing the southeast I found a massive solar array, a dozen rows of dark panels all canted southward. The net effect of the opulence and the energy conservation felt a bit like ordering a giant fast-food meal and topping it off with a large diet drink.

I rang the front doorbell, more to satisfy myself that no one was home than because of any expectation of the door being answered.

No response.

Acutely aware of potential watchers in the homes on either side, I started around the perimeter. Fortunately the houses here were far enough apart that neighbors had a good degree of privacy.

Facing the park was a wide patio with a deeply overhanging roof, perfect for enjoying a meal or a snooze with the park beautifully laid out below.

Lots of expensive houses have alarm-system signs in the yard or windows, partly to tell people right up front it's not worth breaking a window. This home had no such signs. That was no guarantee of the absence of an alarm, but I had pictures of this guy sneaking into my motel room, so if I did get caught, I had at least a weak defense.

I was prepared to break in if need be. As these guys put more and more pressure on me, my inner rule book had more and more crossed-out lines. But in the shade on the patio, on this nice moderate day, two hand-crank windows were open. Neither was screened. The bottom of each window was about waist height. I reached through the gap and cranked the handle, first the wrong way, trapping my arm, and then the right way, widening the gap until I could awkwardly step through the window, more conscious than ever of the gun in my belt.

From inside I cranked the window back to where it had been. If he had an alarm system, I'd deal with the consequences later. Things could not get much worse than they already were. At least that's what I thought at the time.

No alarm sounds sounded when I stepped on to the red tile floor. Maybe if he had one, he used it only when on vacation. Maybe he'd just gone out for milk and would be back any second.

Or he had a silent alarm.

The living area inside the bay of windows was luxurious. Three enormous sets of leather sofas and matching recliners provided enough space for a football team to have ample seating to enjoy the view. To one side was a giant fireplace. Adjacent to the entertaining area was an office.

There I found the bridge of the starship. Five huge monitors faced a central desk chair. On one a cable news channel played silently, its screen filled with so many panels and crawls you'd need to record it and play it back at quarter speed to absorb everything. A couple of the key stories featured renewed Middle-East talks and discussions of possible government corruption, so it was impossible to actually confirm the year or even the decade from just that.

Another screen showed a view of a motel room with the live time counting in the lower right. And not just any motel room.

My motel room.

On the back of the chair near the foot of the bed was a shirt I'd draped there to dry. The view was looking down at the room, so I knew he'd positioned his camera in the air duct I had inspected earlier. This was probably his noon accomplishment. One more checkmark on his evil checklist. Man, I hated these guys.

I took out my phone and captured some video of his layout, especially including the thirty-two-inch invasion of privacy. For good measure I took similar video with my Nikon.

A small black bowl that looked to be onyx or obsidian contained a handful of flash drives. I took one and plugged it in. On one of his other screens, the mouse pointer moved when I moved the mouse. I copied as much of his documents folder as I could fit on the flash drive, then pocketed the drive. I felt like shooting up his whole system, maybe pouring a little concrete. I wondered how much dynamite it would take to level this house, and how many hops I might have to go through to buy dynamite. If for a while you couldn't take nail clippers on an airliner, I imagined that buying dynamite would be like applying for a license to operate your own personal nuclear power plant.

I explored his documents folder briefly. The contents of one folder indicated he went by the name Ross Morse, my new client who conveniently had me send funds to a corporate entity that, thanks to him, supposedly listed me as an officer. Another folder contains enough letters from one single name that I decided his real name was Ralph McFadden. Also on the computer were invoices to a company with "Stuart" in the name, so I almost certainly had a link to show Ben's hand in all this. Again, probably not court-of-law proof since I broke in, but helpful. And possibly leverage.

I left the computer and found my way to the garage. It held an old green Chevy Malibu and a candy-apple-red BMW. To fit with those, his Olds should have been yellow, not silver. I was just closing the door to the garage when the main garage door jerked and started moving upward.

What was it with me and garage doors?

Chapter 41

As soon as I closed the door leading to the garage, I pulled the Glock out of my belt and backed around a nearby corner. I could feel the slight rumbling as the outer garage door travelled upward.

The gun felt alien in my hand. I'd played cowboy and cowboy as a kid, using a cap gun my grandfather had given me. Those days had turned a bit opaque in my mind, a view through a deteriorating mirror, but I remembered feeling excited, happy, even when Billy the Kid had me in his sights. Now I felt dread, fear. I kept my finger away from the trigger. This was not exactly the right time to experiment with the pressure required to squeeze off a shot. If I really needed to shoot it, I'd probably be involuntarily squeezing it hard enough to deform it.

The outer garage door grew silent and then engine noise filled the void. Then silence. The door started rumbling again as it descended. Twenty seconds later the door from the garage to the house opened.

From around the corner came the sounds of both paper and plastic. The door shut harder than necessary, probably shoved by a foot.

The tall man came into view, the same one I'd watched drive the silver Olds. He headed away from me, toward the kitchen. I let him have a comfortable lead.

When I came into the kitchen doorway, he was placing a paper grocery bag and a few plastic bags on the counter next to the refrigerator.

Once his hands were empty I said, "Welcome back. I have a gun, so please be careful."

In his place, I might have jumped a foot. He turned casually, as though someone had just said, "Did you remember the eggs?"

"Well, well, well." His voice carried the slightest trace of an accent, one I recognized, especially in this context.

"Hello, Ross. Or do you prefer Ralph?" His was the voice of my new client, the one whose account resulted in the charge of fraud.

"I'd ask you to make yourself at home, but it would appear that you already have. Can I offer you a beer? You can call me Ralph." Ralph was six or eight inches taller than I was, similarly slim. Brown hair clipped short enough to make his ears seem to stick out more than usual. Slate-gray eyes that blinked only occasionally.

"Maybe later," I said.

This was not going the way I expected it. I thought the presence of the gun would promote agitation, that my presence in his house would cause surprise, confusion. Maybe some of those were there, buried deep, but his outer demeanor was as confident as a president just having won by a landslide.

"I'd like to put some of this food away. Would that spook you?"

"Do it later." I didn't like the idea of letting him pick up a heavy can of beans and suddenly hurl it at me. I didn't even like the idea of letting him grab a grape.

Insolently, he went ahead and put a couple of packages of meat into the refrigerator. If I were going to shoot someone, it wouldn't be for that.

He finally turned, leaned back, and rested his hands on the counter. I conjured an image of a sleepy lion watching a bunny, trying to decide if he was hungry enough to sit up.

"What can I do for you, Mr. Barlow?"

"You've been making my life pretty miserable."

Ralph was silent.

"I'd like to know why."

He said nothing.

"I could start shooting up the place."

"I won't converse with someone holding a gun on me or who might be recording me. Call me superstitious."

With my left hand I took out my phone and squeezed the power button until it made the shut down sound. I had the screen facing him the whole time. It occurred to me that someone could sell an app that made that shutdown sound and blanked the screen. But the market for such a program might only be me.

I popped the battery compartment cover off the camera and ejected the batteries. I held them in the palm of my hand before I laid them on the counter and put the camera with them.

"I still see a gun. Can you shut that down?"

"Look, I already know a lot of it. What's the harm in filling in a few gaps? None of this could be used in court since I broke in and I'm aiming a gun at you."

"You sure you know how to use that thing?"

"You want me to fire a test round?" I adjusted my aim toward the center of his chest.

"You surprise me, Mr. Barlow. I figured by now you would have caved, moved to another state." He pulled away from the counter.

"Would that stop all this?"

"Nope."

He moved a step toward me.

"Stop right there."

He moved another step. "There are some things you apparently don't know, Mr. Barlow."

"Stop moving."

He moved another step. I was getting close to having to decide whether I could shoot a man in cold blood. I lowered my aim to his knee.

"One thing you don't know is that your safety is on."

I started to say, "I'm not falling for that crap. There is no safety on this Glock." I got as far as "I'm not falling for that—"

Moving way faster than I anticipated, Ralph zipped another step or two toward me and slammed my wrist away from its extended position. I got off one round that went wild. Blam! His other fist rammed into my stomach a couple of milliseconds later.

For an instant I was in a different kitchen, years ago. When I came back to the present, I couldn't breathe.

My wind was gone. I couldn't draw in a breath. He casually moved away from me. He kicked the gun farther away. When he reached it, he calmly squatted and picked it up. I vaguely registered the fact that my wild bullet had slammed into a toaster on the counter.

"There are some important differences between us," he said, once I regained my ability to breathe. "I *will* pull this trigger in time if I need to. And I do stuff like this for a living."

I took a few deep breaths. "Yeah, well, that toaster isn't going to burn another piece of toast. And I can tell you how best to prepare for retirement."

He grinned. "I'm doing OK for myself."

"Yeah, but you're doing it by harassing innocent people. Or at least one innocent person."

"You were driving when Allison died, am I right?"

I hesitated.

"You want a beer now?"

"Why not?"

He casually finished putting away groceries. He put some eggs and bacon into the refrigerator and withdrew a couple of Coors in cans. "Let's adjourn."

He angled my gun to show me which way to go. He followed me into the living area I had originally entered, the windows once again the way he'd left them. He put a beer next to an armchair and moved well away from me before he sat. He lay the gun down on a coffee table. I knew I couldn't cover that distance fast enough. I sat.

"Maybe it is time to move to another state," I said.

"Actually, I no longer believe you would. I think you would have cut and run already if that's who you were."

I opened the beer and took a sip. I was oblivious to the taste right now. "Look, I get it that Ben blames me for Allison's death, and that maybe my starting to date Cathy before Ben might have moved on after his wife's death made him angrier. But I've given the police information on the attempts on my life. You and Ben stand to lose of lot if I die."

For the first time I saw movement in Ralph's face. Matching spots on both cheeks puffed out slightly as he clenched his teeth. His eyes narrowed fractionally. "We're not trying to kill you."

"Maybe Kevin didn't get the same memo. Is he working for you or directly for Ben?"

Ralph was silent as I could almost see the machinery clicking inside. "What the hell does this have to do with Kevin? Kevin Mayer, Ben's son-in-law?"

"Come on. What's the point in lying about this?"

"We're not operating from the same information basis. Kevin's just a dumb schmuck who got lucky by marrying way over his head."

"Kevin and his girlfriend have tried to kill me. Three times. You're saying you knew nothing of it?"

"You're crazy. Admittedly, Ben would be pleased to be causing that. But you're not making sense."

"So you're telling me whatever Kevin's been doing is not part of this?"

"What has he been doing? According to you?" Ralph seemed convincing.

"So far, a hit and run, a poisoning, and an attack in Black Forest. I can see his hand directly in those actions. I see evidence of you in the reunion, the case of the concrete car, and the mystery of the flattened house."

"I honestly don't see your angle in this. Why make up stuff like this? The police won't believe anything without evidence."

"You mean your stuff or Kevin's?"

"Kevin is a dick, but he's not capable of stuff like that. He's got a great thing going with Maddy. He wouldn't risk messing that up. And why would he want you dead?"

"I have no idea why *anyone* would want me dead. But I do have proof that Kevin is doing some stuff Maddy wouldn't approve of."

"And what is that exactly?"

"I've got pictures of him and his girlfriend."

"With you?"

"With me," I said, and added a bit too late, "Copies anyway."

Ralph smiled. I have to say I was not fond of his smile. "Show me."

"You have to give me my camera."

"Stay." Ralph got to his feet easily and move silently to the kitchen, keeping my gun trained on me. He went out of sight for a second and was back. I stayed exactly where I was.

The shadow of a cloud moved past the windows.

Ralph put the camera on a table six feet from me and backed away. He then fetched the batteries. He retreated to his original chair and sat. "OK, take them."

I loaded the batteries back into the camera and found the recording I'd made outside the medical center earlier today. I set it to play and put the camera back on the table. When I was back in my seat, Ralph approached and took the camera.

I said as he watched, "You know it's possible to edit photos, but this is video. Surely you must know that's more difficult to fake. I took that around noon today."

Ralph watched the video for a couple of minutes, no doubt seeing the very warm kissing. He smiled again. "Ben will love this. He hates Kevin almost as much as he hates you."

"Will he love it enough to call you off?"

Ralph looked thoughtful. "I don't know. But tell me more about these incidents you mentioned."

I took him at his word that he didn't know about the three incidents that bore Kevin's fingerprints. I gave him a fairly dispassionate account, wanting him to believe me, to find me credible. Maybe there was a chance Ben would call off his dog. That would leave only Kevin trying to kill me for whatever reason.

He interrupted me only a few times. He wanted the address in Black Forest. He wanted to know more about the pills I'd found in Kevin's house.

When I finished my tale, Ralph was silent again. Finally he said, "Without commenting on the incidents you believe I had a hand in, I can tell you straight that these things you blame on Kevin were completely unknown to me." He looked around the room, then out at the park land across the way. "Hang on."

Ralph picked up a phone and speed dialed. Seconds later he said, "It's Ralph. I need to speak to him." Seconds passed. "OK. Have him call me." He hung up the phone.

"Our mutual friend is down for a nap, with firm instructions not to be disturbed. I'll talk to him tonight."

"Is this something that could get him to call off the harassment?"

"I don't know. But I'm going to copy these files."

I nodded. Like I had a lot of choice.

He backed away from me, still aiming the gun in my general direction, but seeming even more relaxed. He stepped into his office, maintaining line of sight, and came back with a laptop computer. A few minutes later, he seemed satisfied that he had what he needed. He put the memory card back in the camera and put the camera on the table beside him.

"Can I have my camera back? And my gun?"

"Maybe. But I want to talk to him first."

"Then when?"

"I'll call you in the morning."

"You need my number?"

"No. I think I have it." He smiled. "I think we're done here, Mr. Barlow."

"Does that mean you're going to shoot me or that I'm free to go?"

"You can go."

He showed me to the front door, from a distance. Before he closed the door, he said, "I underestimated you, Mr. Barlow. I also underestimated Kevin. That concerns me."

"You're concerned about that, but not the concrete car, my house?"

He considered this. "Those, too, actually."

We held each other's gaze for a moment, and I nodded.

The door closed behind me. Apparently he wasn't going to shoot me in the back. Yet.

Chapter 42

I turned my phone back on as I walked back to my car. The car was where I had parked it.

My motel room *looked* untouched, but I knew it had been. I saluted the camera with one finger and brought some fast food into the room. I didn't have the energy to remove the vent concealing the camera and dispose of the camera, so I managed to snag a tee-shirt over the top edges of the vent so the view would be blocked for now. As much as I wanted to call Cathy and bring her up to date, I would not endanger her, so even if the camera came with a microphone, there would be no audio to conceal.

I spent the evening going over what I'd heard from Ralph and trying to make sense of it all. In the morning I would go see Detective Winchester again, with or without the latest camera recordings. I still had little that was certain to stand up in court, but if Detective Winchester were equipped with Kevin's name and Tiffany's name, he could look more closely at tire prints from the two scenes, or make an examination of Tiffany's pickup mirror. Maybe he could request phone records.

I could have called the police already, but I'd dragged my feet partly because I hadn't decided how best to minimize the fact that my trail of evidence included a stop or two for breaking and entering.

~~~

The next morning, a little after 9AM, I hadn't had a call from Ralph, so I decided to drive over to his place before heading down to talk to the police. The morning was heavily overcast, the unusual humidity bringing with it unidentifiable smells that reminded me of one vacation in Maine.

This time I drove right into Ralph's driveway. I pushed the doorbell button and heard a distant chime. But no Ralph.

I'd hoped for a thawing in relations, but maybe that wasn't going to happen. I left. I hoped Detective Winchester would be interested in what I'd found.

I was back on Highway 24, heading southeast toward police headquarters, when something in my rearview mirror caught my eye.

Several cars back was a blue sedan that looked like a Mazda. I slowed, and it slowed. It was in fact a blue Mazda. Like Kevin's car. One of the cars behind me pulled into the other lane impatiently and sped past.

I had gone another couple hundred yards, trying to decide what to make of it, or whether there was a way to use this to my advantage, when *bang!* A tire blew. The car lurched to the right, but I was able to maintain control over the car as I slowed down to a crawl. I pulled over to the right as far as I could and put on my emergency flashers. A right-turn lane had formed for the intersection ahead, so I pulled into it. I tried to grapple with the feeling of déjà vu and another thought that tried to reach the surface, but too much was going on.

The blue Mazda rolled past me at about the same time as a police car appeared, coming the opposite direction. Who says the police are never around when you need them?

The cop started up his lights and most of the nearby traffic started to slow. This section of Highway 24 had no median, so the cop did a careful U-turn behind me. He pulled to a stop, leaving his vehicle sticking out into traffic to protect mine.

With the newfound protection, I opened my door and went around to examine the failed tire. Front right. Again. What were the odds of two blown tires in a year?

The tire was completely flat, part of it shredded. And someone had keyed my car, on the right front fender.

The cop reached me. He was one I hadn't met before. Reddish, short-cropped hair. Stocky. Friendly. "Bad luck, huh?"

"That's the tip of the iceberg."

He looked puzzled. "I'll be happy to help. Driver's license, registration, and proof of insurance please?"

Wow, and I'd figured he was just here to help. "Ah, sure." I got out my wallet and handed him my license. I opened the passenger door and got the rest out of the glove box. Trying to be as far from belligerent as possible, I asked, "Do you always require this info from someone with a flat tire?"

I didn't think he was going to answer, but he said, "We had a report of a hit and run up Highway 24. Blue Camry."

"Gotcha." That made perfect sense. It wasn't my Camry, of course, but I could see his point of view.

While he took my stuff back to his car, I moved to the trunk and popped it open.

I gasped. Adrenaline flooded my body. Lying in my trunk on his side, all bent out of shape, was Ralph.

Ralph had a black-ringed bullet hole in the side of his head. His skin was pasty white. No one could look like that and not be dead.

And next to him was what looked exactly like the Glock I had recently purchased. The one Ralph had confiscated.

I shut the trunk, my mind racing at Indy 500 speeds. *Oh, God. Oh, God.*

My life didn't flash before my eyes, but some very recent events raced through my brain. The odd smell in the air this morning. That smell was much stronger in the trunk. And the keying on the right fender of my car, near the damaged tire and on the side opposite the one I'd gotten in on this morning, the long scrape. Maybe it hadn't been someone keying the car.

Maybe it was someone wanting the Camry to look like a hit-and-run vehicle.

If Kevin had managed to follow me all the way to Ralph's, and if he'd heard our conversation...

My fingerprints were on Ralph's window and a number of surfaces in his house. I'd been to the police multiple times complaining that someone looking vaguely like him was harassing me. He could be traced to Ben Stuart. I could be traced to his house. Twice.

Holy crap. This was going to look extremely bad. And there was no way Ralph had done this.

I looked back at the cop. He had his head down, maybe looking at a readout. Then his head snapped back up and his gaze fixed on me. I was instantly certain that meant the phony hit-and-run call, no doubt made by Ralph's killer, matched my license plate. I was screwed if I stayed here. The cops would have all the evidence they needed to lock me up for however much murder in Colorado got you nowadays.

I glanced at traffic, and I bolted.

Horns blared from cars coming in both directions. The speed limit here was around forty-five miles per hour. Traffic was slowing some because of the cop's flashing lights, but as soon as drivers determined his car was stopped, they tended to speed up again.

I raced across two lanes of eastbound traffic amid screeches, paused for a tenth of a second in the center turn lane, and barreled across the two westbound lanes. I heard more horns, and a crash as one motorist with good reaction times dealt with a tailgater with bad reaction times. They would have needed one of those stop-action, horse-race cameras to see the margin I made it by.

The cop shouted, "Stop!" but his voice barely made a dent in all the chaos.

My sole advantage was surprise. Well, surprise and speed. Well, surprise, speed, and a frantic desire to avoid spending the rest of my life behind bars. The cop probably had to radio in a "Calling all cars" or whatever they did rather than just racing after me. And he had that collision to worry about. Why knock yourself out when an entire team could encircle the neighborhood?

The side of the road I ran to was lined with trees and a six-foot chain-link fence. I ran around the right end of the fence and started following a concrete path down a gentle slope. In seconds I was much less visible to the south. The trees here were all no doubt growing where they were because of the presence of Fountain Creek, which paralleled the highway along this stretch. It wasn't a very big creek most of the time. I was wondering if I'd need to try to jump it or scramble through it when I realized the path I was already on curved and went over a small bridge across the creek. Ahead was a brown bear, on a mural. The bridge was one tiny break to make up for a monumental bad break.

Of course being caught with a dead man in my trunk was not merely a bad break. It had to be the deliberate result of someone's awful plan. Kevin, almost certainly. By now I bet I hated him even more than Ben Stuart did.

As I raced over the bridge I saw that the creek was only a tiny obstacle, at least right then. The water was probably less than a foot deep and two feet wide. I followed the path as it turned left again.

As I ran, my lungs already started to complain. It was a dismal indicator of the events that had pushed me from law-abider to law-breaker that, as I ran from the police, I had the early instinct to shut off my phone. I reached into my pocket and pushed the off switch long enough, I hoped. I didn't want the ringer to give me away, and I definitely did not want law enforcement tracking my location.

The path continued to follow the creek. On this side of the creek and the trees was another chain-link fence, and beyond that a small park, Vermijo Park, I thought. I ran west and then turned north again as I reached a parking lot that connected with a narrow road sloping upward through the trees.

On my left was a large fenced-in area, a garden, not a flower garden, but a big vegetable garden.

I raced up the dirt road and reached a street, actually more like a paved alley with many houses facing out to an adjacent street. Another decision faced me. Which way? A backward glance showed no sign of the cop yet. Maybe he'd just started up his car and taken a left at the upcoming intersection, ready to turn onto the street I was on. I couldn't outrun a car.

I took a left and ran past three or four houses. Then I took a chance and went left again, around a log cabin and though someone's large yard. I reached another concrete trail and realized it was probably the same trail I'd been on. If so, I had wasted some time on a wrong turn. On the other hand, if the cop had seen me running the initial direction, maybe he would direct the search into the wrong area.

I reached the path and turned right. Away from the cop.

The path started angling north as it passed a lot full of RVs. It angled west again.

I kept following the path as it wound through the neighborhood. My lungs burned from exertion and my knee ached. This was not a simple short jog, but a full-tilt sprint.

The path crossed over the creek once again, so now the creek lay to the north.

Finally I reached a point where I could see a major road ahead, a divided road that would take me too long to cross. On my right, on the other side of a band of trees, was the back side of a McDonald's restaurant. Past it was another bridge over the creek. A Taco Bell lay on the other side of the bridge.

This was as good a place as any to hide. I found a spot in the grove, between two large scrub oaks, and I sat.

Slowly my breathing recovered, and I listened to sirens that seemed to come sequentially from every direction. It could have been one car, doing a constant ice-cream-truck sweep, or multiple cars. I would have given anything to hear the tinny, warbling ice-cream-truck music instead.

My thoughts gradually became less scrambled as I sat there. First of all, this seemed to be corroboration that Kevin and Ralph were acting independently. I thought back to Kevin looking around in the medical center parking lot. Someone had put a GPS tracker in my old car. Kevin could have put another in my Camry. He could have been looking at a GPS tracker screen, abruptly realizing I was nearby. He could have followed me to Ralph's without ever having to be in sight. In fact, he could have been right outside, listening to my conversation with Ralph, suddenly understanding that we both had to die before we said anything to Ben. Probably Kevin had my camera now, and he would know that it held the only proof about his relationship with Tiffany.

It also occurred to me that my tire blew out at exactly the worst possible moment. Not only was I carrying a dead man in my truck, along with a gun that no doubt still bore my fingerprints, but my tire blew just as I was about to cross paths with a cop looking for a car exactly like mine. Probably with a scratch like mine. This was as far from coincidence as I was from Bolivia.

So someone, Kevin, I assumed, could arrange it so my tire would blow at exactly the right time. He was certainly following me. He saw the cop coming. Odds were I was bound to drive past a cop sooner or later. And he pressed a button. Maybe some kind of remote-controlled explosive. I imagined those might even be off-the-shelf products sold for testing automobiles experiencing blowouts.

Ralph was not the only one to have underestimated Kevin.

Just as I reached this conclusion, my body went cold with a parallel conclusion.

If Kevin could do this today, he could have been following Allison and me on Monarch Pass and could have done the same thing then. But why?

I could still see the headlights of that car following me that night. How they grew closer before the accident.

Before the murder.

Maybe the transmitter had a limited range. Maybe Kevin had needed to get closer so he could see right when to blow my tire. To make sure he was on the scene first to guarantee that Allison was dead. And maybe to snatch the evidence of an explosive. Or destroy the evidence in a fire.

If Ben Stuart knew about this, he'd hate Kevin even more.

And he might hate me a lot less.

Chapter 43

I needed to talk to Ben. He might have the clout to fix all this, to get the police to listen, to look closely at the tire that blew a little while ago. As long as he believed I didn't kill Ralph and understood who was really responsible for Allison's death. But would he?

Too many questions still puzzled me. If Kevin wanted me dead now, why did he choose to let me live back when Allison died? For the present, maybe having me shot by a cop, or locked up for life, would keep him happy.

A faint whirring noise sounded from beyond the nearest bushes. Seconds later a pair of bicyclists sped past me, racing along the path.

I waited where I was for more than an hour, wishing I had a police scanner or an invisibility cloak. I focused on the invisibility cloak as somehow the more practical of the two. I got up and took off my shirt, leaving just a white tee-shirt to cover my torso. The discarded long-sleeved shirt went under a bush. I had bought it just days ago, so my sentimental attachment was pretty minimal. My phone went into my back pocket. I hoped I wouldn't forget and sit on it.

I walked north, over a small bridge and then through the McDonald's parking lot. I moved as casually as I could, staying on high alert for police cars. Near Colorado Avenue, I stood in the shadow of an evergreen, waiting for the longest possible lull in traffic. A few minutes later, I walked across the street, feeling like a target, but going for casual, nonchalant.

I made it through the parking lot of a 7-Eleven and onto the residential street behind it. From there, I took another chance and headed back east again. A few blocks later I came south. The coast looked clear as I walked past a couple of parking lots, around the corner, and into a west-side surplus store.

The cash in my rental car was gone. The cash in my motel room might as well be in Casablanca. But I still had cash in my wallet and no driver's license was required to spend cash.

A set of camouflage pants and shirt would give me a totally different look. I added a hat as long as I was at it. I would stand out more than in my old clothes, but in a heavily military town, I would not look *that* out of place. Looking a bit unusual was still better than looking exactly like a man matching the description lighting up all the local police cars.

Given what lay ahead, I did some additional shopping. No need for renting a giant searchlight or buying cold-weather gear. But I found a canteen, a blanket, a flashlight, and some other things that caught my attention. I found a small pack that would hold most of my stuff. I paid for my purchases and left.

This was just great. I'd gone in stages, from having my stuff scattered throughout my home, to having my stuff fit in a motel room, to having my stuff fit in a car. And now I carried all my stuff on my back. This was something I was not going to get used to. Bolivia was looking pretty damn good.

I retraced my most recent path, heading north and west again. Between a dumpster and couple of parked cars, I changed pants. The camo pants were a little too long, but I just rolled up the cuffs. The shirt was fine. Now that I had the shirt and pants on, I wished I'd bought some army boots, too, but there was no way I'd go back. I filled my canteen from a garden hose a homeowner had left running into the street.

I walked for more than an hour, staying cautious, generally keeping a block or two off Colorado Avenue, which paralleled Highway 24. I was making my way out of the police zone and slowly toward Ben Stuart.

A small park occupied land near where both Colorado Avenue and Highway 24 shifted paths and crossed one another. The highway rose to an overpass that led up the pass, and Colorado Avenue kept basically level as it snaked toward Manitou Springs. Manitou Springs lay nestled in a valley and spread up the valley sides. I stopped at a large tree stump that was out of sight of traffic.

I sat, resting against the tree stump, facing away from the walkway. The soft sound of creek water burbling and the happy bird chirps from the trees were the most soothing noises I'd heard lately. Amazingly, I went to sleep.

When I woke, the sun was behind the mountains, but there was still plenty of light.

I got out my canteen and took a drink. I had passed up the MREs for sale in the surplus store, but they'd also offered some granola bars, so I now had several tucked away. I ate one. Then another.

Indecision hit me again. I needed to make my way up Ute Pass to see Ben Stuart. But I was unsure whether to risk hitchhiking or just walk it. It might take me six or eight hours, assuming I didn't have to stick to the roads and I could shortcut overland at Crystola. But I needed to see a map.

I didn't want to turn on my phone here and potentially signal my presence.

I started walking north, toward Garden of the Gods. The detour was taking me out of my way, but if I essentially signaled the cops and said I was moving up Ute Pass, I'd be making life a lot harder on myself.

Finally I reached a spot that I thought offered adequate concealment and a choice of escape routes. I would leave the phone on for only a minute, and maybe that wouldn't be enough time for an alert to go out.

Seconds after the phone came up, it chimed for an incoming text. This proved how much a slave to technology that I am. I looked at it.

I was glad I did. It was from Ben Stuart.

"Dave, contact me soonest. I heard from Ralph and I know you weren't to blame for the accident that killed Allison. We need to talk. Come see me."

That took hardly any thought. I replied. "Will do. See you soon." As soon as I was finished, I put the phone in airplane mode, turning it invisible to detection, as far as I knew.

I kept scanning my surroundings as I thought about this.

Receiving a text instead of voicemail raised my paranoia level. The message could have come from Ben, but it could have come from someone else. My reply, indicating I was coming, wasn't binding. I didn't actually have to go. Minutes earlier, seeing Ben had been my highest priority. Now I wasn't so sure. It was like wanting that new car, and then, having rolled it off the lot, being left dealing with buyer's remorse. But if the message hadn't come from Ben, who would have sent it? Only Kevin likely knew enough to do that, and I didn't see his angle.

I still had no better alternative, though. It wasn't like I'd forged such a close bond with Detective Winchester that he'd swim upstream against all the evidence pointing at me. I wanted to get to Ben's as fast as possible, and not be completely tired out when I got there.

I switched airplane mode off, again possibly lighting up a dot on a map I didn't want to be on.

I dialed Cathy's number. I didn't know who else to turn to now. The phone rang several times. No answer. I got her voicemail, but this wasn't the kind of message for leaving a recording.

I switched airplane mode back on and thought some more. Still no flashing police car lights in sight.

I switched it again. I dialed Holly.

After three rings she picked up.

"Holly, I'm calling for a giant favor, but it could cause major problems for you."

"I'm in," she said simply.

"I want you to meet me in your car. Don't say where you think I'm about to tell you. Just tell me if you understand."

"OK."

"At dinner you mentioned a favorite restaurant of yours."

She was silent for several seconds. "Got it."

"I'll tell you more when I see you and give you another chance to say 'no.' Try not to be followed."

"Got it." Again, she sounded as though she were embarking on an adventure, while I was fighting for my life. But she was up for it.

I hung up. Just in case, I made sure I had an offline map of the crow's-flight path between my current location and Ben's. I switched my phone entirely off and got moving, walking as quickly as I could and keep looking casual. I needed to get into Manitou Springs.

Staying off Colorado Avenue still seemed wise, so I got on El Paso Boulevard, which paralleled it to the north. Once there I spotted a path just south of the road, and followed it until it veered too far to the south. At that point I started walking through parking lots, keeping the road in sight to avoid getting turned around.

It was starting to get dark, and the last stretch was a bit like traipsing through the woods, but finally I could see the roof of the Briarhurst. Then I could see more of the Victorian, sandstone structure, the old Briarhurst Manor, now an upscale restaurant.

I kept my hat on as I moved through the parking lot. People were entering the front door. I scanned the cars and didn't see a red Mustang. But I did see the profile of a police car in the lot, its bar lights off now, but unmistakable in silhouette.

I nearly turned around and backed out of the lot. But even cops had to eat meals. Maybe it was someone just off duty enjoying a meal. I gulped and moved toward the front door. Under a tree, I stopped, waiting in the dim light. No sign of Holly.

The festive outside lights made me acutely aware of feeling like an outsider. The only key to getting my life back was a dying man who hated me. The police would very much like to talk to me. I could defend my actions, but I thought of all the people on death row who are exonerated by new evidence found only after decades had passed. The justice system wasn't perfect. Ralph's dead body had been found in my trunk, and he'd no doubt been shot by my gun. And I had been in his house.

I had no interest in being locked behind bars for a long enough time that youth would be a distant memory. My livelihood was on hold, under severe threat. The small stuff, like a destroyed car and home, had dwindled to nothingness in comparison.

A figure stepped out of the front door and scanned the surrounding area. Holly.

I moved toward her. She looked right at me and turned away.

Was that a signal? I halted, unsure if that meant she had seen a cop. Or had already been questioned by a cop. And then I realized. I wore my camouflage outfit and hat.

I moved closer. She turned, reached for the door handle. And I said, "Holly."

She spun. Looked at me again. Then looked around for some other source of my voice. She looked back at me.

"It's me. Dave." I took off the hat.

She came forward finally. "Well, *that* freaked me out. What are you doing?"

I grinned. "I had to change my look. Come over here for a minute, will you?"

She came with me and we went back to the tree I'd waited at. We moved to the far side, out of sight of the front door.

"Thank you for coming," I said. "I need to tell you some stuff, but here's the bottom line. I want to ask to borrow your car, and I want to tell you up front that I'm wanted by the police for a murder I did not commit."

"Holy crap... OK."

"OK, here's the rest of the—"

"I don't care. I said OK."

"Holy crap," I echoed. "That's trusting."

"I've got good instincts about people."

I thought about the reunion incident, but Holly's judgment wasn't at fault. If anything, it was her agent's problem. "Thank you, Holly. I'll make it up to you if I can."

"I know you will."

"OK. Here's my plan. I'm going to drive the car up to Ben Stuart's estate tonight. Either I'll be able to drive it back on my own by tomorrow, or you'll need to have a friend pick it up." I told her where I would leave it. I was taking a chance in trusting her, but I just couldn't accept the notion that she was in on all this.

"Here's what I suggest," I continued, handing her some bills. "You go in and have a nice dinner. When you come out, you'll realize you forgot and left your keys in the car and your car is gone. You'll feel stupid and embarrassed, and you'll report the theft to the police. That's your protection against them claiming you helped me. Tomorrow, either your car will show up and you'll tell the police it's back, or you'll tell them you got a call telling you where to find it."

"Got it." She searched in her purse and came up with the car key. She handed me the key, then pointed. "I'm almost at the end of that second row."

"Thank you. You're sure you don't need the whole story?"

"Tell me later. For now, who's the person you're supposed to have killed?"

"The man that your agent dealt with. Someone killed him and put his body in my trunk."

"Wait, what?"

"That guy's body was dumped in my trunk by whoever is really behind all this."

"Those bastards!"

I couldn't help myself. I flashed on "South Park" and "Those bastards! They killed Kenny!"

"Oh, wait," she said. "He's a bastard, too!"

"I'll explain it all when I can. I might have to do it from prison—"

"Shut up and get going." She smiled.

We hugged and I left her there. On the whole, I would rather be sitting down to a nice dinner.

In the parking lot, I skirted the police car by a wide margin. Probably they weren't there for me, but no sense going right up to an angry dog and twisting his nose.

I found Holly's Mustang right where she said it would be. It looked blacker than red in the dim light. I got in.

In another unfamiliar car, I would have spent a couple of minutes making sure I was clear on the controls, knowing where the wiper lever and other stuff were. Tonight I just made sure the headlights were on and I that could feel the brake and the accelerator.

I started breathing again when I reached Colorado Avenue. No police lights flared. If I was being followed, it was covertly.

I took the interchange exit, and shortly I was heading up Highway 24 into Ute Pass again, the headlights illuminating only a small fraction of the darkness that lay ahead of me.

Chapter 44

I listened to radio news for part of the trip to Ben Stuart's. I was a pretty dangerous character, according to the police. Thank God I wasn't watching the TV news and having to see my awful driver's license photo blown up to full-screen. I swear those picture-takers must have competitions for best deer-in-the-headlights shot, best police-line-up shot, best bad-hair-day shot, and best most-likely-to-kill shot. And don't get me started on my passport photo.

Holly must have filled up the tank right before loaning me her car. I sailed through Woodland Park with the gauge still reading *full*. As I passed a police car going the opposite direction, I concluded I wasn't quite as paranoid as it was possible to be. When I got in Holly's Mustang to make this trek, I'd never thought to look in the trunk.

A mile after having that thought, I pulled over and looked in the trunk.

No body. Not even the typical spare tire. Instead there was a "tire mobility kit" with slime and a pump. I'm too young to be called old-fashioned, but I prefer having a spare.

As long as I was stopped, I looked in the wheel wells for a GPS tracker. Nothing. I resumed my travel.

I took the turn-off from Highway 24 and cut my speed. Out here, with the absence of street lights, the darkness seemed more absolute, more lonely. More threatening. I wondered if somewhere out there Kevin waited with a high-power rifle and a scope.

If he did, he gave me a pass or he was a terrible shot. I reached the edge of the high fence that surrounded Ben Stuart's estate. I pulled to a stop on the dark, deserted road.

I had told Holly I would reach this point, turn around, and park the car about a hundred yards along the road, so I did. It was probably closer to a hundred and fifty when I found a wide enough spot to leave the car safely. I locked up and then put the key on the ground just inside the front left tire so she could find that too.

A nearly full moon, rising in the eastern sky, large and slightly pink, provided the only light. A breeze passed over the landscape with just enough force to produce a soft whoosh through the branches. I dug around in my pack to find my flashlight. I held it directly against my palm as I turned it on, wanting to make sure it still worked but not wanting to start over on my night vision. A dull red line glowed before I turned it back off.

I walked east on the road, wishing I'd seen fewer zombie movies.

At the point where I'd turned the car around, the corner of the fence line, I left the road and made my way carefully along the fence. I wasn't going in the main gate tonight.

The top of the fence was over my head. My backpack held some rope in case I needed it, but I wasn't ready. I wanted to be farther south, well away from any eyes focused on the front gate. I walked up a slight slope for a couple hundred yards and the land leveled off. In another fifty yards, the terrain headed down again toward a distant valley, at a gentle slope.

Maybe fifty yards farther along, was a felled pine tree not far from the fence. It was barely bigger than a typical Christmas tree, making me wonder if a nearby property owner had wanted a Christmas tree far from his line of sight but then found a better choice.

When propped against the fence, the tree made a passable ladder. Of course it gave me help for only one direction—in. But I didn't expect to be coming out this way, assuming I would come out.

I caught that pessimism in my thoughts. Enough of that. People overcame worse odds than this every day. They survived monstrous diseases. They got past terrible pain. Someone had to be buying those winning lottery tickets.

I scrambled over the top of the fence and hung there for just a moment. It was not too late to head for Bolivia.

I dropped.

One foot slid off a rock and I almost turned an ankle. But I leaned on the fence and regained my balance. Until now I'd walked in the shadow of the fence. Now the moon looked like a dim spotlight aimed directly at me. I took a big breath and started east.

I had a sudden image of Mr. Burns releasing the hounds and decided I'd seen too many episodes of "The Simpsons."

I picked my way through the trees. Few of them were close enough to their neighbors to touch branches, but occasionally a trio of trees forced me to walk around. Fortunately, the moon made it easy to keep going in the same direction.

Maybe ten minutes later, a tiny bit of yellow light showed ahead through the trees. The ground continued to rise gently toward the high point Ben had picked for his mansion and the two guest houses.

The guest house on this side of the mansion, the house where Kevin and Maddy stayed when they were up here, was dark.

Lights showed in Ben's mansion, mostly on the side facing to my right. I angled toward Kevin and Maddy's darkened guest house.

At the guest house, I rounded the corner to the north and moved into the shadow of a nearby pine. From there to another shadow. At my new vantage point I could see the driveway and guest parking area for the main house. No police cars. No guest cars. So far so good. I wanted that text to truly have come from Ben, but after all that had happened, I was in hope-for-the-best-but-plan-for-the-worst mode.

I retraced my steps to the side of the guest house and moved around to the side facing Pikes Peak. The peak stood out in the cool moonlight.

I stepped over a two-foot-high rail and onto decking that ran along the side of the house. Multiple wide glass doors lined the wall. Overhead was a deck on the second floor.

I tried the first door I came to. Locked. That mildly surprised me. In such a remote area, in an enclosed estate, I would have guessed locks were just a nuisance to avoid. I moved around a chaise lounge and tried the second door. Locked.

The third door was different. It slid open noiselessly on its tracks. I stepped into the dark interior, wary of being outlined in moonlight, aware that Kevin could conceivably shoot me dead right now, defensibly, as an unknown intruder. The bastard.

No one home. At least down here. The large living area was empty. Multiple sofas and recliners reminded me of Ralph's place.

I eventually found the stairs leading upward, wishing I had a gun and at the same time being acutely aware of how well that had worked out.

The next floor, the floor on a level with the front door where it opened onto higher ground, also seemed deserted. The media room was silent. I heard little but the faint murmurs from the refrigerators.

I went up to the top floor. One bedroom contained an unmade bed. I pegged it as Kevin and Maddy's bedroom. A bedroom facing Ben's mansion was pristine. A guest bedroom. I moved quietly toward the window and reached the curtains, which were parted just enough for my needs.

From my pack I withdrew a pair of binoculars. My camera had a larger zoom, but it was probably somewhere in Ralph's house or police headquarters, bearing my fingerprints.

Two people sat in recliners on the mountain-facing deck on the main house. Ben Stuart leaned back, nestled in a thick blanket. The other person looked to be one of his model-bodyguards. She was covered with a thinner blanket against the cool night air.

Being a sick and dying billionaire must carry its own frustrations. All that potential and not feeling well enough to enjoy much more than a nursing home resident might experience.

Other lights were on, but no one else showed. The house looked quiet, a palace for two. I watched for twenty minutes. No cars came in from the front gate. No one moved in the big house. No sounds came from the house I was in.

I'd seen enough.

I stowed my binoculars and moved away from the window. I descended the stairs as cautiously as a teenager returning too late from a date.

The front door was unlocked. I stood just inside the door, in the semi-dark and turned my phone back on. It finally finished booting.

No signal. I set the phone into recording mode and turned the speaker volume all the way down. I turned the screen off and put the phone back in my shirt pocket.

I slipped out the door, into the moonlight.

The land was still. My first step on the path sounded too loud, and gravel crunched underfoot. I moved off the path.

The front door to the mansion was also unlocked. I let myself in and stood there in the dim light, listening. No sounds of ball games or game shows or TV dramas. No music. Just a quiet, sad house.

I started the familiar trek, pausing in unoccupied side rooms from time to time. In the kitchen I looked in the appliances. In the light spilling out of the refrigerator, I implemented a backup plan. I busied myself in the kitchen. Two minutes later I moved on.

The stairs to the second floor seemed wider this time, the reverse of going home after having been away for a long time.

I wondered how Ben would react to my information about Kevin and Tiffany. All that remained in the way of weak proof were pictures of the texts they had exchanged. But with his clout, if he believed me, he could get to the bottom of this. And if I was lucky, Ralph had briefed him before he was killed.

I quietly walked the long corridor that led back to the room Ben seemed to live in nowadays. The door was open. Once I stepped into the room I could see all the way to the open glass doors to the deck on which Ben and his bodyguard sat in recliners. I moved closer.

I reached the open deck doors and stepped out. The bodyguard glanced over at him, not seeming startled at all. She didn't get up.

I walked over to Ben and sat down beside him. The thick blanket keeping him warm draped over both sides, almost reaching the floor. I leaned forward. Slowly I pulled my phone out of my shirt pocket and set it on the floor below Ben, hidden by the blanket.

"I need to talk with you one last time, Ben," I said.

He opened his eyes. He didn't seem startled, either, and I took that to mean he in fact did send the text to me.

"I don't think it matters anymore," he said. His voice was weak. As he tilted his head toward me, he seemed to be under the influence of gravity far stronger than what I felt. Just turning his head seemed to be an enormous physical effort.

Puzzled, I tried to process that.

"I've got information you should be aware of, Ben. Kevin has a girlfriend. Together they've been trying to kill me. And I think maybe Kevin was behind Allison's death."

For the first time Ben looked startled. His eyes widened. He tried to push himself more upright in his chair, but failed.

I continued. "I've got copies of texts he exchanged with his girlfriend. If you get the police involved, they can verify the texts. They can look for clues that link Kevin and his girlfriend to the attempts on my life."

The overhead light from inside the room was blocked for an instant. I looked up.

I knew this had been too easy.

Kevin stepped out onto the deck. He held a pistol in his hand.

"Well, hello there, Dave," he said. I was really beginning to hate this guy. "It's about time you showed up."

"It's over, Kevin. I've got—"

"You've got copies of the texts. I heard. But I've got the video you took of Tiffany and me. All you have is stuff that makes me look bad, but doesn't prove I killed anyone. And you're still alive. So far."

My mind raced through options. I wondered if I could jump over the side of the deck and survive. I adjusted my position on the chair.

"Before you go off all half-cocked, buddy, there's something you should know." He gestured at something or someone back in the observation room.

I looked where he had temporarily aimed his pistol.

Cathy stood there.

Chapter 45

Cathy looked sadder than I'd ever seen her. Behind her, with a gun, was Tiffany. The lights were in Cathy's eyes. She probably couldn't see me yet.

Tiffany moved closer and shoved Cathy forward. Cathy stumbled, then caught herself. She flashed Tiffany an angry look.

Tiffany prodded Cathy again and together they came closer to the deck where Kevin held a gun on me. Ben and his model-bodyguard stayed in their recliners.

I'd wanted to see Cathy more than almost anything, but not now. Not this way. She stumbled forward again, then righted herself and pushed strands of black hair out of her eyes. She brightened as she saw me. "I'm glad you're here. I've had about all I can take of these two sociopaths."

Tiffany's beautiful, freckled face contorted into a mask of sudden fury and she shoved Cathy again, even harder. Cathy caught herself on the railing. I grabbed her hand and she gripped me tightly. I silently cataloged Tiffany's temper as a weakness.

"Easy, dear," Kevin said. "We're almost all here. Can you fetch our other guest?" He turned to me and said, "Take off the backpack, carefully, and toss it that direction." He gestured over the deck railing, to the right.

I did so. The pack sailed into darkness.

Tiffany moved away and Kevin positioned himself where he could cover Cathy and me. He seemed less concerned about the bodyguard and was completely oblivious to Ben.

Quietly I said to Cathy, "Are you all right?"

Her voice was just as soft, but determined. "Yes. No permanent damage. But I am so glad to see you. These two are real pieces of work. But I almost feel sorry for anyone who underestimates you."

I wished I shared her optimism.

Moments later, Tiffany returned. This time she was pushing Maddy along, ahead of her.

Maddy's lip was split and a small line of blood spilled onto her chin. "Get your hands off me, you—"

Tiffany shoved her again. Maddy moved over to the deck railing near Cathy. From her bloodshot eyes and runny makeup, it was evident that Maddy had been crying.

Kevin and Tiffany each put an arm around the other's waist for a moment. So touching. Kevin said, "OK, the gang's all here."

I looked at the model-bodyguard who still lay on her recliner. "I had you pegged for a bodyguard," I said. "I must have guessed wrong."

Looking very sleepy, she met my gaze, then glanced toward a pill bottle and back to me. Enough valium to make her compliant, no doubt.

I nodded. More things made sense now. I looked at Kevin. He was in motion, walking to a new position, aiming his gun our way, then moving to another position and repeating.

"It's not going to work, Kevin."

The distraction broke his concentration. He gave me an angry look, but he responded, maybe just to shut me up. "Wrong again. Now can you just keep quiet for a minute more? I've got a shoot-out to choreograph."

"The police already know too much. They know about you and Tiffany. They have the texts. They know about her black pickup. They have video of you and Tiffany at the Blue Star."

"Nonsense. I was never in the Blue Star."

"I know. You parked your Mazda in the MAT parking lot, two spaces from the far end of the row."

That got Kevin's attention. "Circumstantial. That is no proof of anything."

Cathy looked puzzled.

"There are still some things I don't understand, though. I do get that you and Tiffany plan a life together, or that she's your temporary help. I get that with no children and Maddy dead, you probably inherit a lot of money. I get that with Ben dead and no other remaining family, you likely inherit even more. That's why you've been slowly poisoning him."

"What?" This was from Ben.

Maddy faced Kevin. "You son of a bitch. You're the reason?"

Kevin looked at me as if he were seeing me for the first time just now. "Ben's autopsy isn't going to prove that. I've been very careful."

"But why did you have to kill Allison?"

Kevin hesitated. "You can thank Maddy for that."

Maddy cried, "What?"

Kevin ignored her. "Tiffany and I had a fight. I don't even remember what it was about. But I hooked up with Maddy and we had some laughs. Once I learned she was one of Ben Stuart's daughters and Ben was sick, Tiffany and I saw the potential. But Maddy put the money at risk. She was tipsy when she hit a bicyclist. Poor guy died. And Maddy fled the scene."

"Because you pressured me to, you bastard! And it never would have happened if you weren't groping me at the time."

Kevin kept talking to me as if Maddy hadn't spoken. "In a way, that was good, because it gave me a lot of leverage over Maddy. But Allison noticed a little damage to the fender. She knew about the accident. I couldn't take the chance that she was going to speak up." He hesitated. "Plus Allison couldn't be around if I hoped to get *all* of Ben's money."

Allison's last dream finally made sense to me. She'd found an innocent-looking cat had been torturing a mouse. In real life, she'd learned something terrible about a sister she loved, and no doubt she was trying to decide whether to tell anyone. "So you put an explosive on my tire and blew it out at just the right time. What were you going to do if the crash hadn't killed Allison?"

I sensed Ben struggling to get up. He couldn't.

"It didn't."

A chill raced down by back. I saw Allison suddenly turn her head toward me in the car.

"You broke her neck. You twisted her neck and broke it."

"See, I knew you were a threat."

"But you were only trying to kill me during the last couple of weeks? Why wait?"

"Before, even if Allison had told you about the hit and run, all you could have was hearsay. But you finally remembered me being at the accident scene. I thought you were unconscious at the time, but I saw it in your eyes when you visited us at the guest house."

"But I didn't really know that consciously. There was some low-level déjà vu, but I didn't *know*. It was only when you started trying to kill me that I started piecing things together."

Kevin laughed. "Well, all's well that ends well. For Tiffany and me anyway. For you all, not so much. At this stage, what's one or two more deaths?"

"It's not going to work."

"You don't even know the plan. You see, Ben has been harassing you, using Ralph and another guy as his henchmen. Ben's done some really nasty stuff to you. Stuff that drives some people to kill to settle the score. You tracked down Ralph and shot him with a gun you yourself purchased. And tonight, with your life falling apart, wanted by the police, you dragged Cathy up here to deal with Ben. To get even."

Cathy looked devastated. "He came to the door. He said you were in trouble and needed help."

Kevin moved to a new position and seemed to imagine himself pulling the trigger from there. He continued as if Cathy had said nothing. "You could anticipate that Ben's bodyguard would be here. But you didn't count on Maddy being here, too. So then you shoot Ben and Maddy and the bodyguard. But the bodyguard is good at her job. Even wounded and dying, she manages to get off shots at you and Cathy. Everyone dies. A 911 call is made during the confrontation, but no one speaks. The police will investigate. Armed with what they already know, they'll be almost there. I can reluctantly fill in the gaps for them." He smiled.

"I race over here from the guest house, having heard the shots. I'm absolutely horrified and devastated. The bodyguard tells me what happened just before she dies. Tiffany of course was never here tonight. If it comes out that I knew Tiffany before, hey, I'm only human. If it doesn't come out, then after a suitable delay, we meet and she consoles me after losing my dear wife and her father. I will be such a tragic figure."

Into the stunned silence, Maddy said, "Dad, a long time ago you tried to warn me about bad boys. I'm so sorry I didn't listen. Did you know that 'bad boy' is just another word for 'asshole'?"

Tiffany moved closer and slapped Maddy.

"Hey, hey, hey!" Kevin said. "Trace evidence!"

"I uploaded photographs to the Internet," I said. "The whole story is there on KevinMayerIsAKiller.com." I was lying, but I needed a bit more time.

"Like hell you did," Kevin said.

"And I suppose you don't care about Ben's whole-house video-recording system?"

"Do I look stupid to you?"

"You will look stupid if you almost get away with this and then find out the truth. Every vent has a camera behind it. I think it started out as anti-theft, but Allison told me she thought Ben started reviewing the recordings all the time. It kind of creeped her out." I felt bad for trashing Ben this way, but I needed more—

Blam-blam-blam. A trio of muffled explosions sounded from the first floor.

"What the hell was that?" Kevin asked angrily.

"Probably the cops on their way in. I'm wearing a wire."

"That's crap," Kevin said forcefully. "You're on the run from the police." He looked torn. To Tiffany, he said, "Keep watch on them. I'll be right back."

Around the time Kevin reached the doorway, one more explosion sounded from downstairs, far louder this time. This one rattled the windows and shook the floor. It was even more than I'd hoped for.

Tiffany looked flustered, worried. Perfect.

Kevin disappeared down the stairs. I didn't have much time before he'd be back.

"Sorry it had to end this way, Tiffany." I said. "When I found Kevin's secret cell phone, I found out he has *two* girl friends."

"Shut the hell up." She moved toward me menacingly. "Keep talking and I will shut your mouth for you."

"You should know you're the disposable one. You're supposed to die here tonight. Elaine Emerson is his true love. She's a model—"

"*Shut up!*" Tiffany wasn't nearly as pretty when she was angry.

"I'm sorry. Well, actually, it feels pretty good, knowing what a sucker you've—"

"*Shut up!*" she screamed again. She stepped in and swung the gun viciously at my face.

Too many things recently caught me off guard, the sudden flash of energy ending even before I even recognized what was happening. *This* I was ready for.

I ducked at the last second. Her swing whistled over my head, and she lurched, off-balance. I rose, slamming my shoulder into her midriff.

I twisted as I pushed upward, putting ten days of frustration and anger and desperation into the body blow.

Tiffany's body lurched upward into an arc and she toppled over the deck railing. I think the only reason she didn't scream on the way down was that I'd knocked the wind out of her.

If I hadn't, the ground certainly would.

I didn't wait to hear a thud. I grabbed Cathy's hand and pulled her with me. We ran.

Maddy sagged onto the floor. I called back to her, "Hide, Maddy!" She didn't move.

Kevin was still downstairs apparently.

"Come on," I said softly to Cathy. I led her to another room. I ducked my head inside. I grabbed the doorknob and pulled the door closed. I moved to the next doorway and Cathy followed.

Again, I pulled the door closed. We moved to a third room.

This one had what I wanted.

We went into the darkened room and closed and locked the door.

"Help me," I said. I started pushing a heavy armoire in front of the door. Together we leveraged it in place, finishing just as I heard footsteps racing up the stairs beyond the door.

I went to a bedside table and lifted the phone receiver. No dial tone sounded, but I dialed 911 anyway and left the receiver off the hook, under a pillow.

Cathy and I were moving toward the window when the sound of Kevin's enraged scream reached us. His agony seemed to vibrate the walls.

I was sliding the window open when we heard three sudden gun-shots. *Blam blam... blam.* Then silence. Cathy gasped. For a fleeting in-stant, I felt sorry for Ben. He'd been deceived by a lie the same as I was. I absolutely felt sorry for Maddy.

Cathy whispered, "Is it too much to hope for that he just shot him-self?"

If only. I'd go back and help him empty the clip.

Below the window was a decorative ledge that protruded three or four inches from the wall. It was still a long way to the ground, though. The land sloped to the south and what was the second floor along the front of the house was the third floor back here.

Feeling like a prison-movie cliché, I stripped the sheets off the guest bed. I handed one corner to Cathy. "I'll hold this in place while you climb down."

"How will you—" The door slammed against the armoire blocking it. That answered our question about Kevin's possible suicide.

"Just do it." I braced my feet against the wall.

She did it. She was on the ground no more than fifteen seconds later.

"Run!" I called as I got back to my feet. "Get as far away as you can!"

Chapter 46

As I called to Cathy to run, at least I knew Kevin was not down there to threaten her. He was still slamming and kicking the door against the armoire. He had succeeded in moving the armoire a couple of inches.

This cannot be happening. I registered the intense fear that was pushing me to collapse in a puddle on the floor, like Maddy, and I somehow forced it aside. I would be afraid later.

I tied a knot in one corner of the sheet and jammed the knotted end into a dresser drawer and closed the drawer tight over it. The other end of the sheet still dangled out the window.

I leveraged myself out the window until I had my toes on the decorative ledge, my arms and chest inside the room. The night air evaporated my sweat.

The pounding Kevin was generating gave the impression that the wolf harassing the three pigs had just gotten a dozen wolves as reinforcements. Man, he was angry. The armoire moved another couple of inches. If I'd had a gun I could have blasted him right through the gap. A thought flashed through my brain.

I pushed myself away from the window, holding onto the sheet. The sheet started pulling the bureau, turning it, and letting the sheet slip out of the bureau drawer. As fast as I could, I slid the window closed, trapping the sheet.

Kevin smashed against the door again. The gap was wider.

I pushed off, trying to rappel down the sheet as Cathy had.

Before my body had dropped a foot, I could feel the sheet starting to slide again. The friction from the drawer and the window were not much of a match for my weight.

I scrambled down as fast as I could. I had dropped maybe three feet on my own as the sheet dropped a couple feet on its own. I was still maybe eight feet off the ground when the sheet gave way completely.

My knee jolted as I landed on a juniper bush next to the house. The pain felt like I had bumped my knee into a table leg, hard.

As I was temporarily paralyzed from the pain, Cathy turned my head toward hers. She said, "Just in case," and kissed me hard on the lips for a full second.

Maybe it was the kiss. Probably it was the fact that I was on the ground, still alive, and a second had passed. Whichever it was, the pain in my knee faded to the point where I could move again.

"I told you to run," I said.

"Yeah, I heard that."

Women.

"Come on!" I yanked her with me as I moved toward the rear of the house. Just in time, because Kevin slid the window open so hard the glass broke and he started firing down on us.

We ran.

We headed for the place Tiffany had fallen over the railing. Or was pushed. Who cared anymore? God help us if she was just waiting there, slightly dazed, but ready to shoot us both.

She wasn't. She was a limp doll now, draped over a potted plant at the bottom of a two-and-a-half-story fall. She'd spilled a lot of blood. I'd never killed anyone before. Directly.

Surprisingly, no image of my mother or my father, bleeding out on a linoleum floor, popped into my brain. If I'd seen something like this a month or two earlier, I suspected things would have been different. What I felt right now was anger at Kevin and sorrow that there had been no alternative to Tiffany's death. Not unless I were willing to let Cathy die. I also felt some guilt, but pushed it aside. I would deal with it later.

"Her gun," I said. "Find it fast!" Some light spilled from the deck above, but the patio and surrounding area were dim.

"I don't see it."

Neither did I.

Footsteps sounded above us, running. Kevin. He was back out on the deck.

I grabbed Cathy's hand. "Come on! We've got to get out of here."

Cathy and I ran. I was never so glad that her tennis conditioning made her fleet on her feet. I was also glad that Kevin was a golfer, not a tennis player.

We raced away from the deck, into darkness, heading roughly for the other guest house.

Blam. Blam.... Blam. Kevin fired at us, presumably from the deck. Where he was firing from wasn't as important to me as the question of his aim in semi-darkness.

"You OK?" I called softly.

"I've been better."

Women.

Blam! This time I felt the shock of pain in my left arm. I cried out involuntarily. Kevin's last bullet had hit.

"Again?" I said. "Doctor Bentson is not going to believe this."

Cathy stopped. I grabbed her arm and pulled her forward.

"Who's Doctor Bentson?" she asked. "That ER doctor? And what do you mean 'again'?"

"Long story."

"Are you all right?"

"I've been better," I said. "He nicked my left arm."

Cathy made me stop on the other side of a tree while she tied a handkerchief just below my elbow. My forearm was slick with blood, and the camo shirt sleeve was moist with blood, but my sense was that as my luck teeter-totted between awful and OK, I had been incredibly lucky again. Seconds later we were back in motion.

The shots had stopped. Kevin must be running back through the house to get out and chase us. For a millisecond I considered going back to look for Tiffany's gun, and another millisecond later I thought about the possibility that Kevin could be doing a feint. I kept running, with Cathy pacing me.

"What were those explosions?" she asked.

"Eggs in a microwave. I set the timer to go in a few minutes just in case. The big one was a bottle of champagne in the other microwave."

"Where did you—"

"YouTube."

We kept running.

"I assume you don't have a phone with you," I said.

"No. And they talked about a jammer anyway."

I'd certainly wondered about that. In addition to murder, they were probably guilty of breaking some big FCC law. I hoped the FCC would throw the book at them.

We reached the other guest house. It, too, was dark. I ran for the front door and Cathy followed. The door was locked.

I slammed a shoulder then a foot against the door. The foot was an even bigger mistake. I used my other foot and the pain was more manageable. Not only did my leg hurt, but pain shot through my arm also. I kicked again. And again. Finally the doorjamb broke loose from the doorframe and the door swung open into gaping darkness.

Cathy said, "But he'll know we went in here."

"Exactly." I grabbed her hand and pulled her with me as we ran past the guest house, farther into the woods.

The moonlight provided good news and bad news. The good—it made it more difficult to run straight into a sharp branch at eye level. The bad—Kevin would be able to see us from a greater distance.

Cathy followed my lead as I changed directions. She certainly knew I'd been on the estate before, and she might have imagined that I had a plan. I wished I did. All I could think of was the current step: *keep away from Kevin.*

We ran down alongside a narrow ravine that angled down the gentle slope. I have no doubt the view of Pikes Peak in the moonlight would have been wonderful. Instead of looking at the peak, I watched the rocks and trees. Occasionally I glanced behind me. Perhaps we'd bought time with the guest-house-door ploy, but Kevin might have heard us scrambling away. I wondered if there'd been a gun in that house, or something else that would work as a weapon. If I got my hands on something that would work as a weapon, I was going to hang onto it.

The notion of a weapon triggered another thought. I veered to the right. Cathy paced me. We were both breathing runner-heavy, not racehorse-heavy, so that was good. I hoped Kevin used a golf cart when he played.

We ran over a rise and paid the price for my miscalculation. The ground fell off more sharply than I'd anticipated. We both scrambled to maintain control as we headed down, and we both lost control. Rocks bit into my back, my arms, my legs, before I came to rest. New pain flashed through my arm. The worst part was the clatter of rocks. I knew that sound would travel.

"Can you still run?" I asked.

"Yes."

We ran. I tried not to think about Ben and Maddy and the bodyguard.

Branches seemed to swoop into our path as we worked our way across the slope. Rocks fell away from where we stepped. In the shadow of one pine, the stump of another tree gave my shin a wallop. I recovered and we ran on. If we lived, I was sleeping in tomorrow.

I got a glimpse of our destination and changed course. Soon a storage outbuilding stood out in the moonlight. The door was in shadow, but I knew it was there.

I didn't have to beat down this door. It was unlocked.

Cathy and I stepped into the dark interior.

"He might not still be on our trail," Cathy said.

"Maybe. But we can't know that." I let my eyes adjust to the deeper darkness. Two of the building's walls sported windows. "Move over there and watch for any signs of him."

Cathy bumped against something in the dark, cried out softly, and kept moving for the window.

I moved off in the direction I remembered from a visit here two years ago, the only Fourth of July Allison and I had shared. For safety, Ben stored a number of potentially hazardous materials out here when they weren't in use, from barbecue grills to unused paint. Last time I was here, there were leftover Fourth of July fireworks, some on a shelf, and some in a pair of tall square crates on the ground.

"Nothing so far," Cathy called.

I moved past a couple of grills to where I remembered the fire-works.

Gone. Nothing on the empty shelf, and the floor right there was bare.

Crap. Time was running out. We couldn't afford to be trapped in here. I had to have a new idea fast.

I went back to the grills and turned right. There was the toolbox. I scrambled to get it open. In the top drawer was a claw hammer. I grabbed it, then looked around wildly. At least I had a close-range weapon.

A couple of hoses on wall were held up with large nails. I took off a hose and tossed it away.

"I hope you know what you're doing," Cathy called.

Me, too.

With the hammer, I pulled a nail out of the wall stud. Almost done.

I knelt between the two grills and fumbled for the controls.

I found a propane canister and twisted the valve. Hardly any sound. I turned to the other canister and did the same. Hardly any new sound. I stood and fumbled for the controls on both grills. One after the other I found the heat dials and turned them upward. The hisses increased and the smell of rotten eggs began to fill the room.

"What the hell are you doing?"

"Time to go."

I met Cathy at the door. "Just a sec," I said.

Hitting a nail on the head in very dim light is tougher than it sounds. I mashed a finger in the process, but I got the nail started. Two more thuds and I was done. I had a nail pounded into the door, as low as I could make it, on the inside.

I opened the door cautiously, praying Kevin wasn't right on the other side by now.

He wasn't. But what sounded like a rock clatter came from the distance. I pointed a direction to Cathy and she crept out the door and around the corner. I pushed the door closed behind me and through the gap I hit the nail twice, downward, until it bent far enough to scrape on the concrete. I reached around and turned on the interior lights, then pushed the door as far closed as it would go, feeling resistance from the nail.

I followed Cathy around the corner. I thought I heard another rock fall back the way we'd come from.

"Keep moving now, very softly," I whispered.

We moved off, hoping the building stayed between us and Kevin. Seconds passed. And more seconds. The trees had been cleared around the perimeter of the storage building, so it took us an agonizing amount of time before we reached the first pine tree. I started breathing easier. If Kevin were coming after us and approaching the building, the more time he took, the better. Gas would keep accumulating until the propane tanks gave out.

We moved to another tree, and then another. Finally, I whispered. "Let's wait a minute." If Kevin were on our trail, he should be reaching the building soon. If not, we could be heading for him now for all I knew. So maybe this was as good a time as any to listen for indications of his presence.

I breathed in and out shallowly, aware of Cathy doing the same. After thirty seconds of silence I moved my mouth to her ear and said, "There are two things I never said to you. One, I am so sorry for involving you in this, putting you in danger. Two...I love you."

Cathy drew in a sharp breath and for a moment her body shook. She could have been laughing or crying. She moved her lips to my ear. "I love you, too."

Seconds later she asked softly, "Earlier, what did you mean 'again'?"

"I, ah, got shot in the leg a few days ago."

"Oh, my God."

"Shhh."

I guess Kevin must have been following us after all. Not five seconds later came the sound of a nail scraping on concrete. I think. It was hard to separate all the individual results.

A monstrous *boom* sounded. The windows blew out. Flames billowed out of the open windows. The roof blew off the top of the building. And one wall started toppling outward.

"Run!" I said. "Either he's dead or he's not going to be able to hear anything for a few minutes." Unspoken was the idea that I was not going to go back to investigate and maybe get shot by a dying man.

We ran.

We were less cautious for the moment about sound. "That was amazing!" Cathy called. "I'll be careful not to mess with you."

Behind us flames still shot into the sky. I hoped we hadn't triggered a forest fire. I thanked Ben for the cleared buffer zone around the building.

A few seconds later two fireworks exploded overhead. *There* they were. I laughed for the first time in too long.

When I first thought of Kevin standing before the opened door to a propane-filled room, I'd had the image of me shooting a bottle rocket or a skyrocket through the door from a distance. The nail worked better.

We took a circuitous path through the property, avoiding clearings and open spaces, trying to keep concealed from anyone with a long view. Kevin could be lying dead next to the storage building, or he could still be on our trail. There's nothing more dangerous than a wounded asshole.

We reached the southern fence and walked westward until we found a convenient hidey-hole nestled among some scrub oak. I put the hammer down, and we recovered our breath to the point that we'd be able to hear Kevin approaching.

Fifteen minutes later we felt more optimistic that the coast was clear. I retrieved the hammer, our only real weapon, and we continued west. We reached the corner of the estate without seeing a convenient dead tree with which to scale the fence.

And then I thought, *I have a hammer.*

Three minutes later, after judicious and stealthy use of the hammer, we had an opening we could step through.

The fence gave us an additional sense of defense against sound and Kevin. We walked north, toward where I'd left Holly's car.

The moon had shifted another half hour or so in the sky by the time we neared the car. By then we had a plan, of sorts.

At the point we'd agreed on, we stopped. I gave Cathy a heartfelt kiss. "We're almost done."

She nodded.

I went on alone. Soon the car appeared in the moonlight, right where I'd left it. I approached it slowly, my empty hands slightly out from my sides.

Maybe we had gotten free. Maybe Kevin really was dead or severely injured back at the storage building.

But no.

"Hello there, Dave. Where's your little friend?"

Kevin stepped out of the shadow of a nearby pine tree. He really looked like a mess. His face and arms were blackened. His shirt and pants in bad shape, tatters hanging in several places. As I'd feared, if he lost us, he must have decided to wait where he figured we'd return. The car almost had to be on the road not too far from the gates.

I said softly, "She's getting the police."

"What?"

I touched my throat as though talking was difficult.

Kevin moved closer.

"Where is she? I want you to see her go first."

"Kevin, I'm the one you want. Just let—"

"I'm going to count to three."

"One of your bullets hit her—"

"Where is she?"

"I'm right here, dipshit," Cathy's voice called loudly from maybe thirty feet away, over Kevin's shoulder.

Kevin was suitably surprised. He whipped his head and torso toward the voice and fired a couple of shots that boomed loudly in the night.

But I didn't consciously watch him turn, or see any muzzle flashes. The instant Cathy had called out, I reached behind me.

The claw hammer was waiting, hooked on my belt. I grabbed it. I swung my arm, aimed at Kevin's head. And I let the hammer fly. Just as hard as I possibly could.

Thud.

The head of the hammer hit Kevin, a solid impact, just above and forward of one ear. The hammer's momentum snapped his head the same direction, and slowly he toppled. He hit the ground hard. The sound was like that of a dropped bag of flour. A large one.

I scrambled toward him to grab the gun and retrieve the hammer. The gunpowder smell reminded me of fireworks. And a kitchen. For a second I found nothing. But then my searching fingers first grasped the hammer and then the gun. I rose and backed up a step. In that instant, years of pain telescoped somehow into a single cathartic release. And that *Terminator* line I had impulsively said to my abusive father just somehow burbled up through my lungs and windpipe and out my lips.

"Fuck you, asshole."

Tears stung my eyes. I swiveled to where Cathy had been. "Are you OK?" I called

Silence. Then a hoot of an owl. Then, "I've been better."

Women.

I started crying in relief. I stayed guard over Kevin as Cathy came out from behind a pine tree and walked shakily toward me.

She stopped next to me and we put our arms around each other. She was so precious. I had almost lost her because of Kevin and his greed. My anger at him flared again. He could have killed her.

I let Cathy go momentarily and turned to Kevin. He might have already been dead. I'm really not proud of this, but I kicked him. Hard.

I looked back at Cathy and said, "Maybe he moved."

She looked at me, horrified for a moment, and then looked back down at the man who had happily killed people who got in his way. The man who had almost killed her. And me.

She said, "I think I saw him move again."

We laughed. In the pale light of the overhead moon, we clung to each other at the side of the deserted road. We were alive. We had each other. Delirium coursed through our veins. We laughed.

Chapter 47

We almost got shot at again that night.

The key to Holly's car had been right where I left it. My phone was still on Ben's deck. We dumped Kevin's still body in the trunk and raced down the road. We overshot the first driveway we spotted. I slammed on the brakes and we slid to a rough stop on the road, dust roiling over the car. I backed up and pulled in at the driveway.

The sprawling house was dark, but that didn't even slow us down.

Together we ran to the door, pushed the doorbell like demented trick-or-treaters, and pounded on the door.

We stood well back from the door then, and we both kept yelling, "Call 911. Please!"

Fortunately the homeowner, a wheelchair-bound retiree, paid more attention to the "Call 911" message than to the pounding on his door. He might not have cared about Ben Stuart's family problems, but shooting us or making the call were the only possible ways he was going to get us off his lawn.

~~~

Cathy and I were waiting at the gates to Ben's estate as the police and firefighters busted through. One of them had the smart idea to break through the fence instead of the gate, so the process went much easier than it could have.

Two cops stayed with the car once we opened the trunk and explained. Kevin's body lay unmoving, his face pasty white. He probably was dead. He could have been alive. I no longer cared. The question was soon answered as an EMT shook his head.

An EMT took a look at my arm. He washed the wound with something that stung a lot and eventually my arm sported a white bandage. At least it wasn't a cartoon-character Band-Aid.

I guess because we were the 911 callers, the cops cut us a little slack. Only one of them felt it necessary to stay with us while the others moved on the more important stuff. They did take Kevin's gun, though.

The rest of the police went in to sweep the mansion and count the dead, while Cathy and I waited outside. As the cops and the EMTs made multiple trips out to numerous emergency vehicles we got updates on what had happened after Tiffany went over the railing and we had excused ourselves.

One microwave was due for extensive cleaning. The other was completely totaled. Some of the nearby shelving would have to be rebuilt. One of the cops went by muttering to another about crazy rich people trying to warm champagne.

Kevin's three shots had not been allocated the way I had imagined. Two had gone into the bodyguard, who was dead. Kevin probably saw her as the biggest potential threat. Or his anger at seeing Tiffany where she'd fallen was so great he just blasted off a couple of reflex shots.

Tiffany was dead also. Her body had still been resting on the potted plant about a foot tall. She'd also fallen on her gun, which was why we couldn't find it quickly. They found my pack, but it contained nothing I cared about any longer. I wouldn't be keeping the camo outfit either. I should have saved the receipt.

Kevin's remaining shot had been for his wife, Maddy. Kevin must have known Ben wasn't going anywhere, so Kevin left without shooting him. The balance of the story was reminiscent of those apocryphal tales of people lifting cars off loved ones. Somehow, as Maddy lay bleeding out, Ben had managed to get out of his chair, crawl his way over to his one remaining daughter, and apply pressure. If you ever have a choice of being Ben's friend or an enemy, I strongly recommend friend.

Maddy was probably going to survive. She was unconscious as they carried her out past us.

The last one wheeled out alive was Ben. He caught sight of me as they carried him past us. "Wait," he called. His voice was weak and raspy, but it still held that command tone.

The EMTs didn't like stopping there, but they did, for a moment. Ben reached a frail hand toward mine and grabbed me. The strength in his grip amazed me.

He said nothing to me, but he nodded. A tear formed in his right eye. I nodded back. *Shucks.*

There was no way to know how much more Ben had in him, but he wasn't going to die tonight.

Not unless he threatened Cathy.

Chapter 48

One Month Later

Cathy and I both took the afternoon off. I had packed a picnic lunch and driven us in a brand new blue BMW 750Li Sedan. Courtesy of Ben Stuart.

In Cathy's garage was a matching red one.

Holly had one, too. Her old car had had a dead body in the trunk. There had been a lot of that going around.

I was probably on the no-rent list with a number of rent-a-car outfits, but I could live with that. I'd gone through worse.

I had found a bottle of the same champagne that had exploded in Ben's microwave. It seemed fitting for today. I refilled Cathy's glass. Her green eyes sparkled as she smiled.

Ben was steadily improving, now that the doctors understood about the extra medication and, oddly enough, some grapefruit juice, that Kevin had been slipping into Ben's diet whenever he and Maddy were staying on the estate.

Maddy had been in intensive care for several days, but now she was out of the hospital. The last time I had seen Ben and Maddy, they were recuperating in matching recliners as they watched the clouds form and dissolve over Pikes Peak and they thought about the future. Neither of them had been doing enough of that recently. None of us had.

On this clear Colorado afternoon, Cathy and I sipped our champagne and sat in lawn chairs as we watched people work.

We were located on a corner of my lot on Mesa Road, watching as a cement truck did something I enjoyed watching. It was sluicing out concrete into prepared forms as workers smoothed the goopy stuff out to the far corners of the foundation.

Ben was having a replacement house built for us. I use *replacement* in the same sense that one would use when saying, "I'm replacing the computer I got from my grandfather with a top-of-the-line, brand new model."

It's good to know the king.

The new house would be the perfect home for a married couple.

A week ago, I'd asked Cathy if she would marry me, and she'd said, "Yes, yes, yes, yes, yes."

This was even after I'd told her all about my history, my mother killing my father, my vow to never have children, my fears, my nightmares. She'd said, "Yes, yes, yes, yes, yes," anyway.

My phone chimed with an email. I almost didn't check it right then, but I had an idea of what it might be about and I was curious. The message summarized the terms of a new investment account I'd recently landed. I glanced at the message and then did a double-take. And then a triple. I showed it to Cathy. Her eyes went wide when she got to the end.

Ben Stuart had finalized the terms he'd demanded. The amount in the fund was staggering, but the most amazing part was that the contract required me to take a minimum management fee every month, and, although gains could be taken out of the account for Ben's use, the principal could not be removed in his lifetime.

Or mine.

The minimum monthly management fee was about what I'd been making every two years.

Ben had also cleared things up with my boss, and the odd accounting that Ralph had set up was forgotten. I never did get my gun and camera back, but I could replace them if I wanted to. I had gotten my phone back, along with Kevin's audio confession, but the testimony coming from the four of us who survived made the recording superfluous. For the official record, Tiffany fell. And the blow to Kevin's ribs must have happened as part of the explosion. But my toe hurt for several days afterward and not once did I regret it. Well, I did regret that when I kicked him he'd probably been dead already.

Allison's death was now in the records as a murder rather than an accident. Every day I gave thanks for the happiness she had infused into my existence. And every day I made a point of telling Cathy how lucky and grateful I was for her presence in my life. Some men might go through their entire lives never knowing a woman as wonderful as the two who had entered my orbit.

I'd had time for a couple more visits with Violet and several work-outs with Bruce. Violet confirmed without even saying, "I told you so," that there was something cathartic and therapeutic about fighting back and conquering one's demons, or at least two villains, because I felt better than I had in a long time. Or that could have been Cathy's doing. Even the small things, like lying with my arms around her and listening to distant train whistles in the middle of the night, were elevated to moments that sometimes just took my breath away.

As Cathy and I sat there enjoying the sounds of progress, a mother from up the street walked by. She had an infant in her arms and a toddler who was interested in every single stone and flower. His blue eyes went amazingly wide when he saw the cement mixer at work. His mouth formed a perfect "O."

He ran toward Cathy and me because we were between his mother and the colossal machine. He stopped there, virtually glowing in the excitement over the enormous apparatus. And he looked at us as though we were heroes, as if this wondrous event were all our doing. We had brought this marvelous machine to Earth just for him to see.

My throat constricted as I looked at his joy and amazement. His mother must be so happy with him. From the corner of my eye I noticed Cathy watching me instead of the toddler.

We assured Mom that he was no bother, and he communed with the construction equipment and with us for a few minutes.

When Mom walked away, and the toddler reluctantly followed, Cathy looked at me intently.

The roar from the cement mixer unexpectedly hushed as Cathy took my hand. "I understand about the vow you made, Dave. About not having kids. You know that was in the middle of a terrible time, when you felt that way."

I looked at her.

She swallowed. "Have you ever—ever had second thoughts about that vow? Do you think it's possible that your feelings about it might change?"

I looked back at the toddler, who was now totally absorbed in staring at a motionless rabbit in the nearby brush. The rabbit no doubt felt that as long as it stayed still it was invisible and no harm would come its way. If only life were that simple.

As I met Cathy's gaze I realized how much had happened since I'd made that vow, how much I'd changed, and I said, "It's more than possible."

We both started crying at the same time.

All my life I'd heard people talk about tears of joy.

So *that's* what they felt like.

Acknowledgments

Life and literature bounce off one another in an endless Brownian motion cascade, with unexpected collisions and unforeseen influences.

The genesis of this novel included death, a rebirth of sorts, and echoes of long-ago decisions.

Those of you who follow my career know this book represents a new period for me. It's the first major new work after a too-long fallow season. Relatively early in that period, my father died unexpectedly. Soon after, we moved my mother to live with us in what turned out to be a couple-year decline as we waged her losing war with melanoma. About a year after her death, as I was starting to feel life returning to something like normal, my wife of many years was diagnosed with uterine cancer. Annette and I fought that battle for about four years before her doctors explained that they had no more tools in their toolbox. She died about four months later.

My brother, Richard, was of incalculable help throughout all of this.

I in no way wish to diminish the effects of PTSD on our wounded military, but by the end of a long series of hopeful and hopeless doctors appointments and hospice visits, I could better empathize with those lost souls, feeling I was going through maybe one percent of their experience. I felt lost and perpetually fatigued, uncertain what the future held.

In the year following Annette's death, the universe worked its unfathomable magic, and I went to a coffee for a political candidate.

There, a friend of Annette's I hadn't seen for maybe twenty years approached me and pointed to Karen, a woman widowed about a year earlier. This friend said Karen and I should talk, and we did. And late in the following year, we married.

Death still visits people in my life, and that's pretty unlikely to stop. My brother's wife, Linda, has died since these events took place, and the friend who introduced Karen to me, Marcy, has also died.

One of the many unexpected things in my life was that at the same time I felt deliriously happy with Karen (and still do) I felt guilty for moving on after Annette's death. That guilt persisted a while, despite my knowing that Annette's two final wishes were that I would find happiness again and that Annette would make her way through her final months with dignity, which she did in spades.

I owe debts of gratitude of astonishing magnitude to Richard, Annette, and Karen, and to my parents. Special thanks, too, to Earle Turvey and Kavin King.

When I was first married, there was much talk of overpopulation, and I realized I harbored strong doubts of being an adequate parent. So I never had children of my own.

Into that gap, thanks to Annette and Karen, have entered a truly wonderful family. From Annette I was gifted with Greg and Chris, two truly great guys. And from thanks to Karen, I was gifted with Jenn, Becca, and Liz, the most wonderful daughters I could imagine. Thank you, too, to Annette's terrific sisters, Mel and Michele. Thank you all for enriching my life and for all the joy you've brought me. And thanks to those in the next generation who are doing that, too. I am so lucky.

Special thanks to my new agent, Sara Megibow, whose enthusiasm seems endless. Thank you, too, to colleagues who provided advance quotes for this book: Diana Gabaldon and Chris Goff.

Special thanks to my editor, Andrew Burt. And to my publicist, Samantha Lien.

Along the way, I've met a great collection of readers who have become friends and at various times have been willing to be first readers, helping me make sure the story in my head is the story that reaches the pages. Thanks to Chris Barili, Nathan Beauchamp, Rose Beetem, Ryan Blaha, Deb Blaha Jones, Wayne Carey, Fred Cleaver,

Susan Crites, Mel Eads, Charles Eklund, Jamie Ferguson, Boots Few, Randy Finch, Ralph Hoefelmeyer, Mark Kielar, Kavin King, Elaine Markley, Pam Martinez, Cliff Morgan, Tyson Mowat, Barbara Nickless, Steve Palmquist, Brienne Bunny Parker, John A. Skiba, MiRobin Webster, and George Wilhelmsen.

Thank you, Dr. Douglas C. Hammerstrom, for looking over the medical aspects of the novel. Thank you, Jeff Thomas, for looking at the financial counselor elements. If any errors remain, they are purely mine.

Karen has been a boundless source of love, encouragement, wisdom, and humor. Thank you more than I can ever say.

About the Author

John E. Stith's works include REDSHIFT RENDEZVOUS (Nebula Award nominee), MANHATTAN TRANSFER (Hugo Award Honorable Mention), REUNION ON NEVEREND, and RECKONING IN-FINITY (on Science Fiction Chronicle's 1997's Best Science Fiction Novels list, on the Nebula Award preliminary ballot). His other novels are SCAPESCOPE, MEMORY BLANK, DEATH TOLLS, and DEEP QUARRY. Naught Again includes a Nick Naught novella and a novelette.

Stith's work also includes best sellers, a Seiun Award finalist, a La Tour Eiffel Science Fiction Book Prize finalist, HOMer Award winners, and Science Fiction Book Club selections.

His work has also appeared on the New York Public Library Best Books for Young Adults list, Science Fiction Chronicle's List of Year's Best Novels, and the yearly Locus Recommended Reading Lists.

His website is www.neverend.com

Follow him on Twitter: @johnestith

Facebook Writer Page: www.facebook.com/pages/John-E-Stith

Personal Facebook Page for interests beyond writing: www.facebook.com/john.e.stith

More books from John Stith are available at: http://ReAnimus.com/authors/johnestith

ReAnimus Press

Breathing Life into Great Books

If you enjoyed this book we hope you'll tell others or write a review! We also invite you to subscribe to our newsletter to learn about our new releases and join our affiliate program (where you earn 12% of sales you recommend) at www.ReAnimus.com.

Here are more ebooks you'll enjoy from ReAnimus Press, available from ReAnimus Press's web site, Amazon.com, bn.com, etc.:

Deep Quarry, by John E. Stith

Manhattan Transfer, by John E. Stith

Reunion on Neverend, by John E. Stith

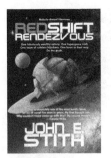

Redshift Rendezvous, by John E. Stith

Memory Blank, by John E. Stith

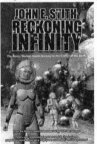

Reckoning Infinity, by John E. Stith

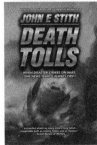

Death Tolls, by John E. Stith

Scapescope, by John E. Stith

All for Naught, by John E. Stith

Walls and Wonders, by S. R. Algernon

The Exiles Trilogy, by Ben Bova

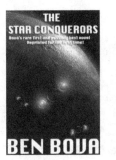

The Star Conquerors (Collectors' Edition), by Ben Bova

Colony, by Ben Bova

The Kinsman Saga, by Ben Bova

Star Watchmen, by Ben Bova

As on a Darkling Plain, by Ben Bova

The Winds of Altair, by Ben Bova

Test of Fire, by Ben Bova

The Weathermakers, by Ben Bova

The Dueling Machine, by Ben Bova

The Multiple Man, by Ben Bova

Escape!, by Ben Bova

Forward in Time, by Ben Bova

Maxwell's Demons, by Ben Bova

Twice Seven, by Ben Bova

The Astral Mirror, by Ben Bova

The Story of Light, by Ben Bova

Immortality, by Ben Bova

Space Travel - A Science Fiction Writer's Guide, by Ben Bova

The Craft of Writing Science Fiction that Sells, by Ben Bova

Vengeance of Orion, by Ben Bova

Orion in the Dying Time, by Ben Bova

Orion and the Conqueror, by Ben Bova

Orion Among the Stars, by Ben Bova

The Starcrossed, by Ben Bova

To Save The Sun, by Ben Bova and A. J. Austin

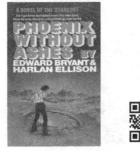

Phoenix Without Ashes, by Harlan Ellison and Edward Bryant

Shadrach in the Furnace, by Robert Silverberg

Bloom, by Wil McCarthy

Aggressor Six, by Wil McCarthy

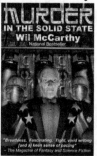

Murder in the Solid State, by Wil McCarthy

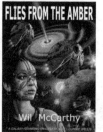

Flies from the Amber, by Wil McCarthy

In Search of the Big Bang, by John Gribbin

Cosmic Coincidences, by John Gribbin and Martin Rees

Q is for Quantum, by John Gribbin

Ice Age, by John and Mary Gribbin

In Search of the Double Helix, by John Gribbin

The Living Labyrinth, by Ian Stewart and Tim Poston

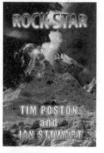

Rock Star, by Tim Poston and Ian Stewart

Wheelers, by Ian Stewart and Jack Cohen

THE EGG
OF THE
GLAK   AND
OTHER
STORIES

HARVEY JACOBS

The Egg of the Glak, by Harvey Jacobs

A Guide to Barsoom, by John Flint Roy

Jewels of the Dragon, by Allen L. Wold

Crown of the Serpent, by Allen L. Wold

Lair of the Cyclops, by Allen L. Wold

The Planet Masters, by Allen L. Wold

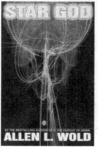

Star God, by Allen L. Wold

**Anthopology 101: Reflections, Inspections and Dis-
sections of SF Anthologies,** by Bud Webster

Woman Without a Shadow, by Karen Haber

The War Minstrels, by Karen Haber

Sister Blood, by Karen Haber

The Sweet Taste of Regret, by Karen Haber

The Science of Middle-earth, by Henry Gee

Commencement, by Roby James

Xenostorm: Rising, by Brian Clegg

The Cure for Everything, by Severna Park

Ghosts of Engines Past, by Sean McMullen

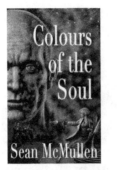

Colours of the Soul, by Sean McMullen

The Gilded Basilisk, by Chet Gottfried

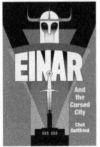

Einar and the Cursed City, by Chet Gottfried

Neon Twilight, by Edward Bryant

Particle Theory, by Edward Bryant

Trilobyte, by Edward Bryant

Cinnabar, by Edward Bryant

Predators and Other Stories, by Edward Bryant

Timeshare, by Joshua Dann

Bug Jack Barron, by Norman Spinrad

The Void Captain's Tale, by Norman Spinrad

The Last Hurrah of the Golden Horde, by Norman Spinrad

Costigan s Needle, by Jerry Sohl

The Mars Monopoly, by Jerry Sohl

One Against Herculum, by Jerry Sohl

The Time Dissolver, by Jerry Sohl

The Altered Ego, by Jerry Sohl

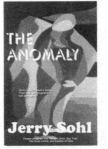

The Anomaly, by Jerry Sohl

The Haploids, by Jerry Sohl

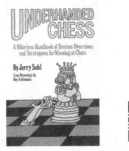

Underhanded Chess, by Jerry Sohl

Underhanded Bridge, by Jerry Sohl

Local Knowledge (A Kieran Lenahan Mystery), by Conor Daly

Bad Karma: A True Story of Obsession and Murder, by Deborah Blum

A Mother's Trial, by Nancy Wright

The Box: An Oral History of Television, 1920-1961, by
Jeff Kisseloff

You Must Remember This: An Oral History of Manhattan from the 1890s to World War II, by Jeff Kisseloff

Biff America: Steep Deep & Dyslexic, by Jeffrey
Bergeron (AKA Biff America)

Side Effects, by Harvey Jacobs

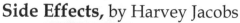

American Goliath, by Harvey Jacobs

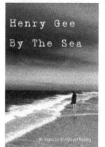

By The Sea, by Henry Gee

Innocents Abroad (Fully Illustrated & Enhanced Collectors' Edition), by Mark Twain

The Sigil Trilogy (Omnibus vol.1-3), by Henry Gee

CPSIA information can be obtained
at www.ICGtesting.com
Printed in the USA
LVHW011133200222
711571LV00007B/82/J

9 780967 298450